THE RETURN OF RASPUTIN

by

Stephen J. Kieran

Special thanks:

Patrick W. Kieran
For being there at the beginning.

Lynne Gessner, Author
Arizona Author of the Year (past recipient)
For shining by example. For everything.

KIKUCHI*DESIGN*
For a great cover that helped wrap it up.

ISBN: 0615737862
ISBN-13: 978-0615737867

Aloha Amber Publishing
Aloha, Oregon

The rise and fall of the title character
are based on actual events.

A Guide to Names and Glossary follow.

For Diane

Your B-o-B

CHAPTER 1

Pokrovskoe, Russia

June 22, 1884

"Misha!" Grigory yelled frantically, "Misha!" His older brother was losing his fight with the white waters of the Tura River. And now Misha was so close, only five meters from the bank. Grigory ran ahead to a spit of land and dove in. When he reached Misha he pulled the fourteen-year-old's face out of the water while shaking the water from his own hair and eyes. "Misha!" he cried, but there was no response.

They floated into a wider section of the river. The slightly slower water offered twelve-year-old Grigory a chance to look for help. There, on the path beyond the bank, a *moujik* walked a team of oxen pulling a straw cart, a swayback horse plodding along behind.

"Ho!" Grigory yelled as best he could, his aching lungs burning in protest. "Help!"

The *moujik's* face turned toward them, but Grigory barely got a glimpse of a long beard before the Tura dumped a wall of water over his head.

Grigory kicked and paddled with his one free hand until he could see again. The *moujik* had stopped and was looking out across the river, probably wondering if he was seeing things.

"Over here!" Grigory kicked up as high as he could and waved wildly.

The *moujik* waved back and moved quickly to untie his horse. He mounted and galloped toward the bridge downriver, close to where the Tura emptied into the Tobol, crying for more help from other travelers on the road.

After what seemed an eternity, the boys rounded the next bend and Grigory saw the *moujik* waiting in the middle of an old wooden bridge. He held a coil of rope. Other men were running toward him. He tied one end around his waist and waited for the boys to come closer, to pass beneath him.

The *moujik* jumped at the perfect instant, resurfaced and wrapped Misha in a tight bear hug. The rope snapped taut, and they held tight—the *moujik* to Misha, and Grigory to them both in the relentless surge and spray.

By now six men had wrapped the rope around bony, callused, farm-tempered hands. They planted their feet and leaned hard against the current. When the river gave them brief respites, they inched their way toward the bank in shuffles and half-steps. Slowly, as the boys and the *moujik* neared the bank, the pull lessened, and finally the rope went slack.

The drenched *moujik* rose and stumbled backward through the river stones, pulling Misha, as the others arrived to help. Quickly they laid him on his stomach and pumped his back.

Grigory stood nearby, dripping, scarcely noticing the blanket one of the *moujik* women had draped about him. He closed his eyes and prayed, asking God for the special light to come that would make everything all right—the light he had seen in the barn over injured horses, the sign that they would stop bleeding and begin to recover.

Then Misha coughed and water sprayed from his mouth. "He'll be alright now!" the group agreed, but Grigory felt sick. The light had not come, and, regardless of Grigory's prayers during the straw-cart ride back to their farm, it never did.

Four days later

June 26, 1884

The day after Misha's funeral, Grigory still didn't have the strength to move off the cot his father, Efim Novykh, set up for him near the stove in the central room of their wooden home. He felt warm and safe, though, and lying amid the hub of household activities helped take his mind off Misha.

As dusk fell, Grigory looked forward to the monthly meeting of neighbors that would be held in the Novykh home that night. His father, who served as village headman, had said Grigory could remain lying near the stove and witness the gathering for the first time. But he had to promise to act as an adult and, no matter what happened, mind his tongue.

Soon a dozen men sat about in the main room. They lit cigars and warmed their vodka with dark, hot tea from the samovar. To begin the meeting, headman Novykh called for anyone with important news.

Igor Dilatov, a poor and simple-minded *moujik*, immediately rose to address them all, "Oh, neighbors, whatever shall I do? A thief has made off with my mare, and now I have no way to pull my cart to town or plow my field. I do not ask much of you— only to keep an eye open for a thief and a nag with one white boot. If I do not get her back I am lost and my family will do without. My unknown enemy has dealt me a crippling blow."

Grigory listened to promises to stay on the alert, and that others would help Dilatov survive the winter if need be. But Grigory felt uncomfortable, as though he had been tricked. There was deception in the room. One of the men knew more than he was admitting, and that man was hurting Dilatov and his family. Grigory saw a familiar twinkle of light over a portly, well-dressed villager.

Grigory sat up in bed but stayed silent. The twinkling grew brighter. Grigory gasped. How could the visitors still sip from their mugs? Why did they not see the light?

"Papa, that man took the horse!" Grigory said, quite accidentally during one of those rare, quiet pauses in a conversation. He pointed at Alexei Prosportin.

Shocked, the elder Novykh turned. "Grisha!" But then he, like Dilatov and the others, looked for Prosportin's reaction to the wild claim. They saw only innocent surprise in his eyes.

"I apologize for my son's words, Alexei Stoyanovich," Novykh offered, "but you know he has been ill with the fever."

Novykh walked to his son's side and felt his forehead. In a quiet voice he asked Grisha to lie back down. "You know nothing about these affairs, son. They are the affairs of men and you mustn't concern yourself with them."

"But Papa," Grigory protested, "he stole the horse. Is it wrong to speak when you know the truth?"

"Son, you still have the water in your chest. And Mr. Prosportin is the last man who would have need of Mr. Dilatov's mare. Please quiet yourself and sleep. You will feel better in the morning."

"But Papa—"

"Sshhh..." Novykh stroked his son's cheek with the back of his gnarled hand. Grigory knew better than to continue.

Prosportin could wait no longer. He stood. "Well. You all have known me for many years, and you've *never* known me to be a thief. But since this bereaved and sickly child has raised a question that must be answered, I will expect you all at my barn in the morning. For now, I bid you good night. I pray a speedy recovery for your boy, Efim Andreyevich." He slammed the door behind him.

The men were torn. On one hand, if the Lord truly had smiled on young Grigory and blessed him with unusual powers, as was rumored, then it was blasphemy to ignore Grigory's words. But on the other hand, Grigory could not have implicated a less-likely horse thief than Prosportin.

One man said, "I have seen young Novykh still the flowing blood of injured horses—it is the gift of *zagovarivat'krov*, and that can come only from Almighty God."

"But Efim Andreyevich is a blood-stiller as well—his son just learned it from his father."

"I taught him only the methods, my friends," Novykh replied, "just as my father taught me. Yet strange-ly, I've lost many horses to bleeding over the years, and Grisha never has. When he calms a horse and soothes the wound, the bleeding stops. Always. I believe the boy has abilities that most men do not."

"Then perhaps the boy also sees things that we do not?"

"He is delirious with fever. I, too, have seen things in such a state," doubted someone else.

"But never a horse thief, you ignorant *moujik*," a friend chided.

Finally Dilatov stood and spoke. "The boy has no reason to lie, and I have no reason to doubt him. After all, only the reputation of our neighbor Prosportin stands in the way of the boy's words, and that is a picture that we ourselves have painted. And, by God, if Alexei Stoyanovich Prosportin has never shown a sliver of dishonesty in his dealings—indeed, if any one of us has forever been above reproach in the eyes of the Lord—" many of the men cast glances downward, "then I will eat my last pair of shoes where I stand."

After a moment of silence the man beside Dilatov quietly said, "I am with you, neighbor, yet I know not what our course of action should be."

"I, too, Igor Ivanovich," said another. "But I have a plan. I think we should not wait for morning to set off for Alexei Stoyanovich's barn. We should go now, before he has time to move the horse, if indeed he has it there."

The three nodded. They stood and bade Novykh, his son and the remaining guests a solemn good night.

The tale of what happened next quickly spread throughout Pokrovskoe. The three crept onto Prosportin's land in the darkness. From a knoll above the barn, they saw Prosportin by the light of his lantern—leading a horse with one white boot from his barn.

Dilatov was the first to reach him. His anger made up for his small size. His hard fists flew in the name of the wrong dealt him and his family. The other two men joined him, and they administered a proper dose of Siberian justice. They left triumphantly. They had recovered Dilatov's nag, and they had an amazing tale to tell of young Grigory Novykh's gift from God.

Four years later

April 23, 1888

The spring sunshine had thawed the permafrost into fertile ground, and for the second year in a row, it was sixteen-year-old Grigory's chore to work it.

Already it was late morning. He stopped their plow horse at the end of a furrow to knot a bandanna around his dark, sweat-soaked hair. He looked back at his work with a critical eye; the rows were crooked and unevenly spaced. "A sign we are working too hard," he said to the mare, "but we are getting there." He took the plow handles and clucked his tongue.

They had plowed only a third of the next furrow when the mare suddenly stopped in mid-stride. She wasn't spooked—she just stopped. Grigory nearly fell forward over the plow. Then, like the sun breaking through the clouds, the brown earth lit up brightly ahead of him. Only there hadn't been a cloud all day. Slowly Grigory lifted his head and looked for the source of the light...and there it hung before him—his light, God's light, twinkling five meters above him, larger than it had ever been.

Reverence overcame him. He fell to his knees. He could not take his eyes off the spectacle. It grew brighter and more intense with every second. It was spinning. Brilliant sparks flew about, landing all around him. Finally Grigory crossed himself. Perhaps his time on earth had come to an end, right there behind the plow horse.

The light exploded. Grigory covered his eyes to protect them, but the sparks did not hurt. Then he dared to peek. He meant only to glance up, but his gaze could not fall back down. He felt terrified and mesmerized and comforted, all at once, and then there was no awareness of time or place or anything else.

Before him, hovering above the Novykh field, was the Holy Mother Herself, the Virgin Mary.

The sweet song of a celestial choir fell onto the land and wrapped Grigory in its angelic grip. Through the glowing aura he saw a golden crown upon Her head, and a golden cross above that. Gleaming, spun gold hung like lace from the crown, framing Her beautiful ebony-skinned face and beyond, cascading down in a rippling shimmer and wrapping Her Child, whom She held close to Her heart.

A string of pearls encircled the high collar of Her purple cloak, which parted gently below Her bosom to expose a shimmering white gown, trimmed in gold and silver and colorful jewels, that trailed off into a sparkling cloud several feet above the earth.

She spoke no words to Grigory, who was still frozen in place. Slowly She extended Her right hand, palm down, and bestowed upon him Her blessing.

Grigory felt a delicate brush upon his head and crossed himself again. The Virgin smiled, and Her devout student's heart soared.

"You bless me," he said quietly, "the Virgin Mary blesses Grigory Efimovich."

The Virgin showed a hint of a smile at his devotion, and then She looked off, over his head, and raised Her hand. Though She said nothing, there was no mistaking Her instructions—She pointed west, to the snowcapped Urals and beyond, and wordlessly commanded Her disciple to venture there in Her name.

Grigory closed his eyes in prayer. There was work to be done in the name of the Virgin, and clearly She had chosen him to serve Her. "Thank you, Holy Mother," he murmured, and when he opened his eyes again, only a swirling, colorful cloud remained, spiraling slowly upward, back toward the heavens.

He remained on his knees, motionless, and again closed his eyes. Now the light did not go away. She had left a twinkling sliver of Herself in his mind, somehow behind his eyes and yet in front of them. The light twirled and spun, there but not there, and it was still there when, again, he opened his eyes. It danced off everything around him. Everything seemed brighter, fresher. The mare seemed a fellow child of God, she who would do anything she could to help turn the dirt to food. Her mane and tail glistened, her coat and muscles beneath were beautiful to behold. Even the earth seemed alive, an investor with his family in the harvest. Tears left tracks down Grigory's cheeks.

He clasped his hands and prayed aloud. "Oh Mother, shall I leave now on my mission? What should I look for once I am on the road? Will the priests help..." but he stopped in mid-sentence, for like all Russians, he knew that Russian Orthodox priests merely lit candles, led prayers and heard confessions. The Lord never called on them for divine missions. They never wandered in search of their souls. They possessed fine beards and proper manners, but that was all. They would be of no help.

But he knew who could be—Russia's *stranniki* (traveling lay-priests) and *staretsi* (religious wise men). Grigory admired these men of God. The *stranniki* were the true spiritual leaders of the Russian *moujiki*, unencumbered by physical possessions, or by family, or by land that needed care. They wandered in search of their souls through all of Russia and more, to the Holy Lands, to ancient Greece and Turkey, to the ends of the earth, exchanging stories of far-off lands and peoples and miracles for bed and board. And when they satisfied their quest for themselves, they stopped roaming and lived in solitude as *staretsi* in monasteries or forests or wherever else they chose. The *staretsi* knew in their hearts who and what God was, and they dedicated their lives to worshipping Him and to blessing and helping those still searching.

The most famous of all *staretsi*, Makari, lived to the west, in the low forests of the Urals. "That's it!" cried Grigory, "That's why the Virgin pointed to the west. I will travel to see Makari and ask his wise advice. It is what the Virgin wishes of me."

Yet what of the work to be done at home? Grigory sighed. His family could not do without him until fall, so he made a solemn promise to both the Virgin and himself: "After the harvest, when Papa can do without me, I will go to Makari of the forest outside the monastery at Verkhotourie. And in the meantime, I will never fail to serve You."

One week later

April 30, 1888

A crowd was gathered in the mid-afternoon mud before a small house on the edge of Pokrovskoe. At its lead was one of the local Russian Orthodox priests.

"Out! Out with you, evil one!" cried Father Peter, a short, plump man with fiery red hair and blotchy skin. "You will not infect our town with the devil's work!"

The crowd cheered Father Peter's stand against Satan and his followers. Grigory stood behind the throng, waiting to see the evil one.

"The Lord will have you face Him!" commanded the priest to chants of "Out! Out!" from the townspeople.

Finally, to the pleasure of the crowd, four men flew past Father Peter and up the porch steps. They kicked in the front door. Seconds later they dragged out the evil one—a small, frightened woman with short black hair, clad in only a nightshirt.

"Whore!" cried Father Peter. "We know you took in a *strannik* last night—he was seen entering your home! You fed him, bathed him and gave him his pleasures! *Prostitutka*! You have shamed yourself and our town in the eyes of God Almighty, and now you shall pay your penance!"

The men pulled her arms wide apart and ripped her thin shirt away. The crowd had full view of her naked body. Grigory was mortified. He'd never seen such treatment of a woman. And the church was right there, leading the humiliation! He forced his way through the crowd, toward Father Peter. Then he stopped in his tracks.

One of the men had struck the woman in the back of her head with his fist, and she fell to her knees. But they still held her arms, and they pulled her right back up. This time the man planted his boot squarely between her buttocks and sent her flying off the porch. Without touching the steps she landed in a twisted heap in front of Father Peter. She moaned, not moving.

Father Peter bent over and said in a loud voice that all could hear, "You are a disgrace to the God-fearing people of Pokrovskoe, *prostitutka*! They shall do as they please with you!"

"Wait! She is injured!" Grigory used his arms and Bible to break through the front rows of onlookers.

Father Peter turned. "What—Novykh! Why are you here? This is the Lord's work, not folly for a false disciple such as yourself. Go home to your horses."

Grigory angrily confronted Father Peter. "You beat this woman in the name of the Lord? You say He would treat her in such a manner?"

"She has sinned and disgraced our town, and she has no need of someone like you. Now stand aside and let the people of our fair town show you what they think!" With that, the crowd surged and scooped up the woman, shoving, beating and pummeling her through its midst until she had passed all the way through. Somehow still on her feet, though doubled over, she stumbled off to the scrub brush at the end of the lane and fell from sight.

Grigory fought his way behind her to the catcalls of the priest. "Your false powers will not help her, Novykh, for her beating was just in the eyes of God! Comfort will be long in coming—true healing comes only from Almighty God!"

But Grigory paid no heed. "You are wrong!" he cried out over his shoulder.

He followed the scuffed trail through the brush until he heard a quiet sobbing and there, curled under the scant protection of a bush, lay the dirty and trembling nude woman. She cowered from him with bruised, tear-streaked cheeks and tried to cover herself.

Grigory stripped off his grey work shirt, dropped to his knees and spread it over her. "They were wrong. The Lord would never hurt you like this." He bowed his head and prayed aloud, asking the Lord to forgive the priest and his followers for their actions.

Her sobbing quieted as Grigory prayed. He asked one more time for the Lord's forgiveness before he again turned to her. He held her bruised face in his hands and saw she was younger than he'd thought, barely thirty years if that, with handsome features that had withstood the beating. There was blood on his fingers. He gently turned her head and stroked a large cut on her scalp. "Please, tell me your name so that I might treat you as the Lord would prefer."

"I am Darlena Igorevna Startov. My husband died—but nothing happened, nothing at all—" she began crying again, uncontrollably. Grigory held her.

"The Lord will help you, Darlena Igorevna. He loves you as one of His children. He will see that no more harm comes to you."

Soon her crying quieted to a sniffle. She wiped the tears from her soiled cheeks. "You are Grigory Efimovich Novykh," she stated almost nonchalantly, startling him. "I have heard of you. They say God gave you special powers."

"I have no such powers, Darlena Igorevna. I am but a *moujik* who believes in the Virgin and follows Her word." He looked again at her cut. It had quit bleeding. Tiny diamonds of light glittered on her damaged skin. Grigory closed his eyes and thanked Her. He tore a strip of cloth from his undershirt and tied it around her head.

"I am going home for food and clothing, Darlena Igorevna. I should be no longer than an hour," he guessed, hoping that, on such a mission, the six *versts* would fly beneath his feet. "Stay here and rest. After dark I'll move you someplace safer."

"Thank you, Grigory Efimovich. You are a blessing." She nodded her thanks as he dashed off.

Later that night, Darlena lay in the crude bed Grigory made for her in the hayloft of the Novykh barn. She watched him work to heal the bruises on her legs. He stroked her skin lightly inward at the edge of the discolored areas, as if persuading the healthy cells to move into the welts and heal them. His eyes were closed, he was lost in prayer.

Darlena reached out, caressing his thigh through his trousers, running her fingers lightly along the long, young muscles. Then she moved her touch to the inside of his legs. His eyes remained closed. She brushed him, and he crawled out of himself. Her fingers danced along its increasing bulk, and as he reached full excitement she touched and squeezed him between her fingers.

Grigory stopped massaging her legs but did not open his eyes. "I am not sure this is right, Darlena Igorevna. What would the Virgin have me do—"

She answered, "The Lord would have you enjoy such treatment, Grigory Efimovich. They probably call you Grisha, yes? The Lord meant you to use your manhood, Grisha, as well as your mind, to comfort those in need. And surely I am one of those in need."

"I want to help you, Darlena Igorevna, but what of the church? Do they not say such things are wrong?"

"The church errs, my Grisha. The church expects men and women to ignore the desires the Lord gave them. They do not understand how they force their parishioners to sneak about behind their backs. It is so wrong." She reached into his trousers and grabbed him. Her eyes opened wide. "My God, you are so big! How can they expect us to ignore this?" She stroked him with vigor until he grabbed her wiggling wrist.

"I cannot ignore it, Darlena Igorevna." He relaxed his hold on her, and she resumed. This time he did not stop her.

She cast the blanket aside and pulled Grigory where she needed him. "Grisha, I want to feel it. It will comfort me."

He thrust his hips with the skill of a natural. She gasped as he did. He backed up and thrust again, careful not to brush the bruises on her legs, but soon neither of them paid attention to bruises or anything else. Time passed without notice.

"You were wonderful, Grisha," Darlena panted at last, "you had what I needed to help me through this. You have such talent, such experience."

"But I have not done this before, Darlena Igorevna."

"What? You jest! No? Then you have done very well indeed, my Grisha. You have taken an important step in your life. Now you know what women need—you'll never again have to wonder about that! People should know of your accomplishment. I shall call you '*Rasputin*'!"

"Rasputin? Please, no! 'The debauched one', the corrupted one? I will not be known by that name. It is against the ways of the Virgin, and it will offend the Lord."

"No, Grigory Efimovich Rasputin. I mean it only as the 'ill-behaved child', for that is what you are! People will understand the difference."

"I will not allow it, Darlena Igorevna. I remain Grigory Efimovich Novykh of Pokrovskoe. Please do not use that other name when you speak of me."

"If you insist, Grisha. But you will always be Rasputin to me." The need for sleep finally won her over.

Grigory returned to his room inside the house. The furious battle within him came out in his prayers. "Am I the wicked one?" he asked of God and the Virgin. "Is that who I am? Is what I did evil in Your eyes? Oh God, oh Mother, tell me it is not so! Tell me how You view such conduct, for if it is evil, I shall never do it again. I will live as the monks do, without women, if You would have it so.

"Yet even animals satisfy themselves, and I know they do not cower in fear of You. Can man be so different? Oh Lord and Mother, I do not understand. Why would You give me such a need for her body, such a need to satisfy her, and her for me, if it is wrongful in Your eyes?"

CHAPTER 2

Four years later

Pokrovskoe, Russia

August 14, 1892

'Rasputin' had been born. Grigory's *tovarishch*, Petcherkin, hadn't thought the nickname evil at all, so over time Grigory answered to it. And it was a name that blew across the Siberian tundra like Russian thistle. Twenty-year-old Rasputin was the Blessed One, and he loved all of God's creatures, as the Virgin would have it so. He helped heal a man's injuries, then engaged him in Biblical debate. And he took special care of the women, whether beautiful or homely, fat or thin. If he found their spirit needed unification of body and soul, he made use of other gifts to help them feel comfortable. Few women rejected his ways, his hypnotic blue eyes, his soothing charm. He dismissed those who did with a wave of his hand. Needier souls awaited.

Along his path Rasputin found that vodka and Madeira wine eased his path. Laughter flowed freely when he and his consorts drank "like true Russians." It loosened many tongues, inhibitions and buttons, and its influence on him became noticeable night and day.

The priests of Pokrovskoe were not amused. Their town was small and Rasputin's activities did not go unnoticed. They warned, "His teachings are false, he is a lost soul. He does not follow the ways of the church, and he will not find salvation."

Their warnings were not heeded. The townspeople embraced Rasputin's healing abilities. His relationship with the Lord and the Virgin was not doubted, and there was nothing the clergy could do. Rasputin became a cruel reminder that the *moujiki* did not expect much of them.

Still, Rasputin was not comfortable with his distance from the church. Several times he tried to explain his anguish to the priests, his battle between spirit and flesh. He asked, 'had not the Lord, through the Virgin, called for his spiritual devotion to Him? And had He not also provided him with such a sexual drive and stamina that, day or night, more than one woman would thank him and beg him to move on to another? Where was the Bible's answer to his dilemma?'

Abstinence, the priests replied, and true worship. They did not budge from their position. If Rasputin fought them with words of Scripture, the priests turned their angry, jealous ears away.

It was useless. Rasputin cried for help from the night tundra, but none came. His forays grew wilder, some involving daring timing and even two women at once.

As the fall harvest neared, Rasputin needed to visit a girl on a distant farm who was promised to another, but who had begged him to instruct her in the ways of true worship. For the days' ride he borrowed a horse from a nearby pasture without permission. When he'd finished his lessons and tried to sneak the horse back, its owner replied with a shovel-blow to the back of Rasputin's head. It was the Siberian way.

The wound confined him to bed for two months and forever altered his speech, slowing it to a stumbling delivery full of pauses and half-sentences. But worst of all, his journey to see Makari again had to be postponed, likely until fall. Over that winter Rasputin studied the Bible like never before, looking for the answers that would assuage his spiritual guilt.

The next summer he took a bride, Praskovia Dubrovina, whom he'd met at the festival in Tobolsk. She was a wholesome, strikingly pretty blonde with deep brown eyes, four years older than he, with a manner well-suited for raising children. Praskovia also was one of the few women who did not submit to his early advances.

Yet even with his new, ever-available partner, Rasputin still found his sexual thirsts unquenched. Even more remarkably, Praskovia understood her husband's needs. "God Himself has given Grisha His blessing—and there is plenty of Grisha to go around," she said to friends and neighbors. Some of the ladies would nod vigorously.

Finally, after the 1893 harvest, the weather grew chilly. The Siberian winter was just around the corner. If Rasputin was ever to visit the mystical Makari, it would have to be now. Praskovia gave him her blessing.

Three days later

The Foothills of the Ural Mountains

October 2, 1893

Rasputin crossed one more ridge and suddenly it lay before him—a dense stand of birch, hidden in a small valley behind an army of fir and spruce. He entered the stand. Dying yellow leaves overhead obscured the cold afternoon sun, they rustled in the breeze like a man's steps behind him. The eyes of the birch, watching from the bark of the thin, white-skinned trunks, followed his every move.

He came to a small clearing, a cove of short grasses and wildflowers. To his left was the first sign of a human he had seen for many *versts*—a small, simple hut of animal skins stretched across thin birch poles. Rasputin approached the hut slowly. No one answered his call. His weary feet ached. He would be grateful had this been the end of his search, but how could a *starets* as famous as Makari live in such a way?

"There are no easy answers, my young friend," came a voice from behind. Rasputin jumped with surprise. He spun around to see he was standing but two meters from an old man seated cross-legged on the leafy forest floor in a rare spot of sun. Long white brows shaded his eyes. His face was long and weather-beaten, his white beard magnificent.

"Father Makari?"

"Indeed, the Lord reminds us to first be sure we understand our questions."

Rasputin squatted and laid down his pack, pulled out a battered tin cup and poured water for the starets. When both had wet their lips Rasputin sat, respectfully distant. "My name is Grigory Efimovich Rasputin . . . Novykh, Father Makari. I come from Pokrovskoe, in the Tobolsk Province. The monks of the monastery at Verkhotourie told me if I fell into your favor, I might beg you to help me with my questions."

"The battle between the soul and the flesh has raged for time eternal, my young friend. It remains for each of God's children to fight it on his own terms. For the monks of Verkhotourie, and for Makari and other servants of the Lord, the battle has quieted, owing to the solitude of the forest. But is that the way for all men? That is what you must find for yourself."

Rasputin stared, gaping, tongue-tied. How could Makari answer questions that he had not yet asked?

"I feel the Lord has already spoken unto you, young Grigory Efimovich. Your confusion speaks loudly, you call yourself by two names. Tell me about your experiences," he said, closing his eyes.

Rasputin coaxed himself to speak and explain his dilemma. He started his story from when he first noticed the light that burned before his eyes, when he was working with his father, practicing *zagovarivat'krov* on their injured horses. He described his brother's death, and how the light had not come to help Misha, but yet it was there to uncover Mr. Prosportin's thievery shortly thereafter.

Makari's eyes remained closed throughout, to the point where Rasputin wondered if the starets was still listening or had fallen asleep. But when Rasputin told of the Virgin Mary's visit, Makari's eyebrows lifted, though his eyes remained closed. Evidently he was listening.

When Rasputin finished, the *starets'* eyes opened, dancing with a fresh charge of spirituality and life. "The Black Virgin Herself! You are a blessed man, Grigory Efimovich, and indeed, I now understand your questions fully. You must understand that the Black Virgin and the White Virgin are both spirits of the Holy Mother, yet they differ, too.

"The White Virgin is the personification of purity, of

tenderness, understanding and motherhood. She accepted —no, she welcomed —God's mission for Her, that is, to bear His Son with modesty and humility.

"And the Black Virgin is no less true in the eyes of the Lord, but She symbolizes the power and sexuality, the passion, of womankind. A fiery temperament and inner strength drive Her to protect both Her children and the White Virgin within Her like a lioness. She is a Queen who serves her King, and you are a fortunate man to have Her appear before you.

"Now tell me, Grigory Efimovich —how have you felt the pull of both sides of the Virgin Mary?"

Rasputin told the story of his rescue of Darlena Igorevna Startov from the angry townspeople, and, red-faced, the loss of his virginity to her. Then his tears flowed. "Father Makari, I feel as though I have sinned, but I do not feel that what I did was wrong! How can this be? Did not the Lord grant us these bodies? And did He not give us a need for the opposite sex that can spring up at any moment?

"Yet the church says I must not —that Darlena Igorevna cannot —for it is wrong in God's eyes. But mere dogs do it in the street! All of His animals do. Are we to be judged apart from them? Do they risk drawing His wrath? Oh, I feel so lost, as though He has placed this obstacle in my path to keep me from contentment." Rasputin buried his face in his hands.

"You must look at your suffering as an invitation to come to know the Lord, Grigory Efimovich. He will point the way for you, but you must decide how to best serve Him. It will not be easy. Begin by recalling what the Virgin said unto you."

Rasputin looked up at Makari while wiping the tears from his face. "She didn't actually say . . . "

Makari interrupted, "Then you were not listening, my young friend. Did she not bestow her blessing upon you?"

Rasputin nodded.

"And did she not indicate your path to travel?"

"That is why I came here, Father Makari. This is where she pointed."

Makari laughed. "Grigory Efimovich, I am an old man in the forest, though I thank you for your compliment. I do not have answers for you. As I said, at most I will help you to ask the right questions. You are so young, and you have seen so little. Tell me, why would the Virgin point you to my humble hut, to a servant who has found the answers only for his own life?"

Rasputin shrugged. "I do not know."

"Then we must ask ourselves to what she was pointing."

Again, Rasputin had no answer. Makari closed his eyes and volunteered nothing. He seemed content to listen to the passing breezes overhead, whispering and gusting, toying with the clusters of dry leaves.

Eventually Rasputin said, "Maybe she was not simply pointing west, Father Makari. Do you think she meant for me to search for my own answers, to become a *strannik*?"

With a faint smile Makari opened his eyes. "That is a difficult choice for any man of God. The path of the inner way, a monk's life of meditation, is more frequently chosen, Grigory Efimovich.

"The path of an underground man is not so easy. Pilgrimage and the life of a *strannik* . . . authorities shall believe you a thief. The church shall call you a heretic, you must live by your wits and charm alone, that and the word of God.

"But if that is your path, the Russian *moujiki* will help you, for they are the most generous people on Earth. They will open their homes for you, and feed you, and allow you to pray in their *sabors*. All they will ask are to hear your tales and learn of your adventures.

"You will encounter other *stranniki* on the road and in those *sabors*, all in search of their paths. And there you will find no end to debate, for the Bible is full of lessons of interpretation. In fact," Makari chuckled, "every man you meet will have an earful, ready for you."

Rasputin smiled, his heart fluttering. "Father Makari, now I am sure my answer lies in coming to know the Lord as a wanderer. I will take leave of my wife. She is a good woman, and she will await me in the home of my parents. I look at myself and the world through new eyes. Thank you."

"It was you who looked within yourself, Grigory Efimovich, not I," Makari replied. "However, I have faith that you have made the right choice, that you will find a way to serve the Virgin. Remember, She will guide your life forever more, no matter how you choose to serve Her. May God bless you." Makari performed the sign of the cross upon him before closing his eyes and returning to meditation.

Rasputin stood and slung his pack over his shoulder. "Thank you again, Father Mak—". He saw a tiny light twinkling over Makari. Further words were pointless. The Virgin Herself was with him.

Rasputin returned home; his faith helped him deal with the passing of his mother that winter. The Virgin would care for her. She would care for them all.

The excitement of pilgrimage burned like fire in his soul. The Virgin Herself was within him, it was all he spoke of. He and Praskovia and their newborn son, Dmitri Grigoryevich, moved in with his father. Efim and Praskovia would care for each other when Rasputin left. It was the Russian way.

Six months later

April 10, 1894

At the first sign of spring thaw, Rasputin set out from Pokrovskoe as a *strannik*, carrying only a change of clothes and his Bible in his pack. It took him little time to cross the Urals and enter the easternmost forests of Western Russia. There, on a path through the wilderness, a wild little man with the curliest hair nearly knocked him over. The little man asked if he carried medicine.

"The Lord's word is my medicine. I am Grigory Efimovich Rasputin."

"This way then, priest. My daughter lies ill by the stove." On the way the stout *moujik* introduced himself as Paul Pavlovich Bakunin. Shortly he took Rasputin's arm and dragged him off the main path, leading him down a narrow trail that ended at the steps of his tiny, one-room home. "Quiet, please. My wife, Anna Sergeyevna, and Pasha Pavlovna are inside."

They entered. Paul shut the door behind them and sat to speak with his wife. A muted glow, barely resembling sunlight, filtered in through four greenish, moldy panes centered on each wall. But an oil lamp burned softly in the icon corner, drawing his attention. He knelt before the two icons hanging there, crossed himself and prayed. The sickly stench within quickly overpowered the crisp morning air they'd let in.

Rasputin finished praying and turned about, his eyes adjusting to the darkness. He saw Anna, a thick, young woman, pressing a rag to the forehead of a bundled child next to the stove. He stood and pulled his bag off his shoulder. He set it beside the hissing samovar on the square wooden table in the corner, and he laid his heavy *caftan* on a bench built out from the walls. As he approached the little girl, Anna and Paul rose and went to the other side of the room.

Rasputin performed the sign of the cross over the child and then took her hand. Her swollen eyelids parted slightly. "I am Grisha, my little one," he said gently, caressing her cheek with his other hand. "The Lord has sent me for you, for you are His favorite. It troubles Him that you are not outdoors with other children, playing horses and riders."

A faint smile formed on her lips. Rasputin bent over and kissed her forehead. "Pasha Pavlovna, we shall speak to our Lord. We shall tell Him of our devotion." His hands clasped together over hers and he closed his eyes. His head rocked from side to side as the Bakunins joined hands. Soon Rasputin shifted so that his back was against the wooden wall, and he pressed his head hard into it.

He chanted gutturally, pushing harder against the wall. The muscles and veins in his face and neck grew visible. A sweat broke out on his forehead and his hands shook with power.

Anna finally looked with concern at Paul, as if to say, 'Who is this man, and do you see that he holds the hand of our sick child?' The heavy creases in Paul's forehead told her of his own doubts, but he took her in his arms, as much to comfort her as to make sure she did not interrupt Rasputin's prayers.

Finally Rasputin stopped chanting and his head nodded forward—but suddenly he cried out and crashed his head back against the wood. Anna cried out, startled. Paul held her tightly. Then Rasputin fell silent. Then he startled them again with his cries and self-abuse. And again.

Two hours passed before Rasputin finished. Pasha slept. Her parents lay on the floor, worn of worry and surprises.

Rasputin opened his eyes. He saw a light twinkling over the head of the young girl. "The Lord has crushed her fever, my friends," he announced, smiling. "You will sleep well tonight."

Anna practically trampled Rasputin in her rush to her daughter. Pasha opened her eyes wide at the touch of her mother's hand. "Mama?" Anna responded with a cry of joy and a smothering hug.

Paul approached Rasputin and knelt before him. "Bless me, Father Grigory, for never have my home and family been in the company of such a true man of God."

Rasputin performed the sign of the cross over him. "Healing is the work of the Lord, not mine," he said humbly. He returned to the icon corner, knelt and said a brief prayer.

"We shall feast in honor of the holy man, Father Grigory!" declared Anna. She rose, kissing Pasha again on her forehead. "I will set to it at this moment!" She spoke with such determination it drew laughter from the men, and she set to her tasks like a whirlwind.

"Bring to the table everything you can find in the oven!" called out Paul.

Rasputin smiled at the old *moujiki* proverb. He knew they were about to prepare a fair portion of their winter food supply, and it would be an insult if he did not eat heartily.

Paul pulled two metal-bottomed mugs with handles down from a shelf on the wall, along with a smaller, simpler cup. He set them on the table and poured pungent black tea from the pot atop the *samovar* into each. Then he added a shot of hot-peppered vodka and steaming hot water from the tap at the bottom of the samovar to each cup. He took the small one to his wife.

"Pray tell, Father Grigory," he said, rejoining Rasputin and passing him one of the men's mugs, "of the travels that brought you to join us here tonight."

Rasputin smiled. He told of his visit from the Virgin amid the smells of cooking cabbage and buckwheat and the strong drink before them. Paul listened with awe, then shared some of his thoughts on the teachings of the Bible. Together they decried the rape of traditional Russian Orthodoxy by Peter the Great and his henchman, Patriarch Nikon. They shared their admiration for the *staroveri* for their armed defense of their traditional beliefs, and they wept for those *staroveri* martyrs who chose mass suicide by fire over conformance. The new Holy Synod, they agreed, was wrong to ban Russians from worshipping as their ancestors had, and to withhold the ordination of priests that they might now follow.

The meal scarcely slowed their conversation. They spoke

through full mouths, all the while shoveling in black bread loaded with gruel and pouring in cabbage soup from wooden bowls.

Paul said, "The *staroveri* cannot be criticized for not returning to the folds of the Russian Orthodox church, Father Grigory. A man must rely on himself to guide his worship to the Almighty."

"And a woman, too, husband," added Anna.

Rasputin nodded, "You are both right, my friends. Just as Makari, of the forest, has found his own path, so must we choose the paths of our own."

"What of you, Father Grigory?" asked Anna. "Do you follow the path of traditional Orthodoxy, or do you follow another?"

"I do not follow the *staroveri*, Anna Sergeyevna. Nor do I follow the ways of the modern church. I find myself with questions that neither can answer. My conflict deals with human need, with the celibacy that people of religion so readily accept. I have to ask, is that really what the Lord asks? If so, why did He give us such an instinct, and such a drive, to procreate?"

The Bakunins exchanged glances.

Rasputin continued, "I cannot believe sexual release is intended only for the purpose of reproduction. The needs of the body are so strong, they are such a part of the human animal— indeed, of all animals. And does the Lord frown on all animals? Surely He does not. Some claim the ignorance of animals saves them from judgment. But I have known many humans, then, who should also be saved from judgment."

The Bakunins laughed loudly. Then, in a timid voice, Anna said, "I have heard of a sect that follows thoughts such as those, Father Grigory. Tell us, do you know of the *Khlysty* beliefs?"

"Wife!" bellowed Paul, glaring.

Rasputin downplayed any offense, "I have heard of them, yes. But I have never encountered *Khlysty* worshippers. It was only this year, at the vile monastery at Mount Athos, that I learned of *Khlysty* beliefs in detail."

"Vile?" Paul asked. "I have heard of the monastery only in high praise, with the holiest of admiration."

Rasputin bowed his head, and in a low voice said, "Let us say, many of the monks suffer from the same anguish as I. And they acknowledge the dilemma. Yet among them are many who have found unnatural answers—answers truly against God's way. I saw them myself, deep in the woods."

"Oh, my!" murmured Anna, blushing.

"Yes. And yet they dare to call *Khlysty* followers heretics! I do not respect such monks. Tell me, how do you know of the *Khlysty*? Do other *stranniki* bring news of them?"

Paul exclaimed, "No! I mean, no, they do not bring news." He and Anna again looked to each other.

"Will you excuse us for a minute, Father Grigory?" Anna asked. "We must check on Pasha Pavlovna. We shall be right back. Paul Pavlovich?" she beckoned, and he followed her to the other side of the stove and crouched over their daughter.

Paul returned to Rasputin shortly. "Pasha Pavlovna is sleeping well, Father Grigory. We shall never leave your debt. I thank the Lord for sending you to us." He fell to his knees before Rasputin, and Rasputin blessed him again.

Paul then took a seat beside Rasputin and spoke in a quiet tone. "Do you know of the penalties that await those who are found to worship in the *Khlysty* manner, Father Grigory? The authorities are harsh, and there are many Russians who would turn you in for reward.

"Yet you are truly a man of God. I have witnessed it, and my wife has witnessed it. We trust you and your word. If you are truly interested in the *Khlysty*, we would introduce you to a man who knows them well. We may leave at any time, if you would have it so."

Rasputin's eyebrows lifted and a smile came across his face. "I would have it so, Paul Pavlovich."

Paul turned and looked over to his wife, and she looked back with in a way that said, 'did I not tell you so?'

Paul turned back to Rasputin and said, "We happily honor your wish, Father Grigory. You and I shall go to visit the *vozhd* at this moment. I am sure he will see you are a man of God."

Four hours later, under a cold sliver of moon and sky of stars, three worshippers trod a winding path through the forest. Rasputin could barely see in the shadows of the tall trees. Finally they came upon a clearing where an old cottage had long ago crumbled under its roof. Beside it a dilapidated barn, too, was heading for the same fate.

Rasputin looked for other worshippers, but there were none. The tales he had heard of the *Khlysty* included many worshippers, dedicated congregations that would push through the snow and rain throughout the year to attend services. So where were they? And where was the *vozhd* he had met after dinner, Zharkov? Not even a light was burning within. Were they the first to arrive?

Rasputin followed Paul and Anna to the back of the barn. Paul stomped twice on a piece of wood that lay near the stone foundation . . . and a moment later he seemed to be pulling at a loose plank on the weathered wall. Rasputin's eyes widened. The plank was actually several in a row, fastened together and discreetly hinged. It was a door, and when it opened they stepped inside. Rasputin looked for a doorman; there was none.

Anna found a candle under a shelf beside her and lit it. The flickering candlelight unveiled the dilapidated tack room they had entered; it smelled of sweaty leather and old hay. Then, near the wall, Rasputin saw a hole in the floor—an earthen stairwell that led down into darkness. A rope came up through the floor near the stairwell, ran through eyelets and was tied to a latch on the inside of the door.

Rasputin suddenly realized what had happened. "Those

below have granted us entry?" he asked, smiling. "All in the name of the Lord, Paul Pavlovich!" He slapped his host on the back. "Let us descend!"

Anna led the way with her candle, stopping on the bottom landing. Another door blocked the way. She delivered a secret knock, and the door creaked open. A towering, leather-faced, slant-eyed Kirzhig blocked their path. He recognized the Bakunins, but he scowled at Rasputin.

"He has met with the *vozhd*, Mashin. Did not Father Zharkov leave word?" Paul asked.

Mashin grunted and moved aside. The door opened into a long, narrow changing room. The air smelled strongly of cabbage, and sweat, too, and clothing hung on wall pegs. Clean white robes hung from other pegs. A long bench built into the floor ran the length of the room.

Anna walked past the bench and stepped behind a tall screen. Paul disrobed where he stood, and Rasputin followed his lead. They chose white robes of the proper size and finished dressing just as Anna rejoined them.

She had loosened her thick hair so that it fell about her shoulders with a pleasing fullness, and she had donned a waist-length white smock with a belt beneath her ample bosom. Below that she wore a floor-length white skirt.

They stepped up to the last door, but Paul stopped before they passed through it. "Again, we allow no man to speak of our worship, Father Grigory. I must ask even you to swear to secrecy."

Rasputin nodded. He crossed himself and swore, "By the Virgin of Kazan, Holy Mother of all Russia, the events I witness tonight are sealed within me."

"Welcome to the *Khlysty*, then, Father Grigory," Paul smiled. He pushed open the door.

A hundred or so small candles burned around the sizable room, they cast a fluttering dance of light and shadow onto the walls and timber ceiling. Even more tapers lit the arc that rose over the *vozhd's* simple pulpit and the icon hanging behind it. The unbroken circle of light inspired a feeling of belonging and of strength in numbers in Rasputin, and he felt goose-bumps rise on his skin.

The air was thick and heavy and stifling, and it was difficult to see, but there were about twenty robed worshippers sitting cross-legged on the ground with their backs to them, chanting their allegiances to Christ.

Paul quietly closed the door and led the way to the rear of the congregation. The three of them sat. He leaned over to Rasputin and whispered, "They have finished the feast and the tables have been stored. Now you will learn how our *vozhd* applies the principles he described for you tonight."

Suddenly the door behind them opened and closed with a bang. The chanting stopped. Rasputin recognized the *vozhd* as he strode past, Zharkov, a tall bearded man. He wore a red rope around the waist of his robe. Zharkov continued past the worshippers to his pulpit. In front of the icon he performed the sign of the cross upon himself, then he turned to his followers. "I welcome you, my friends, in our worship of Christ and His spirit. Now we pray to the Almighty Lord."

Rasputin was surprised to hear prayer after prayer that was harmonious with the Russian Orthodox church. The next hymn his own family had sung when he was a small child. And yet there was something indescribably different here, a type of nervous excitement reflected in the voices.

"Neighbors, I beg you," Zharkov asked them, "forgive those who do not believe that God is always among us. They persecute us in their ignorance of the highest worship of Him. They shall never know the body as a temple of God. They shall never admit that only the drive for survival comes before physical pleasure, and they shall never draw closer to Him!" His clenched fist banged the pulpit.

"We are the chosen ones! We know best the spirit of the Lord, for He is within us! That way we know how to love Him! Now pull—pull His spirit from out of your breast!" He clutched at his chest as though to pull his own heart out. "Hold it high for all the world to see and love!" The men and women stood and eagerly thrust their cupped hands over their heads. They turned and twisted under the divine weight.

"Now let it go! Let go the spirit of the Lord! Free it to the world! Cast it upward!" The worshippers shed the weight away, palms toward the ceiling, shrieking with delight. Rasputin laughed, overjoyed at the spectacle.

"And again!" cried Zharkov, shoveling spirit from his breast and hurling it to the ceiling. "Again! The room fills with His love!" The *Khlysty* frantically followed his lead, shoveling and hurling for all they were worth.

Suddenly the woman in front of Rasputin stripped off her smock and threw it up in the air. Others quickly followed suit and soon there were a dozen bare-breasted women in the room. Rasputin saw that they outnumbered the men.

"To the Lord!" Rasputin proudly called out, stripping away his robe as other men did and adding it to the rain of garments. His manhood flopped about as he danced in frantic worship. He watched excitedly as other robes and dresses flew into the air. The candles flickered and danced, somehow remaining lit.

"Join hands now, my children! We are one with the Lord—an unbroken circle!" The nude men and women encircled Zharkov, who still wore his robe. The wheel of men and women began to turn.

"Faster, faster! For the Lord!" Zharkov commanded. He pulled the red rope off his robe and whipped it at a small woman who was not keeping up. "Faster, sister! Close your eyes and allow Him to pull you along! He is ahead of you! He is behind you! Love them both!"

While spinning in tight circles himself, Zharkov whipped

indiscriminately at whomever was nearest, his open robe flying from his shoulders. Finally one of the women screamed in anguish and broke the circle. She dizzily ran to Zharkov and pulled him to the earth, landing him squarely between her legs.

Rasputin watched the rest of the circle dropping to the ground in pairs and threes. Paul took the woman on his left side, and another woman joined them. Anna watched. Rasputin still held her hand, and she turned to him. In no time they fell together and rolled on the ground, fondling and grasping each other passionately. He kissed her creamy-white chest, pressing her breasts to his cheeks. He had fully hardened. He rolled Anna onto her back and spread her knees wide apart. She thrust him in with both hands, her eyes wide, her breathing fast.

He rammed her over and over, and then a young woman crawled up and sucked at Anna's breasts wildly. Rasputin climaxed at the sight. Then he jumped up and entered the young woman from behind. She gasped, but never even turned around.

Rasputin looked around the room at the scene. Zharkov was now beneath his attacker. Flesh and motion were everywhere. Never had he seen such a sight. Such abandonment! Such a lack of shame! He threw back his head and howled with delight.

Paul looked up to from his dalliance, grinning broadly before the woman pushed his head back down. Rasputin howled again. No one else paid him any attention. "Thank you, Lord, for this heaven!" he said to himself as he refocused on the task at hand.

The young girl ran off to another couple as soon as Rasputin pulled out, and Anna had already found another man, so Rasputin wandered through the room, taking other women as he saw fit. Finally he was the last one not sleeping, for even the woman he now caressed had dropped off.

He pulled up a soft belly for a pillow and closed his eyes. The earth was warm. He felt at peace, exhausted but happy. His member had shrunk back to normal size. No passion remained in his body. "Holy passionlessness," he mumbled, "yes, it draws me closer to Thee." With a smile he added, "And I shall never stray far again."

For the next week, while he awaited the next *Khlysty* service, Rasputin explored the two nearby villages. He returned to the Bakunin's house at night. But a problem arose—Rasputin had seen how Anna and other local women behaved when they had allowed the Lord to unleash their true selves.

"You should release yourselves every day," he told them, but they steadfastly refused. Rasputin did not understand. Did they not worship the Lord always, even away from *Khlysty* services? He did not give up. He would prove that women so lustful in worship could not possibly ignore their desires.

Finally Zharkov himself had to ask Rasputin to abstain from attempting sexual engagements outside *Khlysty* tradition. But Rasputin made no promises. He merely crossed himself as if to say his divine mission allowed him such actions.

When finally the next *Khlysty* service had come and gone, Rasputin's disenchantment with the group was complete. Not only was there no alcohol allowed during service, but, as he explained to Paul, "Last night I saw fathers with daughters, mothers with sons, even a brother with a brother! Yes, to sin and ask forgiveness is the way of the Lord, but you cannot violate the natural laws. There are acts that cannot be forgiven, unholy bondings that cannot be repented."

So Rasputin resumed his westward travels, helping heal when he could, living the life of a *strannik*. Many were the earthen cellar *sabors* he blessed; many were the lonely wives he comforted to snoring husbands' lullabies.

Even women with the monthly curse found themselves cleansed in body and mind, purified and momentarily 'healed'—at least while Rasputin worked his magic. Smiling, they would wave farewell in the morning to the powerful man blessed by the Virgin Herself.

CHAPTER 3

Eight years later

Tsarskoe Selo, Russia

March 17, 1902

The royal grounds glistened under a bright morning sun, every inch of the icy-white marble and stonework shining in a portent of the coming spring.

Tsarina Alexandra danced out a side door of the Alexander Palace and onto the salted walk to the summer cottage. It was only a short stroll, and she paid no attention to her unbuttoned furs as they flapped about. She burst in through the kitchen door, rosy-cheeked, and surprised her best friend, Anna Vyrubova, peeling potatoes in the stove-warmed kitchen.

"Oh, Anyushka!" Alexandra sang, simply bursting at the seams. "Dr. Phillipe says I am pregnant! And he says it's a boy!"

"Oui! Oui! Anna dropped her knife, shrieking with Alexandra. They danced around the butcher block, holding hands and giggling like young girls, one in furs and the other in an apron.

In spite of Anna's heavier figure and homelier features, a stranger might have mistaken them for sisters. Both wore their dark hair high above their squarish faces, both had strong, but not unhandsome, jaw lines. And each was well-rounded in the bosom and possessed the whitest of skin.

Excitedly they went into the drawing room, where Anna belatedly wiped her hands on her apron and took it off. She helped Alexandra out of her wraps and they sat on the fine horsehair sofa.

"Not even Nikolas knows yet, Anyushka. He is reviewing the army this morning."

"After so long . . . Nikolas will be so happy! All of Russia will be happy for you, Alex!" She took Alexandra's hand and squeezed it between hers.

Alexandra could not stop smiling. "I feel as though my face will freeze this way, Anyushka! A boy . . . after four daughters. Just think of it! An heir to the Romanov throne. They will be singing across Mother Russia! And now . . . " she stopped, losing just a touch of her excitement, "well, perhaps the people will think better of me now. Maybe they will not treat me as such an outsider."

"Alex, you stop that," Anna said. "The people love you and you know it. You are Tsarina, the Mother of all Russia. They just don't know you as we do. And that will change now. They'll see how hard you have worked for them, and they will finally show you their love."

Alexandra's eyes lit up. "Do you really think so? Oh, Anyushka, you always know just what to say." She paused, thinking, giggling. "A boy, a boy—"

Anna hugged her again. "Oh, Alex, you have to tell the Montenegrins. They'll want to hear it straight from you. I will send for them at once!"

The elder sister from Montenegro, Grand Duchess Militsa Romanov, was there within the hour. She arrived in a closed carriage behind a *troika* of well-groomed Arabian horses. Olive-skinned, with a thin, upturned nose, she took the news as if she expected it. She smiled through thin lips.

"Of course, Empress, I knew Dr. Phillipe would succeed," Militsa declared. "His power is so mysterious. He is an expert of medicines and the mind. My dear Empress, it wasn't your fault, I'm sure, but it was probably your own mind that was blocking the conception of your son. Dr. Phillipe saw it, you know. The stars help him determine the causes of such things."

"Yes, sister, he was such a find," came a voice from the front door. Grand Duchess Anastasia Romanov had already figured out the gist of the surprise. "And we are lucky that he came to us from Paris. Why, Empress, if I hadn't asked for his help . . . "

Alexandra was home waiting for Nikolas when the army parade concluded. He, too, was overjoyed, but not just to have an heir to his throne. For years he had longed for a son to ride with him at a full gallop across Tsarskoe Selo, to hunt with him for deer and geese at their Spala, Poland estate, to sit with him as the Armies of Russia paraded before them.

Soon the palace was in preparation for the arrival of the boy. Designers created clothing fit for a Tsarevich, and Alexandra chose something from each of them. The nursery was repainted in shades of blue, and miniature soldiers and ponies of Nikolas' choosing were placed in the nooks and crannies.

Only one point of behavior seemed out of place. Alexandra refused to submit to an examination by the royal doctors, and as the months passed, the care provided by Dr. Phillipe raised a few eyebrows. Her special diet, one which Dr. Phillipe claimed to be in tune with the stars, bloated her. And his astrological consultations, tarot readings and psychic exercises required her presence at his tables for hours on end.

Finally, after six months, Alexandra complained to Nikolas that all four girls had begun to stir in her womb by that point in pregnancy. So far, the boy hadn't. Dr. Phillipe told her not to worry, but she couldn't help it. Nikolas called for the royal doctors, and they confirmed the worst possible news— Alexandra wasn't pregnant. She never had been.

The embarrassing episode was deadly to Dr. Phillipe's reputation. He fled the country to avoid a lynching by the angry Russian people.

But worse, by far, was Alexandra's devastation. She mourned for the son she had never carried, and for three weeks she did not rise from bed. Besides the Pages of the Chamber, their servants, she allowed only Nikolas, her daughters and Anna into her mauve boudoir.

"My beloved Alex," Nikolas begged, "we shall have our boy, and he will grow into a strong Tsar. But not this way. We cannot conceive between your tears. You must get up and become yourself again. I miss you, and the girls miss you."

"My Nicky," she moaned, "you are a good man, but you don't know what I've been through. I cannot tell you . . . " She turned her head away and gazed upon the Neva River while Nikolas' chin quivered. Tears rolled into his overgrown moustache and beard.

Three weeks later in the early morning, Duchess Militsa arrived at the palace and requested an audience with Alexandra. To everyone's shock, Alexandra granted it. Militsa went to her.

"Nik-o-las . . . " Alexandra sang out an hour later. He rushed to the room to find her fully dressed and standing gingerly beside her bed. "Nicky, call for a rolling chair," she said as he stood there gaping. "I don't seem to be moving so well."

"Alex!" Nikolas exclaimed. He helped her to sit back onto the bed.

"The chair, Nicky?"

Nikolas looked at his wife in surprise. "You are serious? Whatever for? Where are you going?" He looked at Militsa, but she only smiled.

"All in time, husband," Alexandra teased.

Confused but happy, Nikolas had no choice. "Page! Find a rolling chair and bring it here!" he ordered over his shoulder. "Please, Alex, tell me what is this all about."

Alexandra kissed him. "You are such a patient man, and I love you deeply. You've cared for me while I pined away over an embarrassing incident, but now I feel better. It is a bright day—a lucky day to embark on something new, so I am going out with Militsa. I can't tell you any more than that. Do you love me, Nicky?"

"By God in heaven, I so love you, Alex. I love you more than Russia herself. I just wish . . . "

"But I can't tell you right now, Nicky. Now where is that chair? I'm afraid I'm crippled right now."

Nikolas kissed her cheek and strode out into the hallway, where a page was coming with the chair. Nikolas eased Alexandra into it and pushed her through the palace halls and out through the foyer. After he'd helped her into the Duchess's carriage he tried one more time. "Alex, what is happening?

Where are you going in such a hurry? Who will help you out of the carriage?"

Alexandra kissed the tip of her finger and pressed it to his lips. "The driver will help me, Nicky, and the rest you'll find out in good time. I'll be back soon!" she waved as the three Arabians high-stepped out of sight.

The ladies boarded the royal train at Tsarskoe Selo station— horses, carriage and all—for the short ride to St. Petersburg. In little more than an hour they were clattering into the stone courtyard of the Duchess's palace. The driver pushed Alexandra's chair to Militsa's instructions, into a secluded parlor of a little-used wing of the palace. Anna and Duchess Anastasia were already there, seated and having tea.

"Empress!" they cried. They rushed up and kissed her cheeks, thanking her for coming on such short notice.

"You were right, Empress," Anna said when they had all taken seats. "Russia has her own healers and mystics. We needn't go clear to France to find them. This woman today is from Kazan. They say she is a bit daft, but that she predicts the future in her own way. She is called Matrena the Barefooted."

But Matrena the Barefooted was no help. Her childlike, singing replies to the simplest questions left the ladies in a snickering titter.

Four months later they gathered again. But Mitya Kolaba, an epileptic from the Black Sea, awarded them a writhing and drooling performance-seizure that was both revolting and sickening. A dropped teacup marked their hasty departure.

Then, eight months later, they called for Daria Ossipova. Despite her miraculous foretelling of danger a month earlier at the Nitzhy-Novgorod fair, just outside Tsarskoe Selo, Daria Ossipova's only vision was clouded anger. "You!" she shouted at Alexandra, "You are the German who sleeps with our Tsar! You look down upon our people and treat us like dirt, and you cannot give us a Tsarevich!" Alexandra's mouth fell open; she stepped back from the tiny nightmare.

That night Nikolas held Alexandra's head to his breast and ran his fingers through her long, auburn hair. A log in the fireplace shifted and cracked open a fountain of sparks. Eddies of tiny snowflakes swirled outside the royal bedroom windows.

"Is it worth it, Alex? That woman today, the old barefoot woman, the misfit? All for what, to upset you?"

Alexandra sighed. "No, Nicky, not to upset me, but to make us happy, to give us our Tsarevich. I do it for us, my love."

"Not for us, Alex, not for me, for I cannot be happier than when I am with you and my daughters. Don't you see? I love you more deeply than I can ever say. When you sing like a morning bird, my heart soars! But when you are teary, I am fallen. The blackness of night takes my soul and grips it hard in its fist, and I moan with the pain."

Alexandra sat up and faced him. A single tear crept down his cheek. "Oh, Nicky, I do love you so. And I do not mean to hurt you, I swear. But I must try, I must do what I can to bring us a son. It will not be easy, but you must be strong with me. You have to believe we will find a way to have our son, no matter who we have to get to help us. Nicky, do you believe?"

"Oh God, Alex, I believe! I believe! You are the finest gift ever bestowed on me, and I know you will do the right thing. Alex, have I told you tonight that I love you?"

Alexandra smiled. "I think you'd better show me, my Nicky," she waited for him to move his lips closer to hers. "Oh my! Wait, Nicky—there, on the bed stand!" She pointed to three burning candles.

"What is it?" Nikolas cried out, and then he realized what she meant. "Three candles burning together. That won't do, will it?"

"You know they will bring us bad luck, my Nicky."

He thought for a moment. "I have a question for you, then, Alex. If three burning candles bring us bad luck, would three—" poof! he blew them out with one breath "smoking candles bring us good luck?"

Alexandra nodded in the firelight. Gently Nikolas took her face with his hands and kissed her lips, and she kissed him back, sighing. He kissed her nose and cheeks, her eyes, her ears and jaw, her lips, her neck and shoulders . . .

The snows had quit swirling outside by the time Alexandra again lay with her head on Nikolas' chest. St. Petersburg slept.

But nine months from that night, on July 30, 1904, the city would be rejoicing far beyond that late hour. The church bells would ring and toasts would be made—all in honor of the birth of Tsarevich Alexei Romanov.

Two months later

September 16, 1904

There was a knock at the door of Alexandra's boudoir. It opened slowly and the heavy new nursemaid, Luba Viktoryevna, walked into the room with uncomfortable apprehension. Near the door Duchess Militsa sat in a tall chair of carved walnut and mauve floral silk.

Alexandra lay on the bed, fully dressed, with her lacy white dress flared out over her legs. Mauve silk throw pillows propped up her upper torso as she rocked round-headed little Alexei, cocooned in soft cotton with only his head exposed. Anna and Duchess Anastasia were on the mauve settee at Alexandra's feet.

"Empress, they say they are ready for you downstairs. Shall I watch the Tsarevich?" Luba asked.

"No," said Alexandra, holding her son protectively, "if you should drop him, or bump him . . . "

"She won't drop him, Empress," chided Anna. "Luba Viktoryevna knows how to care for sick infants, believe me."

"She is the best I could find in St. Petersburg," Militsa stated.

" . . . that *we* could find anywhere in Russia, Empress," chimed in Anastasia.

"Good heavens, ladies!" Anna managed to glare at both sisters at the same time.

Alexandra was shaking her head. "I'm sure Luba Viktoryevna is a wonderful nurse, but Alyosha may not take to her. If he cries and fights her, he may start to bleed again." Tears welled in her eyes.

Anna rose and strode to the head of the bed. Sternly she said, "Alex, you hired Luba Viktoryevna for a reason. Let us find out if Alyosha takes to her. If he doesn't, we'll begin another search, but let us find out, right now."

Alexandra glared, but finally she looked down at Alexei and sighed. She kissed his forehead and held him out for Anna, who passed him to Luba Viktoryevna. Little Alexei squirmed a little in the fleshy cradle of her arms, but then he settled into the crux of her wide bosom and began mouthing the white fabric covering her breasts. Luba Viktoryevna beamed, drawing smiles from everyone except Alexandra.

"See?" Anna said. "He likes her. He'll be fine. Now let us go down and meet Dr. Papus. He has traveled far to help the Tsarevich. We shouldn't keep him waiting any longer.

"Luba Viktoryevna," she continued, turning to the nursemaid, "take Alyosha to the nursery until we are finished downstairs. And you," she said to Alexandra, "please get off your royal backside! You know Nikolas has a surprise waiting for us downstairs, and you know how impatient he gets. He's probably watching the staircase and strutting like a rooster as I speak! Now up!" Anna offered her hand in assistance.

Alexandra nodded and smiled. She took Anna's hand, swung her feet off the bed and stood. She hugged Anna tightly. "I must seem so silly, Anyushka. Thank you." She hugged Militsa and Anastasia, too, then she strode to the door and held it open like a doorman. "My friends, shall we meet Dr. Papus?" The ladies mockingly tipped invisible hats to her as they passed into the wide hallway.

They were still tittering when they reached the top of the staircase, a sweeping, curving, terraced sculpture of mahogany and gold, lined with hand-woven tapestries. Below, Nikolas spotted them at once and stopped in mid-strut. Beside him was an older man, lean and balding, who wore eyeglasses set into tiny, round, dark frames.

Alexandra followed her friends. When they reached Nikolas, he introduced them to Dr. Papus, who bowed and kissed their hands. Finally Nikolas presented his wife. "And this beautiful creature, doctor, is my Empress, Alexandra."

Dr. Papus bowed deeply, then rose and said, "I have known your husband since he was a child, Empress. Now I must admit, he is the finest judge of beauty I have ever known." He kissed her hand as well.

Alexandra blushed and looked approvingly to Nikolas. "I am charmed with Dr. Papus, Nicky, but I must know—what is the surprise? What do you have in store for us?"

Nikolas smiled. "Alex, one of my fondest memories is of Dr. Papus conducting a séance to seek advice for my father. As it turned out, the advice was as good as gold. Now he's offered to do the same for us."

Alexandra's eyes grew wide.

"A séance, doctor?" asked Militsa excitedly. "With whom?"

"Someone dead, obviously, sister," Anastasia answered. "But do tell us, doctor, will we be speaking with someone famous? Has he been dead long?"

Dr. Papus held up his hands in protest. "Ladies, please. His spirit will come easiest in a calm, serene setting. The pages have darkened the parlor, and we should go there now. I will explain everything in due time."

Nikolas clapped his hands. "Of course. Alex?" Alexandra took his arm and together they led the way to the grand parlor, to a round table covered with dark cloth. A single beeswax candle burned in the center of the table.

Nikolas seated his wife and sat beside her. Two young pages seated Anna on the other side of Alexandra, then Anastasia and Militsa. Dr. Papus took his seat and completed the circle. The pages left the room, closing the double wooden doors behind them.

The doctor took off his glasses in the flickering light, folded them and placed them in his breast pocket. "Ladies and gentlemen, many years ago, when I was a student of medicine at the University of Paris, I came upon a man working deep in a basement laboratory, Dr. Henri Sangier. Now Henri was a gentle man, to be sure, but he was so lost in research that it was difficult to come to know him.

"Somehow, though, we struck up a kinship, and after a time, he revealed his motivation to me: he had lost an older brother to the disease of hemophilia. Many times I heard him ask himself, 'Why? Why Jacques and not I?'

"He gave himself little rest in search of the answer. In fact, too little rest, I'm afraid, for there was a fire in that laboratory late one night, and Henri did not make it out alive. They found his remains under the frame of his cot."

"Oh, how awful," said Anna, cringing.

"Yes, it was awful," Dr. Papus agreed, "but just as tragic was that his notes, too, were lost forever. And since he confided in so few people, no one knew how close Henri came to finding his answers. I believe it is time that we find out."

"Oh, we should!" extolled Alexandra. The mood in the room lightened considerably.

"Well then," Dr. Papus chuckled, "I shall attempt to contact Henri from the gate beyond, and we shall see if he is able to help the young Tsarevich. Please, Your Excellencies, everyone— we must join hands on the table."

As they did, Dr. Papus closed his eyes and hummed loudly, and everyone focused their attention on him. He tilted his head back at a rigid angle, drawing tight the quivering voice box and sinewy muscles in his neck.

Then he quieted and spoke. "Everyone, please concentrate. Allow only one thought in your head, that of Henri Sangier. Henri Sangier. Henri Sangier. Concentrate with every fiber of your being. Let the power flow through our hands. Let it collect and call out for Henri Sangier!" He resumed humming, his head still tilted back.

For several minutes both Nikolas' and Alexandra's heads wove from side to side as they silently mouthed Sangier's name. Anna's head fell forward loosely, as though it might hit the table. The Montenegrin sisters watched Dr. Papus suspiciously.

Suddenly a booming voice emanated from Dr. Papus, deeper and scratchier than his own. "I am Sangier. Who has called me from my rest?"

"Oh, my," murmured Alexandra, but no one answered the voice of Sangier. They just gasped, at each other and at Dr. Papus' elongated throat.

Finally Alexandra nudged her husband. He managed to stammer out, "I did. I am Nikolas, Tsar of Russia."

"Why do you disturb me?" the voice asked.

"It is my son, Alexei Nikolayevich Romanov," Nikolas explained. "He suffers from hemophilia. Dr. Papus said you might know how to cure him."

"Papus, he is a good man. He can help your son. Provide for him, for he is a true healer. I shall see that he comes to know of my work. But for now, I must rest."

Papus' hands broke the circle and clapped loudly together, then his head crashed down onto them. The candle blew out in the sudden gust.

Anna yelped out a scream, and Alexandra fainted limply in her chair. It was all Nikolas could do to keep her from sliding to the floor. He yelled, "Pages! Pages! Bring us water!"

The double doors flew open; one of the pages was sprinting away, down the hall. He quickly returned with a pitcher of water. While Nikolas tended to Alexandra, the page sprinkled water onto the back of Dr. Papus' head. Soon Alexandra and the doctor had both regained their senses.

"Emperor, what happened?" asked Dr. Papus breathlessly. "Did we find him? Did we speak with Henri?"

Nikolas continued fanning Alexandra with his hand while he turned toward Dr. Papus and smiled. "Indeed we did, doctor! It was wonderful! You are welcome—no, you are requested to live with as we fight this bleeding disease. You may be Alyosha's only hope!"

Dr. Papus looked at the Tsar with a bewildered, though content, expression. "I am happy it went so well, Excellency."

Militsa and Anastasia exchanged quick glances, eyebrows raised.

Eight months later

May 18, 1905

There would be two commencement ceremonies this day at St. Petersburg's Corps of Pages Military Academy. In the afternoon the cadets' family and friends would attend the outdoor commencement, but that was actually an after-the-fact show, staged specially for them.

At high noon the real commencement would take place, with all the military protocol due such an event. In the Academy auditorium the graduating class would sit in the front rows and be called up, one-by-one, to what Headmaster General Prosky called the 'World Stage'.

They would walk the wide, polished stage to receive their Army commissions, their first service orders and a blessing. They would kiss the symbol of the Corps of Pages, a black Maltese Cross that was laid into the face of the white marble podium—kiss it at its center, where the four points of the arrowhead-like V's turned inward and met to form an apex of unity and power. They would feel the sting of the Maltese Cross on their left breast, tattooed there only the night before.

Then, when the last graduate had joined the group, they would stand together as fledgling officers and take the Oath. They would swear Service to the Tsar, and then Friendship Until Death toward all fellows of the Corps of Pages.

Finally, and for the first time as Russian Army officers, they would turn and salute the symbol of the Tsar's presence—the magnificent double-headed black Imperial eagle, of iron and as tall as four men, that hung from massive chains behind the stage, set against the great pleated crimson curtains. She seemed so lifelike that one pull of her mighty wings might lift her into the heavens of Mother Russia.

It was time. At the rear of the auditorium three sets of tall, wide double doors opened simultaneously and spring sunlight streamed in. Tall young men in uniform, two abreast, stood perfectly still outside the portals, hats in hand. At the cue of a crisp whistle they descended, high-stepping perfectly in time, down the long, sloping aisles. The cavernous room shook under the precisely orchestrated parade. Each cadet made an appropriate, well-practiced turn, marched to his assigned seat and stood at attention before it.

After the youngest, smallest cadets had taken their places at the back of the auditorium, General Prosky marched down the center aisle. The doors behind him slammed shut, echoing thunderously over his footsteps. He marched to the stage apron and, with perfect military precision, ascended the steps at stage left and took command of the podium. A second whistle blew. As one the cadets took their seats, erect, with hats and hands in laps.

General Prosky cleared his throat and spoke in a strong voice. "Cadets, as you know, the end of the academic year means many things. But to today's graduating class, it means only one thing—that life truly begins! They shall find themselves in service of their country, strong officers in the Tsar's Russian Army!"

He proudly swept his hand, palm upward, across the rows directly before him, extolling the graduates' good fortune. The rest of the cadet corps stood and applauded until the general signaled them to take their seats.

"So today we honor a very special guest. He personally served Tsar Alexander III as a Page of the Chamber and graduated your Corps of Pages in eighteen eighty-nine. He rose to Colonel in the Russian Army, then returned to his home and was elected to district spokes-man. Earlier this year he founded the Union of the Russian People, and today he is one of the great orators of Mother Russia. I introduce you to Vladimir Mitrofanovich Purishkevich!"

To a standing ovation, a heavyset civilian with a receding hairline and a pointed beard strolled out of the wings toward the podium. He came to attention before Prosky and returned his salute. Prosky yielded the podium and stood at parade rest three steps back.

Purishkevich motioned for the cadets to sit. "Thank you, brothers of the Maltese Cross! What pride and comfort I feel knowing that we are one in support of Tsar Nikolas II!"

CHAPTER 4

One month later

St. Petersburg

October 31, 1905

Steam hissed into the chilly air from beneath a shining black locomotive. Thick smoke rolled from its stack. A long whistle blew, metal couplings clanged taut. The short line of royal-blue and golden cars with gilded double-headed Imperial eagles on the sides slowly pulled out of St. Petersburg station.

Grand Duchesses Militsa and Anastasia managed false smiles for Grigory Rasputin, staring at them from the velvet bench opposite. They did not know him well—they'd met him only once, at a society tea in St. Petersburg three years earlier, where he was rumored to be a mystic of devout holiness and healing abilities. Strangely, he had turned down their invitation to meet Alexandra, saying he had not yet finished the search for himself. This time, however, on his second trip to the capital, he had accepted their invitation.

"Have you ridden the trains much in your travels, Father Grigory?" Militsa asked.

Rasputin shook his head, his beard catching on the rough fabric of his worn *caftan*. His deep blue eyes did not blink as the train jolted into motion, his body swaying like a leaf in a breeze. "The Lord prefers that I travel by foot. It allows Him to speak to me as He pleases. I'm afraid He might not enjoy speaking to me over such a commotion as this."

The sisters laughed nervously, unsure if he was joking.

"Well, we've only twenty-five *versts* to cover," said Anastasia. "I hope the Lord hasn't reason to call out to you in that time, Father."

"He will call to us as He pleases, my little one. Tell me, does He not speak to you?" The sisters stared at him blankly. Rasputin nodded and winked at them, then he leaned far forward in the car and put his hands on one knee of each of them. In a husky whisper he confided, "When you sin and He forgives you, that is when you shall hear His voice."

Militsa drew back in surprise and shifted her leg away from his touch. Anastasia, though, blocked in against the window, could make no such move to escape his grasp.

"What does the Lord sound like, Father Grigory?" she asked innocently. Militsa looked at her scornfully and began to apologize for her sister's impertinence, but Rasputin held up his free hand.

"It is the most beautiful sound you will ever hear, little one. I will tell you of my visit from Our Lady, the Virgin. I was only a boy, tending our fields in Pokrovskoe . . . "

During the rest of the 20-minute ride to Tsarskoe Selo, Rasputin told stories, his steely blue eyes dancing, his hands waving passionately. Even Militsa relaxed as she witnessed his sincerity and fiery passion for the Lord.

The train slowed and pulled into Tsarskoe Selo station. Tall Cossack guards bowed to the Duchesses and helped them step onto the platform. Their *troika* awaited.

The horses trotted majestically down a tree-lined street, past the manors of aristocrats who thrived on the excitement of life near the royal family, until they reached the high iron gates of the Imperial compound. More Cossacks waved them through without delay. They passed by mounted guards and acres of freshly cut lawn on the way to the smaller of two palaces less than a half-*verst* from each other.

"This is the Alexander Palace, Father—the family prefers it to the Catherine Palace," Anastasia said. "They live there, in that wing." She pointed to one of the two sprawling, pillar-lined wings that shot off from the palaces' squarish center-block.

Rasputin glanced over in silence. If he was impressed, he did not show it.

The carriage stopped and they were shown in. A tall Negro wearing a turban motioned for them to wait in the foyer; he disappeared behind double doors into a bright room. Momentarily he reappeared and motioned for them to come.

Nikolas stood near a white linen tea table. Alexandra remained seated and nodded to the guests. The Duchesses politely curtsied and together said, "Your Majesties."

Militsa turned to Rasputin and said, "May I introduce you to . . . ," but Rasputin did not wait for protocol. He strode in the general direction of Nikolas, who, with a confused, surprised look on his face, reached out his hand.

But Rasputin strode past Nikolas without a glance; his eyes were fixed on the icon "Our Lady of Vladimir" that hung on the wall. There shed his *caftan* onto the floor and fell to his knees upon it. He crossed himself and bent over, arms extended, until his forehead touched the ground. He chanted in a loud monotone voice, like a monk, slowly and deliberately.

The rest of them watched, astonished. Nikolas' mouth hung open. Alexandra and the Duchesses cast doubting glances to one another that asked, 'Is this another mistake? Should we have believed the tales that preceded this *strannik's* arrival in St. Petersburg? Are we going to embarrass ourselves now in front of Nikolas, too?'

Rasputin continued praying, his chanting growing in fervor that seemed to pull from the depths of his soul. His head rose and fell repeatedly. The sound of his forehead banging on the floor grew loud enough for all to hear.

Nikolas could not continue to watch Rasputin pray alone. He knelt beside Rasputin and joined him, doing his best to chant in unison. The ladies called for kneeling pillows, and soon they had joined the prayers, too.

Finally Rasputin's head fell to the floor for the last time. His chanting stopped. Twenty minutes had passed since he'd entered the room. Everyone awaited his next action.

Rasputin slowly lifted his head to again view the icon. He closed his eyes and crossed himself, and the rest of them did, too. Then he turned and took Nikolas' head in his large, rough hands.

"*Batiushka*," he said simply, and he gave Nikolas three kisses of friendship and embraced him. Then Rasputin released Nikolas and stood.

He greeted Alexandra the same way. "*Matushka*."

Nikolas broke out in relaxed laughter. Soon the children were sent for, including the infant Tsarevich Alexei. Rasputin blessed them all.

As they sat through tea and cakes, Rasputin told of visiting monasteries throughout Russia, of traveling the mighty River Volga to the Black Sea, of his journey through Greece and his march to the Holy Lands, to Jerusalem.

The family was completely at ease with Rasputin. He seemed one of them. He so enchanted them with his tales and exhibitions of devotion that they scarcely noticed his dirty nails and his uncombed, matted hair. Even tiny Alexei seemed comforted by his voice.

Later that night, after they said good night to Rasputin, Nikolas and his family basked in the warm feelings Rasputin had left behind.

"He measures his words so carefully," Nikolas said.

Alexandra hugged him, beaming, and said, "I feel so—so—alive, Nicky!"

And later, after Nikolas had taken his bath and sipped a late-night tea, he summarized the day in his diary: 'Tonight we have come to know a man of God, Father Grigory, from the Tobolsk Province.'

Two years, eight months later

Tsarskoe Selo

July 30, 1908

To set the stage for Tsarevich Alexei's fourth birthday party, scores of white linens had been spread over the lush lawn at the edge of the Great Pond, and a shady forest of umbrellas blossomed out over them. A perimeter of a hundred or more straight-back chairs framed much of the site, with a lengthy dais at its head and a tiny chair there for the guest of honor. Bright ribbons and bunting hung everywhere, concealing almost completely the gazebo where the Tsar's army brass band warmed up with marching medleys.

Guests from St. Petersburg arrived steadily, nestling in and around the gently flapping fabrics, lying out half-onto the grasses or sitting upright. Princes and politicians, businessmen and the idle rich were all there, fashionable in high-collared shirts, hair cut short, beards grown long. They sat with their wives or consorts in the shade of the umbrellas, and everywhere their uncorked brown bottles and crystal stemware balanced precariously at odd angles on the covered turf amid plates of sweetmeats, fruits and breads.

In marked contrast to their elders, the young girls of the Imperial School of Ballet sat quietly in front of the dais, rehearsed and practicing the manners expected such times.

But standing around the fringes of the linens were small groups of the Tsar's senior army officers, smoking cigars and boasting of hunting, horses and of their length of service to the Tsar. And in their shadows, laughing politely at just the right times but offering no quips of their own, were the junior officers, their training and 'experience' at the Corps of Pages and other military academies paling in comparison.

Suddenly the band rose and struck up at full volume with "God Save the Tsar," halting conversations mid-syllable. The officers came to attention, as did many of the civilian men in their own way. Everyone looked to the crest of the knoll that hid the Alexander Palace.

Count Fredericks was the first to appear, formally marching in his trademark swagger, his riding crop tucked under his arm, his great moustache bouncing with each step.

Tsar Nikolas and Tsarevich Alexei followed, escorting Nikolas' mother, the Dowager Empress Maria, between them. Nikolas and Alexei were magnificent in matching bright summer uniforms decorated with sashes and ribbons and epaulets. Maria glowed in a bright summer dress beneath a wide hat laden with flowers. The three of them strolled together, Alexei's grin warming the hearts of the guests.

Following were Alexandra and her daughters, Olga, now a willowy 13, Tatiana, 11, Maria, 9, and Anastasia, 8, prancing in soft pastel summer dresses and spinning white parasols.

Behind them strolled Anna Vyrubova and Grigory Rasputin, arm-in-arm. She wore a light dress of many layers that improved her shape, and Rasputin had recently parted his stringy hair—roughly though, as if with a garden rake. He wore a gold belt around a purple *bluza* that Alexandra had given him. It looked out of place on him, though, like a fine silver saddle on a milk horse, perhaps due to his wide, shapeless *moujik* breeches and greased black boots.

Grand Dukes Paul and Peter Romanov and their wives brought up the rear of the procession, the brothers in parade uniforms and Duchesses Anastasia and Militsa radiant in summer outfits and flowered accessories.

The entire procession stood at the dais in the traditional order. They nodded and waved to their friends until the band reached its triumphant crescendo, and then the crowd gave them a standing ovation that never seemed to end.

Nikolas finally held up his hands, mouthing "Please, please!," and he gestured up toward the knoll for all to witness: a party of six magnificently bearded, white-and-gold robed clergy, led by the aged John of Kronstadt himself, slowly carried an icon and two painted icon-banners toward them. Any men who still wore hats reverently removed them.

"*Ei Bogu*," Rasputin said quietly to Anna, "it is the 'Icon of the Holy Visage'. What a proper *molebin* it shall be." He dropped to his knees on the platform and crossed himself as the icon approached. The rest of the family followed his lead.

Father John halted the group and carried the icon across the dais to the Tsar. Nikolas kissed the gilded frame. He remained kneeling as Father John placed it into a stand on the dais for all to see. The guests crossed themselves, and two of the other priests planted their icon-banners into the lawn behind the dais. Two more priests placed candles on either side of the icon and lit them, and Father John recited a long, traditional Russian Orthodox prayer. The final priest carried a brush and basin; at the proper moments he cast holy water onto the banners and the grounds, then among the royal family and upon the icon, and then, symbolically, among the guests, too.

As the prayer ended, only the sounds of chirping jays and priests' gowns were evident. Father John bent over and shook the hand of the guest of honor, "God bless you, young Tsarevich."

Alexei blushed and looked to his smiling papa for the right words. Nikolas understood, and he whispered instructions down to his son. "Thank you, Father John," stammered out Alexei.

Then the royal couple thanked Father John—Nikolas with three gentle Russian kisses, Alexandra with but a single kiss, softly planted onto the thinning wisps of beard on the old man's cheek.

"Your son and family are blessed in the eyes of the Lord, Excellence," Father John said, his old blue eyes twinkling between wrinkled folds of skin under bushy white eyebrows. "May you always remember this day's beauty."

"Oh, Father," Alexandra replied, "that was beautiful. Will you stay with us this day?"

Father John shook his head. "The Tsarevich would like his party to begin, Empress, and my days of festivities are long past. And Father Grigory surely knows fine words with which to close the day . . . is that not right, Father?"

Rasputin bowed from behind the royal daughters. "They shall pale in comparison with yours, Father John."

Father John nodded at the compliment. "Then I shall return my favorite icon to its home in Peter the Great's cottage. I bid you all good day."

He motioned to his priests to collect the 'Icon of the Holy Visage', but they left the candles and banners in place as a continuing blessing. The family and guests crossed themselves as the icon was solemnly lifted and carried away. Rasputin again fell to his knees as it passed by.

Finally a spirited murmur rose from the crowd. A porter made his way along the dais with glasses of wine and punch.

"A toast!" cried out Nikolas with his glass in the air.

The guests complied happily, scrambling for their glasses.

"To my son—the next Tsar of Russia!" Nikolas turned to Alexei, and a cheer rose from the crowd. Alexei grinned infectiously. He raised his punch glass and clinked it against his fathers'.

"On my birthday!" he blurted out above the din of the crowd, and they laughed with him.

"To the Tsar!" shouted Rasputin, and the crowd echoed his toast with raised glasses.

Toasts filled the next quarter-hour, until it seemed there was no one or no thing on earth they'd missed.

At last Nikolas held up a hand, "Enough!," only to have one of his officers on the perimeter loudly toast, "To enough!" and raise his glass one last time. Above the belly-laughs Nikolas turned to his son and loudly asked, "Alyosha, this is your party—do you have a special birthday wish?"

Without hesitation, the boy pointed to the back of the crowd, where a table overflowed with gaily-wrapped boxes of every size and shape. "I want to open my presents, Papa!"

The guests approved with applause. Alexei was in heaven. He opened a set of nestling *matroishka* dolls, handsomely painted, with a tiny soldier hidden in the last egg. There were scale wooden models of rifle and cannon, all bearing the seal of the Tsar. He happily strummed a small *balalaika* a few times. He unwrapped a photo album bearing his name and the seal on the cover, yet empty—a condition, he proclaimed, he would soon cure, until it was "even bigger than my Papa's!" He received paints and camel-hair brushes and hand-carved games, including a double-headed Imperial Eagle oak jigsaw puzzle.

Finally, when the presents were all unwrapped, Rasputin stepped forward and knelt before the boy. "Alexei Nikolayevich," he said, reaching into his golden sash, "know always that you walk with the Lord." He presented Alexei with a simple icon, worn and traveled.

With a youngster's charm, Alexei crossed himself before accepting the icon. "Thank you, Father Grigory," he said in the midst of a hug, and then he showed the gift to his beaming father and mother. They also crossed themselves.

"You are blessed, Alyosha, to have so holy a friend as Father Grigory," Nikolas said appreciatively. Alexandra kissed Rasputin on the cheek.

Rasputin stepped back, to the edge of the crowd. He was thirsty, it was time to find a glass of wine. The festivities continued. Alexandra presented her gift to Alexei, an emerald-and-ruby encrusted toy box made to order by royal jeweler Carl Faberge.

Suddenly two young men appeared in front of Rasputin. Both were shorter than he, in their mid-twenties, slender, well-dressed and handsome in the face. And they had a glass of Madeira for him.

"Father Grigory, it is a pleasure to see you again," said one, offering his hand.

Rasputin hesitated for a moment. "Ah, young Romanov—Dmitri Pavlovich, is it not? Nephew of the Tsar, yes?" he asked, declining his hand and exchanging three kisses with him instead, then accepting the wine.

Romanov's teeth glistened. "You remember me, Father Grigory, I am honored. This is my great friend," he presented the other young man, "Prince Felix Felixovich Yussupov, also of St. Petersburg."

"Felix Felixovich," Rasputin echoed, kissing him also.

"I have heard such great things about you, Father Grigory," Yussupov said. "Your powers are strong. You comfort the Tsarevich when he suffers from bleeding. All of Russia is in your gratitude."

"I have no amazing powers, Felix Felixovich," Rasputin answered, his head bowing momentarily to acknowledge the compliment. "The Almighty acts through me. That is all."

"Oh, he is so modest, Misha," Yussupov said, half-turning to Romanov, but never breaking contact with Rasputin's steely gaze. "Tell me, Father, are you also so modest in the gypsy camps outside town? We have heard, you know . . . " Yussupov raised a perfectly-shaped eyebrow that suggested disapproval, but then an almost-invisible smile lifted the corners of his thin lips, and boyish laugh lines appeared around his nose and eyes that might have looked sinister on a more aged face.

"You're a real man among men, Father Grigory!" suggested Romanov, giggling.

Yussupov's smile evaporated. He subtly elbowed Romanov's ribs and said to Rasputin, "I have heard no end to the stories of your—stamina, shall we say? The wine flows, the women dance, and the great Father Grigory outlasts them all! And so many women! How do you do it, Father? Did you bring a magic potion with you from the Tobolsk Province?"

Rasputin did not answer. He studied the faces of the two young men, his cool blue eyes betraying not a trace of his inner thoughts. He took a sip of his wine, then he spoke slowly. "You seem to know much of me, Felix Felixovich. Tell me, hasn't a young man in your position better things to do? I am but a simple *strannik* who follows the path of the Virgin."

"We do not mean to offend you with our interest, Father Grigory," replied Yussupov. "We simply find you a fascinating man. A *strannik* in the court of the Tsar? A dedicated man of God who spends evenings in the gypsy camps? Indeed, there is more to you than meets the eye!"

"Indeed, more!" added Romanov.

Rasputin was hesitant. "What is it, exactly, that I may help you with?"

Yussupov drew up closer, pressing against Rasputin. He spoke quickly. "Come be with us, Father Grigory. We can show you things you could never see, people you could never meet, places you could never go." His excitement was feverish. "You'll never need to seek out common gypsies again."

Romanov leaned in and whispered into Rasputin's ear, "I can give you more than any gypsy, man of men."

Rasputin recoiled, shocked, his eyes wide, his hands rising defensively, spilling his wine. "*Ei Bogu!*" he cried out. "I know you now—you are one with the monks of Athos! You are unnatural, you do not follow the path of the Virgin. Be gone, foolish boys!" Guests glanced their way.

Yussupov and Romanov collected their wits and backed up, murmuring loudly about the madman opposite them. Conversations around them slowly picked back up.

Rasputin watched them retreat far away, beyond the crowd. He finished what remained of his wine and looked about for a fresh bottle—until a fresh, radiant beauty took his breath away.

She was on the arm of a young man in a police officer's dress uniform, but there was tension between them. Rasputin's eyebrow lifted. Their smiles were forced. And after a peck on the cheek, he left her to join the cigar-smoking army officers.

Rasputin could not take his eyes off her. She positively glowed. Her light golden hair was not hidden needlessly under a wide hat, but was exquisitely curled, falling lightly upon her shoulders. Her frame was small and delicate, though full-busted, and she carried herself well, floating where others seemed to awkwardly traipse. She took a seat near the now-cleared dais, waiting, as the ballerinas gathered upon it.

Nikolas came back to join his officers for a smoke, but Rasputin scarcely noticed. He ambled to one of the snack tables near the woman, until he was so close he might have reached out and touched her. His eyesight had not failed him—up close, her appearance remained heavenly.

He stood there for the performance, watching with half an eye. As the ballet ended and a magician appeared, she rose. Rasputin quickly took two glasses of wine from the table and stepped into her path.

"I am Father Grigory, little one," he said, gracefully nodding and offering her a glass.

With a surprised look on her face, she met his blue-eyed gaze. She accepted the wine.

Rasputin's free hand stroked the end of his long beard. "I saw your—husband, is he?—with the Tsar. He looks to be a fine man. And an important one. Tell me his name, so that I might know if he is spoken of in the halls of Tsarskoe Selo."

She hesitated, taking a sip of wine. "Yes, Father Grigory, my Igor is moving up quickly in the St. Petersburg bureau," she said flatly, her eyes drifting in a search for her husband. She located him, but she appeared content to watch him from afar. "He is Igor Igorevich Lipov, *Captain* Lipov," she emphasized with a certain disdain, "and I am his wife, Tatiana Valentinyevna Lipov."

"He is fortunate to have a wife as beautiful as you, Tatiana Valentinyevna. And you are fortunate to have a husband as ambitious as he."

"Father Grigory—" she said as if suddenly realizing with whom she was speaking, "the healer? I have heard of you. Your healing powers have eased the suffering of the Tsarevich, yes? Have you been blessed with a gift?"

"I have no gift, little one," Rasputin answered solemnly, still stroking his beard. "I am only a man who follows the Virgin. If I am blessed at all, it is in knowing the way of my path."

"You must enjoy knowing your path, Father. Many people do not have such knowledge, even those here."

"Everyone must seek their paths, little one," Rasputin said close to her ear, close to the smooth arch of her neck. "The Almighty wants you to find your path, also. It is the true source of happiness."

"I want that, Father Grigory. I want to find inner peace, for I know that happiness is not to be found among these people."

"Then let us discuss the matter, little one. We shall distance ourselves while we have the chance. Come with me."

Rasputin and Madame Lipov stepped from beneath the umbrellas amid more applause and deep, smoky laughter from the men. They strolled over the knoll to the mosque-like Turkish Baths. Rasputin showed her through the entry to a side room, where they knelt and prayed briefly on a mat in the icon corner. They shifted to face each other, alone in the quiet afternoon, still kneeling.

Rasputin lightly placed his large, rough hands on top of her head, covering it. He looked deeply into her eyes, and even farther, into her soul. "Do you wish to find salvation, my little one?" he asked in a voice dripping with devotion.

"Oh, I do, Father," she answered dreamily.

He gently massaged her scalp with his coarse fingers, slowly moving his hands down until he had lightly cupped her ears. His thumbs stroked her temples, his fingers strolled behind her ears and down the soft sides of her neck. Her eyelids quivered, her lashes met as he continued caressing her.

"My child, all happiness is inside you if you carry the Lord. Tell me of your relationship with Him."

"I—I do not know, Father," she answered with a hint of shame. "I believe in Him, and I pray to Him, but I still feel alone. I do not know what to do."

Rasputin's thumbs traced her eyebrows and the delicate ridges of bone surrounding her eyes. "He knows, my child. He knows you and He loves you. He asks only for your worship."

"Please help me, Father Grigory. I do not know how best to worship Him, and I want Him in my life. Should I pray more often? Should I spend more time in the church? How is it I do not hear His voice?"

Rasputin slowly followed the contours of her nose and cheekbones. "Shhhh, my little one. He hears you, and that is most important. Listen to me—the Lord did not build your church. He did not build your *sabor*. *You* are His creation. *You* are His temple. Your *flesh* is His temple. Rasputin's thumbs followed her lips and jawbone.

"I do not understand, Father."

"You must satisfy yourself, my child. Eat the foods He placed upon the earth. Drink the wine as His Son did. Satisfy your urges, for that is why He placed them within you. It brings you closer to Him." His hands dropped to her chest. He traced her breasts.

She recoiled briefly and opened her eyes, but his stare was hypnotically intense. She did not brush his hands away. She closed her eyes and fought to find words. "But is it not wrong to use the body in a sinful way, Father?" she asked between quickening breaths.

Rasputin felt the whole of her ribcage, around to the small of her back. He pulled her closer. "Not when the Lord is in your mind, little one. It is then that you may have a man in the flesh. It is as He wishes. It honors Him—your thoughts of Him sweep away evil."

"Father-" she said, pulling back slightly and looking for truth in his eyes, "I do not understand—sweeps away evil? Adultery itself is evil, is it not?"

Rasputin moved his hands up to her shoulders and caressed them. "How can you sweep away evil, my little one, except by sincere repentance?" He paused, allowing his words to sink in. He massaged her elbows, then stroked her forearms.

She had no answer. Her eyes closed again.

"And how can you sincerely repent, little one, if you have never sinned?"

He set her hands down onto the tops of her thighs, and from there he felt the outline of her dress, reaching back up to her waist. He easily laid her over on her side, and still kneeling, ran his hands roughly over the front of her body. He lifted her dress and caressed her legs through her silken slips, and then he lifted the soft fabrics. Her ruffled underpants were damp and clinging to her, but he easily pushed them aside.

"For the Lord, my little one."

All eyes were on the stage when Rasputin and Madame Lipov returned to the party and went their separate ways. Tsarina Alexandra was in the midst of a rare speech.

"We are all happy that Alyosha is so well and . . . " she choked back tears, " . . . .and healthy for his birthday. God is smiling on him now, and we owe it all to our friend, Father Grigory." She waved to Rasputin, who had just taken a seat in one of the straight-backed chairs. The crowd applauded.

"Without him, our Alyosha might not be having such a wonderful day as this. We are forever in his debt. And with this in mind, we feel it is time to properly honor him. Father Grigory, will you please come to me?"

Rasputin rose, and when he was standing beside Alexandra, she continued. "Father Grigory, you say that when you feel the Lord's strength working through you, you see a light sparkling over the sick one. And you say that you have seen that light over our Alyosha. "So then, so that all of Russia may know you, I bestow upon you the title of *'Lampadaire de Cour.'*"

Rasputin looked puzzled; she quickly translated for him.

"'Court Lampadary' . . . the man of the standing light. I will insist that our Court Physician, Dr. Derevenko, listen to your advice, and that he follows whatever care you prescribe for our Alyosha.

"Our friend, your own concerns will not be forgotten, either, especially those you have for your family and friends in Siberia. You say they lack food and medical supplies, so Nikolas and I have decided to form a council to look into this problem. And we will declare the *Duma* responsible to answer with whatever aid is appropriate.

"Father Grigory, we appoint you President of this new Siberian Imperial Council. Thank you again, and may God bless you." Alexandra gave Rasputin the traditional kisses, and Nikolas did, too.

At the rear of the crowd, Vladimir Purishkevich bit the tip off a cigar and spit it from his blubbery lips, nearly hitting his friend's polished boots.

"What is this rubbish, Igor Igorevich?" Purishkevich moaned. "This monk—this charlatan—will now dictate the *Duma's* direction? This is an outrage! I will not move the causes of my own constituents to a back burner to accommodate his petticoat pursuits!"

Captain Lipov shook his head. "It seems we have no choice, Vladimir Mitrofanovich. You know Nikolas will do as Alexandra pleases. Her hold on him is strong."

"And who is to know," Purishkevich speculated, "exactly what hold 'Father Grigory' has upon Alexandra?"

Startled, Lipov turned and looked Purishkevich in the eye. "Keep such thoughts to yourself, my friend. Even the canvas has ears at such events as these."

Purishkevich nodded. "I suppose so. But since our protection of the Tsar never ends . . . " his voice dropped to a whisper, "what shall we do if his enemies are his own wife and a fellow he calls a priest?"

Lipov did not answer.

Purishkevich went on, "Men with our commitments must adapt to the challenges, Captain. In this case, the Tsar must be protected even if he invites the danger into his own sitting room. The Maltese Cross on our breast holds us to this ideal."

"I am aware of what our Cross signifies, Vladimir Mitrofanovich." Lipov's eyes were on the stage, where Rasputin basked with Alexandra and her daughters. "And I am well aware that it is time to investigate that man."

"Investigate, hell," Purishkevich retorted. "There's no time, and his intentions are clear. He must be stopped before he succeeds in raping the Motherland."

CHAPTER 5

Three and one-half years later

St. Petersburg
Nevsky Monastery, Office of the Archimandrite

December 15, 1911

Bishop Hermogen of Saratov sat frowning behind a simple, wooden desk. He was an immense and worn presence, with a bushy, overgrown salt-and-pepper beard and tired eyes that spoke of a thousand-mile journey to be there. He had arrived only that morning for conferences with his colleagues, Father

John of Kronstadt and Archimandrite Theophan, head of the monastery, but his plans had yielded to this most distasteful of investigations. Hermogen and Father Iliodor of Tsaritsyn were alone in the office.

Iliodor immediately denied any involvement in the reported rape. "It was Rasputin of St. Petersburg, that is who should be called to atone for this crime!"

Hermogen scowled. "I did not hear that Father Grigory was anywhere near the scene, Father Iliodor. How do you come to claim that he is involved in the accusations of Madame Lotkin?"

"It is a long story, Eminence. I shall explain."

Iliodor paced and spoke quickly, his heavy cross and Russian Orthodox medallion bouncing against his dark robes. "It was in June when Rasputin traveled with me to worship in Tsaritsyn, where my congregation flourishes. Then I was to continue with him and travel to his home in Pokrovskoe, in the Tobolsk province.

"We began the journey in a state of friendship. I respected his devotion, as I was sure he respected mine. But when we reached Tsaritsyn, I saw firsthand the methods of his healing. My respect for his ways vanished."

Iliodor's eloquence and delivery seemed honorable. Hermogen nodded for him to continue.

"Rasputin made no attempt to pray with the women of my congregation, Eminence. He simply fondled them! He would approach to give them the traditional triple kiss, but would instead meet them fully on the mouth, with either his hand up here, near his chest, or around behind—" Iliodor demonstrated the motions, his composure fading. "And with two girls that were rumored to be one with the devil—why, he disappeared with them into my quarters, and he allowed no one to witness his healing! Eminence, I fear for what happened there!"

Hermogen lifted a hand. "Father Iliodor, be seated," he commanded, rising to his feet. His beard shook like a hedge as he spoke. Iliodor sat instantly. "We are not here to judge Father Grigory. You have your own actions to explain . . . "

Iliodor interrupted, "I am getting to that, Eminence."

"Well you had better!" Hermogen thundered, "because so far I do not see what your story has to do with this charge of rape."

"You will see, Eminence," Iliodor sat forward on the edge of the chair, constantly shifting, following Hermogen as he walked around the room with his arms folded across his chest. "Rasputin and I left Tsaritsyn as planned, and it took a week to reach Pokrovskoe. In that time we argued endlessly. I defended the church and the ways of the Lord, and he supported—well, paganism, Eminence. He spoke at length of mixing spiritualism with the pleasures of the flesh, though he denied membership in the *Khlysty*. He said he could have any woman he chose, and he demonstrated his ways at every possible opportunity. Worst of all, he showed me letters written by Tsarina Alexandra and her daughters. They were personal in nature. The Tsarina wrote of her devotion to him, and the elder girls wrote of feelings they had for young men in their church—feelings which the Lord reserves for man and wife."

"Father Iliodor, what does this have to do . . . "

"Eminence, after our trip I returned here. Then yesterday, when I heard the confession of Madame Lotkin, she spoke of desire for men other than her husband. Of course, I explained that the Lord does not approve of such thoughts, but she argued with me. She said Rasputin approved of such carnal pleasures, and that since he is constantly in the company of the Tsar, he must know more than I, a lowly priest from a distant district!

"Imagine my shock at hearing Rasputin's false teachings! And then she asked if I, too, had felt the call of the flesh! Well, I had had enough. I opened the chamber door to counsel her face-to-face, and she came out, too, apparently misinterpreting my motives. She began to unbutton her blouse, and—and—I was appalled! I reached out and grabbed her hands, which startled her. She stumbled backward, tearing her blouse. I tried to catch her, but I fell with her and landed upon her. And at that moment several members of the congregation rushed to us. She told them I was attempting to mate with her! Oh, imagine the horror! Of course, I put the story straight and told them of her false worship, and they saw through her lies. They declared that only a *prostitutka* would try to commit such devilry."

Iliodor turned back squarely in his chair, his head bowed. "But I have forgiven her, Eminence. And I have prayed that she recovered from the punishment they dealt her."

Hermogen did not respond. He stood behind Iliodor, his bushy brows furrowed. Finally he returned to the desk and sat, looking Iliodor straight in the eye. "Father Iliodor, you have much to explain. Most seriously, it is unthinkable for you to have emerged from the confessional chamber to face Madame Lotkin. You disregarded the rules for conduct in such a situation—therefore, you betrayed the trust and respect she felt for the clergy.

"Also, I am surprised at your reaction to Father Grigory's tests of your beliefs. I wonder if you are not jealous of his alleged healing abilities, or of his lack of celibacy. You have much to atone for, Father Iliodor. I will have to put some thought to your punishment.

"For now, though, we should work to keep this from happening again. I will summon Father Grigory to account for his teachings, and I will place your matter on hold until he has presented his case."

Five hours later, at nearly eight o'clock, Rasputin burst into Nikolas' study. Nikolas was aghast. Rasputin's eye was bruised, and there was blood on his silk *bluza*. The shoulder seam was ripped open.

Nikolas called for the doctors and bade Rasputin to calm himself. "Father Grigory, sit. You must be still. Tell me who was behind this attack."

Rasputin told him the story of Father Iliodor's attempted rape of a woman the day before—and how Iliodor's bishop, Hermogen of Saratov, happened to be in town and was investigating the incident. Hermogen had called for Rasputin that afternoon, questioning his beliefs and asking of his relationship with the Imperial family. Then Hermogen had called him a heretic for his teachings.

"Has Bishop Hermogen lost his mind?" asked Nikolas aloud.

"Batiushka, what would you have had me do?" Rasputin wondered aloud. "How would you have had me respond to such darkness?"

Rasputin apologized to Nikolas for not turning and leaving at that point. Instead, unwisely, he had told Hermogen that Iliodor's story was a lie, that Iliodor must simply have given in to his urges.

Rasputin continued, describing how Iliodor had burst in from the next room, and how he and Hermogen had tried to 'beat the devil' from Rasputin's soul. But they had accomplished little, since Hermogen was slow as an ox and easily avoided, and Iliodor's attack was like that of a wispy woman.

"They are no longer one with the Lord, Batiushka! Petty thoughts and jealousies have corrupted their judgment. You must protect other men of God from these two Orthodox extremists. If nothing else, allow them to serve you from far away. Distance them from the temptations of St. Petersburg."

Nikolas agreed, disappointed that two such fine priests had fallen so. Hermogen had had a fine record of service before this mental collapse . . . so he decided to banish Hermogen to a monastery famed for its healing waters.

But Iliodor's record was neither as long nor distinguished. Nikolas asked Rasputin if a furthering of Iliodor's education was in order, and Rasputin agreed that it was. So Nikolas banished Iliodor to a monastery known for its scribes. He would copy the work of the masters, and if he held his mind open, in time he would gain wisdom from their words.

The proclamations of banishment were delivered to Hermogen and Iliodor the next morning. Nikolas denied Hermogen's request for an audience. Grace and dignity marked Hermogen's departure.

Iliodor, though, hid in a St. Petersburg basement for two days following his banishment. He copied feverishly—not the work of the masters, as Nikolas had ordered, but letters. Letters that Alexandra and her daughters had long ago written to Rasputin, letters Iliodor had stolen during their brief journey together. He dropped copies of them into the postal system on his way out of St. Petersburg.

Seemingly overnight, newspapers published the letters throughout the Russian Empire. They were the 'proof' that Rasputin, like Drs. Phillipe and Papus before him, was wreaking havoc on Nikolas' personal life. And Alexandra must be, too—her letters to Rasputin suggested that nothing was unthinkable. Even Olga's and Maria's letters to him were shockingly frank.

Scandal rocked the country. Hadn't Rasputin played Nikolas for a fool! Hearts went out to the Tsar, for everyone knew that Alexandra ruled him with an iron hand. Venomous anger rose toward Rasputin and Alexandra—'who wasn't even a Russian in her heart'. She was, and always would be, a German.

Cartoonists showed Rasputin bouncing the royal couple on his knees, eyes burning with evil intent. And craftsman created a new set of hand-painted *matroishkas*—this set featuring not Nikolas at the core of the royal family, hidden in the smallest nestled egg, but Rasputin.

As the scandal grew, the intelligentsia of Russia smugly claimed knowledge of these 'truths' all along. And the working class talked of their suspicions that *something* had been amiss at Tsarskoe Selo—and that now, with the 'facts' exposed, Nikolas would surely take strong steps. He would banish Rasputin, retake Alexandra and regain his dignity.

Only the *moujiki* were skeptical. They knew the stories were lies, meant to bring down the only *moujik* ever to gain royal influence. The *moujiki* knew Rasputin had done much to end food shortages and to begin land reforms—and he would never have taken advantage of Nikolas. Still, some quietly wondered. Had the vicious, big city life clouded Rasputin's eyes—as it had the popular Bishop Hermogen of Saratov?

Two weeks later, Nikolas had had enough. He emphatically proclaimed that Russia's newspapers would not print another word, cartoon or reference to Rasputin. And then he summoned the cause of his troubles into his study.

Nikolas stared blankly out his window onto the Gulf of Finland. "Our embarrassment is indescribable, Father Grigory," he began, slowly and deliberately. "And while we do not blame you for Russia's reaction, your failure to keep our family life secret is beyond our understanding. You should have guarded those letters with your life."

"But how could I have known, Batiushka, that Iliodor was a man of evil . . . ?"

Angrily the Tsar turned, "You should have *known* him as such!" His eyes burned with rage. He turned back to the Gulf. "There are many men of evil, and I do not appreciate them dragging my family through the mud. They have outfoxed you.

"You have angered my friends and amused my enemies with your carelessness, Father Grigory. I cannot trust you any longer. Leave St. Petersburg, for the sake of my family and for your own safety. Return to your wife and family so they may enjoy the comfort of your presence."

Rasputin fell silent. He turned to leave the room, but hesitated at the door. "What of the Tsarevich, Batiushka? If Alyosha should fall and a spell overcome him—"

"Nonsense. We have the finest doctors in Russia. They will administer to him. They will be glad to be free of your shadow."

"And what of Matushka?"

Again Nikolas turned to face him. The veins in his neck and forehead bulged. "*I am the Tsar! You will obey me! I say to you,* leave this city! You are not welcome here now!" Nikolas pointed toward the door. "Go home, Grigory Efimovich Rasputin!"

Rasputin bowed, crossing himself. He paused to perform the sign of the cross on Nikolas, whose arm was still outstretched, finger pointing, then he nodded and turned away.

Rasputin knew the twenty-four-hundred *verst* trip home would not be easy. He would have to cross the frozen Urals, a physical test for any man. But even more importantly, he could not succumb to the angry black thoughts of betrayal in his mind. He would have to find true strength, physically and mentally. And he would have to ask for it from the Virgin Herself.

Nine months later

Spala, Poland

October 2, 1912

Every autumn in the lowlands of Little Poland, sunshine and warm air from Southern Europe and Asia held off the Arctic chill that overcame the rest of the north. Nestled into these lowlands, just north of the Carpathians, larch, ojcow birch, oak and beech basked in the long, extended summers. So, too, had generations of Tsars. Their estate at Spala was a world away from the cold stone and ice of St. Petersburg.

Or just a dreaded quick train ride away, as the oldest girls, Olga, now 17, Tatiana, 15, and Maria, 13, viewed it. The vacation was ending far too soon. They skipped the chilly morning carriage rides with their parents now, savoring the last lazy mornings before their return to long days of study in cold St. Petersburg.

On the other hand, Nikolas, Alexandra, Anastasia, 11, and Alexei, 8, weren't nearly so downhearted. They donned overcoats to ward off the nip and set out to enjoy the turning colors of the trees, those of both of the local countryside and farther off in the northern uplands, where entire hillsides appeared freshly painted. And they took notice of the Carpathian Range's slow donning of a white, winter cap.

But the views wouldn't last much longer. Yesterday they came upon patches of fog so dense they lost sight of their favorite landmarks. And for a few moments they couldn't even see Count Fredericks—who, with his own bearings misplaced, had simply crossed his fingers and let the team guide him for a change.

This morning was even worse. There were few breaks in the freezing fog. Was it finally time to head home to St. Petersburg?

Suddenly scrubby bushes beside the road rustled with life— three wild pigs shot out in front of them, snorting and grunting. The horses reared and bolted, and despite Nikolas' hold, Alexei slid off the front bench straight into his mother's knees. With a moan he slid down onto the carriage floor.

Nikolas was down with his son in a heartbeat, even as the horses raced uncontrollably. In time Count Fredericks had them calmed and slowing, apologizing all the while.

"It is not your fault, Fredericks," Nikolas said as the carriage stopped. He helped Alexei up onto the bench seat to lie down. Nikolas took off his coat and made it into a pillow for him, and then, despite the chill, unbuttoned Alexei's coat, shirt and trousers to examine his midsection. There was a reddening and a slight swelling at the site of an old wound that, two years earlier, had taken three painful days to subside. He redressed his son and closed his overcoat back around him.

"Nicky—" Alexandra said, but Nikolas did not reply.

"Get us home, Fredericks," he commanded with soft urgency, stroking Alexei's cheek. "Damn this fog."

A week passed at the Spala estate, and the blackish tumor in Alexei's groin showed no signs of shrinking. Alexei was dulled by the pain, his cries reduced to weak moans and sobbing. Alexandra rarely left the side of his small brass bed. She trusted the girls to Nikolas' care and he responded admirably, serving as mother, confidante and now tutor, starting their autumn lessons in reading and writing to help take their minds off Alexei's condition.

When Alexei slept, Alexandra knitted to keep her hands busy. Or she would clean and refill the oil lamp beneath the icon, or she would wipe the dust from his tiny Army boots, which would lead to her polishing them one more time, readying them for his next inspection of ranks with his father. Or maybe she would just straighten his hair or tidy his sheets so he would not be sleeping on creases.

She tended to his needs when he woke, sometimes answering his questions of what it was like to die—if the pain would leave, and if God would let him play like other boys did. But other times she wouldn't answer, or couldn't, preferring to chastise him for such silliness, promising that he would ride every sledding hill in St. Petersburg when he quit lollygagging and got up out of bed. They would even build a new sledding hill, she promised, one as tall as the spire on the Peter and Paul Fortress, where everyone in St. Petersburg could see him ride down. His smiles brought her just the slightest hope.

Another two days passed. Dr. Botkin spoke to Nikolas in hushed tones, away from Alexandra, of worsening anemia, of imminent rupture and peritonitis, of the inevitable. But it wouldn't have mattered if Alexandra had heard him. The opinions of others simply didn't matter to her. She couldn't trifle herself with the words of foolish doctors. She wasn't spending enough time in prayer, she told Nikolas, and with that her knitting and other busy-chores fell to the wayside. She prayed night and day.

Early on the morning of October twelfth, a local priest arrived with the miracle-working icon 'Madonna of Vladimir'. Alexandra found an extra place above the oil lamp for Her to watch over Alexei, and Nikolas held her as they sobbed through the administration of Last Rites for their son.

When the priest left she rushed back to her chair to console unconscious Alexei, to tell him that he needn't listen, that he could stay if he wanted to, that God probably wasn't ready for such a little boy. Nikolas stood near the icon, wiping his wet cheeks and beard with his handkerchief. He crossed himself before Her, then he kissed Alexandra and Alexei and left them alone. There were details he didn't want to concern Alexandra with.

Suddenly, frantically, Alexandra called out for Olga, and her eldest daughter appeared quickly. Alexandra asked her to fetch paper and pen, and when she returned, Alexandra hurriedly dashed off a few lines and sealed the paper into an envelope. She sent word for Count Fredericks to ready the team for Olga's errand. Olga divulged nothing to her curious sisters as she donned her overcoat. Alexandra returned to her prayers.

Four hours later

Pokrovskoe

October 12, 1912

Five simple place-settings lay on the yellow-checked cloth. Praskovia peeled and cut potatoes while cabbage boiled.

In the front room Rasputin creaked to-and-fro in his rocking chair, telling his children yet another tale of St. Petersburg. This one was about the horseless carriages that were becoming so common, and how a man filled with vodka had tried to drive home in one, only to crash through the railing of the Moika Embankment and dive nose-first, three meters down, into the canal.

Maria, now 14, and Varya, 12, laughed, their mother's beauty evident. Their clear blue eyes danced just like their father's as he described the drunkard's attempts to climb out of the car, only to fall back into the waist-deep water, and how firemen in a rowboat finally pulled him to safety before the gathering crowd.

Dmitri, 17, didn't understand. He asked what happened to the horses. Rasputin smiled and patted his son on the head.

When Misha was a toddler, a measles fever had burned hot in him, forever affecting his mind. He looked just like his father. His face was wide, his nose large, his ears two sizes too big. From his mother he had received an even temperament; that patience helped him to understand those things that did not, at first, make sense.

Rasputin explained to him that horseless carriages moved under their own power, that they were noisy contraptions, prone to breakdowns, and that they were best-suited for use in cities, where there were repairmen and paved streets.

Dmitri nodded, but it was hard to tell how much he understood. He said only that he was hungry.

"Oh, Misha," Maria chided, "lunch is almost ready. Come, we will wash our hands and take our seats." She stood and led him away, smiling at the wink from her father. Caring for her slower, older brother and younger sister had matured Maria beyond her years. She was the little mother in the Rasputin home—even when she spoke of joining a circus like the one that came to Tobolsk, it would be so she could tame the big cats and care for their 'kittens'.

There was a knock at the front door, and Varya jumped to her feet. "Who is it?" she yelled on her way.

"Telegram for Father Grigory!" came the answer. A young man handed it to her and was on his way.

Rasputin strode to the door and read the message. His face fell.

"Papa—what is it?" asked Varya.

Rasputin did not answer her. He took the telegram into the kitchen and pressed it into Praskovia's hands. "I must pray," he said, and he disappeared through the cellar door to his *sabor*.

Praskovia read the telegram and held it to her breast in shock. She heard his chanting through the floor. There was little she could do but keep the house quiet, so she rounded up the children with a sternness that they dared not question. Once they were together in the kitchen she explained what was happening.

"The little Tsarevich is very sick, and if he is to get well, he will need your father's prayers. We must not disturb him; he prays to our Mother, "The Virgin of Kazan".

"So let us eat quietly. And until Papa is finished, I want you to stay that way, as quiet as mice." They all sat. Praskovia filled their bowls and cut them bread.

Lunch did not take long, and the children did not need reminders. They went upstairs to their rooms afterward, while she walked out to the front room and knelt in the icon corner before the burning lamp and their smaller copy of the icon "The Virgin of Kazan." She did not pound her head to the floor like her husband, but her prayers were just as sincere. She chanted and moaned quietly in congress with his voice.

Two hours passed. Praskovia prepared tea on the *samovar*, sat and waited. At last, Rasputin clumped up the steps to the kitchen. His appearance was shocking—he stood wobbling, his face colored a ghastly white, except for his forehead, which was red and swollen. Praskovia rushed to him and held his weakened frame tightly in her arms. He reeked from his toil.

"The light burns strongly for Alyosha," Rasputin said at last.

"Oh, Grisha—"

"Alexei—Matushka and Batiushka—I must telegram them. "

Alexei suddenly shifted in bed and looked about serenely. He calmly informed his mother, "I'm hungry."

Alexandra was stunned and scared. She tried to soothe him, to snap him out of this 'delirium' by stroking his cheek with a shaking hand. But he shook his head impatiently.

"Mama," he pleaded, "I'm hungry! And I want to go home to my own room!"

Alexandra's jaw dropped. Her whole body shook. She sat back in her chair, unable to speak or move. Tears rolled down her cheeks.

"Papa!" cried out Alexei.

Nikolas found Alexei sitting straight up in bed and Alexandra frozen in place, quivering, watching their son.

"Papa, something's wrong with Mama," Alexei stated matter-of-factly. "And I'm hungry."

Doctors Botkin and Derevenko soon arrived. They examined young Alexei closely, and afterward they could only shake their heads.

"The tumor has softened."

"It's size has decreased."

"But his pain. I don't see how it could be gone . . . "

"He should remain in bed."

"But I'm hungry!"

Nikolas and Alexandra gaped at their son and at each other.

Finally Dr. Botkin spoke up, "By all means, give the boy something to eat!"

Two days later Alexandra was napping; she and the girls had just finished packing for the train ride home. But Alexei saw no need to let her rest. He was bouncing into the room and onto her bed as usual, as though he had never been sick. He knew his mother would certainly want to know about the message that had come.

"Mama, mama . . . .it's a telegram from Father Grigory!"

Indeed, Alexandra opened her eyes and smiled.

"Olga says he talked to God and saved me. Is that true?"

She sat up. "Yes, Alyosha. It must have been him. He is very close to God."

"Then are you and Papa still mad at him?"

"No, Alyosha. We are lucky to have him as our friend."

Alexandra took the telegram from her son and held it where she could focus. It was addressed to she and Nikolas, but he would not be out of his meetings until dinnertime. She read it aloud:

"Batiushka and Matushka,

Have no fear. God has seen your tears and heard your prayers. Do not grieve. The light shines for Alyosha. He will live, I now know it to be Her wish. You will be comforted soon.

- Your friend, Grigory."

She held the note to her breast and said a soft prayer.

"Alyosha, you and I shall respond to Father Grigory at this moment. Come, let's go to the writing desk."

Alexandra thanked him with all her heart. And she begged his forgiveness for their anger toward him. Please, she wrote, would he now return to St. Petersburg? And this time, would he bring his family with him?

Rasputin and Praskovia discussed the idea and decided that, perhaps, it was time for the girls to experience the city. Especially now that the relationship between he and his daughters was so strong . . . he did not want to leave them behind again.

But Praskovia wanted no part of such a journey. Her roots were deep in Pokrovskoe. She and Dmitri would do best to stay at home. They decided to ask Dunia, their housekeeper, to go in place of Praskovia. Dunia agreed. She would to cook and care for the girls when Rasputin was out, and she would keep the family's flat fit for them.

And so it was decided. Rasputin eagerly planned for his return to St. Petersburg. Scandals and ill-feelings would be in the past, he told Praskovia, for once again the Almighty had saved the life of the Tsarevich. Surely none of the Godless ones would bear grudges against him now.

CHAPTER 6

Six months later

St. Petersburg
64 Gorokhovaya Street, flat 3A

April 8, 1913

The Russians who waited behind Rasputin's flat in the western quarter often crowded not only the landing outside his door but all three flights of narrow wooden steps as well, spilling into the courtyard below with dreams and prayers and hopes worn plainly on sleeves.

This spring morning was no different—even a chilly rain did not deter them from want of an audience. They watched coldly as a teary-eyed young lady with a torn dress ran out of the flat, sniffling as she passed through them. They witnessed the next visitor emerge angrily, cursing in a loud voice that he would tell all to the Tsar. They knew Rasputin had seen through the selfish ruses of these two malcontents. The two had received everything they deserved. It was as God would have it.

But they relished the smiles of the blessed ones—those who stepped lightly out the door and gaily bounced through them down the steps. Sometimes those people would wave a note or a handful of rubles over their heads as if to say, 'Do you see? You need only ask Father Grigory, and you, too, shall receive!' Contagious hope and good cheer would spread through the crowd, and they all would climb one step closer toward Rasputin's door.

The simplicity of the flat surprised many. Expect-ing furnishings befitting a royal consul and widely known healer, they would smile through pursed lips when encountering exactly the opposite. They would sit at his sparse kitchen table, and there was no room for modesty. They had to discuss their quandary openly while a half-dozen or more of Rasputin's followers nodded or frowned, and often while Maria, now 14, and Varya, 12, sat within earshot.

Rasputin's judgment decided all fates. If the visitor was a God-fearing modest man, rich or poor, Rasputin would usually grant the request. Often he wrote a simple note, addressed to no one in particular, that read: "Dear Friend, Do this thing for me. Grigory." The visitor presented the note to whomever it was intended, and Rasputin's signature was usually impressive enough to accomplish the task.

But men so presumptuous as to lay a stack of money on the table to buy a favor left disappointed or angry. Their only gift from Rasputin might be one of humility—the opportunity to watch the next poor *moujik* with a dying plow horse be granted the entire amount. Rasputin would smile and say, "It is God's way."

Rasputin held female visitors to a different standard. He asked young ladies to adjourn with him to his bedroom, and on the fox bedspread he would ask that they worship with him. Those who did could save their husbands from transfers to the Siberian plains, or worse.

When it came to older, matronly women, those who tickled his heart had their way with him. But many did not. "God does not come to me for you," he told them as they received some or none of their wishes, "it is His way."

Outside the flat, at all hours, the St. Petersburg police noted the proceedings. They recorded who was in line, how long each subject's meeting ran, and the condition of said subject upon his or her exit. So when the occasional charge against Rasputin reached court, the police promptly produced a record of the plaintiff's visit. But the work was for naught, since no judge ever ruled against the most popular holy man in Russia.

Rasputin and his followers looked at the police in a different way—they had free protection around the clock. Eventually Rasputin came to know all the officers and called them by name, and he bade Dunia to take them tea during long nights of freezing rain and blowing snow. And on those rare occasions when there was no line of people waiting to see Rasputin, more than one officer put away his pad and knocked on the door himself.

So police records officially documented that on this day, Vladimir Purishkevich and Captain Igor Lipov respectfully waited in line and were greeted at 3A by Rasputin at the door.

"Father Grigory, it is a pleasure to see you again," Purishkevich said. "May I introduce Captain Igor Igorevich Lipov of the St. Petersburg police? He and I work together in the name of the Tsar."

Clearly, Rasputin was taken aback by these visitors. "Vladimir Mitrofanovich, what brings you to my home? You have fought my work in the Duma many times. What was it you said—I would fuel the Siberian *moujiki* arsonists with kerosene if they so asked? I never expected to see you here."

Purishkevich laughed heartily. He explained, "Father Grigory, I am a politician by trade. At times, I must speak and act more on behalf of my constituents than myself. Personally," he leaned closer, stroking his beard, "I do not know how you do what you do, but your results are astounding. I congratulate you."

Rasputin relaxed. He exchanged kisses with both of the men. He motioned them to the table and took his usual seat across from his visitors. Then, while Dunia was refilling Rasputin's glass with Madeira, he asked her to bring out a bottle of his father's vodka for the guests.

"First we share the drink of the *moujiki*, my friends," Rasputin said heartily. "For without them, the Tsar is without his people."

"You'll find that both of us are *moujiki* inside, Father Grigory," declared Lipov.

Rasputin raised an eyebrow. "Some of us are one with the land, Igor Igorevich," he replied. "And some of us are not."

Dunia handed Rasputin an unmarked bottle of clear liquid, and he half-filled two glasses for his guests. Then he added hot water from the samovar to fill them full. The concoction's odor spread throughout the room.

"Ah, *zubrovka*," Purishkevich mused before he tasted his drink. He nodded his approval with a smile.

Lipov hesitated. He tried a sip, but he was unable to hide his repulsed reaction to its foulness. He took a deep breath and sipped again. "Yes, *zubrovka*," he stammered. He nodded his approval, shuddering. His lips formed a snarl.

"Yes, now we are all *moujiki*, Igor Igorevich," Rasputin said. His eyes twinkled, but his face remained straight.

Dunia, watching from the kitchen, hid her face in her hands to stifle laughter. In Pokrovskoe, it was said that kerosene had a more pleasant taste than Efim Novykh's homemade *zubrovka*. Once the Pokrovskoe *moujiki* made bets that bison dung was its unknown ingredient. But Novykh would not cooperate—he said only that there was no winner of the bet, and he continued guarding his secret recipe. In his twilight years, it honored him that Rasputin took his *zubrovka* to St. Petersburg to serve to the rich merchants and politicians—but Rasputin never told him of its true value, of how he used it to measure a man's honesty.

"Father Grigory," Purishkevich said, "Let us get to the point of our visit. Of course there are differences between us, but there are also common goals. We both want to still the unrest of the Russian people. We want to see Mother Russia prosper and fulfill her destiny."

"The Lord would have it so, Vladimir Mitrofanovich."

"And how—" Lipov started to add, but his *zubrovka*-shocked voice box failed and he had to repeat himself. "And how could that goal be better accomplished than by asking the Russian people to unite and work together as one?"

"The *moujiki* already act as one, Igor Igorevich. They are the soul of Mother Russia."

"Yes, Father Grigory, they are," broke in Purishkevich. "But we must ask more. We ask them to stand up together for their country, loud and strong, past the Urals and Siberia to Kamchatka, to the Caspian Sea and the land of the Mongols, to the people of the Kara and Laptev Seas. We need all *moujiki* with us—Mother Russia needs her countrymen now more than ever!"

"We *must* unite the people and defend our interests in the Balkan states, especially," added Lipov. "The Tsar has so much at stake. We must stand behind him like never before."

Rasputin was silent and still. Finally he said, "You speak of the Balkans—but they are not the business of Russia. We shall not fight for others, at great cost . . . "

Lipov interrupted, "The cost will be ours to bear if the tide turns against us, Father Grigory. The picture is large, so let me explain . . . our Balkan friends Bulgaria, Serbia, Montenegro and Greece have a disagreement with Turkey. So be it. Good luck to them all, and may they find a local answer to a local problem.

"But what if Austria-Hungary or Germany comes to Turkey's aid? The 'local affair' suddenly grows larger and threatens all of Europe. Russia *must* stop such an action by declaring her support for the Balkans. Would Austria-Hungary and Germany risk our wrath to aid Turkey? No, they would not. They would let Turkey fight its own battles, and that is how it should be."

Quietly, Purishkevich added, "Now think of what this stance would mean for Tsar Nikolas, Father Grigory. His reputation as a decision-maker would quickly rise. Our neighbors would know that Russia takes a stand when she must, that she supports her allies to the death. Think of the *moujiki*! They would be talking about Russian strength and resolve; our internal difficulties would fade away. Mother Russia would be on the way to healing herself without having fired a single shot."

Rasputin sipped from his wine. He said, "You speak war. There can be no healing in such matters."

"There *can* be winners, Father Grigory," Purishkevich countered. "The Tsar, especially, will win when he shows no tolerance for strife so close to our borders."

Rasputin looked him squarely in the eye. "You say Russia will not fire a shot if we choose a side. But what if we must? Nikolas cannot go back on his word—we will have to fight. Yet politicians and policemen like yourselves will not die, only the *moujiki* will. You sacrifice them for your own gain."

"Not for our gain," Purishkevich said, "for the gain of the Tsar and Mother Russia! Do you not feel for your country?" He pounded his chest with his fist.

"We live in different countries, Vladimir Mitrofanovich. You live in a country where war is planned and fought on paper. I live in a country where men pay with blood and arms and legs. I will not ask Batiushka to commit to such a thing. I cannot support you."

"You can*not*?!" shouted Lipov. "If you love Russia and your Tsar, you must! It is our chance to regain respect in the world— and a chance for the Tsar to return to favor with his subjects!"

Rasputin glared at Lipov. "I did not know he was out of favor."

Purishkevich kicked Lipov under the table. "I think Captain Lipov means that the people would come to unite behind him, Father Grigory. Surely you feel how our people are at odds with each other."

"I feel for both the *moujik* and the factory worker, Vladimir Mitrofanovich. So does Batiushka. His concern for them runs deep. He plans to tour Russia in the spring, to demonstrate his good will. That is when the people will unite behind him again. Now then . . . others wait outside for me. If that is all—" Rasputin stood and gestured toward the door.

Lipov rose and stomped off, but Purishkevich stayed behind and exchanged kisses with Rasputin. "Please forgive my friend, Father Grigory. His emotions get the best of him, but he means well. He is a true Russian."

"Igor Igorevich would do well to humble himself. Such men are their own worst enemy."

Purishkevich nodded, smiling. "Lord knows we have enough enemies to fight without adding ourselves to the list. Wouldn't you agree, Father Grigory?"

Fifteen months later

Pokrovskoe

June 15, 1914

"Matushka,

Worry not, for the Lord will guide us and protect us. The war is not ours to fight. Batiushka will be Russia's strength. Life is ours to love.

- Your friend, Grigory."

The clerk took his telegram and Rasputin turned to leave the post office. He stopped at the window and peered out its clouded, foggy panes. Thick, black cloudballs were tumbling in from the north. The air was heavy, soon rain would fall in sheets. It seemed fitting. The news he'd received from Alexandra was dark—Archduke Francis Ferdinand and Sophie were dead, killed by a Serbian revolutionary. Rasputin's heart ached for Matushka. Could there be peace for her German family now? And what of Mother Russia?

He shook his head at the oncoming storm. The Archduke and his wife had been fair and open people, dedicated to peace and true friends of Russia. Now one man had shattered it all, dashing their futures to the bloody dirt. Tensions would worsen. There would be more calls for Nikolas to go to war, and it would be difficult for him to decline.

Praskovia had asked Rasputin not to worry about war, but that would be impossible now. He saw young men in the street hurrying about, some dragging small children, trying to finish their business before the clouds let loose. Rasputin wanted to tell them not to bother, that the weather didn't really matter. War was coming. When the announcement came, every Russian's heart would sink to where his own now suffered. The *moujiki* would die again.

Rasputin stepped outside. It was only five o'clock, but it seemed like dusk. The air was damp, mildewed. This would be a big storm. Praskovia would have a fire kindled and a wonderful dinner for them.

A small beggar woman approached him, her head covered by the hood of her *caftan*. She held out a shaking, dirty palm. Rasputin dug deep into a trouser pocket for some coins. As he did, he caught a glimpse of her other arm lifting, almost imperceptibly, from her side. His reaction was slow, his right hand mired impossibly deep in his pocket. Her hand neared him, and he saw a dark reflection of the clouds on the knife blade. His left hand could not move fast enough to block it, and her hands joined on its hilt as the blade approached. She thrust it deep into his belly.

"For Iliodor," she hissed.

In an instant Rasputin's breath was gone, as though a horse had kicked him. Enraged, eyes wide, Rasputin clamped his large left hand over both of hers and wrenched the blade from his gut. Her hood fell back as she fought for control of the weapon. She was ravaged by syphilis—her bony face was covered with ugly lesions, and no lips hid her broken and missing teeth. Her eyes burned red, her thin blond hair was pasted flat against her skull. She was death.

Rasputin's chest froze in place. He opened his mouth to cry out for help, but no sound emerged. Finally he managed to pull his right hand out of his pocket and hold her at bay.

There were shouts, men running toward them. Someone wrapped the woman in a bear hug, others stepped between them and disarmed her. One man threw Rasputin's arm over his shoulders and helped him remain standing. Others dragged the disfigured woman into the street and delivered Siberian justice.

Other men helped Rasputin down the block to his home, his feet dragging behind him.

Maria, Varya and Dmitri watched their father's delivery through the front door, screaming when they saw his wound and the trail of blood he left across the hard-wood floor. Praskovia held them back, barely able to see through her tears. She ordered them to lay him on the cot near the warm kitchen, and for Dunia to put water on to boil.

Rasputin drifted in and out of consciousness. He needed a doctor, but the nearest one was in Tyumen, six hours away. One of the men raced back to the post office and telegraphed him. In the meantime, Dunia did what she could to stop the bleeding. There was little to do but wait.

The doctor was there in just five hours, and he repaired what damage he could. But he cautioned that Rasputin's prognosis was not good. He needed hospitalization and immediate treatment for peritonitis. The doctor insisted they ferry him across the frigid plains to Tyumen; if any man could survive the trip, it would be a man as strong as Rasputin.

Praskovia and Dunia packed all the blankets and pillows in the house, and they instructed the younger ones to wear every piece of clothing they could button on. Then they all lay together in the back of the wagon, as much to keep warm as to cushion Rasputin from the merciless road.

Dawn broke before they reached Tyumen. Rasputin still breathed, and for now that was enough. The doctor took him to surgery immediately, and the rest of the family was led to a warm, quiet room. They closed their eyes and slept. So far, the Virgin had taken care of Her favorite son. It was all in Her hands now.

One month later

Pokrovskoe, Siberia

July 13, 1914

Rasputin refilled his wine glass, emptying the bottle of Madeira. It rocked on his nightstand when he set it down and finally fell over. He drank half the glass in one swallow—he had no reason not to. He was a prisoner in his own home as he healed, a student of humility, completely dependent on others for his care. Even his bodily functions were not his to command. Rasputin, who had helped to cure so many, could do nothing to speed his own recovery.

At least the pain was lessening this week. A cough no longer brought tears to his eyes—just a knotted pull in his abdomen. But in a way the lessening pain was a curse, since now he had so much time to think and no way to act upon his convictions.

He finished his glass and rang his bell. Dunia brought him another bottle. Alone again, he wondered if the forces of heaven were working against him. Did the Virgin want to see Russia go to war? It must be so, for She had made it impossible for him to fight its call. By now the cabinet ministers would have convinced Nikolas of the need for war, and Alexandra would have severed her ties to Germany to stand with him. Rasputin knew it was so. If Batiushka and Matushka had chosen otherwise, Rasputin would have heard from them.

But Rasputin found it surprising the local *moujiki* had accepted war, too. His visitors told him they wanted Russia to fight her foes, to defeat those who would stand against her. His arguments made no difference. Their minds were set.

Rasputin took his pad to write another telegram:

"Batiushka,

The strength of Mother Russia is in her people. They mus"

The point of his pencil snapped off and Rasputin threw it across the room. "*Ei Bogu!*" he cried, and he threw the pad of paper, too. Again, the forces above had stopped him.

"Papa?"

Rasputin looked up. Dmitri, now 19, stood in the doorway. He looked afraid. "Come in, Misha. I am all right."

Dmitri walked slowly, cupping a rag in his large hands. Rasputin lifted the top flap of cloth. Beneath it lay a quivering baby lark, more dead than alive. Its beak sluggishly opened and closed once.

Softly Dmitri asked, "Will he live, Papa?"

Rasputin took the bird into his own hands. It was so fragile, so light and helpless. He covered it again and patted the bed beside him. Dmitri sat. "We shall pray, my son," Rasputin said, and they both closed their eyes.

Rasputin hummed and chanted, sending his thoughts to the Lord. For several minutes the two of them did not move, and then Rasputin fell silent.

"Is he all right now, Papa?" Dmitri's face was full of innocent hope.

Rasputin did not answer. The light had not come.

Dmitri lifted the cloth to see the bird. He sniffed back tears. Rasputin looked—the tiny lark was still, its mouth wide open. He pulled the cloth back over it.

"He has gone to the Lord, Misha. We must be happy for him. Come now," he brushed his son's face with the back of his hand, "we shall hold a service in the yard—"

Dmitri was devastated. He got up and held out his shaking hands, and Rasputin set the bundle into them. Dmitri carried it away as carefully as he'd carried it in. Rasputin could see out his window as Dmitri dropped to his knees in the backyard, gently laid the bird down and dug a grave with his hands.

Rasputin sighed. He swung his feet out of bed and shuffled to the kitchen.

Praskovia and Dunia were watching Dmitri, too. They turned when they heard Rasputin. Their eyes were misty, and this time they did not chastise him for being out of bed. Instead, they helped him walk out to the sunny yard. Maria and Varya were there now, too.

Dmitri finished digging. He crossed himself, and the rest of the family followed his lead. He laid the bird and its shroud gently into the grave, then filtered dirt through his fingers until the hole was filled. He stuck a stick into the ground as a marker.

"Papa, would you—?" he asked, looking up. His face was covered with dirt, muddy trails lining his cheeks.

Rasputin nodded. He crossed himself and asked aloud that the Lord accept the tiny bird, for it was one of His finest creations. But for the first time in his life, he did not know if Anyone was listening.

CHAPTER 7

Five days later

Pokrovskoe

July 18, 1914

Rasputin could not yet negotiate the stairway to his *sabor*, so he shuffled to the icon corner and knelt before the small "The Virgin of Kazan." Aloud he begged Her to take pity on those who had led Russia into this conflict, and that She return the fighting *moujiki* to their families and lands.

But for now he must wait. He was quietly crossing himself when there was a knock at the door. No one else was home. He willed himself up and called for the person to enter.

It was a delivery boy with a telegram from Alexandra:

"My friend,

These are truly the saddest of times. I cannot tell you how my heart sinks when I think of warring against my own people. I long for the comfort of your words in times like this, even though Nicky thinks you stand against him. But besides the terrible declaration, there has been other news here today that I must tell you of. One of the maids called me into the Alexander Hall to look at our favorite icon "The Virgin of Kazan." Tears were falling from Her eyes! We are positive it was so. There was no rain or dampness that could have explained it otherwise. The Virgin cries for Mother Russia. I feel it is a sign from the Almighty. May His spirit remain with us throughout this ordeal.

- A."

Rasputin again crossed himself and knelt before the icon. He gazed deeply into Her eyes, desperate to witness even one tear. But there were none, of course. This was only a copy. The famous original, 'The Weeping Virgin', hung in the Alexander Palace; it was only She who ever weeped for Mother Russia.

He returned to prayer, pressing his head to the floor. Suddenly it mattered less that the light was gone. If the Virgin took it, She must have had good reason. And one day She would return the light to him if She so pleased.

Before dinner, Rasputin took pen in hand:

"Batiushka,

This is a day of great sadness. The storm has engulfed Russia. Her people will spill their blood in her name. The Holy Mother weeps for Russia. The Lord knows how all will end. I beg you, stop this madness while you still can. Only you are strong, and only you can show the strength of your resolve.

- Your Friend, Grigory."

Two months later

St. Petersburg

September 11, 1914

Nikolas still refused to grant Rasputin an audience, but, oh how the gypsies welcomed his return. Night after night they cavorted in the *Novaya Derevnya* camp on the banks of the Neva, pouring themselves and Rasputin full of wine and vodka, dancing to the music of *akkordeons*, dulled to the dropping temperatures and concerns of war. During quieter moments Rasputin told of his travels as a *strannik*, and many were the ladies who waited their turn to worship with him in the tents that circled the fires.

The police noted that he usually returned to his flat between dawn and noon, often babbling and stumbling up the steps. And although they were fewer now, his visitors lined up in the afternoon to see him before he would again leave for the evening. Everyone knew Rasputin would not be out of Nikolas' favor for long.

His critics were mystified. Keeping hours such as those, how could Rasputin still hold 'court' around his kitchen table? Did he not sleep? Did he not need recovery time from his shenanigans in the countryside? From the number of female visitors, they knew his stamina was at full strength. Had he really been stabbed? And where would his madness lead?

Three months later

Petrograd (formerly St. Petersburg)

January 6, 1915

Rasputin hastily packed several items into his bag, including his pocket-sized icon 'Our Lady of Miracles'.

"I am ready," he told the Tsar's driver. The two of them dashed from Rasputin's apartment to the Imperial carriage and set off. It would be a long, bumpy trip.

The afternoon was fading to evening. Snowdrifts along the way cast long shadows across the white road. The air grew chillier by the minute. Above, the sky held dim, hazy light, and black smoke rose into it from the south, in front of them.

Twenty minutes passed, and they came upon a section of the road crowded with bystanders, buggies and horseless carriages. Farther on, fire brigade wagons blocked all but the narrowest of lanes for them to pass through. Between the wagons and horses Rasputin caught glimpses of the train that now lay on its side, its blue and gold cars charred and twisted dark and ugly, turned up at odd angles or dug into the hard permafrost. It seemed unreal, an impossible vision. Rasputin winced and crossed himself.

The black smoke was pouring from the engine and steam hung about the rest of the train. Men walked on the cars, stepping over the Imperial eagles on the sides, avoiding the broken windows. Others walked on the ground, entering or leaving the cars through gaping holes in the metal skins.

As they passed the fire brigades, Rasputin saw a row of linens on the ground, perhaps fifteen or more, some reddened, that outlined human forms. He pulled the icon from his bag, crossed himself again and chanted prayers for the dead.

He said prayers for Anyushka, too. From what the driver told him, she lay trapped for quite some time, constantly calling for Father Grigory before losing consciousness. And even though she was now free of the mangled steel trap and under care at the palace, she was close to joining the unfortunate ones under the linens.

They continued on to the hospital at Tsarskoe Selo, and the driver led him straight to her room. Rasputin's stomach tightened at the stale odors of alcohol, sweat, blood and urine, but there was work to do, and adrenaline carried him through. He paid no attention to Alexandra, who sat sobbing on the far side of Anyushka's bed, or to Nikolas, in his general's uniform, who stood with bloodstained Imperial surgeon Prince Gedroitz nearby. He had not come for them.

Anna lay unconscious. Most of her head was wrapped in bandages, and all the color was gone from what little part of her face was exposed. Her legs were grotesquely large under the blankets.

Rasputin fell to his knees beside her, placed his icon on her pillow and mouthed a silent prayer. After several minutes he lifted his head and looked at her. He then stood and took her hand in his. "Anyushka—Anyushka, look at me," he said firmly.

She did not respond, but no look of anguish came across Rasputin's face. He closed his eyes and stood his ground, waiting, swaying slightly. He muttered an almost imperceptible chant. Then suddenly he barked out, "Anyushka! Look at me! I am here!"

Everyone in the room jumped. Anna opened her eyes a sliver and saw him. She squeezed his hand. "Father Grigory," she whispered, "thank God." She closed her eyes again.

Rasputin laid her hand down and wiped a bead of sweat from his brow. He finally looked at Alexandra and Nikolas. "She will live," he said, "but she will always be a cripple." He did not elaborate. He turned and walked unsteadily from the room. He took a seat in the polished hall, his hands on his knees, his head bowed.

Alexandra followed him out. He looked up when she put her shaking hand on his disheveled hair. Her shoulders were quivering, her tears flowed. "Father Grigory—" she sniffled.

Rasputin stood and hugged her. She burst out crying, uncontrollably, almost violently. Rasputin held her head to his shoulder. "Let it out, Matushka," he said soothingly. "The Lord would have it so."

Nikolas came out, too. He didn't speak, but he nodded and put his hand on Rasputin's shoulder to thank him.

Oddly, a smile had lightened Rasputin's face. Nikolas looked at him puzzled. He asked, "Father Grigory, do you smile for Anyushka?"

Rasputin nodded. "I smile for Anyushka, Batiushka. I also smile for the Lord and the Virgin. For They hath giveth, and They hath taketh away."

Nikolas looked alarmed. "Taketh away? I thought you said Anyushka would live."

Rasputin still smiled. "So she shall, Batiushka. They tooketh from *me*. And today—over Anyushka—They have returned to me the light. The light of the Virgin again burns strong before my eyes."

Nikolas smiled for him. "Father Grigory—" he hesitated. It had been a trying afternoon and evening for Nikolas, and his voice was shaky as he searched for the right words. "We have always known the light burns within you. How could we have doubted you for so long? The girls and Alyosha would love to see you—won't you come home with us to eat and rest?"

Alexandra jumped back with excitement, "Oh, my friend, won't you? Alyosha is always asking for you, and the girls have missed you so much."

Rasputin nodded. "If you would have it so, I would be honored."

Alexandra hugged him, and Nikolas slapped him on the back. Finally they were friends again. If it weren't for the blasted war, it would have felt like a return to life as usual.

Fourteen months later

Petrograd
The Duma, Office of Vladimir Purishkevich

March 16, 1916

Only here could Vladimir Purishkevich and Captain Lipov speak freely; opportunists lurked everywhere else, especially in the halls outside the door, full of up-and-comers seeking position in the country's illogical hierarchy. For in the scant six months since Nikolas' departure, two new paths to political power had completely replaced the old—impress Alexandra and Rasputin with one's religious conviction, or show one's allegiance to Russia by turning in those who spoke unkindly of her.

"Look what has happened since Nikolas left for the front lines, Igor Igorevich. The list of ministers who have come and gone has hit fifteen. One was dismissed even before he was sworn in. How can Nikolas tolerate such chaos?"

"He must not know . . . ", Lipov replied, "for who would be brave enough to tell him? His German wife? Rasputin? Nikolas would banish *him* from the capital—again—if he knew the mad monk was dismissing ministers for the color of their suits."

Purishkevich nodded. "Banishment would come not a moment too soon." He leaned back in his chair, stroking his beard, staring at Lipov. "We should consider banishing him ourselves."

Lipov closed his eyes and dropped his head. Suddenly he slammed his fist into his open hand and stood. He turned his back to Purishkevich and said over his shoulder, "Banishment to hell is what I would prefer, Vladimir Mitrofanovich. I have reason to kill him for something that happened long ago. And with his new position in the capital, I cannot reach him to avenge my honor."

He paced the room, too embarrassed to look Purishkevich in the eye. He told of learning that Rasputin had 'worshipped' with his wife at Tsarevich Alexei's birthday party in 1908. When he finished, he strode to Purishkevich's desk and leaned over onto it. "I will kill him for that, my friend. I will have it no other way." Fire in his eyes testified to his resolve.

"Then it shall be so, Igor Igorevich, and you shall never hear me discuss your motive. Please, sit down, and let us consider our options."

They agreed, first, that Rasputin's mix of sex and religion certainly confirmed his membership in the outlawed *Khlysty*. He belonged in prison, not Tsarskoe Selo.

Second, that Nikolas' absence had left Alexandra completely under Rasputin's control. That meant he was 'worshipping' with her, and possibly with Nikolas' daughters, as well. The news would devastate Nikolas when he learned.

Third, that Alexandra's German heritage could not be ignored. Was she purposely undermining the war effort with her selection of incompetent ministers? Had Rasputin persuaded her to choose Germany over her husband?

"The evidence points that way," Lipov said. "I think we have only one alternative—and that is to remove Rasputin, permanently."

"I already have a plan," Purishkevich said, smiling. "To begin, we need Doctor Stanislaus Andreyevich Lazovert transferred here from his medical train at the front. He is a first-rate doctor, and he wears the Maltese Cross on his chest. I am certain he will provide a slow, painful method of execution . . . one that leaves no trace of foul play.

"However, I do not have a location or plan to lure him from Tsarskoe Selo. I know he returns to his flat in the city occasionally, so we might begin some sort of watch of the premises. Perhaps your contacts in the Petrograd police—"

"Of course. We will establish his routine—for his safety, I will announce. When we can predict his schedule, we will set our date. As to the location of his execution, let us take our time. We will know the right place when we find it."

Eight months later

Petrograd
The Duma, Main Hall

November 20, 1916

Purishkevich roared from behind the podium, "As more and more of our men shed their blood, we must ask ourselves, are we doing all we can to prevent it? Is this what Mother Russia's people shall become—sacrificial offerings to those who would kill them? Our people are tired, cold and hungry—both at home and on the battlefield. Yet the countries we fight are not suffering so! Should we remain in this war? I say no! Let us withdraw before all of our young men are buried in the trenches of Poland!"

Thunderous applause broke out, and much of the Duma stood. There'd been private debate on whether Purishkevich would be first to air these words publicly and tempt the consequences.

"Stand with me then, leaders of Russia! Together we can make a difference. The Tsar has been away too long—he no longer knows what we feel at home. Yet do I blame him? Certainly not. He loves Mother Russia, and he will forever do what he feels is in her best interests. But his communication lines have been cut off. And without his knowing what is wrong, we cannot expect him to make repairs.

"Fellow champions of the Motherland, it is here, at home, where we must focus our energies. Each of you must consider how and why the Tsar has grown out of touch. And when you do, you will reach the same conclusion that I have—we have a cancer at our center. A cancer unlike one we have ever seen, a cancer whose tentacles reach out and choke the arteries of Mother Russia. Worst of all, this cancer assumes the shape of goodness, of Godliness. It is convincing those who listen, and they stand behind its facade. But we cannot. We must excise it, and we must do it soon. The Tsar and the Motherland depend on us to perform this act. Our true enemy, my friends, is within us."

Without another word, Purishkevich strode off-stage. Every eye was on him, many mouths open with astonishment. Never before had a politician so publicly guillotined Rasputin. Purishkevich was doomed. And anyone who supported him was doomed as well.

Two more speakers addressed the Duma before it recessed for the day, but little attention was paid by the smirking, whispering politicians.

As Purishkevich was collecting his papers to leave, a young man approached him, his hand extended. He said he was impressed with Purishkevich's speech and he would like to help Purishkevich in his cause. He introduced himself as Prince Felix Felixovich Yussupov.

The next day

Petrograd
The Duma, Office of Vladimir Purishkevich

November 21, 1916

Purishkevich paced, shaking his head. "How can we allow them to work with us, Igor Igorevich? He would not speak of his motives—and my God, he is a prince! Surely he is a spy for the Tsarina." Purishkevich took a seat on the edge of his desk.

"I think not, my friend," Lipov said. "Yussupov has come to our attention many times. He and young Dmitri Romanov, the nephew of the Tsar, have quite a reputation in some parts of the city." He leaned forward in his chair. "Yussupov is married to the Tsar's niece, but don't let that fact fool you. He and young Romanov are more than partners in crime . . . they are faggots in every sense of the word. Some call Yussupov the 'Prince of Perversion.'"

Purishkevich raised an eyebrow. "And you think such 'men' have a place in our plans? What value could they be? And why would they want to see the demise of Rasputin?"

Lipov smiled. "If memory serves me right, a couple of years ago Yussupov emerged from the gypsy camps with a bloody nose. And there was mention of his male companion being dressed as a woman. Apparently they were drunk and had tried to take Rasputin by force.

"And consider these points, Vladimir Mitrofanovich— Romanov, as a member of the royal family, is shielded by law from prosecution for any crimes he commits. And the Yussupov family owns more mansions throughout Russia than I can count. Their palace in Petrograd is quite private, and it is equipped with its own security force. It would be perfect for our needs. Yussupov and Romanov could literally get away with a murder there . . . in a manner of speaking."

"In a manner of speaking," Purishkevich echoed. He was silent for some time. Finally he sighed. "Then let us begin."

One month later

Petrograd
The Yussupov's Moika Palace

December 16, 1916

Yussupov shivered in the frigid night wind, fumbling to unlock the door to the servant's quarters below the palace. Finally he shoved it open. Romanov, Lipov, Purishkevich and Dr. Lazovert followed him in.

"Misha, you'll kindle a fire?" Yussupov asked as he slammed the door shut.

Romanov nodded. He peeled off his sable greatcoat and hung it on the stand behind the door before setting to work.

"As I promised, Vladimir Mitrofanovich," Yussupov said, "our purposes shall remain secret. After my staff decorated these quarters, I granted them holiday for today and tomorrow. And my wife is in London at Windsor."

Purishkevich nodded, stroking his beard. A polar bear rug lay between the satin couch and chair and the fireplace. A portrait of the Tsar hung over the mantle, and two sets of floor-length purple drapes covered the windows. Tucked into one corner was a bar equipped with a silver serving dish, a samovar, a wine decanter and stemware. Beside it was an ornate gilded table and chairs. In the other corner, on the far side of the room, was a small landing and the two doors Yussupov had described—one that led outdoors to the private courtyard, and other to the staircase into the palace.

Purishkevich unbuttoned his coat. "From servant's quarters to comfortable apartment . . . this shall suit our needs. Igor Igorevich, please light the lamp below that icon—it hasn't a trace of soot about it."

Lipov nodded. He crossed himself before the small painting and golden crucifix and lit the burner.

Purishkevich asked Yussupov, "And where is the stockpile of Madeira wine? You were to have stocked plenty?"

"There is a case of the swill behind the bar," he answered, "plus the cakes, which were baked just today. Perhaps the doctor would like to begin his preparations?"

Lazovert, bald and thin as a lamppost, nodded and carried his black bag to the bar. He lifted the cover from the serving tray and found seven cupcakes iced with chocolate. Eight more were plain, with no icing. He glanced at Yussupov. "I thought you said we would have pink—"

"Pink icing, yes. There should be a bowl of pink icing somewhere behind the bar. Please use it after you have treated the cakes."

Lazovert went to work. No one spoke, but there were anxious smiles and glances when he pulled the vial of potassium cyanide from his bag. He lightly sprinkled each plain cupcake, then he carefully spread the icing over it.

"Is that enough poison, Doctor?" Lipov questioned. "He is a strong man, and surely we need not skimp—"

Lazovert scowled, his thin lips twitching. "Skimp? If you were familiar with potassium cyanide, Captain," he said, "you would know each dusting on these cakes could kill ten men.

Would you like to sample one?" He held out a pink cupcake for Lipov. The rest of them smiled nervously as Lipov retreated.

Yussupov asked, "And the wine glasses, Doctor? Or do we need bother?" but Lazovert had no chance to reply.

"We surely do need bother!" retorted Purishkevich. "The animal has driven Mother Russia to the brink of civil war, corrupting every aspect of her government along his way. Yes, we shall bother!"

Lazovert pulled another vial from his bag—this one a clear liquid. He set a thin glass rod into a wine goblet and dribbled drops of the poison onto it. They spiraled downward and formed a tiny, clear pool at the bottom, virtually undetectable. Then he showed Yussupov the goblet's position behind the bar.

Only occasional snaps and cracks from the growing fire broke the murderous silence, and one or another of them seemed to jump with each spark. Finally Romanov stood back and surveyed his work. Yussupov went and paid him a quiet compliment.

"Now then, Felix Felixovich," Purishkevich said, "show us to our quarters and we will settle in."

"Of course. Gentlemen, follow me please."

Romanov retrieved his coat and Yussupov led them all to the landing and through the door, up the stairs into a luxurious drawing room directly above the servant's quarters. Paintings of Romanovs and Yussupovs graced the walls between oriental tapestries. Satin-upholstered settees and carved tables were sprinkled about, and gilded accents glistened in the lamplight.

With a gleam in his eye, Yussupov stopped at the gramophone. "No party is complete without music, my friends," he said. He turned the crank and set the needle onto the cylinder, and scratchy strains of "Yankee Doodle" resonated from the horn.

"That will be fine," Purishkevich said. "Now we should review our plans one last time." He motioned to himself, Lipov, and Romanov. "The three of us will keep the music playing and pace the floor as the poison takes effect. Felix Felixovich, you have your plan to ensure Rasputin will come back with you tonight?"

"Yes. I know he thirsts to meet my wife. He accepted an appointment with her once, but she had to put him off. I am sure that if I offer him the chance to come to our home tonight and pray with her, he will come. And quickly."

Purishkevich nodded. "The thought of his perversion makes me ill, but it will be his undoing." Then he turned and addressed Dr. Lazovert, "Stanislaus Andreyevich, you will have to serve as Yussupov's driver. You're the only one of us Rasputin does not know."

"Surely not," Lazovert objected. "I agreed to serve as your doctor in this affair, and that is all. You know my terms."

Purishkevich glared at him, then took him by the arm and led him to the corner of the parlor. They stopped and faced each other defiantly.

In a low voice Purishkevich said, "Now see here, my friend. We go back together a long time, and you have my utmost respect. But as a fellow of the Corps, you are bound to aid us in serving the Tsar."

"We took a vow of Friendship *Until* Death, my friend," Lazovert replied, "not Friendship to *Cause* Death. So clearly I am past the boundaries of our youthful pledge. And I remind you that I *was* serving the Tsar—beside him, at the front lines, where death raked us by the thousands. Perhaps it would do you well to see it for yourself."

Purishkevich's face reddened. He tightened his grip on the doctor's arm and his words poured out like an avalanche. "Need I remind you . . . I arranged your transfer to Petrograd on one condition—that you agree to help us in our mission. And you agreed to that condition. So then, you will look at serving as our driver as simply another task in the mission. Look at it as such or I will see you returned to the front lines tonight!"

Lazovert glared at Purishkevich but he did not reply. Purishkevich turned about, and Lazovert shook his arm free. They returned to the others.

"Now then, Felix Felixovich," Purishkevich snorted, "you and your driver should be off. Bring us the cancer that infects Mother Russia."

CHAPTER 8

Thirty Minutes Later

December 16, 1916

In the open cockpit of Yussupov's horseless carriage, Lazovert twisted into the biting swirl of ice and snow blowing off the Moika Canal. Yussupov sat behind drawn curtains in the passenger compartment. Soon they reached relative calm amid the buildings in the heart of Petrograd. The western quarter of town, and 64 Gorokhovaya Street, lay not far off.

Lamps burned in Rasputin's windows as they turned into the courtyard. Lazovert stopped the car at the bottom of the staircase and shut off the engine. He retreated into his furs, licking at the frozen snot on his upper lip.

Yussupov leapt out the door enthusiastically and hurried up the steps. Soon light from 3A spilled out onto the porch.

"Ei Bogu! Yussupov!" Rasputin tried to shut the door, but Yussupov managed to get a foot in.

"Please, Father Grigory—" he protested, wincing in agony, "listen to me! I have changed! I have asked God's forgiveness for my past life. May I not beg the same of you?"

Rasputin did not reply, and he did not take his weight off the door.

"I swear to you, I have found the Lord's way. My Irisha and I have found it together. Please, may I not speak?"

Rasputin's face appeared, stern and intolerant, at the crack of the door. "What is it you want?"

Yussupov smiled affectionately. "I know you may not be able to forgive me, Father Grigory, but the Lord has. He has blessed my life now, for without His blessing I would not have come here. I know how you hate me . . . "

"I do not hate," Rasputin interrupted, his voice no less softer. "I feel only sorrow for you. You are not one with the Lord."

"*Was* not, Father, I *was* not one with the Lord. But now I am, and my happiness knows no bounds. Except—except where Dmitri Pavlovich is concerned. Naturally we have parted company, but he has not renounced his evil ways. I fear for his soul." A tear rolled down his cheek. "Tell me, will Misha find redemption before the Lord?"

Rasputin sighed. He opened the door and motioned for Yussupov to enter. They took seats at the table. Rasputin topped off his wine glass and poured Yussupov a warm vodka.

"Only the Lord Himself can save him, Felix Felixovich. Dmitri Pavlovich would do well to follow your lead. He must ask the Lord for His forgiveness. Tell me, how did you come to seek salvation?"

Yussupov's gaze dropped. It was a moment before he spoke. "I was going to lose her, Father Grigory. My Irisha had had enough of my behavior, and she was going to leave me. She forced me to choose—I did not act on my own volition." He blew his nose and snuck a peek at Rasputin, who was nodding.

"I can never thank her enough, Father Grigory—and my love for her has grown so! What wonderful feelings I have come to know! In this past year my life has become fulfilled."

"You have been blessed, Felix Felixovich. The Lord smiles upon you."

Yussupov's grinned. "I knew you would under-stand, Father Grigory. Now, before it grows any later, I must ask a favor of you."

Rasputin raised an eyebrow, listening.

"I know you and Irina Pavlovna have never met, but she feels she knows you from the stories she has heard." Yussupov's voice cracked, "And right now, she is crying inside. She learned today that a friend is dying, yet she is hosting a party at our palace that could not be canceled. Oh, her pain is so great, yet she must hide it for tonight. Father Grigory, she has asked—" he hesitated.

"She has asked what?"

Yussupov shook his head. "No, I cannot. It would be such an imposition."

"What is it Irina Pavlovna asks of me?" Rasputin demanded.

"She asks to see you, Father. I am sorry to tell you this, for I know it is late and you are a busy man. Yet—she begged me to come find you, and to bring you to our home." Yussupov stood and continued, apologetically, "I could not refuse her request, Father Grigory, for I know her heart is heavy, and I will be honest with her when I return home. I'll tell her you might see her on another day, at a more proper hour."

Rasputin shook his head. "The Lord would not have me wait. His children know no clocks for their pain. We shall go."

Yussupov's eyes lit up. "Oh, Father Grigory! My Irisha will be so relieved—your prayers will mean so much to her."

Rasputin stood and threw the rest of his wine down his throat. "I will get my *caftan* and boots. We shall go to worship with Irina Pavlovna."

At the palace, Yussupov showed Rasputin a basement door where he could enter without attracting attention from the guests. He helped Rasputin out of his *caftan* and pointed to the table. "Please take a seat, Father Grigory. May I suggest a glass of wine while we wait?"

Rasputin shook his head. He walked to the icon corner and crossed himself before the Virgin's image. He turned to Yussupov and said, "No wine. I must see Irina Pavlovna now."

Unflapped, Yussupov went to the bar and poured two glasses of Madeira. He took a seat at the table and set one of the glasses near an empty chair, motioning for Rasputin to join him. "My Irisha will be down soon," he said. "The driver sent word we have arrived, so I am sure she will be down quickly."

Rasputin nodded. He cocked his head; faint music and footsteps came from above. He went to the table and drained half his glass.

"What a true Russian you are, Father Grigory," Yussupov said, again motioning for Rasputin to sit. "I miss drinking with so able a partner. Let us enjoy our own company before the woman arrives and turns us to softhearted fools."

Rasputin finally pulled out the chair and sat. He emptied his glass. "I pray Irina Pavlovna will not be long."

Yussupov nodded and finished his wine, too. "Oh, I nearly forgot—I ordered cakes in case you were able to come tonight."

He stood and walked behind the bar. "I'll bet they are already here. Yes! They are Pierre's specialty!"

Yussupov took the tray to the table and bit into a chocolate one. Rasputin took little notice of the pastries, though. He seemed anxious, staring first at the icon in the corner, then at the portrait of the Tsar, then into the crackling fire.

Suddenly he turned to Yussupov and said, "We shall go and find Irina Pavlovna. She must become one with the Lord."

Yussupov stalled, wiping the corners of his mouth before answering. "She will soon be down, Father Grigory. We must allow her latitude. She could be distressed by her other troubles—let us give her a little more time. I know she wants to meet you."

"Other troubles? Tell me how she suffers so that I might help her. I have prayed with many women, Felix Felixovich."

Yussupov hesitated. "Father Grigory, her other troubles are of a personal nature. But then again—perhaps you *should* know of them. She should not have to keep secrets from you."

"The Lord would have it so. Allow me to pray for her."

Yussupov refilled their glasses, and the two of them drew up the space between them. Yussupov spoke slowly, in a low tone, looking Rasputin straight in the eye. "Since I've returned to Irisha, she has experienced a problem concerning—well, her womanhood. She wants to take me in, to satisfy my needs, but there is pain for her, pain too great for her to ignore. Yet she asks me to disregard her cries! Well I cannot, Father Grigory! As she cries beneath me, and her fair hair swirls and clings to her teary cheeks—"

Rasputin sat on the edge of his chair, engulfed. He wet his lips frequently with wine, and then he reached for a cupcake—a pink one. Yussupov paused a moment, watching Rasputin bite into it, but quickly he looked away. He spun another erotic tale, of he and his wife's first time in bed together, and another of their experiences in the company of others, and yet another of her wavering preference for men over women. The stories seemed to fuel Rasputin's appetite, and soon none of the pink cakes remained.

Yussupov continued, pausing only for sips of wine. Each tale came out a little faster. He invented lusty dreams for his wife, and he told how sometimes he wished he were two men, so he might truly satisfy her. But suddenly he slammed both hands on the table.

"I must check on my Irisha!" he declared. "She must not keep you any longer. I shall return quickly, Father Grigory." He stood and hurried off through the door to the palace.

Rasputin nodded and belched.

Yussupov flew up the steps two at a time, flung open the door into the parlor and rushed in. He leaned back against the door as he shut it and froze there—his skin white as milk, his breathing irregular, his eyes wild and unfixed.

Purishkevich was the first to reach him. He whispered ferociously, "What is it? What is wrong?"

Yussupov could not answer. Purishkevich grabbed him by the collar and slapped him. "Speak to us! What is happening?"

"It's not working!" Yussupov finally blurted out. "He's not dead!"

Purishkevich stifled him with a hand over his mouth. "Lower your voice, my friend, before I cut out your tongue. You say the animal is not dead. Is he even ill?"

Yussupov shook his head. Purishkevich released him and glared at Lazovert. Romanov came to Yussupov's aid, helping him take three steps to the sofa.

"Perhaps he needs a little longer, Vladimir Mitrofanovich," Lazovert said, "but he *will* lose consciousness—as long as he actually consumed the poison, that is." Everyone looked at Yussupov, who nodded vigorously.

"Then we shall all be there to witness his fall,"

Purishkevich declared. "Felix Felixovich, return to him, alone. The rest of us will assemble on the steps just outside the door and wait for your shout to enter. We will either subdue him if he remains unaffected, or we will carry him off for burial if he succumbs. In fact, it would seem easier to help him stumble out of the room before he dies than over our shoulders after the fact."

"No!" cried out Romanov effeminately from the sofa. "This has gone too far—Rasputin must be protected by the Lord! We must stop this nonsense!"

In the blink of an eye Lipov pulled his pistol and aimed it at Romanov. Purishkevich addressed both Romanov and Yussupov, "I should never have agreed to include you women in this group. If you want out, there will be plenty of room in the river for three. Will you be going for a midnight swim?"

Neither answered. Purishkevich motioned for Yussupov to get moving, and Lipov returned the gun to his holster.

As they left the parlor for the staircase, Lipov stayed on the heels of Yussupov and Romanov, his hand on the gun. Purishkevich followed them, and Lazovert left the parlor door slightly ajar behind them so the soft parlor light would light the steps.

Just before Yussupov reached the basement door, Romanov suddenly stopped and bent over, as if suffering from a cramp. When he rose he held a derringer he'd pulled from his boot. He handed it to Yussupov.

Yussupov waved the tiny gun above him and addressed the others in a whisper. "I want him, gentle-men," he proclaimed. "He is mine for having offended Misha and myself, and I will personally see to his death."

Lipov looked back to Purishkevich for instructions, but there were none. Purishkevich could only nod. This was no time for commotion. "Fine, but do not miss or you will pay in hell."

Yussupov tucked the pistol under his shirt, into the small of his back. "I never miss, he's as good as dead." He turned his back to them, marched down the last few steps and through the door.

"My Irisha is on the way, Father Grigory," he announced loudly.

Rasputin was still sitting at the table, but now he held his head in his hands. Yussupov pretended not to notice.

"Irisha did have one request—she asked that you pray for her before her favorite icon. That is what she begs of you until she can be with us."

Rasputin looked up slowly and slurred, "Irina Pavlovna deserves her wish fulfilled." His face was ashen and shiny with sweat, his eyes red, his hair more rumpled than usual. He struggled when he tried to stand. Yussupov came to his aid and helped him to the icon corner.

Rasputin knelt, swaying, eyes closed, and slowly crossed himself. Yussupov stood beside him, watching, then took two steps backward and one to the side. He pulled out the pistol. He pointed it at the back of Rasputin's heart, and he fired. The bark echoed throughout the stone room. There was a small amount of smoke in front of the gun. Through it Yussupov watched Rasputin fall forward heavily, onto his chest. There was a spot of blood on the back of his bluza.

Yussupov stepped up and stood with his legs spread over Rasputin, pointing the tiny gun at him with both hands. "He is dead! Rasputin is dead!" he shouted.

The group burst in like stampeding cattle. Romanov was the first, and he jumped down the landing steps shouting, "Felisha! You did it, you did it!"

Yussupov turned his head to them. His hair was wildly askew, his eyes a shade of blood-red and his nostrils like those of a winded horse. Strands of saliva bridged the gap between his lips. Romanov pulled him from the body; the two of them launched into a frolicking free-for-all of dancing, hugging and slapping.

Lazovert pushed them out of the way to get to Rasputin. "I can find no pulse," he announced.

"Let us see his face," Purishkevich ordered. Lipov helped Lazovert roll Rasputin onto his back. There was no blood or sign of an exit wound.

Rasputin moaned.

Yussupov and Romanov stopped dancing. No one spoke. Finally Romanov muttered, "He's alive—"

But Rasputin went silent again. They all waited to for the next sign of life, but none came.

Suddenly Romanov grabbed Lipov's pistol from his belt and ordered, "Get away from him! Get away from Rasputin!" He waved the pistol back and forth, covering Purishkevich, Lipov and Lazovert. The men neither obeyed nor resisted.

Behind Romanov, Yussupov appeared insane. His gaze was fixed on Rasputin as if the body was taunting him. The saliva now frothed at Yussupov's mouth, his chest heaved.

"Get back! Now!" Romanov screamed again, and the other three men obeyed him this time.

Yussupov kicked Rasputin back over onto his stomach. With adrenaline-enhanced strength he pulled the body toward the center of the room, stopping at the sofa. He managed to lift it up, bending it across the padded arm.

Romanov drove the men to the door. "Out! All of you out!"

Rasputin's head landed on a cushion, his feet were still on the floor. Yussupov tore down Rasputin's trousers, exposing his backside.

"My God, Yussupov," Purishkevich stammered. Lipov made a half-hearted attempt to rush Yussupov, but Romanov cut him off, driving him back with the pistol.

Disgusted, Purishkevich, Lipov and Lazovert turned and walked through the doorway but stopped on the lowest stairs. It seemed they could not leave but they could not stay.

Finally Purishkevich turned and said, "You'll both burn in hell—", but he stopped in mid-sentence. Yussupov had rolled the body off the sofa, onto its back on the polar bear rug. He knelt sideways on its chest, holding a knife high above his head. A satanic grin lit his face.

"No!" Purishkevich cried, "you've done enough!" He lunged back into the room toward Yussupov, but Romanov screamed he was going to shoot.

Yussupov grabbed Rasputin's genitals in one hand and pulled them up hard, away from their foundation, and brought down the knife in a furious slice. Yussupov held the meat high, like a trophy, then flung it across the room. It left a spotty red trail to where it plopped down near the coat rack.

Lipov vomited on the steps. Purishkevich and Lazovert were right behind him, coughing and gagging.

They wiped their mouths on their sleeves and vaulted up the stairs to the parlor. Lipov, out of breath, said, "We have to dispose of the body before they march around with his head on a stick."

"Surely they are finished now," Lazovert muttered.

"In a way, he received his just desserts," Purishkevich said. "That's how he treated Mother Russia, our wives and daughters, and probably even the Tsarina. It is Judgment Day for Rasputin."

But then the three of them froze. A mortifying scream of a dying animal rose from below them.

"Felisha, I need you right now," Romanov cooed into Yussupov's ear as they stared at Rasputin's remains. "Please, let's—now, Felisha, right now—"

Yussupov turned and took Romanov in a lover's embrace. "We did it, Misha. Rasputin offended us, and we have killed him. This is the most important day of our lives—maybe the most important day in Russian history."

"Yes, Felisha, we have done it. We have killed—"

Yussupov waited a moment for Romanov to finish what he was saying, so he filled in an appropriate description, "the devil, Misha. We have killed the devil."

Romanov went completely limp in Yussupov's arms. "Misha? Misha?" he questioned, "What is wrong—"

Suddenly there was hot breath on the back of Yussupov's neck. Terrified, he spun around, dropping Romanov without realizing. Yussupov's eyes widened in disbelief. Before him stood a nightmare—one with matted hair, crimson-red eyes and poison-baited breath.

Rasputin reached out and crushed Yussupov in a tight bear-hug, cheek-to-cheek. Rasputin's mouth opened, and from it burst a cry of death, warm, from the depths of his lungs. Yussupov shriveled, quivering and urinating.

Just then the derringer tucked into the small of Yussupov's back popped loose and clattered across the stone floor. It was enough to catch Rasputin's attention, and Yussupov took full advantage. He kicked his right foot back, then brought his knee up hard into Rasputin's mutilated crotch.

Rasputin howled in agony and released him, and Yussupov flew backward. He landed on his rear and rolled back toward the bar, then sprang to his feet and in two steps he was atop the landing. He threw all his weight onto the courtyard door and burst through it, falling onto the frozen grit outside. He rolled to his feet and ran as though all the fires of hell burned behind him.

He slowed just enough to turn his head and look behind him. Rasputin stood in the doorway. He found the strength to call out, "Alexandra will know! You have killed Mother Russia herself!"

Yussupov turned his head and continued running across the vast yard, his open mouth making unintelligible sounds.

Purishkevich was the first to fly through the door and into the servant's quarters. Romanov lay on the floor. Purishkevich picked up Lipov's pistol just as Lazovert yelled, "The courtyard!"

They raced to the door. There, in the moonlight, they saw Rasputin rambling off, doubled-over.

Purishkevich stood sideways and pointed the pistol. He squeezed off two shots at the weaving target, but they twanged off cold stone in the distance. The third shot stood Rasputin upright. The fourth felled him.

They rushed to Rasputin. He lay on his side, and even in the moonlight the damage to his body was easily seen. His entire midsection was a bloody mutilation, his bare legs and hands were colored dark, and blood soaked the front of his *bluza*. His face was a sickening blue and white color. Blood trickled from his mouth.

Purishkevich kept the gun trained on him, ready for another surprise. Rasputin's icy eyes were open, as if he had been watching his assassins approach. And then his lips moved. Lazovert quickly jumped between Rasputin and Purishkevich, kneeling near Rasputin's face.

Purishkevich said coolly, "Out of the way, Stanislaus Andreyevich. You cannot save him."

"Just give the man his last words," Lazovert replied, moving his ear close to Rasputin's discolored lips.

But there was no need to draw so close, for loudly enough Rasputin said, "You kill all of Mother Russia."

Lipov kicked Lazovert out of the way, and Purishkevich answered Rasputin's charges with his boots. Over and over he thumped them into Rasputin, kicking his body and head. Then he and Lipov each took an arm and they dragged him back inside.

On the way, Yussupov joined them from the shadows of the courtyard. He babbled of how he'd kept Rasputin from escaping, but it sounded comical as he shivered inside stained trousers.

They dumped Rasputin's carcass just inside the door and rolled it down the steps. Purishkevich ripped down both sets of purple drapes, and Lipov pulled the cords loose to use as rope.

Romanov was awakening, shaking his head, and he joined Yussupov near Rasputin's body as if demonstrating his fear was now gone. But it was Yussupov who screamed when a long, low groan escaped from Rasputin. This time Yussupov didn't run away. He kicked Rasputin's head violently until he lost his balance and fell, even then swinging his arms hysterically.

Romanov tried to pull Yussupov away, but he had such a hard time that Lazovert came to help. Together they fell over backwards when they finally separated Yussupov from Rasputin.

Purishkevich and Lipov laid the purple shroud over the drapery cords, and together they rolled Rasputin onto his back in the center of it. They moved his thick, limp wrists together, over his abdomen—and suddenly Rasputin's eyes opened wide. His bloody hands shot straight for Lipov's throat.

Lipov gasped, blocking his face. Rasputin's hands landed on his shirt, ripping it and clenching the fabric like talons. Lipov's naked chest—and the Maltese cross tattooed there—were the last thing Rasputin saw. His eyes closed for good under the renewed rain of Purishkevich's bloody boots.

Purishkevich helped Lipov tear his shirt from Rasputin's grasp, then they held his wrists and tied them together.

Purishkevich pulled the sides of the drapes across the body and secured it with ropes at Rasputin's shoulders, waist and ankles. Finally he looped a rope around Rasputin's neck several times, then wove it through other cords before tying it to Rasputin's feet.

"Get our car into the courtyard!" Purishkevich yelled at Yussupov. Romanov went with him.

When they were gone, Purishkevich spoke to Lipov and Lazovert. "We are finished, and may God judge that we have done the right thing. We must separate as soon as we have disposed of the body and forget ever having been here tonight." His voice shook noticeably.

As soon as the car rumbled up outside, they tugged the body up the steps and out the door. Purishkevich spit onto the frozen ground when he saw that Yussupov remained in the driver's seat. He turned to Lazovert and said, "Stanislaus Andreyevich, take the wheel. I'll not ride behind that poor excuse for a man."

Then he called out to Yussupov, "We will take Romanov to return us home and return your car. You will stay here and eliminate all evidence from the room."

He and Lipov heaved the body onto the floor inside before climbing in themselves.

Lazovert, with Romanov beside him, drove to the prearranged site, the Petrovsky Bridge over the Neva River, where Lipov had spotted a hole in the ice earlier in the day. It was near enough to the Gulf that surely the body would wash out to sea. They met no one on the roads at that time of morning—it was nearly three-thirty—and soon the bridge was in sight.

Lazovert drove to the middle of the span and stopped the car. Purishkevich and Lipov got out, and in the moonlight they spotted the ice hole. They returned to the car for the body.

"Dammit," swore Purishkevich, "we did not fill his pockets with the chains before we wrapped him." He ordered Romanov to get them from the trunk.

Romanov found the box of chains and took them to Purishkevich, who told him, "Help me weight him. Weave them under the ropes and into any seams—"

Finally they were done, and it took all four of them to hoist the bundle onto the wide, icy railing. But Lazovert lost his grip on the slick drapes and the body fell back onto its assassins, sending them tumbling.

"*Ei Bogu!* The man refuses to go!" cried Lipov.

They got back to their feet and this time sent the body over the side. To their relief, it slipped through the hole in the ice and disappeared.

Then Purishkevich cursed again—one of Rasputin's greased boots had wormed its way out of the purple shroud and lay at his feet. He picked it up and heaved it after its owner.

Below the ice, the frigid water shocked Rasputin to consciousness. The biting cold stung every wound in his body. He flowed with the current, struggling violently to escape the drapes, bouncing between hard ice and river rocks. Finally his right hand came loose, and he worked to loosen the rope that bound his left.

He slowed as he entered shallower water. He felt himself tangling in brush, and the water continued to shove him in tighter. Finally he stopped moving altogether. A burp-sized swallow of cold water shocked his oxygen-starved lungs, and his eyes bulged in their mushy sockets.

Then, suddenly, through his swollen eyelids, he 'saw' a man and a child floating in the bright river just an arm's reach above him. Their shadows fell across his face as they passed before the sun.

Rasputin tried to blink back the surreal sight. He tried to work the muscles in his eyelids to clearly see the image. It could not be real. Was there a hole in his shroud? A hole in the ice? Who were the ones in the river above him?

He twisted and squirmed in his bonds, straining for a better view, one more believable, but one did not come. And then it struck him—he no longer felt the bite of the icy water, nor did he have need to breathe in more of the Neva. All was quiet.

The swimmers passed and the sunlight returned, bathing him in warmth and comfort. It occurred to him that he served an entity far more beautiful and loving than any on earth.

Rasputin calmed in his restraints. He slid his right hand up his abdomen and laid it over his heart. He formed the sign of the cross with his first two fingers, and the sun seemed to glow brighter, its light twinkling in the water.

A string of other objects followed the swimmers. There were two dozen of them, rounded on the bottom like harvest pumpkins. They were tied together with space between. Rasputin was so close he might have reached out and touched them, but his quiet comfort was such that he need not. After they'd passed the sun again shone above him again, brighter than ever. Its intensity engulfed him.

And then the sun burst. Sparks flew in every direction. He wanted to shield his eyes but could not. Through swollen ears he heard voices—no, singing—the sweet harmony of angels! It lifted his heart.

The sparks touched down, landing before his eyes. The Black Virgin of Kazan stood before him, impossibly, in the frigid river.

She was a splendor to behold, just as he remembered. Love filled his heart. Her golden crown sparkled, the veil framing the ebony skin of Her face and wrapping Her ebony Child close to Her bosom. Her purple cloak was magnificent, Her jeweled white gown was incomparably more beautiful than the finest in the Russian court.

"Grigory Efimovich."

The Virgin spoke to him, yet Her mouth did not move and She used no words. It was as if She planted Her thoughts directly into his mind. Rasputin's heart soared. Her 'voice' was a flowering song that caressed his senses, and he longed to hear more.

"You shall suffer no more. Your body has endured the injury of others, yet your spirit has remained true to the Almighty. You are released from your pain."

Rasputin nodded, accepting Her words. "I am ready to come to You, Holy Mother."

The Virgin smiled, Her teeth shone like polished ivory. Divine happiness glowed within Her, a radiance so strong it could almost be touched.

"And you shall, Grigory Efimovich, when your destiny is fulfilled."

"I do not understand, Holy Mother. My pain is gone. Am I not dead?"

"Only your time as a mortal has come to an end. Your destiny has been interrupted, it remains unfulfilled. I have further need of you, my child. You will serve again in the name of the Motherland."

"I do not understand, Holy Mother."

"One day, the Russian people will again rely on your faith and your strength. You must be ready. Prepare for the calling that will come, and answer it. Only then, afterward, will your soul will rest in eternal salvation. I have great faith in you, Grigory Efimovich. I know you will follow the true path."

"I have been so chosen? How—why—I am dead, am I not?"

"Only your body, my child, not your spirit. I know you have many questions, but be patient as I ask one of you. By your answer you will learn of your destiny.

"Tell me, what penance would you have your assassins pay?"

Rasputin did not answer. What did penance have to do with Her mission for him? He did not understand.

"Would you have them fall to disease? To assassins? Would you have their children scorn them? Would you have them suffer through eternity?"

Rasputin shook his head. "I do not believe those are the ways of the Lord, Holy Mother. I do not wish them such punishment. I only wish—" he paused.

"Yes?"

"Holy Mother, I wish only that the people come to know those men for what they have done. They must not be allowed to rise to power in the country, for that would lead to the fall of the Tsar and the Motherland. Mother Russia must survive at any cost, for she—and You—are all the people have."

The Virgin nodded, smiling. "You do not disappoint me, Grigory Efimovich. Have faith. Soon you will find yourself in a strange land. Do not be afraid, for I will be at your side. You will come to know of your mission then, and only your love of the Almighty and Mother Russia will guide you. Overcome the temptations and deceptions that will stand in your path."

"I will honor You, Holy Mother."

The Virgin smiled again. She extended Her left hand, blessing him, and in a swirling cloud She left. He watched as She returned to Her place in the sun, high above the water.

He took a moment to pray. He thanked the Lord for a second chance to serve Him, and he thanked the Virgin for Her blessing.

When he finished he looked up, and the water swarmed with commotion. The man and the child were back above him, kicking, suspended between the oversized pumpkins. There was a boat, too, a stream of water shooting from its stern.

Rasputin watched, mesmerized. So much activity! The churning water behind the boat suddenly quieted, and it coasted toward the man. Soon someone in the boat pulled the child off the man's back.

There was something about the man that fascinated Rasputin. He wanted to get closer. He felt himself slowly rising, as if his thoughts commanded his motion. He drew closer. He saw the man's frame was long and lean. He drew closer still. The man was young, in his twenties or late teens. He had dark hair.

He drew closer still. Too close. He tried to slow or stop, but he could not! He was going too fast!

"*Ei Bogu!*" he cried as he crashed into the man. He was surprised to feel flesh and bone, to feel them both cart-wheeling through the water. And then there was nothing.

CHAPTER 9

Four hours later

Tsarskoe Selo
The Alexander Palace

December 17, 1916

A crowd of servants stood in the main hall before "The Virgin of Kazan", some praying, some gaping open-mouthed. They parted as Alexandra passed through them—and there it was, an unmistakable teardrop, clinging beneath the Virgin's eye. Alexandra carefully touched the tear and set it onto her tongue.

"It tastes of salt—call for Father Grigory!" she ordered excitedly to none of the servants in particular. "He must know 'The Weeping Virgin' cries for Mother Russia!"

Alexandra crossed herself and knelt. She prayed aloud to the Virgin, asking why She cried and to deliver a message to Father Grigory to help them understand Her tears.

Several servants scurried off and rumors exploded within the palace. Something serious was wrong. Only war had ever brought tears to the eyes of 'The Weeping Virgin'. Perhaps the Tsar had been injured or killed, or a maybe a bloody battle had been lost, or even the entire war. They wondered what Father Grigory would have to say, and whether the Virgin had already spoken to him. She probably had, of course. Everyone knew Father Grigory was one with the Almighty.

At that moment

Petrograd
The Moika Palace

Yussupov worked frantically to remove the evidence, but with time eternal he could not have succeeded. Too much blood had poured from Rasputin. Crimson accents painted the room.

Now Yussupov just wanted to sleep. But that, too, was proving impossible. He was already upstairs on his featherbed, fully-clothed, exhausted, staring into the azure satin canopy above. Soon Rasputin's angry blue eyes were staring back at him. Desperately he whipped his head to the side and looked out across the massive room, past the inlaid-marble pillar to the fireplace. There he saw a fire that refused to die. He swallowed hard. On gilded chairs sat red velvet cushions, that certain deep shade of red that by now was only too familiar. And when he shut his eyes, other ghastly images came.

He so wanted to sleep and wake up to a fresh day. He wanted to spit the sour taste of revenge from his mouth. He wanted to forget how the sight of Misha returning the car had repulsed him, how he sent Misha home crying. But most of all, he wanted his heart to quit racing with fear. He wanted to surrender to the unkillable man, to admit that he had, in the end, lost.

Already the sun was climbing in the morning sky, and the heavy drapes did not block out near enough light. He would never sleep in this daylight. Dearest God, he wondered, what had happened last night?

Suddenly it seemed the sun came out from behind a cloud. It was like a torch, hot, lighting the stone wall above his headboard. Were there no drapes on the window at all? The sunspot grew impossibly brighter, hotter, like fire, then sparks burst from it in every direction.

Yussupov sat straight up in bed. He had never been a particularly religious man, but he knew who She was. He crossed himself, shaking.

There was no choir singing behind Her, and the Virgin did not smile. She was silent for the longest moment, then She said unto him, "Felix Felixovich, your sins are great."

Yussupov could not find his tongue; he could barely breathe.

"I pray that you come to find the Lord, Felix Felixovich."

Tears ran down his cheeks. "I—I will, Holy Mother. I am so sorry." He buried his face in his hands and sobbed. "It was wrong—it was so wrong," he cried.

The Virgin was unmoved. "Felix Felixovich, Grigory Efimovich does not seek vengeance against you. He would have you given a chance for redemption. Do you wish such a chance?"

He looked up from his hands. His eyes were red, his face was a teary smear. "Oh, yes, Holy Mother. I will do anything to right the wrongs I have committed. Please tell me how I might save myself."

She nodded. "The followers of Grigory Efimovich are many, and they will deeply mourn his loss. Despair will fill their hearts. And know now that they will seek vengeance in his name—for many are the clues to your group's identity. Their hatred of you could rise to challenge their love of God, and I will not allow such darkness.

"His followers must know that someday, Grigory Efimovich will return to them and to Mother Russia. He will finish his mission for me. He will work to save the Motherland, and he will do so in the name of the Lord. You must placate his followers with this truth. You must speak out in the name of Grigory Efimovich."

Yussupov nodded, accepting the unbelievable.

"Your words alone will not accomplish the task. You must bestow upon his followers a special gift."

"A gift, Holy Mother? What gift is that?"

The Virgin smiled. "Present them with my icon "The Virgin of Kazan" that hangs in the home of the Tsar. Announce to them that when my tears again fall, they will be tears of happiness, for Grigory Efimovich will have returned to them. Only then will they believe you have repented your sins."

And in a swirl of morning dust She was gone.

Yussupov closed his eyes in shock and disbelief. He crossed himself and prayed, announcing to the Lord a new-found devotion, asking for His forgiveness of many, many sins. He prayed that Nikolas would find it possible to forgive him as well, and that Alexandra, the girls and young Tsarevich Alexei would, too.

Finally he slept, comforted by hope. In his dreams his mind replayed the Virgin's visit over and over, until every detail lived in his memory.

When again he rose, he dressed quickly and set off for Tsarskoe Selo. The meeting with Nikolas would be difficult, but it would be his first step from darkness to daylight. He would begin by telling the story.

Two days later

Petrograd
The Neva River embankment

December 19, 1916

Nikolas himself went to see Rasputin's body. He needed to see it was really him, before it was moved and made presentable in any way, to see if the corpse bore evidence of the atrocities Yussupov described.

He knelt and pulled back the purple shroud. There was little sign of his friend from Siberia. Rasputin's long, dark hair was caked with blood and viscera and plastered to his misshapen skull. His face was an ashen-purple color, puffed and gouged and covered with jagged tears. And dangling from the crushed left socket was a washed-out blue eye, staring.

Nikolas looked lower, to Rasputin's chest, and saw his coarse fingers had formed the sign of the cross over his heart. Nikolas crossed himself weakly. A tear rolled down his cheek. He lingered long, as though trying to remember his friend from the pieces he had before him, but the rotting stench finally overpowered him. He turned away and was sick.

But Nikolas knew he had to remain objective. Personal feelings could not guide his actions. He had already placed the alleged assassins under house arrest, all five of them. They were not going anywhere; Rasputin's corpse would be considered further evidence of their guilt, nothing more. Just like the policeman's account that had reached his desk that morning—the man had heard gunshots outside the Moika Palace that night, and he'd been warned by Purishkevich shortly thereafter to hold his silence.

But personally, Nikolas had no more doubts. His own nephew and Prince Yussupov had led the group that killed Father Grigory.

He lamented his choices. As members of the royal family, Dmitri Pavlovich and Felix Felixovich could not be prosecuted for their atrocious acts. Royalty was never subject to Russian law; it had always been so.

Purishkevich, Lipov and Lazovert, however, enjoyed no such privilege. But Nikolas' ministers were adamant—many Russians were looking upon the murderers as righteous, their callous acts defensible in the name of Russian reforms. If Nikolas were to put them on trial, they could become heroes to the uprising. To put them to death could create martyrs of revolution.

Three days later, after an autopsy, the Romanovs buried Rasputin under the altar of the new Imperial cathedral under construction at Tsarskoe Selo. The ceremony was beautiful, simple and private. Only his closest friends and the two families who loved him were present.

As the service drew to a close, Nikolas and Alexandra badly wanted to forget the macabre details of their friend's death. But they knew the matter would not go away on its own; circumstance was forcing them to address it one last time. So as the grieving attendees rose and embraced, they quietly spoke with the only person more affected than themselves.

"Praskovia Dubrovina, we are so sorry. You and your children have lost far more than we have," said Alexandra. "But please, join us this morning for tea. We have news we must share with you. Your daughters and Misha are welcome, of course, but we must speak alone. Perhaps we can have the servants give them a tour of the palace while we meet. So please, when you are ready ... "

Slightly mystified, Praskovia nodded.

The Emperor and Empress crossed themselves and bid farewell to Rasputin. They left the widow and her family alone with their memories.

Seated at the table in the Alexander Palace sunroom, Nikolas and Alexandra described for Praskovia the details of Yussupov's visit and his unbelievable vision—especially that the Holy Mother had foretold the return of Father Grigory.

Praskovia was bewildered and incredulous. "She says that Grisha would one day return to Russia? How . . . why would that be?"

Nikolas shook his head. "It is beyond us to know these things, Praskovia Dubrovina. But Yussupov claims his redemption will come when he forms a group for all Russians who mourn Father Grigory—he would call it 'The Union of Tears', and he would present them with the icon 'The Weeping Virgin' in his memory.

Alexandra added, "But we cannot allow Prince Yussupov to proceed without your consent, Praskovia Dubrovina. Every Russian will hear that your Grisha is destined to return to the Motherland. Would you be comfortable with such a thing? After all, we cannot be sure that Yussupov has not gone mad. Could you, and can we, for that matter, accept this legacy attached to Father Grigory—knowing that it could be false, or that we simply may never see it become truth?"

Praskovia was simply overwhelmed. Her tears would not stop, and Alexandra took her onto her shoulder until she could speak. "Prince Yussupov—he would place the icon in a shrine where all might worship Her?"

Nikolas nodded. "He has already found the proper building, the old stone church at the corner of Nevsky and Sadovaya Prospekts. He would purchase it and 'The Union of Tears' would be headquartered there. All that delays him is our decision on whether we would have it so."

Alexandra sighed, "This has been so hard on us, and we know it must be far worse for you and the children. It's all so unbelievable, so tragic. And now this . . . we want to know what you feel. Would you have us believe Prince Yussupov? Should we put faith in his story of the Holy Mother's visit, and how She will return your Grisha to us one day?"

Praskovia shook her head. "I am but a simple *moujik*, Your Excellencies, who was blessed with an extraordinary husband. I do not know of things like this. I do not expect to witness the prayers of my Grisha again, or that I ever should. But tell me . . . you say the Prince did ask the Holy Mother for forgiveness, did he not?"

Nikolas nodded. "He asked our forgiveness, also."

"Then I would allow him to serve the Virgin as he proposes, Excellency. If he has been truthful, She will grant him the forgiveness he seeks. And if not . . . well, then She should be the one to pass judgment on him. I believe that is how Grisha would guide us, were he still here."

Nikolas nodded. "Your words are wise. We would do best to continue following his path."

Praskovia stood, and the three of them embraced tightly. The journey was not over.

That afternoon, Nikolas granted Yussupov permission to proceed as he had requested. And he released the others from home confinement. He would not pass judgment upon them. It was better that he leave such matters to the Holy Mother. If She so chose, She would have Her vengeance. It would have been Father Grigory's path. It would be theirs.

Four days later

Petrograd
The Duma, Office of Vladimir Purishkevich

December 26, 1916

Disgusted, Purishkevich slapped the newspaper onto his desk. His eyes were fixed on a large photo of Yussupov and the headline that read, 'Prince Apologizes to Russia'.

"What is that idiot up to?" Purishkevich asked Lipov. "He claims the Virgin of Kazan paid him a personal visit—so now he is sorry? Well, I'll say he was sorry that night."

Lipov shook his head. "Did you read the rest of the story? It is all back-garden talk, of course, but the *moujiki* are claiming that Rasputin cannot truly be dead—legend says a 'saint' cannot drown. And that's why Yussupov's group will pray for the *return* of the animal."

"Ha! They should have seen him slip under the ice that night. If he didn't drown," he paused, snorting with delight, "then hastily he grew gills. What idiocy. They're elevating the devil to sainthood, whatever could . . . " but Purishkevich fell silent.

A moment later he continued quietly, "We must not forget it is Yussupov behind all this nonsense, my friend. The spoiled child. The Prince of Perversion. I don't believe a bit of this newfound religious manure he is spreading.

"Is he working to escape the Tsar's wrath? If he and Romanov go unpunished, will the Tsar deliver death sentences for us tomorrow? Next month, or next year?

"I think it is imperative that we expose Yussupov's motives for all to see. Think now . . . how will Yussupov profit from this falderal? Would could he possibly have to gain? We must learn more, Igor Igorevich."

"Perhaps he and Romanov simply have a perverted taste for *stranniki* now," Lipov said without humor. "I say, let us allow him to organize these *moujiki* that mourn so pitifully. Let him have his church and his worshippers, let his plans unfold. We need only observe from afar to learn his true motives, and when we decide to end his charade, we shall. I will order increased surveillance immediately. Tell me again, Vladimir Mitrofanovich, why we did not send him swimming that night?"

Purishkevich closed his eyes and shook his head. "It would have been so easy. But not now."

Two months later

Petrograd
The Admiralty Hall

March 7, 1917

"You must choose, Vladimir Mitrofanovich," Lipov said flatly, unblinking. "The time has come." He sat behind the desk in his new office and folded his arms across his chest. He wore a new uniform of gray with red and the insignia of colonel.

Purishkevich refused to sit. He glared at Lipov. "Do you expect me to betray the Tsar as you have, Igor Igorevich? I stand as I always have, in support of our true leader and the Motherland. I do not know how long your Minister L'vov and his Constitutional Democrats will hold the roles they have assumed, but as long as the Tsar lives, I will maintain my oath and support him."

Lipov shook his head. "I, too, support the Motherland, my friend, but the future has arrived. The people have spoken, and Russia needs your support. Think of it—Mother Russia truly belongs to us now. We shall elect our own leaders, and all people shall have the same rights. Nothing is more important than these freedoms. I ask you again to join us."

Purishkevich shook his head. "I fight my battles in the name of Tsar Nikolas, not for Mensheviks or revolutionaries. I do not believe in their teachings, and I do not believe your leader will be good for the Motherland. In fact, I think you have changed your stripes far too quickly."

Lipov jumped to his feet. He slammed hardened, scarred fists into his blotter. "Where is your Tsar now? Where is the outcry for him? He has been under house arrest in Tsarskoe Selo for a week already . . . where are his supporters? Are you the last who remains? I think so! You are the only man calling for the Russia of old, for the inept German wife and her lover, Rasputin, to run the country. For war losses so great our fields go untended, for factory workers striking and children going hungry.

"No, Vladimir Mitrofanovich, I have not changed my stripes too quickly. I am happy to purge Russia of such a past. Nikolas will be forgotten, and you will be, too, if you do not come to your senses. I give you one day to rethink your position. If you do not report back to me with your support, I will have you arrested as an enemy of the people. Do I make myself clear?"

Purishkevich said nothing. He turned abruptly, leaving Lipov waiting for an answer, and strode confidently through the great corridor of the Admiralty. He shoved open the huge wooden doors at the end and stepped out onto the cobblestone, turning up the flaps of his greatcoat as the cold afternoon breeze chilled his ears.

As he passed under the Admiralty's great arch, he stopped and looked up at the double-headed Imperial eagle still perched there. It amused him to recall that skeptics predicted the arch would collapse under its own weight. It had not, and Purishkevich knew it would not. And neither would Russia. He would see to it himself. He would stand there forever, if need be, below the Imperial eagle, his arms extended, helping support the arch while White and Red Russians danced above, trying to crush it all.

He turned and purposefully strode off to task. Somehow, some way, he would find a path to Nikolas. He would return his Tsar to power. And the people would be behind him, for true Russians loved no one as they did their Tsar.

Lipov seethed. Purishkevich had no future. He belonged to the old times with Nikolas and Rasputin. What a farce. Lipov thought back to the circus that night at the Moika Palace. Purishkevich. The failed poison, the shots. Yussupov, Romanov. And years before that, to the birthday party on that spring day. That was where it really started. Purishkevich had declared Rasputin must be stopped; for once he had been right. If only they had moved faster. Maybe they could have kept that bastard from taking over Russia.

Lipov's anger grew; his wife was with Rasputin that day. How could she have done that to him? What kind of spell did Rasputin cast? How did he trick the women so? And seemingly rational men, too, who thought him blessed? And now even

Yussupov, claiming that the animal would return one day . . . Ha!

But the thought forced Lipov to consider the ramifications. Nothing would be worse for New Russia than Rasputin tricking the *moujiki* back to the old ways. The hard-fought victories of the people would be in danger, and the return of the Tsar would not be far behind.

Cold calculations overcame his anger. Obviously Yussupov's claims of the Holy vision were false. But 'The Union of Tears' was providing a possible nightmare of hope to a now-silent faction. Their hope could spread. And in time, they may not remain silent.

Any chance, any *hope* of Rasputin's return had to be stopped. And ever so briefly, the image of Rasputin atop his wife flashed through his mind.

At dawn, Lipov and his men pulled Rasputin's casket from its tomb below the cathedral. When they opened it on the frozen lawn and rolled the body out, the scarves that covered their noses and mouths did not protect them from the egg-rotting, nauseating stench.

Lipov brought his horse around and threw the end of his rope to the men. Stomachs heaving, they looped it around the corpse's ankles; it cut easily through the rotting flesh as they tied it tightly to bone. Chunks of flesh marked the trail as Lipov set off on a circuitous gallop.

He happily took his time. When finally he reached the site of the pyre next to the Great Pond, Lipov guided his horse to drag the remains to the center of the woodpile. He and his men doused the remains with kerosene, and Lipov flipped a match. The smoke could be seen from the confines of the Alexander Palace. The day had passed before the wind carried away its final wisps.

Lipov slammed the note to his desk. 'The Union of Tears'. He would see their prized icon relegated to a closet in his office. He put on his coat and hat and left his office the back way, via the wooden boardwalk past the dry docks from the shipbuilding days of Peter the Great. He paid scant notice to the gulls and the crisp sea air. The church of The Union of Tears was only a short walk away.

Lieutenant Andladrov greeted him at the door. "Colonel Lipov, 'The Weeping Virgin' is not at the altar. We have been questioning the congregation—" There were about fifty believers crowded together in a corner of the church. Andladrov's squad had rifles trained on them.

"This is no congregation," Lipov interrupted, "these are devil-worshippers. You—" he pointed to the first *moujik* who caught his eye, "come here."

A stooped old man limped over to Lipov and Andladrov. When he stopped a few feet away, Lipov reached out and grabbed the collar of his simple *bluza* and pulled him closer.

"Where is it?" Lipov demanded. "Where is the icon you worship?"

The *moujik* shook his head. He responded in a language of gibberish, with a questioning look at the end. Lipov slapped him hard across the face. Moans and cries for mercy came from the others.

"Speak Russian, you fool!" Lipov ordered, but the man just cowered, shaking his head. Lipov shoved him hard, back toward the others. "Who among you speaks Russian?"

A large man, younger, stood behind the old *moujik*. "I do, Colonel."

Lipov eyed him warily, then ordered him to step forward. The man did, and Lipov asked him the same question. "Where is 'The Weeping Virgin'?"

The man shook his head. "It was taken last night. We do not know who took it."

"Liar!" Lipov strode to the man and slugged him in the stomach, doubling him over. Lipov asked him again, "Where is the icon you worship?"

The man did not answer, but as he began to straighten up, Lipov unbuttoned the flap on his holster. In a swift motion he pulled his gun and grabbed the man by his hair. He ground the barrel into the man's temple.

"For the last time, *moujik*, where is the icon?"

The man slowly shook his head, moving Lipov's hand and gun side-to-side with him. Then suddenly, loudly, the man cried out, "You killed him, *pivo*! You killed Father Grig . . . !"

Lipov's proud nose twitched visibly. He fired. An explosion of noise echoed off the cold stone walls, cutting off the rest of the man's words before Lipov had to hear them. The man crumpled; blood and viscera stained the floor and the people behind. The wailing congregation covered their eyes and turned away, shaking with sobs. Some had the presence to cross themselves.

Lipov held the smoking gun before his chest. "Who is next?" he called out. He walked closer, testing those who would look him in the eye. "I am looking for 'The Weeping Virgin', *moujiki*, and I *will* find it. Come now, you know where She is . . . " He pointed his pistol at an old woman sitting on the floor. He motioned her to rise. "You. You know where the Virgin is, yes?"

She stood, crossing herself as she left the group. Several men voiced objections and started to move forward, but Andladrov's squad took fresh aim at them.

Lipov smiled. "You'll get your turn, my friends," he said to them. But his smile quickly faded. "You'll all get your turn if we do not find 'The Weeping Virgin'! Come now—who will speak up and save this old woman?" He put the gun to her head.

CHAPTER 10

Rushing Wells, Idaho

July 19, 1998
9:45 am

The thing would fly kinda like a hammer, Nick figured, flipping around its heavy end if he spun it hard enough. So he took a savage two-handed grip on the old exhaust pipe, locked his arms straight out in front of him and—after a quick glance back to the edge of the cliff, just to be sure on distance—he spun once, twice, and "uggghh...!" let it sail. It was perfect! Inertia spun the pipe around the heavy old muffler with a 'whooump, whooump' a couple of times. A feathery cloud of rusty soot puffed out and floated lightly as the rest of the mess spiraled thirty feet down into the sparkling, pristine ripples of the Snake River.

"Yes!" Nick pumped his fist, but shrill shrieks and childish laughter suddenly echoed up the canyon. "Oh, sh..." He hadn't even checked upriver, at the park next door, to see if anyone was there. He squatted low and cautiously shuffled along the cliff face. He knew just where to stop and peek around the bulge in the canyon wall.

Sure enough, little kids and towels and kickboards were spilling from the doors of the lone SUV in the Snake River State Park parking lot, a white-legged mom and overweight dad in flip-flops clumsily scrambling to control the chaos.

But nobody was looking his way. Thank god. Nick stood up straight and walked back the ten feet to his family's private observation deck, the polished ledge near the lava-stone bench and barbecue and oak-plank table his grandpa and dad had built so long ago, where in happy times their family swum and picnicked and watched the river float by, summer after summer.

He peeled off his dirty hoodie and brushed back a renegade lock of thick, black hair that, just like his dad's, fell into his blue eyes when it got too long. He straight-ened out his grimy tank top and shorts and stretched, tall and lanky, into the climbing sun.

"I hate that thing." Yesterday some kid with the Parks Department had anchored the old swimming dock out near the orange rope and barrel-buoys—within sight of Nick's scenic viewpoint. Covered with worn fake turf and dipping low at one corner, the dock was an oversize eyesore, a moldy chia pet out in the middle of pristine mother nature.

"That's so frickin' lame." Maybe he could shoot it with a flaming arrow and put it out of its misery. Didn't they know it'd be an irrestible base for some idiot's dives out past the ropes and into the main current? He shook his head. For years he'd jumped from their ledge. He knew the river looked calm and peaceful, especially in the short stretch from the park to their place. But the water flowed fast below the surface; he learned from a young age to swim hard to their lower landing, or to the last-resort climbing ropes beyond, if necessary. The alternative was scary. The lava cliffs rose fast downriver, up and up, into a nightmarish hallway a quarter-mile high. No beaches, no place to rest for miles. That's why they kept a couple of inner tubes on the landing when they were swimming. Dad would say, "...Nikolas, you just never know."

Crap, he'd been spotted. The bald, fat dad in a way-too-small swimsuit and two kids were on the dock and pointing at Nick. Their kickboards parked beside them like cars, the little girl with water-wings and her even-smaller, life-vested brother were waving like mad.

Grudgingly, Nick waved back. "Great, just great," Nick muttered, sure that now he'd be known as the That Guy on the Rocks, or some stupid thing, the reward for tourists and toddlers that made it out that far, their welcoming committee. And sure enough, between jumps, shrieks and rocking the dock, the kids tried again and again to catch his attention. At least the dad had bowed out, content to bloat in the sun for a while.

Nick retreated to the bench and kicked off his shoes. He needed to cool off before getting back to the garage and his car, but a quick dip would have to do. He peeled off his ankle socks and stepped back to the ledge. It just wasn't the same with a crowd, no one should have to sacrifice their space like this. He'd move that frickin' dock tonight. And if someone caught him, he'd say it was just too close to the ropes.

He looked over one last time. The girl was hopping about, flapping both arms...when she lost her balance on the tippy surface and flipped backward, head-over-heels. She came up with a scream, already half-way to the rope.

Nick watched it unfold in surreal slow-motion. Dad half-rolled, lunging to the edge toward her, flattening and stretching but just missing her hand as the dock dipped hard under his weight and the other side flew up, flipping the little boy toward shore. Dad's head spun at the sound of the splash, but he quickly turned back to his daughter yelling, "The rope! The rope! Grab the rope!" but she was facing the wrong way and it hit her in the back of the head. Nick saw her clawing fruitlessly, her head dropping below the surface just as she passed under it, the backs of her hands flailing to no avail. And now the boy was floundering, screaming in the water on the other side of the dock.

Oh, God, Nick thought, this is happening, it's really happening. He cupped his hands to his mouth and yelled, "I'll get her! She's coming right to me!"

Nick wondered if the man had heard him, but he waved back like he had. The man rose and jumped in toward his son.

Nick watched the girl float toward him for what seemed like forever. She grew ever closer, treading water, eyes wide open, searching for him. It didn't look like she was in real trouble. She bobbed still closer, slowly, still out of the main current.

He cocked himself on his ledge, ready, waiting, every nerve alive. He had to time his jump perfectly—for god's sakes, to not land on her, but to not have to swim too far to get her, either.

But a little eddy stopped her where she was, toying with her. It slowed her, then it kicked her out into an arc, very much the wrong direction, toward the current. She was just so small and light! Nick tried to guess which way she would go, but it was impossible. She finally slowed a little, still back from his ledge but further out in the river than he would have liked. He couldn't wait any longer. He leapt in an arching dive, aiming farther out than he'd ever dared before.

He body-slapped the cool water and kicked hard in her general direction, straining to spot her legs through the turbulence. For an instant she was there. He clawed, but grabbed only water. She was gone, but she had to be close-by. He rose fast, his head shooting to the surface.

He shook the water from his eyes. He was already even with their landing. The two thick, knotted climbing ropes were still waiting further down, lifelines against the rock. So there was time, but he was far out in the river. He splashed around in a circle. Where was she? Then she bobbed up further out, on the fringe of the main current a couple of yards away.

"*Ei Bogu!*" he cried, absent-mindedly mimicking his Bushka. He kicked and launched toward her, and several hard strokes later he had her. She clamped onto his chest and neck, coughing and crying. Nick held her firmly, spinning with her in the Snake, kicking to keep their heads above water. Now they were well past the landing, already even with the first rope. There was still time... but... he... just... couldn't... move! He simply could not roll onto his back to kick them against the push of the water. Onward they traveled. Downriver. Into the rising walls. It seemed like they were floating downhill.

"I want to get out," the girl sniffled. "I want my daddy."

Nick held her tighter. "We'll be out soon," he told her. "We'll be okay." He felt his own eyes tearing up. His legs ached. It was hard to breathe.

He looked down to the next bend. Well. This would be an easy trip in a boat. Great fishing. Cool in the shadows.

But uncontrollable panic set into the girl. With surprising strength she tried to climb higher and farther from the water around her, clawing and scratching his face, her breathing shallow and fast. She pulled his hair and kneed him in the stomach on the way; her tenacity hit Nick completely unprepared.

He worked to hold her back and keep them both upright, but down they went, the wrestling continuing underwater. Finally he bear-hugged her and they rose, coughing, out of the Snake. He pried her off his face and pulled her back down his chest. They bobbed together, tired and breathless, backward in the current.

Even his eyes hurt now, they felt like they were bleeding. Everything was turning orange... wait! Orange! His heart skipped a beat.

"Yeees!" he cried. An unmanned chain of bright orange barrel-buoys floated behind them in the river. With fresh energy he spun them around and kicked hard into the current, the girl seeming weightless.

In no time they were surrounded by the barrels, and Nick worked feverishly to knot up the rope and shorten the distance between a couple of them. He left just enough room for his shoulders to squeeze in, and with a couple of hard kicks he lifted high enough out of the water to catch the rope sideways with an armpit.

Now, even though they were dangling at an odd angle, the girl obeyed him and crawled up, around onto his back. Nick flung his other arm up and over the rope, and breathed a little easier. This would have to do. And they both rested like that, without a word, continuing into darkening shadows.

In time Nick asked the girl her name, but she didn't answer. At least she'd loosened her grip a little.

"Hello up there," Nick tried again, but he got no response. "My name's Nick—but you can call me Nicky if you want." He never let anyone call him Nicky anymore, but this seemed to be a rare occasion.

Child-size snores answered him. Nick smiled, adjusting himself on the rope, closing his own eyes. They had a couple of hours to kill, and she had the right idea.

The rope felt like a hot branding iron in his armpits, but Nick shifted around the best he could, and they'd traveled most of the way down the canyon, when the drone of an engine startled him. He looked up and saw a boat approaching, and it ran wide around them. It was tan-and-white, a sheriff's rescue boat.

"Hey, you all right?" someone yelled.

Nick couldn't answer but he moved a hand slightly. "Thank God," he muttered under his breath.

The boat drew closer and they killed the engine. A deputy reached out over the front, grabbed a buoy and started pulling Nick toward the boat.

"Hang on, kid. We're going to grab her off your shoulders," a man called to Nick.

It felt like a ton had been lifted off. Nick took a deep breath, relieved. He straightened out his burning arms and happily slipped under the surface.

The cool water felt good, no longer threatening, and for a moment Nick didn't bother to kick back to the surface—but then wham!, a watery blast from below hit him hard, shocking his body to the bone.

Good God—what was that? The boat propeller? A shark? Was he still whole? Nick kicked hard and surfaced ten feet behind the sheriff's boat. His heart beat wildly. He checked his limbs, all were still there. And there was no blood in the water. Then he remembered they'd killed the boat engine as they were floating up, and, of course, it was still off. Couldn't have been the prop. And he'd never heard of river sharks.

Nick's heart slowed just a little. He felt relieved, but he just wasn't sure...he kept checking his arms and legs for blood.

"Take the pole, kid!" One of the deputies splashed a shepherd's hook in front of him, and Nick grabbed it. It was

Delwith, Deputy Fred Delwith, who'd pulled him over for speeding just last week. He pulled Nick to the skier's bench beside the engine, then gave him a hand up into the boat.

"Nick Brody? Is that you? Well, you're safe now. Just relax."

Nick never felt so relieved to see that buzz haircut, that Charlie Brown-face with the St. Bernard jowls. He almost said thanks, but it just wouldn't come out. The girl sat wrapped in a blanket on a seat facing him, and as Nick sat and pulled his own blanket around him, she introduced them to each other quite matter-of-factly.

"I'm Jenny, and we're safe now, mister Nick," the girl said. "The sheriff said Mommy and Daddy are waiting, you know," she announced. "Can we go see them now?" she asked Delwith.

"Sure thing, missy," he grinned.

As they neared the public boat ramp and docks below the bridge, Nick saw people everywhere. They pointed and cheered as the deputies brought the boat closer, into the slip.

Jenny's parents anxiously pranced on the dock, arms extended, and they quickly scooped her from Delwith's arms. They gave her a quick once-over before smothering her with hugs and kisses. Her mother carried her off to two paramedics ashore while her father waited for Nick. Thank god he'd put on regular shorts by now.

Nick stood in the boat and there were more cheers. Jenny's father took Nick's hand and helped him out onto the dock, then pumped his hand incessantly.

"Young man, my name's Levelsworth, Herbert J. Levelsworth," he said, his face shaking with excitement. "That was my daughter you saved today. Dear Lord I'm grateful you were up on that cliff. We would have lost her, we would have. Now, what is your name?"

"Nick. Nick Brody."

"Well, Nick, I'm forever in your debt. The little woman and I..." he pointing her out to Nick as she, Jenny and the small boy were climbing into an ambulance, "well, we're going to do something real nice for you. You deserve the best. Now say, I sell cars up in Boise, and I want to give you a good deal on a Navigator, just like the one we've got here. How does that sound? And how about we start you a college fund? It's yours. Hell, a good-looking boy like you with a nice ride and some bucks in the bank? You'll need a stick to keep the ladies away!"

This was all too much. Nick struggled for something to say.

"No, thanks, mister," he finally stammered. "I don't need a car, I've one I'm working on. And I'm getting a scholarship for college. I don't want anything. I just want to go home."

"Oh, come on, Nick! And call me Herb! Didn't you hear me? I have to do *something* for you! You *have* to take a reward now, you hear? How about lunch? You hungry after that trip, huh? You hungry?"

"Nope. I just want to go home."

Herb nodded with some difficulty. "Good enough." He pulled the blanket tighter around Nick, threw an arm around him and walked him ashore. The paramedics looked him over and asked if he'd like to rest in the hospital overnight. Nick said no.

When he heard that, Herb yelled, "Larry! Larry!" off to the edge of the crowd. Fat, balding Larry answered with a "Yo!" and Herb yelled at him to bring up the car.

"You don't need to—, Nick said.

"Nonsense, Nick, like I said, Herbert J. Levelsworth is now at your service."

Nick was getting frustrated. "Look, I just need to get home."

Then a cameraman and a guy in a suit with a KMVT-branded microphone stepped their path. "How about a few words for the Magic Valley, young fella? How'd it feel out there in the river today?"

Herb shielded Nick from the interviewer. "Outta the way, you blow-dried leech! Can't you see the kid's exhausted?"

The insistent reporter kept firing questions—"Did you think you were going to die? Is the Snake River State Park unsafe? Will you ever swim in the river again?"

Herb brushed the reporter aside and escorted Nick through the well-wishers to the car. Herb opened the door and gave Nick a hand up into the back seat, then climbed in right after him. As he did he explained, "That's my brother Larry driving and he lives around here, so you just tell him where you want to go."

Larry turned around and smiled a big mouthful of yellow teeth. Nick recognized him as one of the shyster salesmen at the used-car lot across from the high school.

Nick wanted it all to end. "I live back up next to the park. Just go back the way you came."

"Well you heard the boy, Larry! Let's get a move on!"

Nick couldn't get the trip down the river out of his mind, especially that jolt he felt underwater after it was all over. Did he imagine that? Was he that tired? No way. Maybe it was a clump of river weeds or something. Yeah, the boat stirred up some river weeds and...

Suddenly Herb asked, "Who the Sam Hell is that, Larry?"

Nick looked over the front seat and out the windshield to see for himself. An old man with flowing white hair and beard stood in the ditch facing them. He held a floppy hat over his heart with one hand and a book in the other. There was a small white cross planted in the ground before him, and a shovel leaned against his bicycle. As they blew past, it was apparent the man was reading aloud from the book.

"That's the Gravedigger, Herb! Didn't I tell you about that loony Russian? They say he used to be a real gravedigger years ago, but now he's just a drunk that buries roadkill. He gives 'em a ceremony, then goes off to the tavern for the wake!" He laughed at his own story and slapped the steering wheel. "He's an oddball, ain't he?"

Herb laughed, too, slapping Nick's knee. "You got a real character there, Nick. He beats the ones we've got in Boise hands down!"

Nick nodded, not smiling. "My house is up on the right, there, under that sign."

Larry saw the arching span of wood mounted between two tall poles and read it aloud, "'The Motherland.' You a Russian, Nick? How'd you get a name like Brody?" He slowed the van and turned it into the dirt driveway, past two weed-choked gates that hadn't been shut in years. They drove through a maze of lilacs, fruit trees, birch and round-bottomed evergreens, all in need of pruning. There was barely room for the big SUV to pass through.

Nick didn't answer; he was picturing Bushka's reaction to these two.

"Nick?" Larry called out.

Nick was staring out the window. "Oh. Well, my grandpa and great-grandma's last name is Brodyaga. But my dad shortened ours to Brody before I was born."

"Wait a minute," Larry said, "Brody. Brody... you're Ivan and Cathy's boy? I'm sorry, I didn't know."

Nick was quiet. "Don't worry about it," he muttered.

The uneasy moment didn't slow Herb at all. "Well young man, I'm going to have to tell *someone* what you did today. Who do you live with, an aunt, or foster..."

Nick interrupted, "I live with *them*— grandpa and great-grandma! But he's never home, and Bushka, my grandpa's mom, she's not doing so well."

"I'll bet Bushka is short for *babushka*, eh, Nick?" Larry guessed, proud of himself.

Nick nodded. "I couldn't say it when I was a kid."

Herb continued, "Well, I'll bet your *babushka* would love to hear what you did today. I really do have to tell her."

Nick shook his head but Levelsworth didn't care. Past the last overgrown hedge the drive opened into a clearing in front of a ramshackle old house. The roof was high and steep, cedar-shingled, sagging in the middle, swooping down in the front like a visor over the dark, wide porch. Larry hit the brakes.

From the porch, behind the railing near the steps, a cloud of blue smoke rose into the sunlight. The brothers saw it, and almost as one they chimed, "What the hell—"

Nick knew if he made this quick it would be a lot easier on everyone. He bolted up and out the door just as Larry cried out, "It's an old lady up there! She's smoking a stogie!"

Herb reached up and whacked his brother on the shoulder. "Shut up, you idiot!" He turned back in time to see Nick land and try to close the door behind him. "Is that your *babushka*, Nick?" he asked, catching the door before it latched.

"Bushka's not well, like I said. She just..." He backed up a couple of steps toward the house as he spoke.

"She looks just fine to me, son, and I'd like to meet her," Herb he stepped out. He put a vice-grip lock around Nick's shoulders and walked him toward the porch.

"Ma'am," Herb called out as he neared, "ma'am, my name's Levelsworth, Herbert J. Levelsworth, and I understand that this here is your boy—"

She didn't reply, but Irina Brodyaga's eyes locked firmly onto the stranger. She pulled a half-smoked cigar from between her lips with twig-like fingers, held it there a moment, then spat a brown NO TRESPASSING warning onto the top porch step.

Herb stopped, shocked. "Ma'am, I'm only here to tell you—"

She ignored him. "(Nikisha)!" she called out in harsh Russian, "(where have you been)?"

Nick tried to answer, but Herb drowned him out. "Now ma'am, the boy's done good, he's done real good."

Irina ignored him. "(It is almost three o'clock and you have not been to the market yet! Ei Bogu! You are becoming like Boris

Grigorevich. If only your father knew—he would crop you good for such misbehavior)!"

Nick turned to Herb. "Look, just leave, okay? I mean, Bushka doesn't care much for strangers. I'll tell her about today later. Really."

Herb took Nick by the shoulders. "Nick, I apologize. I should have listened to you. I mean, you saved my daughter's life—you know what you're doing." He chuckled. "You know I can never repay you, don't you?"

Irina rose to her feet. "(Get to your business, stranger. Nikisha has chores to do)." She spat again, even farther, out into the dirt, then stuck the cigar back between her lips and puffed like it held his ashes.

Nick nodded reluctantly. "I don't want anything! Just let me go!" He twisted out of Levelsworth's grip.

The man was relentless. "Son, if you're ever in Boise, you just give me a call," he said, starting to follow, but he reconsidered before reaching Bushka's range. "I'll give you the best deal you've ever seen. And I hope your *babushka*—" he glanced at Irina, "well, I hope you both do real good. I'll be seeing you." He slithered back to the car.

Both men waved as Larry let off the brakes. The van crept off and disappeared into the overgrowth.

Nick trudged up the steps staring at his feet. When he reached the porch he looked over to see if Bushka was glaring at him. She wasn't. Her eyes were fixed on the trees, swaying in the high summer breeze.

Fine. She was like this too often now, irritated and irritating, her checkerboards of deeply etched skin and wispy strands of thin white hair simply revolting. The less she said to him at times like this the better. He pulled open the screen door.

"(To the market, boy)," she ordered over the door whapping shut.

CHAPTER 11

3:15 p.m.
Friday, July 19

Nick parked their beat-up Ford pickup in the dirt at the end of the Rushing Wells Mercantile wooden sidewalk. He cringed a bit when he stepped up onto the planks—his legs felt like they'd run a marathon. But he willed them toward the entrance, careful not to bang any of the oversize bumpers, winches and spare tires that jutted from other dirty farm trucks along the way. His arms ached when he pushed through the door. If he'd had his way, he would have put off this trip until tomorrow.

"Nicky!" a familiar voice called while he untangled a shopping cart from the row. Nick looked around, his stiff neck balking.

"Over here!" From the produce department Colleen Dillinger waved a head of lettuce at him, then looked at what she was doing and giggled. She tossed the lettuce into her cart and hurried over.

"Nicky, I just saw you on the news—you're a hero! You were marvelous!" Her pretty green eyes danced with excitement. She leaned in and kissed his blushing cheek.

All around them activity came to a standstill. Smiling shoppers even gave him a smattering of applause.

Chills ran up his stiff back. He waved uncomfortably to everyone, but the spotlight was too bright. He motioned for Colleen to follow him up the canned goods aisle.

"You're such a ham, Nicky Brody," she teased, passing him and crashing her cart into his, "but I love it. It's nice to see you lighten up a little, you're always so serious."

"I'm not *that* serious. And my name is Nick. I don't like to be called Nicky anymore." He brushed the lock of hair up out of his eyes.

"I know, but you still seem like Nicky to me, and you are *too* serious, I mean, you're the only guy I know who's *busy* all summer long—so how come you never leave your house? What's so important there? I mean, this is like the first time I've seen you anywhere this summer. What do you do all the time?"

The questions embarrassed Nick. "I'm fixing up my car, Colleen, I thought you knew that. And I work on Saturdays, I study for the SATs, I've been on the computer, I take care of our place . . . "

She shook her head, smiling. He knew it wasn't what she wanted to hear, but what else could he say? It was like the truth wasn't good enough. He felt his face growing warm.

"Look," he said, "I'm not gonna go sit in the park all day like everybody else. I'm tired. I gotta go, okay?" He tried to go by her but she blocked him.

"Well, Nicky, if you're working so hard, then how come you went swimming in the middle of the day? So that's not sitting around, or what? I mean, what's the difference between you and everybody else . . . that you don't have any friends to ask to join you? I wonder why *that* is! Open your eyes—maybe other people might like to do stuff with you, you ever think of that?"

Nick was speechless. Did she mean her? Or what? What was this all about?

She wasn't smiling any more. Her voice dropped to a loud whisper. "Think about it. Maybe you're missing out an a few things? Like having a little fun? Like . . . duh?!"

He was too tired for this. She seemed to live to torment him, but he could play that game, too. "Oh, like you . . . " he taunted, "barrel-chasing or whatever it is you do all the time? Don't you get tired of going in circles like that?"

"It's barrel *racing*, Nicky, not chasing. Gawd. And no, I don't get tired of it. Maybe you should try it . . . or try *something*! *Anything*! Play football! Frisbee! Skateboard! Do *something*! I mean, like, get a life!"

"I have a life, Colleen! I know what I want—"

"Which is . . . nothing! You're gonna run into a lot of brick walls with your nose always buried under some hood or in some book. Now listen—you're a hero for a while, whether you like it or not. People are going to expect you to act like one."

"What does that mean?" Nick felt like she was headed somewhere with all this. As usual. Then, against his will, he swallowed, his larynx rising in his throat like a ball of sandpaper. Damn it! Why did she always make him feel so nervous and defensive?

"Well, for one thing, don't be so rude! You wouldn't even talk to that guy on TV."

"They showed that?" he replied hoarsely. "But I didn't feel like talking. I was tired. I just wanted to go home."

"Exactly, you cow brain!" Colleen's light freckles hid under a crimson flush. "Like usual! Like every morning when you move the sprinkler lines in our pasture, you don't ever stay long enough to talk. You've always got *something* to do at home. Well, Nicky Brody, you better learn that your car or your cows and all your other lame excuses will keep. There's a whole world of things out there!"

"I know, but . . . "

"But nothing!" Her thoughts spewed fast and hot, "you can't just ignore people, Nicky—interviewers *or* neighbors. Especially now that people are looking up to you! Can't you try just being a *little* more friendly? Just for a while? You know, stop and talk a little? Stop staring off into the clouds?"

Nick didn't answer. It was too late—she was on a roll.

"Well maybe you can't! Maybe you're so self-centered or mad at your family or embarrassed or whatever that you can't see anything until it reaches up and smacks you right between the eyes!" Colleen stormed off, abandoning her shopping cart, stomping past the peas and yams and out the store. Her cowboy boots amplified the furious bounce to her steps, her ponytail danced like an angry red snake.

Nick didn't move. He watched her pickup streak out of the parking lot, chaff flying off bales in back. Good God. Would she ever just leave him alone? He shook his head. Maybe she was right sometimes, but then *she* didn't have to live with Bushka and Grandpa. No one could know what *that* was like. The sight of her clomping off down the aisle in those boots replayed in his mind over and over.

He finished shopping, forcing himself to talk a little to people that asked him about his adventure. Finally he was alone again, on his way home, pulling into his driveway. Irina sat on the porch, sipping from her usual cup of peppered vodka-tea.

"(Nikisha)," she called out. Nick stopped with his bags at the door. "(Olga Sergeyevna from church called. She tells me, 'Irina Ivanevna, a reporter on television says your Nikolas Ivanovich was a hero today—that he saved a small girl from the river.' Is that true)?"

"(I did jump in after her, Bushka, when it seemed she would be swept away in the current)."

"(Then you were already at the picnic ledge, yes? You abandoned your chores, yes? Do not think that you are any kind of hero for putting off your work. I expect the fence to be fixed tomorrow, and if the steers get out tonight you'll be chasing them until morning)."

He'd forgotten all about the fence. He was planning on doing that earlier, before everything else had happened.

Then Irina added, "(The Virgin looks kindly upon you for saving the girl. Now put away the food before it spoils)."

She rose and followed him to the kitchen. Cabbage was already on the stove; Nick unwrapped the sturgeon steaks and set them on the counter.

As usual, Boris was not home for dinner. Nick and Irina sat and crossed themselves, said a short prayer to the icon 'The Virgin of Kazan' that hung on the wall above the table, and ate in silence.

Nick took care of the dishes and kissed Irina on the cheek goodnight. He told her he was going to bed, but when he got to his room he plopped onto the bed, still fully-clothed. He couldn't take his mind off the river. Or off Colleen, or off Bushka. Crap. What a life.

In what seemed an instant later, the phone rang and startled Nick awake. 9:10. It was past Bushka's bedtime; he grabbed the cordless and answered the call. "Hello?"

"Is this the Brodyaga house?" asked a gravel-voiced man. Loud country music twanged in the background.

"Yes," Nick replied, "who's this?"

"This is Max down at the Sudspot—we've got a problem with Boris. I don't want to have to call the sheriff on him, but in about three minutes I'm gonna have to. And maybe the undertaker, too. Why don't you save us all the hassle and get his butt out of my bar? Make that two minutes." Click.

"Dammit, Grandpa," Nick slammed down the phone. He slipped on some shorts and dashed to the mudroom, crammed his feet into a pair of rubber irrigating boots, grabbed a sweatshirt off the hook and slid it over his head while stumbling blindly outside. The truck keys were in the ignition. The Sudspot was only a mile or so down the road, beside a gas station out in the middle of nowhere. Just like they were.

"Please, Grandpa—be outside, out of trouble, waiting for me," Nick wished aloud. But then he spotted the ugly old bike leaning near the dark side door, and his stomach sank.

He parked in the gravel lot and hefted the heavy Schwinn into the bed of the truck, spilling the small white crosses and a tattered old bible from the basket.

Still no sign of Grandpa.

Nick's heart started beating faster, his head pounded and he had to pee. But he couldn't put this off, he had no choice. He turned the knob and pushed open the door.

Slide guitar blasted his ears. He squinted into the smoky light. A pool table in front of him was empty, but halfway toward the front door there was a small crowd.

Nick approached. U-shaped booths separated by high wooden partitions lined the wall. Big Max stood with his back to one of them, smacking a baseball bat into the palm of his hand. It looked like he was guarding the booth.

Nick pushed ahead. His feet were heavy, like they were magnetized to a steel floor. Soon he could see four cowboys wanting into the booth. Their women were gaggled up behind them.

He froze in place. Dammit, Grandpa, he thought, what have you done? Are you going to get us all killed tonight? Nick dragged himself a little closer, to where he could hear the angry shouts.

"Outta the way, Max—we're gonna teach the 'Gravedigger' some manners. But we'll take him outside so he doesn't mess up your bar."

Max slapped the bat again. "Shut the hell up, Clyde! You ain't teachin' nobody shit. Hell, the four of ya? Against this old man? You'd kill him."

"Sounds good to me, Max—and how about you boys?" Clyde's friends hooted in agreement. "Who's gonna miss one more Russian, anyway? Especially the 'Gravedigger'? Not a goddamned soul, that's who. It'd be the best thing to ever git done in this county!"

"Got your own grave ready, Gravedigger?" another cowboy yelled into the booth.

"The Lord is not ready for me," slurred Boris, "but those fine ladies will be better off when *you* all meet *your* Maker!"

"Sonuvabitch! Sonuvabitch!" The fuming cowboys shifted restlessly, but none of them dared test Max's reputation with the Louisville Slugger.

Max finally caught sight of Nick. "Hey boy, get over here! Get this drunken idiot out of my bar!"

Nick gritted his teeth. Cautiously he inched toward the lynch mob.

"Hey, it's the hero, the one from TV!" yelled one of the girls.

"Oh yeah, from the Brody Bunch or something—saved the little girl," said another.

"Yeah?" Clyde belched. He took a step toward Nick. "Well you're gonna have to be one tough little hero to get this old coot past us, boy. You got the balls, you little chicken-shit?"

Max whacked the wooden booth partition with the Slugger. "Clyde, boys—I'm gonna make two points. Point A is, if you assault this minor, you're down the river for ten years, and that's no bullshit. It's automatic. Point B is, if you touch this minor inside my bar, I lose my license for letting him in—and you lose your life, and that ain't no bullshit, either. Now, which of you wants to get in the way of this kid getting his grandpa out of here?"

No one volunteered. Max whacked the partition again, and the gang backed up a step.

"Get him outta here, kid."

Nick slipped behind Max and into the booth. He scooted around, but Boris retreated from him, holding a vodka bottle by the neck, ready to break it into a weapon at the slightest provocation. His red eyes glared at Nick from beneath the brim of his hat.

Nick couldn't believe it. "Grandpa, it's me! Nick! Let's get out of here!"

Suddenly Boris' guard dropped and he laughed. "*Ei Bogu*, Nikisha! What are you doing here? Let me buy you a drink," and he tried to wave as if to signal the bartender, but Nick grabbed his arm.

"Grandpa, come on! We have to go!"

"Look at the crazy old Russian!" jeered Clyde. "Barely even recognized his own kin!"

"Rescue him, hero, he's drowning, too. In vodka!"

They laughed, but Nick didn't pay any attention. He slid back out the booth the way he came, dragging Boris' arm with him. Finally he was out, standing behind Max. He pulled Boris out onto his feet.

"I'll show 'em all, Nikisha," Boris bragged with horse-killing breath. "I'll show 'em how a Russian whips dogs like these . . . "

"C'mon, Grandpa," Nick shuffled and pushed him to the door, then outside. All the while Max covered their back-sides. Nick poured Boris into the passenger side of the pickup and sat him fairly upright.

"Don't come back here, Boris," Max said. "You're not welcome anymore."

"Good night, Max. Good night, John-boy," Boris slurred.

Nick got in and rolled down the window. "Thanks for saving him, sir. I'll make sure he doesn't come back."

"You make sure he don't, kid. You know, one day that old coot ain't gonna make it home." Max slammed the door.

"A beer for the Lord, bartender," Boris ordered as Nick started the truck, "and I will have one, too. Three." He fell over, his head crashing onto Nick's thigh. His long white hair covered his face, his hat rolled onto the floor.

Nick moaned and worked around him to get the truck in gear. Before they hit pavement Boris was snoring. Nick leaned his head into the wind, as much for the noise as the fresh air.

He looked down at Boris and groaned. Lord, what had he done to deserve this? He braked and turned into The Motherland. Boris started sliding off his lap and down onto the accelerator, but Nick grabbed him just in time, holding him until he could stop the truck and kill the engine.

"Let me free!" Boris suddenly demanded, "I will fight them, I will fight them all!" He tried to yank free from Nick's grasp, but his head bounced off the bottom of the steering wheel.

"Fine!" cried out Nick. He let go. Boris slid back to the floor and resumed snoring. "Stay there all night!" Nick slam-med the truck door and stomped toward the house, but it looked too confining. Instead he turned and ran to the barn. He felt his way through the darkness to the loft ladder and climbed it. He unlatched the big, wide doors at the end of the loft and swung them open. A moonlit view of the canyon and river unfolded before him.

"One more thing," Nick told himself. He pulled a dusty old porch swing out of the corner and put it right in the middle of the opening, a couple of feet back from the edge.

He sat with his elbows on his knees, his hands joined, his toe tapping the wooden floor, his body tense and hard. Far below his fingertips the Snake flowed. On its jet-black waters, whitecap crystals sparkled in the moonlight. Some-times it seemed that the river wasn't really moving at all—it was just stirring and mixing, preparing for the next day.

"Oh, Ivan, it's so beautiful up here." Nick could still hear his mother's voice that first night, after he and Dad had hoisted the swing with a block and tackle. The three of them fit so perfectly into it. Dad sat in the middle, his arms around his 'two most precious things in the world'.

A tear rolled down his cheek. He brushed it away, but another followed, and he sniffed back even more.

"Dammit," he told himself. Then he yelled, "Shit!" across the canyon and followed with a scream of pure frustration. He sprawled back into the swing, his hands covering his face as the tears flowed. Why? Why was he stuck with a drunk and Bushka, who didn't care about him at all? Why couldn't it be the way it was? Why did God take his parents but leave him behind?

He remembered the night Bushka told him his Mom and Dad wouldn't be coming home, not ever again.

"(The Lord puts people to work for Him in many ways, Nikisha. He knows we are saddened when they leave us, but He takes them to a better place. Your Mommy and Daddy are with the Virgin and Her angels now, helping boys and girls and big people everywhere)."

"(Angels? The Virgin)?"

"(Yes, the Virgin, Nikisha. They're with the Holy Mother and Her angels, blessed and happy to serve Her. Come with me and I'll show you)."

Bushka had lead him down the creaky, narrow stairs to the root cellar. There, behind a heavy door, was her *sabor*, her sanctuary, where he was never allowed to play. She took him in, lit the oil lamp and told him several quick stories about the icons on the walls.

Finally she crossed herself before the last icon, 'The Virgin of Kazan'. She was silent for a moment; he could see that this one was special to her. Slowly she began to speak. She told him how the original icon had been lost, then was unearthed in Kazan, Russia, hundreds of years ago. The Madonna and Her Child were found to be painted black of skin, representing a side of Her maternity rarely iconized—still of goodness, of course, but of fierce protection and loyalty to Her children.

In time, the icon 'The Virgin of Kazan' became known for answering the prayers of those who believed in Her, and Her worshippers built the beautiful Cathedral of Kazan as Her shrine. Even more miraculously, the icon was seen to 'weep' real tears when tragedy struck those She loved. Faithful Russians adored 'The Weeping Virgin', and hand-painted copies of Her could be found throughout Russia. Even the Tsars were believers; eventually they moved the original 'Weeping Virgin' icon into their palaces for protection and guidance.

"(The Virgin is my guardian, Nikisha, and 'The Virgin of Kazan' is, to me, the truest icon of Her spirit. She is an angel of miracles. I have seen it with my own eyes—She once bestowed great powers upon a man I knew, Father Grigory. He performed wonderful miracles in Her name. He truly was blessed by the Virgin Herself.)"

"(Father Grig . . . Gri-gory)—"

Bushka smiled at his difficulty, "(Grigory, Nikisha, Father Grigory)." She took his hand and they knelt together on the thin prayer rug. "(Nikisha, you must believe in the Virgin, too. And you will when you hear the story of Grigory Efimovich Rasputin)."

CHAPTER 12

Rushing Wells, Idaho

Friday, July 19, 1998

Midnight

Nick smiled. Bushka knew how to tell a tale. He remembered the tears in her eyes, the laughter, her gypsy toes tapping, aching to dance again.

The two of them had knelt before the icon and prayed to the Virgin. They asked Her blessing for his parents, and Irina asked Her to watch over Nikisha in place of his mother.

Little Nicky believed in the Virgin with all this heart— Bushka even moved it upstairs for him. He prayed to Her daily, he knew Mom and Dad were with Her. If only some of the crying adults at the funeral had believed that, too. They'd needed to know mom and dad were fine, but they just wouldn't listen.

A tear fell through Nick's smile. The Virgin sure hadn't been the answer to everything. He could use a miracle right now, he thought, one that would get him out of this house and away from Bushka and Grandpa. Maybe he needed to become a *strannik* like Rasputin, just leave everything behind and start walking.

He shook his head, remembering how saintly Bushka had described Rasputin in her story. She practically stood him side-by-side with the Virgin Herself. Now *She* was something; he understood and believed stories about *Her*. The entire Christian world prayed to the Madonna. And if Russians believed in praying for miracles from Her icon 'The Virgin of Kazan', he wasn't going to question it.

But Rasputin? He could heal anything? See lights over people? Well, right. Whatever. But the guy seemed more con man than saint. If he were around today he'd be working with the Levelsworths selling used cars and wearing lots of gold jewelry. And he was going to return? To what? Mother Russia broke up long ago. Rasputin's going to come back from the ashes and save it. Uh-huh.

Nick wondered why Rasputin's followers never saw his nasty, evil side. What, all those people ganged up and killed him for no reason?

Well . . . those cowboys at the Sudspot were ready to kill Grandpa tonight, so did that make *him* evil? "Nope, just freakin' crazy," he told himself. And to hell with him, anyway. "I'm not gonna rescue him again. The world'd be better off without him."

The warm summer night was *too* relaxing. Nick swung his feet up and laid across the swing, dangling his legs off the end. Even without a pillow he was comfortable, and soon the darkness captured him. He dreamt of lands that were foreign, yet eerily familiar—he dreamt of Russia, of the Tsar and the vast tundra, of slant-eyed Mongolians and gilded onion-dome churches. There was no strife, no war, and everyone loved the Motherland. Cabbage cooked in big pots, and there was always plenty to feed the occasional visitor—a *strannik*, if God would have it so.

And there were young women in town, plenty of them, with full Russian breasts that layers of clothing did not hide. A dozen of them took Nick on a picnic, into an open field of wildflowers below towering mountains. They spread blankets, wine poured. They flirted with him. They undressed themselves, laughing, running about . . .

Rasputin awoke.

A foggy shroud numbed him; quiet peace surrounded him. He could neither move nor feel. But he'd been dreaming, he knew that much, reliving a picnic in the foothills of the Urals like it was yesterday.

The Virgin's words came back to him, " . . . soon you will find yourself in a strange land. Do not be afraid, for I will be at your side . . . overcome the temptations . . . "

Rasputin prayed. He asked for Her guidance, but She did not come. He felt the need for caution; he would have to proceed slowly and carefully. Surely more would come to him later.

The frolicking girls fought with him, trying to pull his clothes off, gaily and forcefully. Nick never felt so wanted. He laughed, begging them to stop. He hoped they wouldn't. They rolled him over, fighting for him . . .

Suddenly Nick fell out of the swing and landed with a thud. "*Ei Bogu!*" he cried, barely catching himself, a couple of inches and a balancing act away from falling out the loft doors to the cliff below.

"*Ei Bogu?*" said Rasputin.

Nick froze. Something echoed in his head. He must have banged the floor pretty hard. God, what a dream. It seemed so real.

"(You are Russian, yes)?" asked Rasputin in his deep voice, in Russian.

"What?" Nick cried out, "Who said that? Who's here?" He scrambled to his feet and scanned the dark loft. "I've got a gun!" he lied.

Rasputin felt the fear in Nick's voice. He answered in English, the language of the Tsar's court, "Do not be afraid, little one. I am one with the Virgin. She has sent me to you."

Nick dropped to his knees behind the swing. Fear thickened his tongue and dried his mouth.

"I am called Rasputin. I am on a mission for the Virgin. I feel your fright, but you need not fear me. Tell me your name."

Nick answered, hard as it was, "Nick. Nick Brody. Come out! You're really funny, you know."

"I am out, and I am not funny. My spirit is within you, Nick Brody. The Virgin has placed me here. I am one with Her. You need not fear me."

Something about the voice calmed Nick. For a moment he considered the possibility it might not be a joke. Impossible. "Okay, sure you are. Come out *now* and prove it."

"Prove it? I know not how. I am who I am."

"That's what you say, but how should I know that? You want me to just take your word?"

"My word is all I have. That and my faith in the Virgin."

It was the runaround. Nick fought it. "I need more."

"What would you have me do? Tell you of the Holy Lands? Of the Emperor and Empress?"

"No." Nick thought hard. Anyone could know those things. *He* had to ask the questions here. There had to be something he knew about Rasputin that the voice didn't. He tried to recall just one tiny, trivial detail from the story that Bushka told him so long ago. But nothing came. Only the murder stuck in his mind. Maybe that would be enough to expose whoever this was. "Let's say you really are Rasputin. How did you die?"

"Purishkevich and Yussupov and the other evil ones murdered me in 1916. Their last act was to throw me into icy water. The Virgin came to me then."

Nick didn't have another question. It was all too unbelievable.

"What year is it now?" Rasputin asked.

"1998."

"Is this Mother Russia?"

"No. This is Idaho. America." Wait a minute, Nick thought. The voice—there had to be a speaker and an amp up here somewhere, maybe a microphone. Good crap, somebody put a lot of work in this. "All right, I've had enough, whoever you are," Nick said loudly, striding across the loft and flipping on the lights.

"Ahhh," Rasputin approved. "I can see now. And your movements feel good to me. I have long been motionless."

"You can see now? Prove it." Nick stepped into an empty corner with his back to the loft. He checked behind him, over one shoulder and then the other, looking for a camera or something. *Anything.* But there was nothing unusual. Of course, he thought, he wouldn't see it if it was long-range spy gear. So he hunched over, hid his hands and made the shape of a V with two fingers. Again he looked behind him, and up at the ceiling, too. There was no way a camera could pick up what he was doing. The joke was about to end. "Tell me what I'm doing," he challenged.

"You are looking behind and above yourself," Rasputin answered. "I see bales of hay and the darkness outside."

"No, with my fingers! What am I doing with my fingers?"

"I know not. You are not looking at your fingers."

Nick groaned. He straightened his head and looked down onto his fingers. "Okay. Now I am."

"You have stuck out two of your fingers, as if to poke a man in the eyes."

"And now?"

"You leave your middle finger out."

"Yeah, that means fuck you." Nick pulled the finger back into his fist and leaned his head against the wall. "I must be crazy," he muttered.

"You are not. The Virgin sent me to you. She has a mission for me. She would not have chosen you to help me if She did not believe in you."

"Help you? Who said anything about that? I just want you out of my head. This is crazy. God." He paused for a moment, thinking. "Okay, I've gotta take a leak. Stay where you are."

Rasputin didn't answer.

Nick went to the upper loft doors and took care of business.

"That feels good," said Rasputin.

"God, leave me alone!"

"I cannot, Nick Brody. I know not how to leave you. And anger will not help. We will have to exist together. Let us drink wine. It will ease our spirits."

"My name is Nick, Rasputin or whoever you are. Just Nick. And I don't drink. I'm not like Grandpa."

"One glass of wine will not hurt, Nick Brody. It takes many glasses to do that. Come now, the Virgin does not frown upon wine. One glass of Madeira. I have been asleep for eighty years."

Nick thought about Bushka's wine cache in the root cellar. She'd shown it to him after telling the Rasputin story, emphasizing her faith in the legend. She said all Union of Tears believers had stocks of Madeira for Rasputin. Strangely, he felt like trying some. He was right, one glass couldn't hurt. Why not?

"All right. But I've gotta go to the house for it." Nick climbed down from the loft and headed for the root cellar.

"You have fine land," Rasputin said as they crossed the dark yard.

Nick nodded. 'Yeah, but try living here for a while,' he wanted to say but didn't.

The wine was right where he remembered it.

"A welcome sight, my little one," Rasputin said as Nick blew the dust off a bottle. "You have a corkscrew and a glass as well?"

"Yeah, in the kitchen. Come on, we'll get 'em. Just keep quiet, would you? God, this is so weird." He went back upstairs.

"I really cannot keep quiet, Nick Brody. The Virgin shall use me as She sees fit. I cannot do otherwise. Now come, let us sit and fill our glass now."

Nick smiled. "No, we'll go back to the swing. It's the only place I like to sit at night. You'll see."

They were back in no time, and Nick set to work opening the bottle. Even with help from the voice, spongy shrapnel and half a cork floated in the bottle when he was done. But it was open. Rasputin whooped once while Nick poured a glass.

He sipped. It wasn't what he expected, but it wasn't bad. Kind of like strong, bitter juice. "Okay, now what?"

"More," replied Rasputin. "It is an old friend."

Nick obliged. "So how does it feel?" he asked.

"Feel? It tastes good."

"No, not the wine. To . . . you know—to die."

"I hurt no longer."

"You were pretty beat up, huh?"

"The evil ones shall stand before the Lord for their actions. Or they already have. The Virgin told me the Russian people would come to know of their crimes."

"You really did talk to Her?"

"She blessed me with two visits in my lifetime. Are you one with the Virgin, little one?"

Nick nodded. "I guess She helped me when my parents were killed. Tell me more about Her . . . what does She look like? Does She really speak?"

Rasputin described Her visits to him, how he understood Her even though She did not speak. Then he told Nick other stories—his visit to Makari of the forest, his wandering and prayers, his life as a *strannik*.

Nick twice emptied and refilled his glass during Rasputin's stories, draining the bottle. Rasputin asked him about the girls he knew, if they were one with the Lord.

"I don't know," Nick said. "I don't know that many."

"Have you worshipped with the ones you do know?"

Nick shook his head. "No."

"Have you not lain with even one?"

Nick blushed. "Piss off. I don't care. I've got plenty of friends who are girls. I'd rather just do what I do and get a scholarship and get out of this place."

Rasputin laughed. "You have a cherry on your manhood, yes? Yes? You have a cherry all right!"

"Fuck off." Nick replied. "Sex is a good way to die these days. Besides, I almost had Leeza—" He stopped. Why should he tell Rasputin something like that?

"Leesha? Tell me of her. She likes you, yes?"

Nick took another drink. What the hell. He told Rasputin how Leeza Cummings asked him to the Snowball dance last winter—the dance where the girls ask the guys to go. Afterward they were down by the river, sitting on the tailgate, and one thing led to another, and then . . .

"Yes? Yes?"

"Well, I didn't have a condom. It was pretty stupid."

"A what?"

Nick explained condoms, how they prevented AIDS and pregnancy and whatever.

"Such as syphilis!" Rasputin exclaimed. "Guseva, the disfigured one, suffered from syphilis. It drove her to madness, and she knifed me in the name of Iliodor. But now, what of this wench Leesha? Did you find yourself with a rubber sleeve on your next visit with her?"

Nick sighed. "There hasn't been another visit. She started going out with fricking Jerry Shalikov after that. She must have thought I was pretty stupid not have any condoms."

"Nonsense, little one. She feels just as strongly for you now as she did then. She merely has forgotten."

"Forgotten? How do you know? And how can she forget what she feels?"

"You must remind her of how she feels, Nick Brody. She will remember much if you present yourself to her."

"Whatever." Nick didn't know what to say.

"We must find her, Nick Brody. You cannot wait for women to search you out, for many men are after their favors. We must go to her. Do you know where she might be?"

"Tonight? You're kidding. It must be two o'clock in the morning."

"We should venture to look. After all, it is never too late to spread God's word."

Nick shook his head. It felt thick, heavy, overloaded with people. "God's word? This is all so crazy."

"There is something else, little one. Before we go out, there is something we should try."

"I don't know. I'm getting too numb to try anything. What are you talking about?"

"I am feeling more of my senses, Nick Brody. The Virgin placed me in your head, yes? And now I feel She will allow our spirits to trade places within you."

"Huh?"

"Think of your body as a carriage, little one. Our spirits are drivers. I feel the Virgin will allow us to trade our seats. I would move to the driver's seat of our 'carriage'. We should try such a thing."

"You want me to give you the driver's seat? Complete control over me? You think I'm nuts? You'd probably banish me off to Siberia or outer space or something, and I'd be a floating soul for eternity. I've seen that in movies."

"Siberia is beautiful in the months of summer, I assure you, Nick Brody. But I have no such intentions. I swear to you, and to the Virgin, that I will return control of your carriage to you on your command. But if we do not try it, we will not know if such a thing is even possible."

Nick thought about it. Rasputin's word to the Virgin was worth a lot, he knew that much. "No ifs, ands or buts?"

"The moment you request it."

"Well, this seems to be a night for trying new things," He took a long drink, emptying the glass. "Give it a shot."

It happened. Nick found himself without form, resting like virtual baggage. But he wasn't alarmed—it actually felt pretty comfortable on the inside, like sitting in one of those heated, vibrating recliners in Sharper Image and playing the world's most lifelike video game.

"*Ei Bogu!*" cried Rasputin. He pranced around the room, practicing a few steps from a gypsy dance. "I am whole again!"

"You're gonna make me throw up," Nick said. "Sit down for a while, would you?"

Rasputin shook his head. "I shall not heave the wine, Nick Brody, and I care not to sit. We must go out and worship with young Leesha tonight. We must give her a chance to repent her sins—she must become one with the Lord. Now more wine, yes?"

Nick laughed. "Whatever. I don't care. Just don't fall down."

Rasputin ventured forth. Soon he held two bottles of Madeira by the necks. "You'll see how wine helps with worship, Nick Brody." They headed outside.

Rasputin froze at the mudroom mirror. "Ah! There you are, Nick Brody." Only half his face was lit by the pale yardlight, but it was a flattering, shadowy portrait. His chin and nose were perfectly proportioned, Romanesque, strong, dominating his face. His eye stared back with a taint of innocence, his eyebrow unsure. That lock of hair had fallen loose again, too.

"I, too, had hair that would not tame," Rasputin said, brushing it up. "You are so young, Nick Brody. But you are not hard to look upon. Many will be the women who worship with you."

Nick changed the subject. "The truck's outside. I don't suppose you know how to drive?"

They headed out the door. "I have driven a little, when carriages first were without horses. They are loud, obnoxious machines. We would do better to take your horses."

Nick laughed. "Well I'm not gonna ride any damned horse to town at two o'clock in the morning. Our truck might be loud and obnoxious, but it's gonna seem like a limousine to you. Come on . . . oh, wait, is Grandpa still passed out in there?"

The truck was empty, and Nick was relieved. Cool. Boris always seemed to find the way to his room, no matter his condition.

Nick described how to bang the driver's door near the handle to get the latch to work, and Rasputin pulled it open.

With a little coaching Rasputin got the engine started. "Lucky this truck's got an automatic transmission, Rasputin. You'd be hell on a gearbox."

"I would enjoy you calling me Grigory Efimovich, Nick Brody. It is my given name and the given name of my father — just as Brody is the name of your father, yes?"

"Well, that's our last name. His first name was Ivan. What did you say — Greg what?"

"Grigory Efimovich. Or Grisha, if it is easier for you."

"Okay, Grisha."

"Okay, Nick Brody — Nick Ivanovich, to me. Point us in the direction we must travel."

Nick had him turn on the headlights and showed him the basics — the accelerator, brake and how to put the truck into gear. Rasputin took it from there. They headed down the driveway — scraping a couple of branches on the way — but they made it to the road. Rasputin pulled out and straddled the centerline, creeping at little over an idle.

Nick groaned. "You gotta go a lot faster, Grisha. And get on your own side. We're gonna get run over."

Rasputin said nothing, but he picked up a little speed and moved over a couple of feet.

Nick groaned. "You can't drive worth a crap. See the speedometer? You need to get up to fifty miles an hour. And the whole truck has to be on this side of the yellow line. Trust me, it's how we all drive now."

"It is so fast!" Rasputin exclaimed as they approached forty.

"Nothing moves slow any more, Grisha. You'd better get used to it."

Rasputin took a drink from the bottle and swallowed his fear. He was getting good at keeping the truck between the lines when he ran the stop sign at the four-way intersection outside Rushing Wells.

"Shit! Look out! You just ran a stop sign! Slow down, we're getting into town. Listen, Rasp . . . Grisha—if you see a red sign or a light, stop! Yellow means slow down and green means go. You *have* to obey the rules of the road or we'll get pulled over. And don't drink from the bottle while you're driving. You'll get us thrown in jail. If you can't do this right, I'm gonna boot your ass out of the driver's seat."

"I shall do this right, Nick Ivanovich. I am enjoying your world."

The highway expanded into a wide, two-mile stretch of extra lanes, streetlights and storefronts. "Okay, slow down to twenty-five," Nick said. "This is Rushing Wells, and there's cops here. Just keep cool."

"I am cool. Your streets are lit like daylight," Rasputin commented, "brighter than St. Petersburg on a cold winter's day. And full of color," he added, mesmerized by the neon store signs. They drove Idaho Street to the end, but no one was out. The cruiser hangouts—the bowling alley and grocery store parking lots—were deserted.

"It's just too late, Grisha. Or maybe there's a party out in the sticks somewhere. Wait a minute -" He caught sight of blond hair in the 7-11. "Maybe . . . "

Rasputin pulled into the lot and killed the engine. They walked into the store and there was Leeza, alone, absorbed by an old pinball machine. Rasputin stopped in his tracks. Leeza wore sandals, short cutoffs and a thin shirt with its tails tied below her ribcage. She rocked up on her toes, grinding her hips into the machine, swaying and pushing. She did not look up. Arousal came quickly to Rasputin.

"That's her!" said Nick, full of Rasputin's contagious excitement. Rasputin took a step in her direction, but Nick yelled, "Wait! Stop! Go down the other aisle, over there."

Rasputin had to work at it, but he stopped and turned as commanded. They came to a large display of condoms on a peg-board. "We'd better be prepared this time," Nick said.

"Ah, the rubber sleeves," Rasputin said quietly. "We shall need several."

Nick laughed nervously. "Just get a box. Get the Trojans. They're 'ribbed for her enjoyment'."

Rasputin nodded. Nick made him grab a six-pack of 7-Up, too, for wine coolers—Rasputin couldn't understand the concept until Nick explained that that's what girls liked these days. That's all it took; they went to the front and paid.

"Now we may approach Leesha?" Rasputin said quietly.

"Lee—za, za," Nick corrected. "She'll probably want you to get her name right. Remember, it's been a while since she's seen me. Tell her you just happened to be in town, looking for trouble. And I'd drop the worshipping stuff if I were you. She's gonna think I'm a holy roller, and I don't think holy rollers don't get too far with girls like Leeza."

Rasputin nodded. He strolled up to her and said carefully, "Lee—za. What a pleasure it is to see you again."

She looked up. Her face was not really pretty—her nose was too big and her mouth too small—but she made the most of what she had, and she wasn't hard to look at. "Oh, hi Nick. What are you doing in town? I thought you never left the farm."

"I happened to be in town and wanted to find trouble. I wanted to see you. It has been too long since we enjoyed each other's company."

She stared at Rasputin while the machine tallied her points. "You seem different. You got a cold or something? Your voice is like, deeper."

"Much has changed since you saw me last."

"Oh, really." She turned back to the game and sprung a new ball into play.

"Ask her where everyone is tonight, Grisha. And tell her she looks good."

"You look well, Lee—za," Rasputin said. "Where are the other people?"

Leeza looked at him strangely, and the ball dropped down between her idle flippers. "Everybody's at Metallica in Boise. Me and Jerry were going, too, but he got too fucking drunk and passed out this afternoon. He's such a lightweight. So I'm just hangin'." She put her last ball into play. "You know, Nick, you're really acting weird. You got something good outside or what?"

Nick told Rasputin to mention the wine. "Yes, we—I have Madeira in the carriage, my little one."

Nick groaned. "The truck! You've got wine in the truck! And no 'little one'!"

"I mean I have wine in the truck, Lee—za."

She stared at him again, losing her last ball, too. The machine totaled her points. She didn't get a match, the lights went out. "Well, I could use a drink. It's been a shitty day. Come on, let's get out of here."

"Yeah!" Nick shouted to Rasputin.

Rasputin pointed the way and followed Leeza out the door. He never took his eyes off her small, heart-shaped backside.

"You were right, Grisha! She forgot she liked me! You're all right for an old dead guy."

They drove to the river, where Nick and Leeza parked back in April. She made herself a wine cooler while they talked about little things, nothing. And when she grew chilly in the night river air, Rasputin put his arm around her. He kissed her softly on the ear, and below it. She melted. Her clothes quickly fell away.

For almost two hours Rasputin granted Leeza's every wish, spoken and unspoken, on the bench seat of the truck and eventually back in the bed, between blankets. And not once did she complain of being cold. Rasputin satisfied himself three times, and Nick learned from the best of teachers.

Leeza did, too. "God, Nick, where have you been hiding? I've never had anyone—not like that." She shook her head and took another drink. "I've got to get home, though, okay?"

Rasputin nodded. They dressed and he started the truck.

She asked him to park down the block from her house, and she kissed him long and hard once they stopped. "Call me tomorrow, Nick. We'll go out and do something. See ya," she sang out, and she stumbled off stiffly.

"Now you have learned the ways of a true Russian, Nick Ivanovich."

Nick laughed. "*Ei Bogu*, Grisha. That was great. I still can't believe it happened. And she wants more!"

"They always do, little one. But you must spread God's love far and wide. All women deserve such satisfaction. They should know holy passionlessness. It relaxes them, it brings them closer to Thee."

Leeza waved as she wobbled up her driveway. Rasputin waved back, smiling.

"Passion. Less. Ness," Nick said slowly. "I'd like to spread some passionleshnesh to Colleen. She could stand to relax a little."

"There is another woman who needs to know the ways of true worship?"

Nick hesitated, but he was drunk on sex and wine, and he continued in spite of his better judgment. "Colleen is—I don't know. She's my neighbor—our neighbor," he corrected himself. "I've changed the sprinkler-lines in their fields for the last couple of summers, and she's always trying to get me to stay and talk to her, but—"

"But what, Nick Ivanovich?"

"But it's like, she's really friendly sometimes—she's cool, she's into horses and racing and all that—but then she blows up

at me for the smallest reason. She's mad at me right now, actually. And she wants to know everything about everything! She
asks me about Bushka and Grandpa, and I don't always feel like
talking about them. Then she'll say it's better to talk about
things you don't want to, but to me it's not. I think she reads too
many of those girls' mystery books, you know, drama queen
stuff. Oh—I guess you wouldn't know."

"She is mysterious, yes?"

"No. Well, yeah. Maybe she just imagines a lot. It's like she
thinks up all these hypothetical situations, you know? She asked
me once, if The Motherland—that's what Bushka named our
place, you know—was all mine, what would I do? Keep raising
cows? Sell it? Grow crops? And if I had a son someday, what
would I name him? Or a girl? What college would I go to? What
do I want to do some day? Jeez, she just goes on and on."

"She is consumed by curiosity, then."

"Too much curiosity. She makes me feel like I'm on trial.
Sometimes I just don't know the answers to all her questions,
and then she gets irritated when I tell her that! She gets mad a
lot, actually. Like when that guy from TV was asking me
questions. *She* might have stayed and talked to him all day, but
I'm not like that."

"TV?"

Nick sighed. "I guess none of this makes much sense to
you."

"I know only that she holds your interest, little one. I know
you would have her if you could. Is she easy to look upon?"

Nick lost his train of thought. "Um, yeah, I guess so. Yeah,
she is. She's tall, and she used to be kinda skinny, but not
anymore. Really, she looks pretty good—but we need to get
going. I'm tired." He had sort of a phantom yawn, where he felt
his muscles stretching and air rushing into his lungs.

Rasputin yawned and started the truck. "You do not face
how you feel, Nick Ivanovich. You do not understand her, yet

you feel for her. Such a situation is dangerous. I felt as such for Praskovia Svetlana—and I made her my wife." To Nick's relief Rasputin stopped at the stop sign this time.

"Well don't marry me off yet, Grisha. I'm just saying she's cool. She needs to relax a little, that's all." He yawned again. "Can you find the way home?"

Rasputin chuckled. "I have wandered the tundras of Russia, Nick Ivanovich—I will find our home without problem. Sleep now. And trust me."

CHAPTER 13

Saturday, July 20

4:10 a.m.

Nick dreamt of a gypsy camp on the cold Neva riverbank. Singing men and women sloshed around a roaring bonfire, dancing to *akkordeon* music and slapping backsides. A bearded man stepped into the firelight and sung above the din, his bawdy lines drawing hearty, drunken laughter:

A priest and wench, they were married,
Inside her his babe she carried—
    She'd said unto him,
    I need forgiven,
N'long on the altar they tarried!

Oh! Marry a man who crosses himself,
    For one with the Lord is he.
Marry a woman who crosses herself,
    Blessed shall you ever be!

There was a farm-boy pitching hay,
Who thought of big bosoms all day—
    A young girl did watch,
    Her eyes on his crotch,
She went out and gave him his pay!

Oh! Marry a man who crosses him . . .

Nick sang joyously bad with the crowd, swinging a half-empty stein in time with shuffling feet. He turned to take the hand of the girl next to him—it was Colleen! Nick couldn't believe it. She was there with him! The shock of it startled him awake.

"Dammit," Nick said to himself. He tried to go back to the dream, but then it hit him—something was wrong. The song was so loud . . .wait—it was Rasputin, it was *him*! *He* was singing!

"What the hell?" Nick wakened in an instant. He saw what Rasputin saw— they were standing outside the truck at Colleen's house, not thirty feet from her front door.

Terror gripped him. Colleen's! Oh God! Lights flicked on in the second story windows.

"What are you doing?" Nick yelled at Rasputin.

Rasputin paused. "I sing to the woman you love," he said, taking a deep breath and continuing, "And blessed . . . "

"Stop! Stop! Get out! Give me back control!"

In an instant Nick returned to the helm, the song still full in his chest and throat. He cut himself off and ducked behind the truck. He heard the Dillinger's front door open.

"Who's out there?" Rocco Dillinger's big voice boomed. "Show yourself!"

Nick heard the pump of a shotgun.

"Come out, now!"

"Dammit! Dammit!" Nick cursed. He had no choice. He stood and waved clumsily to Rocco, the darkness concealing his red face. Mrs. Dillinger, Colleen and little Mikey looked out the front windows.

"Nick? Nick Brody? Is that you? What are you doing out here this time of night?" Rocco lowered his shotgun.

Nick couldn't answer. He just kept waving, as if that was his response. Think, think, he thought. "Ahhh— " was all that fell out, and involuntarily at that.

"Tell him you love his daughter, Nick Ivanovich. Tell him you want to look upon her beauty. He will understand such a thing."

"*Shut up!*" Nick said through clenched teeth.

"What's that?" asked Rocco.

"Oh, ah—nothing, mister Dillinger. I'm just out here—ah, looking. For my dog," he suddenly came up with, "for my new dog. Have you seen him?"

Rocco didn't answer. He stared at Nick.

"I got a new dog, a pup. But he's gone. I thought I saw him go through the fence and come over here." Nick turned and pointed at the fence, then looked about and clapped and whistled, calling for the pup.

Rocco shook his head. "I thought I heard you singing."

Nick hesitated, "Well, ahh—I've ahhh—I've been singing, yeah. To him. To my pup. He likes it, I guess."

"You guess? Well it's too damn late to be out here singing, Nick. You get on home. We'll let you know if we see your dog."

Nick breathed with relief. Basically, it was over. "All right, mister Dillinger. I hope you see him over here. I don't want him to get run over or something." Nick waved again. "Sorry . . . .!"

The Dillingers turned in the doorway and went inside.

"I don't believe you, Grisha," Nick said under his breath as he banged the driver's door and got in. "I can't believe you were doing that."

"True love is unbelievable."

"Quiet!" Nick yelled, turning the key and stomping a few times on the gas pedal. "You're such a jerk! You don't go singing in people's yards at four in the morning!" The engine wouldn't start. He'd flooded it.

Nick grimaced and banged the wheel. "*Ei Bogu*! I don't believe this!"

"As I said, true love is . . . "

"*Shut up*!" He turned the key so hard he bent it. This time the engine started. "Leave me alone! Get out of my head forever!"

He needed air. He started to roll the window down and look out at the mirror on the door before backing up— Colleen was standing right there, her shocked face not two feet away.

Nick froze. He felt her anger warming the night air. Chills ran through him.

"Leave you alone? Fine, Nick Brody! After I beat you to a pulp!" She grabbed the door handle and tugged, but she couldn't pull the door open. She reached in, but Nick scooted away, and finally she settled on slapping the door. "Fine! Get out of here! Get out of *my* head forever!" She turned and stomped back to the house, her bathrobe billowing behind her.

"Nice job, Rasputin," Nick muttered. He put the truck in gear and turned around. They drove home without a word.

Nick fell into bed fully clothed, dawn's rays already lighting the window. Sleep came easily.

He dreamt of the river. The little eddies below his ledge were giant whirlpools, roaring, sucking funnels that pulled in him and Jenny. Around they went, inside, spinning in tighter and tighter circles, deeper, faster, gasping and choking on spray and fear. The sun and sky were at the end of a tunnel above him now, impossibly far away. They would die there, churning and swirling. Jenny screamed. So did he.

They dropped out the bottom of the whirlpool onto the boat dock. TV cameras took aim at him, their lenses were shotgun barrels. The blow-dried reporter tried to push him to where the cameras would get easy shots, but Nick twisted away. He ran through the crowd, Colleen now chasing him. She called for him to stop, to stand in front of the cameras and offer himself to the people. He would not.

He found a door to open and ran in. His eyes adjusted to the darkness, his lungs felt the smoke. No one paid attention to him. A man wearing an accordion swayed between round tables, playing fast Russian music to drunken men in colorless clothing with hookers draped over them, they all laughed too loudly and couldn't fix their eyes on anything.

Nick sat at an empty table in a corner below a smoke-stained icon. Suddenly the accordion player took over a clearing in the center of the room, playing with the vigor and volume of a full band. The men clapped in time as the hookers collected themselves and stumbled into a chorus line. They joined arms in a circle and, facing out, kicked high and often, only too happy to show off white ruffles and black stockings.

Then a set of saloon doors banged open into the lounge. Men in cowboy hats strode in, six in all, spurs jangling. The music stopped. The cowboys searched the darkness. They found him. Nick wanted to hide, or to run, but he was cornered. They approached. No one slowed them. One reached over the table with an impossibly-long arm and lifted Nick from his chair, planting him before them. Not a word was spoken. The other arm came around with an impossibly-large fist at the end of it. It slugged him in the stomach, hard.

Nick fell to the floor. The next cowboy lifted him up, planted him and hit him in the face. He fell again. And again. They all wanted a turn.

The last of them pulled Nick up for a second dose. But instead of hitting him, the cowboy pulled a mirror from the wall and held it in front of Nick's face. "Here's the face of evil, boy! Look at it! And listen up—don't you ever take one of our women down to the river again. Don't you drink wine unless you can fight like a man, and don't you ever step foot into this saloon again. We don't want no fucking children in here. Come in again and we'll blow you away."

Nick looked in the mirror. His face wasn't bloody or broken. It was different, though, and he couldn't put a finger on what had changed. The harder he looked, the harder it was to tell anything, until finally his focus drifted and he watched himself age years into the future. His nose gin-blossomed, his cheeks reddened with burst capillaries. His hair grayed. A beard grew, long and white.

Nick closed his eyes. He felt ugly and confused. His stomach tightened, he wanted to get away, to be anywhere else. The stench of cheap whiskey-breath reflected back at him, but it only made him want to drink more of it. He looked again at the face in the mirror. Old. Tired. Deathly. Then suddenly the image grew very clear. He looked exactly like Grandpa. He had become the Gravedigger.

Five hours later

Saturday, July 20

10:50 a.m.

Nick opened his eyes in terror, but he was not in a saloon, and no cowboys were holding a mirror in front of him. He sat straight up in bed, still fully clothed under his bedspread, his heart racing. He felt his nose, his cheekbones. They weren't smashed or cut. Wow, he thought, remembering Grandpa's face staring back at him. What did that mean? Is that what he was going—

But the stale wine in his bloodstream hammered his brain, a penalty for sitting up too fast. "Oh, god," he moaned, holding his head and falling back to the pillow.

"Next time we shall fill our stomach before enjoy-ing wine, Nick Ivanovich," said Rasputin.

Nick moaned. He wished Rasputin would disap-pear like those cowboys just did. "There isn't going to be a next time," snapped Nick. He wondered how he would ever face any of the Dillingers again. His stomach twisted and gurgled. He felt the morning sun warming his bed, a pressing heat on his legs.

Heat? In the early morning? "Oh no!" Nick cried. He looked at the clock. "My class! I missed my class!" He jumped out of bed and stumbled to the kitchen, all the while holding his pounding head. There was no meal cooking, no sign of Irina or Boris. He dialed the Rushing Wells Community Center and asked for the director.

"I've overslept, Mr. Cole. My class— ?" he asked timidly.

"They're fine, Nick. I had them work from their books and gave them a lesson for next week. But you know my Russian's nowhere near as good as yours. Something I said got everyone laughing, so you may get some questions on that next week. You will be here next week . . . right?"

"Of course," Nick assured him. He apologized again before hanging up. Nick's head felt suffocated, spun hard in the dryer. He went to the bathroom for aspirin and Alka-Seltzer, then went back to his room and shut the door.

"You teach the Russians, Nick Ivanovich? That is good. The Virgin smiles upon such things."

"Right. Then why did you make me miss class—oh, to hell with it. Look, teaching that class is called commun-ity service. It'll help me get into a better school, and I need all the help I can get. I don't need you or anyone else screwing this up.

"Look, I've gotta check my e-mail. We'll talk about this later."

"Anger does not suit you, little one. Tell me of this he-mail."

"Not he-mail . . . e-mail. The Internet, the computer? Cripes, I'll show you. Let's look up your name and I'll show you what it's about."

Nick found the Collier's Encyclopedia CD and put into the drive. He typed in 'Rasputin', and up popped the biography with a photo of Rasputin performing the sign of the cross.

"*Ei Bogu!*" cried Rasputin. "I remember the day the man took that photograph! I do not read English well, what does it say there? And how can I be within a box like this?"

"Actually, you're in the computer. Everything is. Okay, it says here, 'Rasputin, Grigory Efimovich (Novykh), born . . . '" and he went on reading the story with frequent interruptions and corrections from Rasputin. Nick killed the window when he was done. "Okay, more later. I've got no e-mail and my head hurts."

"Ah, but we did enjoy our night out, yes? Now we must pray to the Virgin to forgive our excesses."

"Our excesses? If anything, we better pray that that last broken condom doesn't mean I'll get AIDS, or it could kill me.

Kill *us*. Or that Leeza doesn't end up getting pregnant. Crap, I don't want to have to marry her. I'd be like everybody else around here — married too young, fixing fences and watching the cows, divorcing, fighting over kids, working for nothing 'til I die— that's definitely *not* what I want."

Nick was quiet for a moment, then added, "I can't believe what happened last night. The wine, Leeza, missing class— I even dreamed I was turning into Grandpa, drinking and fighting cowboys.

"You know, this isn't right, Grisha. I don't wanna live like you do. Or like you did."

"You must choose your own path, Nick Ivanovich. Come, let us pray to the Virgin. You must tell Her your concerns so She may point the way to your path."

"No. I don't feel like going to church. My head hurts. My whole body hurts."

"Have you no *sabor*? No place of worship? I beg your favor in this matter."

Nick thought of Bushka's *sabor*. It was just what Rasputin wanted. But the guy's screwed up his entire life in one night— and now he asks for favors?

"I also must ask the Virgin for guidance," Rasputin added. "Long ago She told me I would have a mission in this time. Perhaps, if we pray to Her, She will tell me of that mission. It will be all the sooner that I leave you in peace, Nick Ivanovich. You would like that, yes? So come, let us pray to Her."

Nick nodded. Anything to get back to the way things were. "Bushka's *sabor* is in the root cellar. We can go down— but I want to make sure she's not here somewhere first."

Nick snuck a quick glance into the living and dining rooms to make sure Irina wasn't quietly knitting or something.

"Wait!" called out Rasputin.

"What?"

"There, above the table— the icon 'The Virgin of Kazan'. We must pray before Her."

"No! We have to go down to the *sabor*. If Bushka sees me she'll send me outside to work. And what would I tell her? 'Sorry, but Rasputin needs to pray right now, Bushka?' See what I mean? You want a chance to pray or not?"

"Of course. We shall simply take the icon with us. It is my favorite."

Nick frowned. What a hassle. He snuck down the icon and hurried through the kitchen, down the creaky stairs to the heavy door. He pushed it open. Mustiness washed over him, his feeble stomach churning. Cobwebs draped the corners and water pipes. Obviously Bushka wasn't coming down much any more. Nick hung 'The Virgin of Kazan' amid ribbons thumb-tacked to the plain wallboard, beside 'Madonna of Vladimir', above 'Mary with the Seven Swords of Sorrow' and 'Redeemer with the Wrathful Eyes'. Again he crossed himself.

"I have only one more favor, little one. I must take control in order to pray."

Nick gasped. "What? No way! You went crazy on me at Colleen's! You think I'm going to sit in the back seat again?"

Rasputin did not get excited. "Never shall I embar-rass you in my prayers to the Lord. I ask only to pray."

Nick shook his head and paced the room, careful to avoid walking on the worn prayer rug in its center. He wanted to deny Rasputin's request, to deny him any further earthly pleasures. He knew it was in his power to do so. Many people would. Finally he stopped pacing and faced the icons.

"We don't leave this room— got it?"

Rasputin agreed, and Nick nodded. Instantly they swapped.

Rasputin lit the oil lamp on the small shelf below the icons. He fell to his knees and crossed himself. He hummed and moaned deeply, testing the range of his vocal cords, then began a calming chant, pressing his forehead to the floor. He raised himself, gazed upon 'The Virgin of Kazan' and began anew.

Nick felt relieved. This wasn't like the night before, when his adventure with Rasputin was like a ride through a forest on a runaway horse, darting through trees, ducking low-hanging limbs, hanging on by luck, muddy-headed with wine. Now he could relax. He enjoyed the soulfulness of Rasputin's prayers. He believed in the same Virgin that Rasputin so reverently looked upon. He remembered his love for Her, his love for his parents. This was like praying with a priest, with one who enjoyed privileged communications with the Lord.

But then Rasputin looked to the ceiling and filled the *sabor* with a disturbing, anguishing shriek. He paused, refilling his lungs, and cried out again. And again. He bowed to the Virgin, chanting and shrieking, pressing— even striking— his forehead to the floor ever-harder.

Aghast, Nick wanted to cover his ears. He did not want to witness this— Rasputin's humility, his confession, his apologies to the Lord. Nick thought of Bushka and Grandpa. What would they think if they came inside the house? Would they come rushing down to see what wild animal was trapped in the cellar? How would he explain?

The last of Rasputin's shrieks was one long, horrifying cry of despair. Then he rested, chest heaving, his head on the floor, his hands clasped together above.

Maybe Grisha is finished, Nick thought. He wanted to ask, but he held back. He felt he should not interrupt prayers even as bizarre as these. Maybe they would work, maybe they would be forgiven for their excesses of the night before.

Then Rasputin lifted his head and crossed himself. Nick looked with him upon the Virgin. She looked brighter, almost— happier! Could it be? She seemed alive, like She was dancing in the flickering lamplight. Nick couldn't believe it. Was it just an illusion? His heart lightened at the sight.

Rasputin suddenly burst into song, into Russian psalms. Nick was elated. Salvation! Forgiveness! Redemption! Now the pureness of their being was undeniable, their cleanliness shone. None of last night mattered now. All would work out for the good. He felt the sun come out from behind a cloud outside. It had to be so.

Then Nick heard the door to the *sabor* creak open. Who was there? Rasputin did not miss a beat of the psalm, nor did he look to see who had joined them. Nick fidgeted nervously. Who— who— ?? Then a rusty old voice sang with Rasputin, high, female.

Bushka!

Nick thought fast— Bushka had found him in her *sabor*, singing like she had never heard him before. Why didn't she interrupt? Did she know what was going on? No way! Never in a million years could she guess what the truth was. But what *could* she be thinking?

Rasputin and Bushka finished the song on the same note, then silently bowed to the floor together. They paused a moment, then began a chant at exactly the same time, almost on cue.

Nick moaned, wanting the suspense to end. Why was Bushka toying with him? She knew he didn't pray like that! He had no choice but to wait it out. He phantom-sweated.

Twenty minutes passed before Rasputin and Bushka finally threw up their hands in a sky-shaking tribute. He turned to look at her, and she at him.

"(Father Grigory. Your prayers floated up to me, even though I no longer hear like a young girl. I have waited so long— is it really you? Have you returned, as the Virgin promised us)?" She searched the eyes she had known so long as Nikisha's for a clue. "(It is I, Irina Ivanevna)."

"(My Irisha)?" Rasputin exclaimed. "(My loving gypsy)?" He performed the sign of the cross upon her. "(It is I, dear one. My heart sings at seeing you again. You were the most beautiful girl in all the gypsy camps)."

They hugged, wetting each other with tears, squeezing each other with joy and sadness at the years that had passed.

"(It feels good to find an old friend)," Rasputin said.

Bushka could not take her eyes off him. "(But how? You are inside my beautiful Nikisha?— for the voice I hear is not his. Is Nikisha well, also?)."

"(Yes, of course. The Holy Mother has brought me here, little one, and I share the body of Nick Ivanovich. We trade places at its helm, at his direction. The Virgin has a mission for me, Irisha. A mission in the name of the Motherland. Thank God She has allowed us to be together again)."

Rasputin took her hand and helped her up. "(We should go upstairs and sit. We have much to talk about.)"

Bushka beamed, remembering, "(Wine! I have Madiera for you, Father)!"

"(I would enjoy some wine, Irisha— if Nick Ivanovich shall allow it)."

Nick laughed, relieved that he didn't have to try and explain anything to her. "Whatever, I don't care. You can drink some with Bushka. But don't try anything," he joked.

Irina led Rasputin out the *sabor*. She opened the wine cabinet and gasped. "(Someone has stolen three . . .)"

"(It was I, little one. I found your wine last night)."

Irina smiled. "(I have saved it for you for many years, Father. I knew always that you would return)." She hugged him again, this time breaking down and crying profusely.

As Rasputin comforted her, Nick wished he could have left them alone. Bushka was like a little girl, all emotions, and not really the same old woman he'd known all his life. And he didn't enjoy feeling her old body in such a lengthy embrace.

Rasputin kissed the thin cushion of hair on her scalp, and they went up the stairs. They sat closely at the kitchen table, where the samovar was already hot. Bushka poured herself tea and spiked it with her peppered vodka, and Rasputin had his wine.

But scarcely a moment passed before Boris rambled into the kitchen from the hallway. His white hair laid flat against one side of his head as if starched, the other side stuck all up and out. He said nothing. He took a glass from the cupboard and his own bottle of plain vodka from the refrigerator, poured, and cut the drink with a shot of tomato juice. He took a big gulp.

"(Boris Grigorevich)," Irina said. He looked at her with crimson eyes. "(There is someone special I would like you to meet)."

Boris looked at Nick, then back at Irina. He took another drink.

She continued, "(Do you remember the legend of the return of Father Grigory? The Virgin's promise that one day he would return to us)?"

Boris' eerie blank stare usually indicated an angry hangover. And from the way he passed out in the pickup last night, Nick was sure he was suffering much more than he. But this stare was more.

Boris took another drink, then replied, "(I see no legends. Only Nikolas)."

"(It is the word of the Virgin that he would return, Boris Grigorevich, and he has)." She turned to Rasputin. "(Please, tell my son it is so)." She sat back smugly.

Rasputin stood and gave Boris the traditional three Russian kisses. "(I am Grigory Efimovich Rasputin, little one)," he said in his deep voice. "(I am one with the Virgin)."

Boris' jaw dropped and eyes widened, but just for a fraction of a second,. His brows lifted in disbelief. He closed his eyes and mouth and swallowed back the sight and the voice with his red vodka. "Well so am I, so don't try to fool me with some goddamned trick, Nick," he said in English. "I've been around longer than you know, and I've seen every trick there is."

Rasputin performed the sign of the cross on Boris. "(Take not the name of our Lord in vain, Boris Grigorevich. Such an act offends Him. And believe that the Virgin sent me here on a mission. I share the body of your grandson, Nick Ivanovich. Come, pray with us in the *sabor*. You will come to know the truth)."

Boris didn't answer. He just stared back, bewildered. He looked Nick over from head to toe, trying to figure out the voice and strange mannerisms, but there seemed no obvious answer. He slammed back the rest of his drink and plunked the glass on the counter.

Rasputin made one last try. "(May the day come when you find the beauty of the Virgin)."

Boris turned back to face Rasputin. His blood was rising, swelling the veins in his neck and temples. Nick had never been afraid of his grandpa, but right now he wanted to back off a couple of steps. Rasputin held his ground. "Piss off," Boris snarled.

"(Boris Grigorevich)!" Irina chided.

Boris looked right at her. "(Ei fucking Bogu. You believe this crap)?"

Irina stood, her wiry knuckles on the table. "(Don't you talk to me like that)!"

"(Then don't try to feed me full of bullshit. I don't know what you two are up to, but I don't want any part of it. I have work to do— real work, in the name of the Lord)."

"(You call what you do the work of the Lord? Burying animals? That's insanity. The Lord doesn't ask us to bury the unclean)."

"(They are not unclean—-they are unburied souls. Would you have them wander eternity without rest? Like my friends in the sea? Or do you think *they* are unclean, also? I bet not. No, I will see all beings returned to the earth. I don't care *who* gives a shit)." Boris left, slamming the screen behind him.

Rasputin and Irina exchanged glances. She sighed. "(He was in the big war, World War II. He was a sailmaker in the Navy, and one of his duties was to make burial shrouds for men killed in action. He fitted many shrouds to friends, and the nightmares have never left him. Please try to understand. It has affected his mind)."

"(Of course, little one. His heart is pure— he works in the name of the Lord. I find no fault with Boris Grigorevich.)"

Irina smiled. Rasputin sat at the table again. They refilled their glasses.

Rasputin took her hand. "(Tell me what became of you after the evil ones took my life. Did you marry? How did you come to leave the Motherland)?"

"(Oh, Father—)" Irina's eyes welled up. "(There is so much to explain. After you were— were killed, they killed Nikolas, they killed Alexandra, and all the children . . .)" she cupped her eyes with her hands, she shook with emotion.

Rasputin looked to the heavens and crossed himself. He closed his own eyes and mouthed a silent prayer, then knelt beside her chair and put her head to his shoulder. "(They have been one with the Lord for many years, little one, and I have known of them. They knew their destiny. They went unto Him with honor. Batuishka would have had it no other way. Remember him so).

"(Now please tell me . . . your own husband, he was such a man of honor, yes? Tell me of he you married— tell me that I might know of your joy. Come, my Irisha, speak of your happy times)."

Irina shook her head behind her hands. She did not answer.

"(Come now, my little one. The Tsar would have you dancing with his spirit, not saddened by what he could not control)."

Suddenly she dropped her hands. Her aged eyes were red and wet and swollen, but there was a hardened resolve to them. "(Don't you see)?" she asked. "(No man could ever be what you were to me, Father. No man sang or prayed or healed like you— there was never another man with your gifts. You were the only one)."

Rasputin wobbled. He groped behind him for the chair and pulled himself back onto it. "(Surely you jest, my Irisha! You were the fairest of the young gypsies! Every boy wanted you. And yet you took) . . . "

Irina shook her head. "(No one else)."

"*Ei Bogu*," he muttered. "(I would not have had it so, my little one. You were so young, so full of life. You could have made a man very happy)." He thought for a moment. "(Then Boris Grigorevich) . . . "

"(Yes. He is your son. Our son)."

Suddenly she looked alarmed. She tried to look past or through Rasputin, around his hypnotic blue eyes, to speak to Nick. "(My Nikisha, I'm so sorry. I never told you. I've never told anyone, not even your father. I could not)."

Nick didn't hear her. His mind had raced far ahead, freefalling through voices and Dad and wine and Grandpa and icons and Leeza and prayers and Colleen. And Rasputin. Not only was he host to a ghost, he was the great-grandson of Grigory Efimovich Rasputin.

CHAPTER 14

Bushka described for Rasputin the painful fall of the Motherland. The Godless ones had moved quickly, transforming the near-sighted, thick-headed *moujiki* into a million-man inferiority complex with red books in one hand and Mosin Nagant rifles in the other.

This was all old news to Nick. He heard little. Everything had changed. His family's shadows were taking form with faces and personalities; clues that had been there all along now meant more. Like how Bushka had never talked about her husband, Nick's great-grandfather. All she'd ever said—and this was to Nick's dad, not to Nick—was that he was killed in the Revolution. No details, no stories. So seemingly, no pride. But who would have believed the truth? How *could* they have believed her?

And so it was no wonder that Grandpa never talked about his dad. Bushka hadn't told even *him*; Grandpa didn't *know* who his father was. Did he even care? But now, in this light, Nick saw their shared DNA as one and the same—a pair of drunken, praying, pains-in-the-asses.

Good God, Nick thought. Rasputin and the Weeping Virgin. It was like a fairy tale that had come alive, like Jack's Beanstalk had sprouted overnight from their garden.

Irina lit a cigar and freshened the wine and vodka. She told Rasputin, "(Purishkevich never apologized for what he did. He claimed he and Captain Lipov were working in the interests of the Tsar and the Motherland—though I am sure Nikolas would have disagreed! Finally he did try to free Nikolas and the family at Ekatarinaburg. But it was too late. The *Bolsheviks* had become too strong and he was caught. They sent him to prison, then banished him to the south of Russia with the *Mensheviks*. He died with them, of typhoid, I believe.)"

"(Vladimir Mitrofanovich was not one with the Virgin.)"

Irina shook her head. "(Neither were the rest. Captain Lipov, especially. After the revolutions, he followed whoever was running the country. He was powerful in the *Cheka* and, after that, the KGB—the new Soviet police forces. We had no worse enemy.)"

Rasputin snorted, "(Lipov was Purishkevich's monkey, and others' as well. He no courage to follow his own agenda. What became of the others—the doctor, young Romanov . . . ?)"

"(The doctor? Oh, what was his name—I cannot remember. Little is known. Some said the Soviets returned him to the Army. It was still wartime, after all.

"But the Tsar's nephew, Romanov, did not fare so well. When the Bolsheviks came to power he wept at their feet. He renounced his heritage before all of Russia, and the Reds took all he owned. The *moujiki* would not feed him because of his offenses against you and the Virgin, and it was said he took to life on the back streets of St. Petersburg. Eventually syphilis took him. He was alone, it was winter.)"

"(Dmitri Pavlovich was a weak soul. He was not a man. If it were not for his friend Felix Felixovich . . .)"

"(Oh, Prince Yussupov!)" she cackled. "(His is the best story—you simply won't believe it)!"

"(Surely no better fate awaited him. He, too, was an offense to the Virgin.)"

"(Then you would guess Who came to him in a vision?)"

Rasputin shook his head blankly.

Irina leaned forward and whispered, "(The Virgin—the Black Virgin!)" Her eyes danced, her quivering lips hinted a smile. She sat back and continued, "(She came to him soon after your murder, in his bedchamber. She told him his sins were so great that, if he sought Her redemption, he would have to calm the Russian people with prayers in your name. He would have to proclaim that you would return to serve Mother Russia!

"Oh, my! Imagine our reactions—first we lose you to a band of Godless murderers, then we are told the Holy Mother shall return you to us! Oh, Father, it was so hard. I never stopped missing you) . . . " Her eyes had grown misty and wet. Rasputin nodded, covering her hand with his.

"(There is so much you should know)," she went on. "(The Virgin told Yussupov that he must unite your followers and grant them Her icon, 'The Weeping Virgin' from the Tsar's palace. The people would crave to worship Her, and you would need the icon's guidance upon your return.

"But it was difficult to know our path. Those of us who had prayed with you were torn . . . what were we to do? We could not trust Yussupov's words, yet we could not ignore the wishes of the Virgin—for you would not have had it so! There was great debate. Many called Yussupov's story a lie, saying he was used the Virgin's name to escape prosecution. And true enough, no charges were ever filed.

"But in the end, I think what swayed us was Yussupov himself. He was truly changed after the Virgin came to him. He spread Her words to many, many Russians, from the *moujiki* to the shopkeepers on Nevsky Prospekt to the Royal Family. It was just incredible to hear his story. Such emotion and passion!

"So we placed our faith in him. We joined and became 'The Union of Tears', and Nikolas and Alexandra presented us with 'The Weeping Virgin' for our shrine. Oh, you should have seen the crowds! Many Russians joined with us, and I was proud to tell them of our times in the gypsy camps. I missed you so terribly, Father, I think I cried all the time)."

Rasputin smiled. He half-rose and kissed Irina on the top of her head. "(And the icon? Do the people still worship Her)?"

Irina shook her head. "(Yes, but only the peoples' copies of Her icon remain. You see, the February revolution changed everything. After the Tsar fell from the throne, the Godless ones closed our churches and began burning. It was terrible, and we knew they would not spare 'The Weeping Virgin'. But we had pledged our lives to save Her—and we did so just in time. We had just hidden it when they came to seize it)."

Her eyebrows lifted. "(Oh, how that infuriated the *Okhrana* and Captain Lipov! First he tried forcing information from the faithful, but they would not talk)." She lowered her head and crossed herself. Rasputin did the same.

"(Then he posted a huge reward for Her return, but that didn't work, either. And soon there came a miracle—another sign of Her love, we were sure . . . just before the October revolution closed our borders, we were able to smuggle Her out of the country. I was with the believers who carried Her in a suitcase to Paris, and we found Her a home in a fireproof safe, hidden in a farmhouse basement.

"Lipov sent agents from Russia everywhere looking for Her. They were posing as collectors of art—imagine, trying to fool the French when it comes to art! It was laughable. Regardless, She was not found.

"As time passed, Europe seemed headed for war and we were worried that Paris might fall. So we moved Her to America, far away from the tensions and the Godless ones. Her spirit was with us, we were sure. But Lipov never did give up his search. He was ruthless)." She paused, her face lifting when she whispered, "(Imagine his anger when he realized he would never crush 'The Union of Tears')!"

Rasputin smiled. "(It honors me to have prayed with you and those who are one with the Virgin, my Irisha. So tell me of 'The Weeping Virgin' . . . where is She now? And does 'The Union of Tears' still exist? I am fearful of the many years . . .)?"

"(Not *that* many years)," she interrupted, playfully offended. "(I'm sure She's fine, Father. There are many of us who survived and long to pray to Her again, just as we have longed for Her to return you to us . . . and it is high time for both! Shall I call for Her now? Of course! Of course! I have waited so long—and to think you've come to my home, to my Nikisha! Oh, my! Everyone will be so excited)!" She rose from her chair, kissing Rasputin's hair as she floated by. She sat at the phone desk with its jammed nooks and cubbyholes and pulled a timeworn notebook from way at the top.

Her finger shook as she picked through the pages. She found a name and placed a bookmark sideways under the name and number. She looked back at Rasputin, smiling broadly. She picked up the phone, raised her chin to focus her bifocals and carefully punched in a long set of numbers.

"(Tatiana Andreyevich? It is I, Irina Ivanevna Brodyaga! Yes, I am well, but Tosha, you must prepare yourself! Listen to me — the Virgin Sings! Yes, I know what I am saying, and I say it again — the Virgin Sings! Come, bring the suitcase! It has happened! Tosha, you have to believe it, because it's true! Yes, yes, come to Idaho, to my farm. There is plenty of room. It will be like the old days. We must let everyone know . . . please do, Tosha. Call every-one you can think of, and have them call others. Now I have much to do, so I must let you go. I will see you soon. Praise the Virgin)!"

Two hours later

Moscow, Russia

Sunday, July 21
9:52 a.m.

On a sunny, windy plain outside Moscow, in a craftsman's *dachau*, an ancient rotary phone rang in a mahogany-trimmed study.

He picked up the phone, "Dah," standing to full height, gazing out a wall of windows to manicured grasses and smooth concrete retaining walls. Silver hair. Smoking jacket, silk trousers. Reindeer-trimmed slippers.

"(Colonel)," the caller began, "(please pardon the intrusion. There's been an odd report from America. An operative reports activity involving a stolen icon and a group called 'The Union of Tears'. Sir, the computers have no description of this group and icon. There is only a note that any reports be delivered to you personally)."

The man replied, "(I'll take the matter from here, Captain. Route further updates directly to my office. And alert the pilots of departure at 1500 hours. That is all)."

He hung up and turned to face the photographs on the wall behind his desk. One was an older man in a pre-WWII KGB Colonel's dress uniform, with the Soviet hammer and sickle flag in the background. The other man, younger, wore the WWII uniform of a Russian Army Captain.

"(Grandfather. Father. I remember well what you taught me. Now we will end this charade. He will no longer tarnish our family's honor)."

Mikhail Lipov would drive to Moscow himself. It was sooner than he'd planned, but neither his grandfather nor his father had lived long enough to see this day, and he wasn't going to waste a moment's time. He wanted that icon back on Russian soil. And he wanted to uncover whatever sham was being pulled off in Rasputin's name, to terminate it before Russia's *moujiki* had mustered around holy-water revival tents to challenge legitimate leadership.

He wanted the matter dead for personal reasons, too. A Lipov had accidentally helped create the tales—"a saint like Rasputin could not die by drowning," "Rasputin was protected by the Virgin Herself"—and a Lipov would be there to end them. He would recover the icon that his grandfather and father had not. The time was right. Russia was again a great country, long past the turmoil of Tsarism. This last, embarrassing chapter of Her history would be closed.

Of course, his professional duties would come first. 'The Weeping Virgin' would be found and returned to Russia. Only then, if he had time, would he attend to personal duties, like correcting the black mark against the Lipov name.

He gathered his things. Last was his grandfather's heirloom 9mm pistol from the gun cabinet. He loaded the magazine. How appropriate. It had shot the animal once, and it would do so again. He wondered what had triggered these amusing lies of Rasputin's return. Ha! It didn't really matter. The end had come.

The next morning

The Brodyaga home

Sunday, July 21
6:15 a.m.

The rolling hilltops were lit with sun by the time Nick's alarm went off. He rolled over and covered his head with his pillow. "*Ei Bogu*," he moaned.

Rasputin was waiting for him. "This will be a big day, my Nikisha," he said softly.

Nick liked hearing his name roll off Rasputin's tongue. "Nikisha. My Nikisha."

Nick bolted upright . . . he smelled smoke. Smoke? He dashed to his window for a look—and there, in the side pasture, two campfires burned amid five tents. One more was rising that very moment. Four men huddled with cigarettes and steaming cups, two others were piecing tent poles together.

"Ah, they arrive," Rasputin said.

"They? Who are they?"

"The *stranniki*. The wanderers. They come to pray to the Virgin, Nikisha, they know of Her icon. Come, let us speak with them. We will give thanks to the Virgin together. I may take over now, yes?"

Nick was impressed. Eighty years of condemnation as the mad, drunken monk who brought down Russia, and Rasputin still drew *stranniki* like this. And overnight, no less.

Nick nodded his approval and again, instantly, he was sitting in the passenger seat. It would take some getting used to.

Rasputin bounded out to the kitchen and through the side door toward the pasture. He strode toward the men with a confident gait. They were old and traveled; their clothes haggard, worn grays and browns. Wordlessly they watched him approach and perform the sign of the cross upon them as he arrived.

"(I am Father Grigory, of Pokrovskoe in the Tobolsk Province)," he announced.

The men stared warily. One, a grizzled old piece of chew-leather with a navy stocking cap and thick white stubble, spat tobacco juice. "(We were told we could camp here)," he said with a heavy Russian accent. "(We came to see Father Grigory)."

"(I am he. Are you one with the Virgin)?"

No one answered. Their skepticism was obvious.

"(I say a man's wisdom knows no age, my friends)," Rasputin said. "(Tell me, who among you has trekked the Siberian Plain to the Urals? Walked the birchwoods of Makari, tasted the olives of Greece? Have you danced on the banks of the Neva, or dined at the Tsar's table in Alexander Palace)?"

"(You enjoyed Greece, yes)?" asked another man, older than the rest. He wore a bandana around a mane of long white hair, his skin was engraved with age and sun, and he had no teeth. "(Tell me, did you worship with the holy monks of Athos)?"

"(With some of them, yes)," Rasputin responded, "(but with others, no. I saw the way they worshipped with each other, deep in the woods. They must have misunderstood their vows—they became one with each other, not one with the Lord)."

A couple of the men chuckled, but the old man dropped to his knees. "(My father told me of your visit to Athos, Father Grigory, just as you told the story to him. Forgive me. I did not mean to doubt who you are)."

Rasputin performed the sign of the cross upon him. "(I take no offense, little one. Come, we shall pray)." He motioned toward the house, and the old man rose. The others hesitated.

"(Come, my friends. You have nothing to lose in worship, do you? If you still doubt me after prayers, you may expose me as the schoolboy you see. Come, the *sabor* awaits us)."

They hesitated, but they followed. There was barely room in the *sabor* for the seven men, but Nick noticed it actually felt *right*. It seemed more intimate and reverent when so many packed in and knelt before the small icon, 'The Virgin of Kazan'.

Rasputin's voice dripped with excitement as it rose and fell with fellow *stranniki* for the first time in so long. He bowed his forehead especially low and long, and the other men followed his lead. Together they brought in the day, paying respect to the Virgin and the Lord as people of the earth.

Nick reveled in the prayers, his heart light and strong. He felt them join together on a shared, spiritual plane. They had found each other at that place, and they would find comfort and faith and strength always in this worship today. They were, indeed, one with the Virgin.

Every couple of hours, Rasputin led a fresh group of followers to the *sabor*. Whenever the kitchen door opened and the American boy appeared, those gathered outside bowed with respect and love. Clearly there was no longer a question of Rasputin's identity. Those who had already prayed with him made sure of that—they anxiously sought new arrivals to tell of their prayers with Father Grigory, worship that had led them into the arms of the Virgin Herself.

Nick felt Rasputin's pleasure with all of this, his enjoyment with leading the faithful as master of ceremonies. There would be little rest in the days to come, at least until, well . . . who knew? What *was* the mission he had returned to?

As dinnertime approached, one old and bent *strannik* did not return to the field after prayers. He shuffled sideways into the warm kitchen instead, where Irina and Olga sat peeling potatoes amid pots of boiling cabbage and spiced beans. They looked up as he approached, wary, their knives momentarily still. He bowed as low as his frame would allow.

"(Excuse my intrusion, my ladies)," he said, "(but I seek Irina Ivanevna Brodyaga)."

Neither answered, but Olga glanced at Irina. The stranger figured it out.

He was old, perhaps as old as Irina, his hair a mangy mess, his loose *caftan* and dirt-leather boots like those of the others outside. He bowed again, this time to Irina alone.

"(Indeed, the Weeping Virgin sings)," he declared in an old western Russian dialect, rising. "(She sings like a bird in a blossoming St. Petersburg cherry, delirious with the warmth of new life)."

Irina did not reply. She appeared nonchalant, but when she tried to place her knife on the counter, it fumbled to the floor. "(Who are you)?" she stammered. "(How do you know these words)?"

"(My name does not matter)," he replied humbly but without condescension. "(I am but a servant of the Virgin. The keepers of Her glorious icon have sent me)."

"(The keepers? The Union of Tears)?"

He nodded almost imperceptibly.

Irina looked at Olga and tried to tell her what was happening, but nothing came out. So instead, trembling as she was, Irina rose from her stool and hugged the man grandly. In time she cried, "(The Virgin sings . . . the Virgin sings!)"

Olga still looked lost. Finally Irina kissed her on the cheek. "(The Virgin shall come to us)!" she said, then she turned to the old man and asked, "(You *are* calling for the icon, 'The Weeping Virgin', yes)?"

He nodded, his eyes dancing with excitement. "(I shall notify the keepers immediately. They must know Father Grigory has returned. Praise the Virgin—She has fulfilled Her prophecy)!"

Boris coasted off the asphalt and down the overgrown driveway—but suddenly skidded to a stop. Tents were in the pasture beside the house. Smoke rose from campfires. Men milled about, and some had seen him. One turned toward him. "Brother! Have you heard?" he called, approaching.

Boris jumped from his bicycle and it crashed to the ground. Bible in hand he shouted, "Be gone! Be gone!", and he waved the bum back with wildly flailing arms.

The man slowed and stopped, but he would not 'be gone'. "Brother," he called out again, "Father Grigory has returned, as the Virgin said he would. Come, pray with us."

Boris would have none of it. He bolted toward the man, shouting and waving his arms. It was too much for the *strannik*. He turned and ran toward the pasture, Boris in hot pursuit. Now everyone had seen Boris; all eyes were on him. He waved his arms and shouted, ready to run them off his land. He rushed toward the men nearest the kitchen door, yet they had just come from prayers and were not so timid. They simply crossed themselves and blessed him.

Disgusted, Boris pushed his way through them and burst into the kitchen. Irina and Olga's excited conversation halted mid-syllable. "(Who are these dogs? Why do you feed them our scraps)?"

Irina halved a cabbage head, smacking the cutting board with her cleaver. "(Sit down, Boris Grigorevich)," she commanded sternly, and he did. "(These men are our guests. They are here to worship the Weeping Virgin of Kazan, for a miracle has occurred here)."

Boris glared.

"(Do you remember when I told you about Father Grigory and 'The Union of Tears')?"

"(I remember your fairy tale. Just as the cow jumped over the moon, the prince climbed up Goldilocks' hair and strangled her with it)."

She ignored him. "(Father Grigory has returned, just as the Virgin said he would. He has come *here*, but I know not why. These *stranniki* see it too. They are here to worship with him. You will accept this and leave them alone)."

Boris shook his head. "(So where is this Rasputin? This mad monk who bedded the Tsarina and her daughters)?"

Just then the door to the basement opened and Rasputin stepped into the kitchen.

"Nikolas!" Boris cried out. "What do you know about this?"

Rasputin ignored him, turning instead to open the door so the *stranniki* behind him could to return to the field. One by one, as they stepped out, the men crossed themselves before Rasputin, and he blessed them.

"What the hell . . . " Boris said loudly. "That boy's no preacher, you idiots!"

But no one paid attention. When the last man was outdoors, Rasputin softly closed the door on those who still waited.

He turned. "Boris Grigorevich, you are not one with the Virgin. Come, pray with me in the *sabor*. Find the peace within." Rasputin extended one upturned palm to Boris as the other motioned to the cellar door.

"Piss on you, boy. I don't know what kind of bullshit you're trying to pull here, but I ain't buying."

Nick felt ill. Here was Rasputin, well-intentioned as could be, trying to make sense to Grandpa. It wasn't going to work. "Rasputin, I need back in control. I need to talk to Grandpa."

And it happened just that fast. "Grandpa," Nick said, and the sudden change in his voice startled them all. His mannerisms changed, too—his thumbs dove, hooking into jeans pockets, his eyes lost their fire. "Grandpa, it's no joke. It happened in the river. Somehow Rasputin got inside of me, and he's still here. We can trade places . . . "

Boris spit on the floor. "Don't lie to me, boy. Tell your stories to somebody else. I've got no time for this crap." He stomped out of the kitchen, through the living room and out the front door, slamming it behind him.

From her second-floor bedroom window, Colleen Dillinger watched Boris pedal off. This was getting stranger by the minute—exactly *what* was going on? Tents and campfires, men in old, baggy clothes. She had to know more but Nick's phone was constantly busy. She went downstairs and out to the side yard.

Quietly, bent over low, she crept to the dense bushes that separated her yard from Nick's pasture. She listened carefully and peeked through the branches in the fading light. Russian voices filtered through—excited, fast talk, but she did not speak the language. This was one big family reunion, she thought, but why were there so many old men? Was there something else going on? Did it have to do with Nick saving the little girl?

She moved around and tried to get a better view, hoping to discover Nick in one of the nearby groups. She wanted to call out to him, she wanted to let him know she wasn't *that* mad at him. She just wanted to know what was going on. She could keep trying to call him on the phone, but then again, maybe he wouldn't talk to her at all after what she'd said the night before last. No, it was better to wait. She'd find Nick by himself *somewhere* and let him stammer out an apology for waking them all up—and then telling *her* to be quiet. Colleen sighed. No one had ever sung to her before. Not in her yard, in the middle of the night, standing beside a pickup truck. And certainly not in front of her whole family. Never. She tried again to catch sight of him through the bushes.

CHAPTER 15

Two days later

Tuesday, July 22

11:00 a.m.

Irina and her friends from church were back in time, their memories and excitement rising with the kitchen steam. They relived the old days in Moscow and St. Petersburg and Kiev while layering the next kulibyaki with fish and mushrooms and chicken, stuffing pelmini, stirring cabbage, tasting the cucumber soup. They'd glance outside and shake their heads in amazement—the thick-bearded men of Mother Russia were gathered directly outside, mugs in hand, arguing the ways of the Virgin.

Suddenly the door from the cellar door flew open with a bang. Rasputin stood in the doorway positively electrified, nostrils flared, shaking with excitement. "She arrives," was all he could say as he flew past and barreled out the kitchen door. The women crowded to the windows, watching him dart between various surprised *stranniki*, down the driveway and into the overgrowth toward the blacktop.

Rasputin looked east, then west. Chrome glinted in the distance. It drew closer—it was a Greyhound bus. Nick thought, 'false alarm', but then he heard the bus shift down a gear. It was slowing, and his heart skipped a beat. Wow, was he this excited, or was it all Rasputin?

"She comes to us now, little one," Rasputin said.

"On a bus?"

"The Lord might have chosen a mule, it matters not."

They stood beside their mailbox as the bus groaned and hssshhhhhed to a stop. The driver slid open his window. Nick saw that behind the sunglasses and the polished black brim, this driver was old, like the old relic from The Twilight Zone playing kick-the-can. "I'm looking for the Brodyaga farm. Can you help me?"

Rasputin nodded calmly, then he clasped his hands, stepped back and bowed deeply. Then he rose and performed the sign of the cross upon himself, then upon the driver, who sat frozen, staring.

"Ei Bogu" the driver said. "You are . . . "

Nick watched the tinted outlines of passengers crossing themselves as they realized the identity of their greeter. Chills raced up his spine. It was coming true—it was all coming true! 'The Weeping Virgin' Herself was on the bus!

Rasputin signaled for the bus to follow him. He led the way and the bus crept behind him, scraping and pushing, heaving and pitching through the potholes, beating back brush from one end to the other.

Finally Rasputin turned and ran ahead, whooping and yelling. He rounded the last corner of the driveway, into view of the faithful who milled about. "She is here! 'The Weeping Virgin' is here!" he cried.

He ran into the kitchen and landed near Irina, still at the windows with the other women. Short of breath, he commanded, "The Virgin, Irisha! Come, come at once!" taking her hand to make his point clear. She nodded, and Rasputin was careful not to pull her over in his rush out the door and down the steps.

The bus pushed through the last foliage endlessly, forever long, an anomaly of proportion as large as the Brodyaga house itself. All watched as it crept slowly, a kaleidoscope of sunlight reflecting from glass and silver and chrome.

Rasputin still held Irina's hand as he danced in place, until the bus finally stopped and the tall door swung out. He then leapt inside, bent down and kissed the driver, then turned to perform the sign of the cross upon the worshippers. Rasputin lead them in a quick prayer, offering his soul to the Virgin so She could again save him. "We are all one with the Virgin, my little ones," he said, beaming, when he'd finished. "And tell me, have you brought Her to us today?"

Behind the driver, an old man with heavy, squared-off black glasses above a full white beard cleared his throat. Rasputin sat down beside him. "You carry the Virgin with you, yes?"

The man did not answer, he just stared into Rasputin's eyes. Then, finally, he nodded. "(Your soul is alive, Father Grigory, I see it clearly. Come, we must leave the bus. Let us gather out-side)."

Rasputin looked confused, but he did not argue. He led them out. The last to leave was the old man, and when he was outside he pulled a small gadget like a garage door opener from his travel bag. He pushed the button and a small panel near the luggage bays slid open. There was a worn leather satchel inside, and the man motioned for Rasputin to retrieve it. He did, slowly and carefully. The satchel was not light, and it was not much larger than two feet square.

Rasputin carried the satchel to the bed of the old pickup truck and carefully set it down. Trembling, he untied the string and unfolded the top flap. Nick thought his heart would burst from adrenaline. There was a wooden box within, plain and unadorned. Rasputin pulled it from the bag and laid the box onto the leather. He lifted the lid and pulled aside a soft cloth.

Rasputin crossed himself the instant he saw Her. Nick couldn't believe it. Her image shone like angel wings, strong and comforting, Her dark, understanding eyes so lifelike that Nick felt he might offend Her by staring. She was performing the sign of the cross with Her right hand, a gentle gesture of blessing and goodness that cascaded warmth. And Her left arm cradled Her Child, a smiling, beautiful creature with the same magnetic eyes, no smaller than His Mother's.

Nick's heart raced. He looked closer. Tears had traveled Her cheeks. It could not be a hoax, not like this. He could almost picture Her sadness, Her grief at the death of a beloved, be it Her favorite Father Grigory or Mother Russia herself.

Rasputin finished his brief prayer and lifted the icon from its box. He held it to his chest, outward, and turned it toward Irina, who crossed herself silently, intently gazing.

And so Rasputin walked among the crowd, clutching the icon proudly, displaying Her image for all to see. The stranniki dropped to their knees and prayed, even the younger ones who grew up in a time when She didn't officially exist. None of that mattered now. She was real, here and now, a dream of faith, the reward for commitment in the face of the Godless ones.

Through binoculars Colleen watched Nick's slow walk around the grounds. "What is he doing?" she wondered aloud. It didn't seem like a family reunion anymore, unless his hundred or so uncles always dropped to their knees and prayed to Nick's paintings. And since when did he paint, anyway? She swung the binoculars toward the bus. What kind of family would come by bus? How many grandparents could anybody have? Or aunts and uncles? It was just too much. She couldn't wait any longer.

She slid into her Wranglers and pulled on her boots. Tight plaid shirt with ivory snaps, the top two open. She leaned over and combed out her hair, first all forward and then straight back. A fresh ponytail with a silver clasp that matched her saddle ornaments. A spray of "Cowgirl." And downstairs she went.

Colleen went the long way around, like a stranger. But when she got to the bus she stopped. It just didn't seem like Nick's house. There were so many people milling about, all of them in gray or dark clothes, seedy-looking and hairy, half-hidden in shifting smoke or behind makeshift horse-blanket tents. It gave her the creeps. What if . . . no, Nick's family had to be okay. He would have warned her.

Goosebumps popped up as she neared the house. She felt cold. A crowd of men were gathered at the kitchen door— waiting for what, food? Some of them had noticed her, and they were staring. Suddenly Colleen felt unsafe and unwelcome, out of place.

"Oh, Nicky," she thought loudly, her lips even moving, "Where are you . . . oh, Nicky where are you?" She put her hand over her eyes and surveyed every direction. No Nick.

But just then the kitchen door opened, and there he was. His mannerisms were majestic, slow and deliberate. He performed the sign of the cross on the men below, and they accepted it with bowed heads. Colleen's jaw dropped. She took an awkward step forward, then another, approaching the crowd.

She caught Rasputin's eye in an instant. Red hair in the sunlight, bright clothing, young in years.

"Ei Bogu!" yelped Nick, "Quick, switch me, it's Colleen!"

"Ah, your little one? She wishes to be the first to pray with 'The Weeping Virgin' in your sabor!" he laughed as they traded places.

Nick barely heard him. "Nope, that'll have to wait," he replied, jumping off the landing and leaving the stranniki behind, bowed heads and all. He hustled to Colleen and turned her around, away from the crowd.

"Nicky . . . what is this? It looked like you were preaching to those men! But you haven't been to church in, how long? . . . I mean . . . I just don't . . . "

"I know it looks funny, Colleen, and I want to tell you what's happening, but I'm kind of, uh . . . " He glanced back and saw the stranniki watching him. "Let's get away from all this. Down to the river, c'mon."

She nodded, her face red with sun and bewilderment. Nick took her hand and led her through the pasture toward the river, through the barbed wire to the picnic ledge. They sat on the bench. Nick didn't know where to begin.

"Okay, so what's up? What's with all the people at your house . . . what exactly is up with you?"

She didn't waste much time on small talk, and Nick felt his face redden. "Oh, God, it's such a long story. You're not going to believe any of it."

"I'll decide that for myself, Nicky! You've been so weird! What was that song you were singing the other night?"

"What . . . oh, that one song?"

Rasputin started singing it to Nick, very softly, "Blessed are those who cross themselves . . . "

"Um . . . I'm not sure, Colleen. I guess it just came out of nowhere."

"You freaked out my dad. He almost shot you."

"I wish it had never happened." Nick wanted to be anywhere else but here. How could he tell her what was going on? He didn't even know himself.

"He's worried about all the old men camped out in your pasture, too. Are they mental? Homeless? How come they all speak Russian? Dad thinks they're gonna take one of our cows and barbeque it or something, I mean, you know how my dad is. Are these people safe, Nicky? Who are they?"

Nick tried to explain, "Well, they're all, like, priests and stuff. You know, like missionaries? Russian missionaries."

Colleen shook her head but said, "Okay . . . "

It was so quiet they could hear a mom scolding her child in the parking lot at the State Park.

"Nick, what are you not telling me? What's with the preaching and religion and stuff? You're not telling me half of what's going on. I'm not stupid, you know."

"God no, Colleen, I don't think you're stupid. I'm just can't . . . I mean, I'm not trying to hide stuff from you. It's just that there's something really big going on, and it's really weird, like fucking unbelievable."

"Unbelievable? Nick, you saved a girl's life on Friday, you're drunk and singing to me Saturday morning, then you're preaching to a bunch of Russians on Tuesday. And you've never cussed like this, either! It's all unbelievable, I'd say."

Her eyes sure were lit up. She wasn't pissed, but she wasn't happy, either. "Colleen, um, somebody's come to visit. Me. He's come to visit me."

"So . . . "

"Well, he's a preacher, or I mean a priest, kinda. And a healer. And see, he's been, uh, kind of out of sight for a lot of years? The Russians all want to pray with him and the Virgin."

"The virgin?" Her eyebrow cocked funny, "what virgin?"

"No, not a virgin," Nick said, "the church Virgin, the Virgin, the Holy Mother, you know? It's an icon of Her, the Virgin of Kazan, the real one from Russia. They say it's a miracle-working icon, that it actually cried in the Tsar's palace in Russia way back when."

"Cried? The painting cried? I think you're getting heatstroke."

Nick shook his head. Great.

Rasputin quietly told him, "She must pray with us, little one. She must come to learn the ways of the Virgin."

"Look," Nick said, "I'm not crazy, and I told you this is really unbelievable. The icon's here now. It's for real. Those hundred people camped in my yard are praying to it, they're members of 'The Union of Tears'. The priest has taken the icon down to Bushka's sabor, her shrine in the cellar, and now everyone's expecting some kind of miracle. They don't know what the miracle's going to be, or when it will happen or anything else. They just know that this is what the Virgin predicted eighty years ago when the Communists took over. The icon and the priest would reappear to save Russia."

"So the priest is like, what, 150 years old? And he runs the Union?"

"No. They're the other Russians, the ones who hid the icon all these years."

"Hid it from who?"

"I don't know. The Communists, I guess."

She was quiet a moment. "You know, if this is all true, then that icon sounds pretty important—is it national treasure or something? Are the Union guys grave robbers? Did they break into old crypts and take gold, too? Maybe there's a lot you don't know, Nicky. They shouldn't have taken stuff from anybody, especially from churches."

Nick sighed. "Well, that's their own deal. The Union's had the icon for a long time. In fact, Bushka told me all about this stuff when I was a kid. All the Russians know these legends. Bushka just didn't know that all this would all happen to us, at our house. That's what's so weird."

"So where's the old priest? Who is he?"

"Father Grigory Efimovich Rasputin, little one," said Rasputin to Nick.

"Rasputin, little one," said Nick absentmindedly, "Crap, I mean . . . "

"Little one?" she snorted, giggling. "Rasputin . . . I remember him from history class. They couldn't kill him, I think the story went."

"Yeah, but it's no story. The Virgin saved him and now She's brought him back. That's who has come to visit, Colleen. Rasputin."

"Rasputin? The Rasputin? He's dead, Nicky! They did kill him . . . don't you know that?"

Nick shook his head and stared at his boots. "I know, Colleen." Quietly he added, "Look, this is really hard. I told you you wouldn't believe it."

Colleen sighed. She took his hand. "I don't know what to believe, Nicky . . . only that you wouldn't lie to me, so you must be telling the truth. But maybe there's more going on than what you know about? Can we believe that, too?

"How about this . . . can I meet him? Rasputin? Maybe he could tell me why you were over at my house the other night."

"Yes, my little one!" Rasputin said in Nick's head, but Nick didn't repeat it this time. He blushed and cleared his throat.

"You know, Nicky, you don't always have to sit so far away," she said, scooting closer. "I really don't doubt what you're saying, really. But you're right . . . it's so hard to believe. I just want to know if someone's messing with you, okay?"

Nick looked over, she was looking him in the eye. She really meant what she said. He wanted her so bad.

Rasputin jumped in, "Go ahead, little one, kiss her—she wants you to!"

Nick didn't have to think about it. He leaned over to kiss her cheek but she turned and met him head-on. Her lips were moist and soft and supple and her face was warm and all was perfect on this sunny afternoon at the river.

They parted, each a bit breathless. Then Colleen leaned over and kissed him again, longer, deeper.

"She wants you, little one!" Rasputin yelled to him. "Ei Bogu! Give her your manhood, be the man she needs!"

Nick was lost in sensory overload. Colleen so soft, kissing him for what seemed an eternity. Rasputin so excited, shouting, "She must sin, she feels the need! Allow her to sin so she may confess to the Virgin!"

It was all good. Nick reached out. He wanted Colleen now. He did want to give her his manhood. His hand landed on her straining shirt, on a flattened breast beneath. He tried to cup his hand, to pull in his thumb and feel for the prize in the center, but Colleen suddenly leaned back, eyes wide open, her right hand flying from nowhere and landing with a smack! on his cheek.

"Nick Brody!" she yelled. "I am not here for that! God, is that what you think? One day you're drunk, then you're feeling me up . . . " She struggled up to her feet and brushed herself off. "I think I'll just go home now, Nicky. Thank you very much." She turned and stomped off, following the canyon over to her place.

Rasputin broke into laughter. "Ah, she likes you, little one. She shall be yours as you like."

But Nick was furious. "Bullshit! She's not mine, all you did was make me piss her off. Nice job!" His cheek still stung, and he rubbed it with the back of his hand.

"Ah, Nick Ivanovich, you have much to learn. Think for a moment—if you were not hers already, would she have given you the chance to hold her? Certainly not. She had to be sure you want her, and you showed her you do. Ha—that is good. Now she knows you are a man. Do you see all of this now? She is a lady, little one, and ladies act in such ways. You must learn to recognize what they say between their words."

"What, and get slapped all the time? No thanks. I'll just do things my way, all right?"

"She excites you, little one, and she knows it. So yes, do things your own way. Just give her the chance to catch you when she tries."

"What? When she tries to catch me?"

Rasputin laughed. He said no more.

Nick shook his head, but he started grinning. Was Rasputin right? Colleen liked him that much? He'd dreamed about her. Wow.

That night the prayers felt great. Nick was used to Rasputin's ways by now, so he asked the Virgin for things on his own . . . in fact, for anything he could think of—to help him figure out Colleen, to help him deal with Bushka and Grandpa, to help him discover his life's path.

In turn, he pledged his faith. It was so easy. Rasputin's prayers were live and electric, as if he had his own connection to the Holy Spirit. It was never like this in church, and Nick had had plenty of time to think about it—he really enjoyed praying now. Maybe it was the candlelit sabor, maybe it was the Virgin's presence, maybe it was the unshakable faith of the stranniki, so devout and patient, so knowledgeable in their prayers.

They came up the stairs once again. Six men trailed them. "Please, let's finish in the morning. I'm beat," Nick told Rasputin, but it did little good. Rasputin showed the men to the door, and on the landing, in the fading light, he performed the sign of the cross on them, one by one, as they passed. Now just five stranniki waited. Rasputin bade them to follow, and he led them down the creaky steps to the sabor.

"This shall be it for tonight, Nick Ivanovich," Rasputin said quietly so the men would not hear.

As they entered the sabor, the last believer pulled back her hood and unleashed a shoulder-length blonde mane. Her wide brown eyes were possibly the prettiest that Nick had ever seen. He couldn't help but stare. They all did, frozen in place.

"(Am I not welcome to worship the Virgin)?" the thirtyish woman asked in perfect Russian.

"(We are all one with the Virgin, little one)," replied Rasputin. "(Please, worship Her with us)."

And she did. She bowed as low as any of them, and her forehead was reddened as proof. But Nick could feel Rasputin's distraction with her. His concentration wasn't near as strong, and he raced through prayers he had dwelled upon earlier.

Then they were finished. The woman tailed behind as Rasputin led them all back upstairs, and as he performed the sign of the cross upon her she asked quietly, "I have many questions for you, Father Grigory. May we talk?"

Rasputin nodded and glanced back across the kitchen. The living room lights and the television were on. He motioned to a chair at the kitchen table. "Come in, little one. I always have time to speak of the Virgin."

Nick objected, "Wait a minute . . . what are you doing, Grisha?"

"Please, rest a moment," Rasputin told the woman. "We shall share wine, but you will pardon me while I attend to business first?"

She smiled and sat as Rasputin left for the bathroom.

"Now wait a minute," Nick said once the door was closed, "I don't want to get a drunk on tonight. I've had enough."

"Then we shall not, Nick Ivanovich. I shall only wet my lips as I console this young woman."

"Console her? Is that what you call it?"

"Nick Ivanovich, she wants to speak of the Virgin. I cannot refuse such a request."

"Especially not when she looks like that, right?"

Rasputin paused. "Her appearance matters not. She has a soul, and she must come to know the Virgin. That is all."

Nick held his tongue. No sense arguing, they were in the bathroom, after all. "All right, but not much wine. I don't want to go through a hangover again."

They left the bathroom and Rasputin went to say goodnight to Irina. She snored lightly in the living room recliner. He whispered, "My Irisha," and she woke. "Irisha, you must retire. Please, now, off to bed with you."

"(No, Grisha)," she answered, "(tonight I sleep in the sabor. The Virgin is here now. I will protect Her as the Union has all these years. I thought you might join me there when you are ready)."

"(Of course, my Irisha)."

"(Please, then, help me set up the beds. Everything is already downstairs)."

Rasputin nodded. He walked Irina through the kitchen, past the young woman at the table. If Irina noticed her, she did not mention it. Rasputin helped her down the cellar stairs.

Irina's camping blankets and foam pads were stowed on the shelves above the boxes of Madeira. Combined with the cots that leaned in the corner, these beds would be sufficient. Rasputin carried everything into the sabor and set them up the cots against the wall opposite the Virgin.

As Rasputin placed the pillows, Irina slipped back out to the cellar, to a hidden nook, and brought out a dusty shotgun. She cracked it open. It was loaded.

Rasputin gasped. He strode over and put his hand on the barrel. "(Goodness, Irisha, you'll not need that here)."

But Nick saw the way Bushka glared at Rasputin—at him, as it were, for that was probably who she saw there at that moment. Nick knew there would be no discussion about the shotgun. "Give it up. She's not going to budge," he told Rasputin.

Rasputin backed off with little argument. Obviously, he knew Irisha, too, Nick realized. Or else—of course, that's what it was—Rasputin's guest was upstairs, waiting.

Rasputin escorted Bushka back into the sabor and helped her into bed. Bushka wore long flannel pajamas, and long underwear below those. She handed Rasputin the shotgun and he stood it in the corner near the door, not two feet from her head. Then he kissed her gently on the cheek. "Good night, my Irisha," he said, and her eyes were already closed. Gently he shut the door behind them.

"Now, in the name of the Virgin . . . " Rasputin whispered, climbing the stairs two-at-a-time.

"The Virgin, huh? Well, remember, She loves us sober, too."

"Yes, Nick Ivanovich. Too much wine does no man well."

In the kitchen their guest had removed her oversized caftan and brushed her hair. It positively shone, a golden waterfall cascading onto her white, sleeveless turtleneck. She sat sideways to the table, legs crossed, half a cigarette dangling from her bright red fingertips.

Rasputin rushed to her side and took her other hand in his. Nick just stared.

"Tell me of your needs, little one. Are you one with the Virgin?" Rasputin asked.

She blew a puff of smoke. "I don't have much to do with virgins, actually. But I've heard of you—you're supposed to be Rasputin, right? My father told me stories when I was a kid, and I've read the books. When I heard he was coming to see you, I jumped on the bus with him. I hope you don't mind."

"The Virgin welcomes all, little one. Call me Father Grigory," Rasputin smiled hungrily.

She ground her cigarette onto a plate. Then her eyes met his. "I've heard of your 'powers', Father Grigory. You could heal the sick, and you bedded half of Russia."

Rasputin smiled. "It was all in the name of the Virgin, little one. Long ago, She came to me in a field. She passed unto me the need to sin, yes, but also the need to seek Her forgiveness. It is Her way . . . She asks that as we enjoy our weaknesses, we also seek redemption. For if we do not know our weaknesses, how can we become stronger?"

"Oh? And what are your weaknesses, Father Grigory?"

"My weaknesses matter not. It is you who has come to seek forgiveness in the eyes of the Virgin."

She had no reply.

"Is it not true?" Rasputin nodded knowingly. "Seek forgiveness from the Virgin, little one. You shall be freed from your sins."

She could not quit looking at him. "Yes, Father Grigory, I seek Her forgiveness. I think She knows I've racked up enough sins over the years . . . "

"Come now, little one. Tell me, what do they call you?"

"I am Roxanne."

"Come then, Roxanne, we shall pray." He took her hand and she stood willingly. He led her to Nick's room and closed the door behind them. He stood there, taking her in. "Now, come to me," he ordered.

"Oh? And why would I?"

"It is the way, little one. We shall enjoy our physical selves, we shall awaken our senses. Our passion shall move us to new heights." He flipped off the light and they floated together in the light of the screensaver on the computer. He ran his hands down her back and rested them on the swell of her hips. "And we shall be forgiven when the sun rises again." He looked up, into her eyes.

An alarm went off in Nick's head. "Funny, I don't remember praying like this before," he said to Rasputin.

Rasputin answered aloud, "The Virgin's ways know no bounds, little one. You shall see. You, too, shall become one with Her."

Nick paused. This was no snow job—Rasputin truly believed in what he was saying. And his prayers were so devout, the Virgin must know and approve. It had to be true.

CHAPTER 16

Half-an-hour later

Tuesday, July 22

11:35 p.m.

The campfires were crowded with singing, drinking Russians, but all was quiet near the house when a man in black slipped inside the kitchen door. Only his salt-and-pepper beard stood out beneath the black cap pulled down to his eyes.

He opened the only door in the kitchen—it was a stairwell to the root cellar, typical of *moujiki* homes and exactly as he'd calculated. He lit the way with a small flashlight. His feet hugged the walls, but the old steps still creaked. He leapt nimbly past the last few and landed catlike on the throw rug below.

There was the heavy door to the *sabor*. A gentle glow filled the crack beneath it. He turned off his flashlight, tucked it into his waistband and pushed on the door. It opened a crack. He could see the icon immediately—it was hard to miss, centered on the wall and trimmed with ribbons. He pushed the door open further, wide enough to squeeze in, and crept inside.

"(Don't move)," hissed Irina. She stood in the corner, mostly hidden by the door. Her shotgun was leveled at him.

But he took a chance anyway, diving to the floor and rolling once, springing to his feet beside 'The Weeping Virgin'.

He stood there, sideways against the wall, and afforded Irina just a slight glance. His fingers were working around the icon, feeling its weight and how it hung. "(Shoot me if you must, babushka. You will destroy Her icon as well. Are you willing to pay the price)?"

"(You speak Russian, yet you would steal our people's icon. Come away from it now.)"

Suddenly he wretched it off the wall and turned, holding the 500-year-old bodyshield to his chest.

"(You cannot shoot me, old one, without destroying Her icon. Please put down your weapon. No harm will come to you)."

Irina glowered; she did not lower the shotgun. "(Who are you? What do you want with Her)?"

"(I work for the Motherland, old one. Come now, let us live to talk about this day . . .)." He shifted behind the icon, freeing one hand to reach for his silenced pistol. It fat barrel emerged below the icon, trained on Bushka.

She paid little attention, though. "(You will not leave with Her, *pivo*)."

"(And you will not stop me, old one. Come to your senses before it is too late.)"

Without warning, he fired. The bullet clanged off the shotgun and landed beneath her breastbone with a red dot on her pajamas. Irina was stood up straight against the wall by the impact. She looked down toward the wound, eyes wide open, and dropped the shotgun with a clatter. It did not fire. Her hands rose to her belly; she attempted to cross herself before crumpling to the prayer rug.

Quickly the intruder slid the icon under one arm and stepped past her. Pistol leading the way, he dashed up the stairs to the kitchen door. He glanced outside—all was clear—but the bright moon was certainly not his ally. He turned so the icon would be as concealed as possible and slipped outside, hugging the house until he could do so no longer. Then he turned and strode across the bright pea gravel, covering ground quickly until he disappeared into the shadows of overgrowth.

"All right, Nicky . . . where are you . . . " Colleen swung her binoculars from fire to fire, looking for the reveler who didn't fit in with the rest. He *had* to be drinking with them. Good god, what else would make him start acting so . . . weird? She remembered the real Nicky, the cute guy who blushed like a tomato and did anything he could to avoid the subject—any subject, anything that really meant anything.

But surely he wouldn't be drinking himself stupid. He *really* wanted to different than his grandpa, at least that's what he claimed. So hopefully this was just a phase, he was just having fun with all the old men, whoever they were. Still, she'd never have guessed he'd be drinking with them. She hated to think of it . . . but it sure would explain some things. She grinned. He was *such* a boy, *so* touchy-feely, extra-heavy on the feely. It made her giggle. "Oh Nicky-boy, where are you? . . . "

A flash of moonlight off the kitchen door caught her eye. She focused on it. "Hello, you're not Nicky . . . " She noticed the big, squarish item he was half-hiding, but she also saw the silhouette of the pistol in his hand. "My God . . . Nicky!"

Colleen flew down the stairs, out the door and across the sideyard. The fence hardly slowed her. "Nicky! Nicky!" she cried, flying past the tents. She glanced at the fires but still didn't see him, and her voice didn't rise above the drunken din.

She ran toward the house, then slowed, torn. Follow the burglar, or go inside and look for Nicky? She wanted to know that he was all right . . . but what if he wasn't there? The famous painting would be long gone. Her heart was pounding hard. The burglar was getting away, he was already out of sight. Nick was probably over by the fires, but he could be inside, bleeding . . . or worse.

Suddenly she jumped—Boris was coasting in from the road, through the shadows, unaware of whom he'd just passed.

"Help, Mr. Brodyaga!" she cried, "that man! He's got a gun and I think he's got your painting! Come on, we've got to follow him *now*!"

Boris braked and stopped. He stood there, flat-footed and staring, glassy-eyed beneath his floppy hat. "Well," he slurred, "what's in it for me, little lady?"

She heard a car engine start up on the other side of the overgrowth.

"Dear God . . . Boris, wake up! That guy was in your house . . . I think he took your vodka, too!"

"In my house?" He turned half-around, thinking about the man he'd just passed. "My vodka? . . . " He turned back and stared at her blankly.

"Your pickup truck . . . you can drive, can't you?"   Boris nodded.

"Then come on! He's going to get away!"

Boris threw his bike aside and met Colleen at the truck. He banged on the driver door and it popped open. Colleen jumped in through his door and slid over, way over. Boris followed.

"Come on . . . " Colleen sighed. Why did it have to be Boris she'd found? She wished it was Nicky instead; she wished she wasn't leaving him behind. She didn't want to think about whether the thief had had to shoot his way out.

Boris hit the gas and the headlights. The tires spun in the gravel.

"No lights!" Colleen ordered. "We won't be able to keep up if he thinks someone is chasing him."

Boris grunted.

They tore out the driveway and paused at the blacktop. To the right, red taillights faded into the distance, then disappeared below a rise in the road.

"There! Go!" she yelled.

Boris turned the truck to the right and gave it all she had. The road was bright enough in the moonlight, all they had to do was catch up enough to keep him in sight.

Colleen sat on the edge of the plastic seat cover, hands on the hard metal dash, carefully scanning the road and every driveway they passed. "Go . . . go . . . " she said softly, "come on . . . "

"I know the Virgin's ways know no bounds, Father . . . and I don't, either," Roxanne panted. "But I think I'd rather become one with *you*!" Her voice was deep, that of a wanton gypsy, with a delicious upper-crust Boris-and-Natasha Moscow accent. She smiled as Rasputin massaged her breasts through her shirt.

This was *not* what Nick expected. This time he didn't feel comfortable watching and participating. This was *nothing* like the joy he felt in the *sabor*. "You're not really going to pray with her at all, are you?"

Rasputin dropped his hands. "I work in the name of the Virgin, little one. She wants to forgive our sins."

"Oh, I know," said Roxanne. "And a few more here and there, what's the difference."

"What bullshit!" said Nick. "You're creating sins for the Virgin to forgive? There's no way She thinks like that."

"I pray for our sins, little one," Rasputin said, "I pray to the Virgin as I know best."

"No virgins here, Father G," Roxanne sat on the bed and kicked off her boots. She lay in the shadows, impossibly long and lean on Nick's bed.

"Oh shit . . . " Nick was tongue-tied.

Rasputin knelt on the bed, straddling her knees. She sat up, and he helped her pull off her turtleneck. Big, full breasts, bra working overtime, small tummy.

Nick stared. This just didn't seem . . .

Rasputin massaged her breasts again, through her bra, then he pushed it up and over. She reached back, arching, and unsnapped it, and Rasputin gladly removed it before resuming his mission.

"Oh man," Nick moaned.

Rasputin paused to straighten himself in his trousers. Roxanne smiled, lifting her arms and combing her hair back with her fingers.

Nick blurted, "Look, this isn't what you said. I don't want to do this. We don't even have condoms."

Rasputin choked on his breath, muttering, " . . . don't think you want to do this?"

"Don't think I want to do this?" Roxanne asked.

"No . . . I'm not gonna do it!" Nick shouted. "You're not gonna pray, you just wanna get laid, and christ, she's old enough to be my mother. Do you give the slightest crap that *I'm* here, too?"

"I am going to pray, little one. You shall see."

"Yes, I'd *like* to see," she moaned, tossing her head as he pinched her nipples.

"No, I don't think so," Nick said. "What if Bushka comes up? What would you tell her, 'oh, I'm teaching Nick how to have sex?'"

"She sleeps, little one," said Rasputin.

"No, she does not sleep, she needs more of you . . . " Roxanne cooed, again laying back flat.

"Bullshit, Grisha. Look, you were right. I want Colleen, and I hope she wants me. But she's so pissed off at me right now, or well, at *you*, that maybe that'll never happen now. Does that matter to you in the slightest? I mean, what if Colleen finds out about this? She's already gonna hear about Leeza, I *know* that's gonna happen . . . so how many girls are you going to make me apologize for? You're going to ruin my life. You're gonna go back to wherever you came from and leave me to clean up all your bullshit. No way."

"Yet the Virgin frowns when we ignore those who need us most, little one." Rasputin unsnapped her jeans. Her zipper lay flat and tempting, a delicate chain-mail barricade bending up and over her curve.

"So don't ignore me, then, Father G-spot."

Rasputin began to unzip it. The metal links parted. He brushed her contours with the back of his hand.

"I said no!" Nick yelled, "I mean it! I want control, now!" And they switched. Nick quickly hopped off the bed and hit the lights.

Roxanne covered her eyes with her hands. "God, we could have done without that . . . "

But Rasputin gasped. There, between those magnificent breasts, was a finely-detailed tattoo. "*Ei Bogu*! The Maltese Cross! She is one with the devil!" he cried out. "She works with Purishkevich and the evil ones!"

"Purishkevich . . .? " Nick repeated, staring at her tattoo.

At the sound of that name, and at the squeakier voice that delivered it, Roxanne bolted upright. The color had drained from her face. "What did you say?"

"Your Maltese Cross . . . " Nick stammered, "Purishkevich?"

"My God, how do you know that name? And why do you sound so different?" She reached for her turtleneck and held it to her chest, belatedly trying to hide the evidence.

Rasputin told Nick, "One of the evil ones, Lipov, wore such a cross on his chest. I saw it there, the night he and the others sent me into the river."

Nick looked Roxanne straight in the eye. "Rasputin says one of the men who killed him, Lipov, had a tattoo like yours."

Her eyes were wide, her mouth fell open. She had absolutely no answer. She reached for her bra and as she put it on, she asked nervously, in her own, true voice, "So it's true? I mean, Rasputin really *has* returned? How else could you have known . . . " She pulled on her shirt.

"Look," Nick said, "who are you? What are you doing here?"

She moved and sat on the edge of the bed. "Well, first of all, we're on the same side. Don't worry. Here, sit, we've got to talk." She patted the comforter beside her.

Nick stood where he was.

"All right, be that way. You still have to know."

"Know what? That you're a spy, is that it? Is Roxanne even your real name?"

She shook her head. "You Americans, you're all the same— we're all spies, right? My real name is Sonia. Sonia Mikhailevna Lipov."

Rasputin gasped. "As I told you, Nick Ivanovich . . . "

"My great-grandfather was Igor Igorevich Lipov. Yes, *that* Lipov. He helped kill Rasputin—he really *has* returned, hasn't he? Of course he has, you've already proven it to me."

"Proven it? How?"

"Never mind. Look, we don't have time—things are already in motion, and the icon's in danger."

"What?"

"Listen to me . . . the icon's going to be stolen *tonight*."

"Who's gonna steal it? And why should I trust *you*? You were probably going to steal it yourself."

"We must trust her, Nick Ivanovich," Rasputin said. "She tells the truth; the icon must be in danger. *Ei Bogu*— Irisha!"

Nick bolted from the room and flew to the cellar, Sonia close behind. An strong odor hung in the air, stale and burnt. Nick pushed open the door. Her blood had run unchecked, pooling beside her, yet Irina was still able to turn her head toward them.

"Bushka!" Nick cried. He knelt beside her, caressing her face and hair in his hands. "Oh, Bushka, what have they done?" Tears rolled down his cheeks.

"Nick, I'm so sorry . . . " Sonia said.

Bushka was trying to speak. Nick put his ear to her lips. "(Save the Virgin, don't let him hurt Her.)"

"(I won't, Bushka. Come on, let's get you up on the cot)." He started to move her, but she cringed with pain. Instead, he rolled her onto her back and put a pillow under her head, and he laid a blanket out over her. The icon—he looked up and, indeed, there was a hole in the festive bunting where She'd hung.

"Call 9-1-1!" Nick said to Sonia, who dashed off.

Suddenly, louder and more clearly, Irina said, "(Save the icon, Nikisha, She must be saved)!"

"(No, Bushka, I can't just leave you here) . . . " He could hear Sonia upstairs telling how there'd been a shooting in the basement at the Brodyaga house, to send an ambulance.

Rasputin said, "Come, Nick Ivanovich, Irisha is right. We must save the icon for the Motherland."

Nick fought the idea. "No, we wait for help right here, dammit."

Sonia came back downstairs and knelt beside Nick. "They're sending someone, Nick, but I can't stay. I've *got* to get out of here."

Nick didn't answer. He stroked Bushka's scalp, rearranging her hair on a head that once seemed so hard and unforgiving, but that now felt so fragile and thin, like an onion-papered egg.

"Nick," Sonia said, putting her hand on his shoulder, "I have to leave, I can't be caught here without papers. I'm going after the icon and I could use your help. Please, let's go!"

Bushka swore under her breath, just loud enough to catch Nick's attention. She was mad, and he knew it. Leaking blood all over the place, and now she was pissed off . . . God, she never made things easy.

"She will survive, Nick Ivanovich," said Rasputin. "She has made it so far, and help is nearly here. Come, let us save the Virgin's icon for the Motherland. Let us catch the swine that shot Irisha as well."

Bushka nodded firmly, her eyes telling Nick there'd be nothing to discuss if she were her normal self.

Sonia said, "I can drive us, Nick. I know where my father was going with the icon."

"Your father? Your fucking father shot Bushka?"

She wasn't shaken. "I'm sorry, Nick, but he'll shoot us, too, if he finds out I've betrayed him. Look—stay here if you have to, but I'm gone." She stood. "Last chance . . . "

Bushka was practically showing him the door with her eyes. "Christ. I can't believe I'm doing this," Nick muttered, shaking his head. Bushka relaxed and closed her eyes. She was smiling when Nick kissed her forehead and left the room.

Sonia took his hand and pulled him up the stairs and out to the driveway. She led him to where the visitors' cars were parked, near the barn. She settled on a full-size sedan, and she had it running in no time.

"Just a little trick they teach you in Russian spy school," she admitted. "Get in."

Nick sat in the passenger seat, tightly against the door. He stared into the night as Sonia crept carefully, without dust or headlights, out to the road. She turned right, toward the twisting canyonlands, riverbanks and orchards. Past the first big bend she flipped on the headlights.

"He's headed about 20 miles off, Nick, past Hagerman to a cabin on the river. You know where I'm talking about?"

Nick nodded. He wished he'd grabbed his gun before they'd left. He'd like to blast the son-of-a-bitch right between the eyes. It'd serve him right for shooting a harmless old lady like Bushka.

"So what's it like, Nick, you know, with Rasputin? Is he like a ghost, or . . . ?" She sounded like a star-struck teenager.

Nick shook his head. "I'd trade all of this in a minute for things to be back to normal."

Sonia thought for a moment. "Give it time, Nick. It's not your fault—it's just something that's meant to be."

"The path of courage is not for the weak, my little one," said Rasputin.

Nick finally turned and looked at Sonia. "Why did you say you know it's true? That Rasputin really *has* returned? What else do you know about Rasputin and all of this?"

Sonia glanced over uneasily and shook her head. "It's the Maltese Cross, Nick. There's a lot more to it . . .

"Rasputin was right about my tattoo. It's the same one my great-grandfather had until 1918—when the Communists took over, he had it turned into an ugly birthmark. All the old Pages had them covered up somehow. It was a matter of survival. No one wanted to be known as having served the Tsar."

"The Pages?" Nick asked, "Wait a minute—the guys who killed Rasputin worked for the Tsar? I thought the Pages were the good guys."

Rasputin was adamant, "Those dogs did *not* work in the name of Batuishka, Nick Ivanovich. They worked in the name of Satan."

Sonia shook her head. "No, but they *did* start out that way. The Maltese Cross was the emblem of The Corps of Pages, a school in St. Petersburg. They were supposed to be the best of the best, you know—breeding, pedigree, "Friendship Unto Death" . . . "Long Live the Tsar," all that crap. The Tsar used them in his palaces as servants, and he made them officers in the army after they graduated. And nobody messed with them— fighting one meant fighting them all.

"But after the revolution, they denounced their school and their training, and the Corps of Pages disappeared. And that would have been the end of it if one old-timer hadn't held out— an odd fellow named Purishkevich."

"Purishkevich! *Pivo!*" Rasputin shouted, rattling Nick's eardrums.

"I think Rasputin remembers him," Nick said.

"Vladimir Mitrofanovich Purishkevich," Sonia said. "He really *was* devoted; he *did* try to help the Tsar and his family escape from Ekatarinaburg. But he failed, and after they were killed, he was sent to White Russia. Even *then*, in exile, he published a newspaper that supported Tsarism, and *that* almost got him killed. So he went underground, and eventually he died of typhoid. *But*—in the meantime, he'd raised his son under the teachings of the Corps of Pages, and the two of them created 'The Order of the Maltese Cross', to keep the traditions alive.

"Purishkevich knew no traditions," said Rasputin.

"So that was years ago, okay? . . . and then fate stepped in," Sonia said. "I met Vlady Purishkevich when I studied at Moscow University fifteen years ago. Full name: Vladimir Mitrofanovich Purishkevich, great-grandson of the original. We couldn't believe we'd found each other, knowing our histories as we did."

Rasputin scoffed, "Old Purishkevich could not have found his ass with both hands." Nick shook his head at the intrusion.

"In time we became close and he explained the Maltese Cross on his chest. That's how I came to learn about the Order. His family *still* believes in Tsarism, and they kept the Order going during all those years of Communism.

She laughed affectionately, "I learned so much from their stories. I prayed and wept with them for our lost Russia. And it wasn't lost on me that some of *my* family had worn the Maltese Cross, too. So eventually, I joined them. I became a member of the Order, and they trusted me, even knowing who my father was. For a long time, Vlady and the Order were my *real* family."

"*Were*?" Nick asked.

"Well, it didn't work, Vlady and me. He wanted a *matushka* at home in kitchen, mending his socks, while he worked in the name of Russia." She glanced over at Nick. "So that was that. Vlady and I went our separate ways. I changed my studies to the law, and after university, my father brought me into the Russian Security Agency, the new KGB. I covered my tattoo with makeup when necessary—in a way, just like what my great-grandfather had done."

"Why didn't you just have it removed?"

Sonia looked at him. "I dumped Vlady, Nick, but not the Order of the Maltese Cross. That's *still* who I am. There are others, now, many others, who are my family in the Order."

"But if you're in the police now..?"

"My pledge to the Order is that I will fight for the Motherland, Nick, and I do, from the inside, from the RSA. But I'm just one person. It'll take many of us to inspire the Russian people again, especially the millions of *moujiki*, so we can help ourselves and our country. We *have* to show them that together, we really *can* fix what's wrong. But it's going to be a hard fucking job—we've been mistreated and lied to for so long that no one believes anything, especially that anything could ever gets better."

Her frustration was clear. Her fingers gripped the steering wheel tightly, and Nick didn't know what to say. He felt small. This was life in the *real* world, problems that made his little tiffs with Bushka and Grandpa seem like child's play.

She looked over at him. "Anyway, when my father told me he was leaving to investigate this 'Rasputin thing', and that the long-lost icon had been called for—that's when it hit me. The Order needs that icon, Nick. We *have* to return it to the Russian people—*that's* how we'll help them find their faith again!

"And think what that could mean—we could do anything! We could demand the return of a Tsar and have our first real leader in almost a hundred years, we could return to prosperity, we could eventually rejoin the modern world!"

She looked at Nick, her emotions unchecked, "The people *will* remember who they are, Nick, and the icon will play a huge part in that . . . I just *know* it."

She paused to breathe, but only for a moment. "Obviously, I couldn't pass up this chance. I got hold of Vlady and he saw it the same way, so we came up with a plan: I would do as my father asked, to help steal the icon by distracting the guards. Then, once we got home, the Order would take the icon and return it to the Russian people. But now . . . " She fell silent.

"But now? But *now* . . . what?"

She sighed. "Things have changed, Nick. I mean, this Rasputin thing, for one. It's personal in my family. They've wanted the legend of Rasputin dead for eighty years. And now, since Rasputin's inside *you* . . . "

Nick's eyes opened wide. "Then your dad's gonna kill me?!"

"No! He can't, he doesn't know you, and he doesn't know *how* or even *if* Rasputin has actually 'returned'. He only knows the icon was called for and tracked to your house. He was

counting on me for the rest. I was supposed to report back with
. . . "

Nick scowled. " . . . me? With me? That's why I'm here?"

"No, Nick, that's not why—I just can't stick to the plan." She
was quiet, she was starting to cry. "I never liked the idea of my
father and I going back to Russia with the icon . . . I think
Vlady's going to have to kill him to get it. And things could go
really bad, I mean, they could end up killing each other. Now
I'd prefer my father stays here, in jail, for shooting Irina. At least
he and Vlady both stay alive that way. And I can just take the
icon home myself."

"But I won't stay alive! Not if he figures out who I am!"

"That won't happen, Nick! Listen, I've got a plan that'll take
care of you, you'll stay safe. We just need . . . "

"Whatever it is, no! Your dad's got the icon, you've got me,
you're taking me to him, and he wants to kill me. And you're a
fucking spy, remember? I mean, do I have 'Stupid' written
across my forehead? Just stop the car and let me out. That's how
you can take care of me. You don't need me for nothin'."

Sonia sighed. "No, Nick, I don't think you're stupid—so I
know you'll be smart and consider this: my father wants to bury
Rasputin again, one way or another, it's a vendetta. So whatever
happens, you're in danger until we stop him. If he gets even one
of those stranniki at your house to talk . . . well, I don't know if I
can protect you after that—and don't ask me to kill my own
father! I just think I've got a better plan."

"Well, whatever, but I plan to stay alive. How are you gonna
stop him from doing anything?"

"Like this . . . you get on the floor in the back seat. We go to
the cabin, I tell my father that Rasputin's in Rushing Wells,
hiding out. After we leave, you find the icon wherever he's
hidden it, take this car and go hide—and call the cops. Tell them
who shot Irina and what he's driving, and I'll give him the slip
the first chance I get. After they catch him, I'll meet you back at

your house. You'll be alive, he'll be in jail, and I'll be out of here—how's that? *Now* will you trust me?"

Nick smoldered. He didn't answer.

"I trust her, little one," Rasputin said softly. "I will help you find where She is hidden, for I feel Her when She is near. Such an action would allow me to work again for the Motherland. The Virgin told me it would be so."

"What?" Nick cried. "Grisha, *you* want to help <u>her</u>? What about me? You can't help *anybody* if her dad kills me!"

"Nick . . . ?" Sonia said, but Nick raised his hand to quiet her.

"And why would you trust *her*, anyway? *They* stole the icon. *She* distracted *you*, remember? Like *that* took much effort. In fact, if you hadn't wanted to get laid, none of this shit would be happening at all. Bushka wouldn't be half-dead in the *sabor*, and we'd still have the icon. Way to work in the name of the Motherland! I mean, really, why should I trust you at all any more? Wait—you still want into her pants, don't you? I'd trust *that*! So just go to hell, would you?"

Rasputin did not answer, and Sonia did not speak.

They drove on. Nick knew he had to make a decision. He thought of Bushka, telling them to save the Virgin. He shook his head. He quietly asked Her to watch over her.

"Irisha is in good hands, little one," Rasputin answered. "You need not worry for her."

"Just. Shut. Up." Nick told Rasputin through gritted teeth.

"What?" Sonia asked.

Nick glanced at her blankly, then back to the road. He forgot, she couldn't hear this irritating voice in his head. How could he ever get out of this mess?

Suddenly he caught a flash of motion out the corner of his eye. They'd passed a girl running towards them on a gravel side road, red hair, arms flailing.

"Wait! Stop!" Nick yelled, his head spinning. "That was Colleen!" he lost sight of her in the darkness.

"What? You know her?"

"Yeah, she's my neighbor!" Nick yelled. "Go back! She's always nosing around, she must know something. Why else would she be out here in the middle of the night?"

Sonia hit the brakes hard.

CHAPTER 17

Moments earlier

Colleen couldn't get Nicky off her mind. She'd made the wrong choice, she just knew it. Nicky wouldn't have let the guy get away without a fight. She should have gone and found *him*; Boris could've followed this guy by himself. Because really, what were they gonna do if they caught him? Fight him? He had a gun. And she had . . . Boris. Not good odds.

The taillights were about a hundred yards ahead. The guy couldn't know they were there, he was still driving like he was going to church. But they needed a phone or *something*. Colleen thought hard. This sucked. There was a pay phone up in Hagerman, but he'd see them in the streetlights and be gone before she could finish dialing.

The burglar slowed at a stop sign and turned right, toward town. There wasn't much time left until he'd know he was being followed. Think . . . think . . . think . . . she told herself in perfect timing with the turn signal.

"The blinkers! My God—turn 'em off!" Colleen yelled. They were lighting the ditch and the stop sign and everything else— and the sedan sprinted off like a jack-rabbit.

Boris cursed and canceled the signal. "Dammit! That was my fault," he admitted.

Colleen watched the lights fade into the distance. "Don't worry about it," she sighed. "Let's just keep going. Maybe we'll see where he parks or something . . . I mean, he must live around here, right? Why else would he come this way?"

Boris nodded.

They passed moonlit fields of endless furrows, perfectly straight, that seemed to go forever. Colleen chewed her nails. This was just hopeless; he was long gone. And she'd left Nicky behind for what, this? God, what a mistake. She should have known better.

But then in the squinty distance, almost parallel to them, she saw a long, rising plume of dust—and a fast-moving car in front of it, almost invisible. No lights.

"Boris, look! Way over there!"

He looked and nodded. "He's on the canal road! We can go back and get onto it . . . " Boris wheeled the truck around in a wide driveway and they headed back to a small bridge.

Soon they were fishtailing onto a narrow, gravel service road beside a gleaming-white concrete canal bank. The air tasted gritty; they were eating his dust, and the feel of it on her teeth made her heart pound. Her mind raced ahead—so many things could go wrong. He was going to take this personally. He hadn't shaken them, he'd be mad as hell. "This is crazy," she said, mostly to herself.

Boris grunted, staring into the darkness. The windshield was growing dusty, harder to see through.

"What are we gonna do if we catch him?" she asked.

The truck drifted slightly through a corner, but it whipped out straight again. She looked over at Boris, "Um, never mind. Maybe you should slow down a little . . . ?"

Boris shook his head, but suddenly he reared back in his seat, eyes wide. "Oouuttt . . . Jump!" he cried, grinding the transmission into low gear to try to slow the hurtling truck.

Almost too late, Colleen saw it, too—a sharp left bend in the canal, unmarked. An embankment dropped off on Boris' side, and water lay off hers—they were going in.

Everything moved in slow motion. She reached for the door handle and pulled. The latch clicked . . . and the metal handle came off in her hand. Good Lord! But she felt the door loosen. Her feet dragged through molasses toward it. And just as the truck left the road, when she couldn't stay even one second longer, she shoved hard and leapt into the night.

A cold, disorienting turbulence engulfed her. And it took a moment, but when she finally popped her head above water and tried to regain her bearings, the truck was gone. She scampered up the rough concrete bank and looked around . . . there it was, the top of the roof still above water, but barely. Bubbles rose around it. It was sinking.

"Boris! Boris!"

She glanced around to be sure he wasn't lying injured in the gravel somewhere. No luck. He *had* to be in the truck; he'd been holding onto the steering wheel for dear life. She took a deep breath and jumped in.

She fumbled about, trying to see through the upset murk — suddenly the sight of swirling white strands in the cab shocked her backward. But she couldn't be scared! She got closer to see if it was real — yes! There, amid the hair, was Boris, kneeling on the seat, head against the roof, breathing in an air pocket.

She rose for a breath and returned. She grabbed the driver door latch and pulled . . . it wouldn't budge, even with Boris pushing from the inside. She rose again and returned, this time planting her feet against the bed for better leverage. No way. She rose again. Dammit! She knew the passenger door didn't work from the outside, and who *knew* where the inside handle had landed . . . why didn't Nicky ever fix anything???!

Now the roof was underwater. Boris couldn't last forever, she knew that, but at least he'd have the air pocket for little longer. She splashed to the bank and climbed out. "Oh, God, help me, please help me," she cried, water slogging from her shoes and clothes with every heavy step. The road wasn't that far back. Someone would come along and help save Boris.

Sonia hit reverse and gassed it. Nick rolled his window down and stuck his head out. "Colleen? *Colleen*!!" he yelled.

Sonia weaved as she slowed, and Colleen approached, out-of-breath, panicked and surprised. "Nicky?! Oh my God! Is it you?"

She leaned heavily onto the roof above his door. "Quick — it's Boris . . . .!" she panted. Her face was muddy and streaked, her hair a jumbled mess of mossy weeds. "He's in your truck, under water. Come on . . . we've gotta go . . . "

"What!?"

Colleen pulled open the door and shoved him over. "There's no time! We've gotta go *now*! That way! Go!" She pointed the way.

There was no arguing. Nick nodded at Sonia, and she headed up the gravel. Nick could hear Rasputin praying.

"God . . . I'm . . . so . . . cold" Colleen stuttered, shivering. Sonia blasted up the heat, and Nick looked around in the car. There was an old blanket on the back seat floorboard. He grabbed it and tucked it around Colleen; he put his arm around her and pulled her in tight.

"Ahead . . . there's a turn . . . go slow."

In half-a-minute they were there, and Colleen was pushing open the door before they'd even stopped. Nick followed her out. "There!" she yelled, pointing, " . . . right there!"

Sonia had a flashlight and she lit the water—the truck's roof was under a foot of water, barely visible.

Colleen agonized, "I know I shouldn't have left him . . . "

Nick dove and felt for the driver's door. Suddenly, as the turbulence cleared, there was Boris in the window—one foot away, face-to-face with him, wide-eyed and staring back.

"*Ei Bogu!*" yelled a startled Rasputin.

Nick's heart skipped a couple of beats. This was bad. Grandpa was like the bloated head floating in the gashed hull in "Jaws" . . . but he looked again—and Boris nodded! He was alive!

Nick looked closer. Boris had a black hose in his mouth—it ran out the vent window and up, into the crisp night air. Nick grinned widely and went back up.

"He's alive!" Nick yelled. "He made a snorkel!" Excitedly he spun about and went back under. Those chunks of radiator hose had been rolling out from under the seat forever, and he'd kicked them back up, out of the way, a zillion times. Who'd have known they'd come in *this* handy?

Nick swam around so his butt was against the door and his heel was below it, holding him in place. He raised his elbow high and brought it down hard. And though the water was like tar, holding back his swing, he hit the driver door in just the right spot, with just enough force, to jar it loose. Boris pushed it open wide and calmly swam out.

They crawled up the bank together. But when they reached the gravel, Boris immediately knelt and crossed himself. He gave thanks to the Virgin, loud enough that all could hear.

Nick wiped the water from his eyes and stared. What the heck? Since when did Grandpa pray to Anyone?

Rasputin knew why. "He has become one with Virgin," he said, and Nick scarcely noticed Colleen putting her blanket over his shoulders.

Boris finished his prayers. He crossed himself and stood, and he smothered Nick in a giant bear-hug and traditional kisses. "Thank you, my father."

Nick was speechless. His mouth hung open.

"So, you see." said Rasputin. "He now knows . . . "

"Knows? Knows what?" Nick asked, forgetting that no one else could hear what Rasputin had said.

"She came to me, my father, like a dream, but real," Boris said, face and hair dripping. "She was beautiful, wrapped in a thousand stars of night, and She asked that I serve Her. So I shall. I am so blessed . . . " He looked innocent and bright-eyed, and completely sober.

Nick was floored. Nothing was making sense, but he could see it wasn't canal water that was running down Grandpa's cheeks. He was crying real tears. *Something* had happened.

"There is no greater beauty," Rasputin said.

"Okay, everyone, please . . . " Sonia interrupted, frustrated. "Everybody's all right, now we have to go! We have to hurry or my father will *know* something's wrong!"

"Ahem!" Colleen stepped in front of Nick, "Nicky Brody, are you going to tell me what's going on? Like, who *is* that? . . . " she nodded toward Sonia, " . . . and why should *I* care if her father thinks something's wrong? I mean, *duh!*, there is!—we just *crashed*, hello?

"And what in the heck is Boris talking about? And aren't you wondering what I'm doing out here with him in the middle of the night? Well, I'll tell you . . . your painting's been stolen, and we almost caught the guy that did it—*that's* what *we're* doing out here! What about *you*?"

She paused for a teeth-chattering half-a-breath, "You know, this is *all* really weird! I mean, first I think you could be *dead*, then *her* father's going to be upset—like that's some big deal— and now Boris is calling you *his* father?"

Nick looked her straight in the eye. "Colleen, look . . . right now you've *got* to trust me. Her name's Sonia, and Grandpa's going to be fine; there's just a lot more going on than you know about. But, really, we don't have much time, so I *have* to explain it all to you in the car—please, will you get in? *Right now!?*"

She didn't answer, and she didn't budge. She just fumed. Sonia headed around to the driver's door and Nick tried to lead Colleen by the elbow, but it was useless.

"*Ei Bogu*, Colleen . . . "

Nick shifted gears. He opened the back door and held it wide. "Grandpa, please? Will *you* get in?"

Boris nodded, "We shall work together in the name of the Virgin," he said. He followed Nick's lead and took a seat.

Nick closed him in and returned to face Colleen. He didn't have a choice, he had to tell her; he had to quit trying to *not* think about it. "Colleen . . . look, um . . . " his gaze dropped to the ground, and he knew tears would be coming. "Um, Bushka's been shot . . . " his voice cracked. It was all so real again, the image of her lying there was all he could see. "So, um . . . we really need to go now . . . okay?" He fumbled blindly behind him for the door handle.

"My God, Nicky! What? How . . . ?"

This time Nick was silent. He couldn't have talked or looked up if he'd wanted to; he just opened the door and held it there.

"All right, then," she said softly. She wiped tears from his cheeks as she passed, and soon they were chirping back onto the blacktop.

Nick knew she was staring at him, waiting for him to say *something*, but he didn't know where to begin. How could he explain *any* of this?

"Nicky? Is she . . . is she hurt bad? Is she still alive?"

Rasputin said, "Ask for her prayers, Nick Ivanovich. She must pray for Irisha, and she must pray to help save the icon."

Just as Nick was clearing his throat to answer, Sonia whipped the car into a wide spot and parked. She gave him no chance to answer. "Nick, I'm sorry, but we've got a more immediate problem . . . the cabin's right around the corner and our plan's dead—you can't *all* hide in this car. So we'll put our numbers to work and surprise him instead. It's the only way."

Nick shook his head, but at least the subject had changed. "What? I don't have *any* idea *what* you're talking about."

Sonia sighed, exasperated. "Look, I'm going to tell him that you all were chasing him, but that you crashed, and I found you before you could call the cops—got it? It makes perfect sense, and it explains everything. I'll tell him *other* people also saw him leaving, and that *they're* on their way, too. He'll *know* we have to leave fast, so he *can't* go back for Rasputin. It all *works*!

"So I'll ask him to tie you up so he and I can leave. When he does, and when I'm 'covering you', we'll make our move. We'll tie *him* up instead, then call the cops. Trust me, it'll work. The four of us just have to stick together—we'll have the element of surprise on our side."

Nick and Boris nodded, but Colleen defiantly shook her head. "What? You trust *her*, Nicky? Weren't we just chasing *her* father—and now we're going to be, like, *her* prisoners? I don't *think* so! Trust her all you want, but I don't have to. Just get your icon without me—I'll hitch a ride home." She started to open the door, but Nick covered her hand with his.

He swallowed hard and glanced at Sonia, but she just turned away and stared out the windshield.

"We don't have much time, Nick," Sonia said. "You'd better let her know what's going on, but talk fast."

Nick knew he had to start somewhere. "Colleen, do you remember down at the river, when I told you someone else had taken over inside of me, the guy who was singing that night?"

Colleen nodded sharply. She was fuming. "The same guy I slapped later, right?"

Nick blushed. "Um . . . no." This might get bad. "That was me. I was just listening to him."

Colleen couldn't believe it. "You were just listening to him— yeah, okay. Nicky, are you on drugs? Or do I just *look* like an idiot?"

"Colleen, you've *got* to believe me. Rasputin's spirit is inside here," he tapped his head. "He's come back, like they thought he would. And Bushka's almost dead—I swear to God, I'm not making *any* of this up. You'll find out soon enough, and I wish none of this was happening, but it is—and I can't do *anything* about it. Now you're involved, too. Yes, Sonia's father is the guy you were chasing. *He* took the icon, and he shot Bushka. But Sonia's on our side, and she's going to help us get it back."

She was nearly speechless. "From her dad."

"Yeah."

"Well, like I believe *that*! Why would she help us take the icon from her own dad?" She searched Nick's eyes for an answer, for a sign that he was insane or messing with her in *any* way. "So tell me why those old men are at your house, Nicky, treating you like some kind of priest, and why Boris is calling you 'father'! Jeez, do you know realize how *nuts* this all sounds?"

Rasputin jumped in, "Tell her my story, Nick Ivanovich. She must know what is happening. There is too much danger for her to remain unaware."

Nick took a deep breath. "Okay, Colleen, look . . . here's the whole thing. Just let me talk . . . " Nick touched on everything: the icon 'The Weeping Virgin' of Kazan, Rasputin's murder, the Order of the Maltese Cross and how Rasputin was destined to return to serve the Motherland.

Then he told Colleen how he'd been knocked silly in the river when he was saving the little girl—a blast that *was* the return of Rasputin. The legend had come true. Within him. And he wasn't especially happy about it.

Finally he explained his parentage: Boris was Rasputin's child by his great-grandmother, Bushka. So Rasputin was his . . .

" . . . great-grandfather." Colleen finished the sentence for him. "Nicky, is this all true? Do you *swear* it's true?"

Nick nodded, "On a stack of bibles."

Colleen wasn't finished. "So Boris, you saw . . . what? The real Virgin Mary, the Virgin of Kazan? In your truck?"

Boris nodded. "She came to me, little one. And She floated the tubing right before my eyes."

Colleen turned to Sonia. "And you—you're a Russian. You're one of the Maltese Cross people?"

"My last name is Lipov. We are descendants of Igor Igorevich Lipov, who helped kill Rasputin." She lifted her shirt and showed Colleen her tattoo. "And yes, I'm a member of the Order of the Maltese Cross. We've waited for this day for nearly a hundred years."

Colleen shook her head. "Your father stole the icon and your family helped kill Rasputin—and now you're working for Russia . . . or like, old Russia? This is, like, *so* unbelievable. I don't know what to say."

She turned back to Nick. "You *swear* Rasputin is inside you and that he took over and was singing that nasty song? Then let me hear him talk."

Rasputin said, "I shall be happy to," and Nick nodded for him to take over. But nothing happened. Rasputin remained in the background.

"What's wrong?" asked Nick, slightly panicked.

"We cannot switch places, little one. The Virgin must wish it so."

"Well, why would She do that?"

"*Ei Bogu*, Nick Ivanovich. As the Virgin giveth, She also taketh away. It is as She chooses. But you need not worry, for She is strong within you. Perhaps you need me no more."

"Oh, man," sighed Nick. He looked at Colleen. "It's not working. He can't take over right now, and we don't know why. But it's all true, you've *got* to believe me."

Colleen snorted and shook her head.

Nick was desperate. "Look, Colleen, we have to get the icon back—I promised that to Bushka. And I swear to God that all of this is true. I'd never hurt you or lie to you. I want you to . . . I mean, well . . . I want *you*, Colleen! I'd do anything for you. I'd spend the rest of my life with you if you'd let me."

Her eyes opened wide. "Nicky, you've never said anything like that before."

Nick cheeks grew warm. His gaze dropped and shivers ran up his spine. Good Lord, did this have to come out in front of everybody? "I guess I just thought you knew."

"Well, I didn't," she said. "So this is all for real? Everything? Are you leaving anything out?"

Nick nodded, "No. Or, I mean, *yes*—everything's real! It's true, it's what's happening, and I can't help any of it." He dared sneak a glance at her.

She was reaching for him. She took his face in her hands and pulled him to her, and she kissed him on the lips for what seemed forever.

Sonia's patience was at an end. "All right, all right! Let's go!"

Nick pulled away slowly. His heart was beating like it never had. Wow. He and Colleen's eyes were still kissing.

Sonia jumped out. "Okay—please! Nick, you drive. Boris, up front, hurry."

Boris got out and took Nick's place, while Sonia took over the back seat by herself. She pulled her pistol from her purse and laid it in her lap. "Okay, let's go. Remember, everybody, follow my lead. Nick, he's at the Stone Creek Cabins—in the last one, down by the river."

Nick nodded and put the car into gear. Colleen rested her hand on his knee, gripping tightly as they slowed and turned at a weather-beaten sign, a faded fish leaping over crudely-drawn cabins.

Nick idled in, passing camp trailers, fishing boats and monster-mudder pickup trucks that dwarfed the first few one-room shacks. Lights were out, laundry lines bare and lawn chairs tipped up against the dew. They crept onward.

Sonia leaned up and whispered, "Okay, we're getting close. Remember, you're supposed to be my captives, so that's how I have to treat you or he'll be suspicious. Colleen and Boris, put your hands on your heads and lock your fingers together."

Colleen glanced nervously at Nick, but she and Boris both did as asked. They wound through the last bend in the road. Ahead at the turnaround, beneath a yellow security light clouded with mosquitoes and gnats, sat a dusty black towncar that seemed out of place, like a suit among fishing suspenders.

Cabin 11 looked empty as they passed, but a light was on in Cabin 12. The door was ajar, and then a shadow behind it moved. He'd been watching them approach.

Nick parked and shut off the car. He put his hands on his head and swallowed hard.

"The Virgin is with us, Nick Ivanovich," said Rasputin. "Do not be afraid."

Sonia put her pistol to Boris' head. "Out, old man, out now!" she commanded. "Get outside the car!"

Boris slowly opened the door and got out. He put his hands back on his head and stood there motionlessly.

The cabin door opened wide. A trim man in dark clothing stepped onto the porch and folded his arms across his chest. He held his pistol like an extension of his hand.

Sonia leaned forward, her pistol inches from Nick and Colleen's ears. "Now you two. Go."

Nick and Sonia opened their doors and stepped out simultaneously, then Colleen slid over and followed Nick. Sonia covered them both from a few steps away. Nick and Colleen, hands on heads, walked around the front of the car.

Lipov stepped off the porch. He motioned with his barrel for Boris to get out of the road, to move toward the far side of the cabin.

"Follow the old man, you two," Sonia commanded. She joined her father and walked side-by-side, pistols extended.

"(You are late. Who are these people?)," he asked Sonia.

She kept her eyes on her captives. "(Those two are the ones who followed you, father. And the boy, he lives at the house. He is of concern, but it may be insanity—he is the one who started the talk of Rasputin's return)."

"(Really). Stop there," he ordered.

"(Why did you bring them here. And why are they wet)?"

Sonia shook her head mockingly. "(They crashed into a canal while chasing you, father. I found the girl near the main road—it was better to grab her than give her the chance to call for help. And it seemed better to bring them here, to you—perhaps you can get them to tell us what they know about Rasputin)."

Nick looked over at Colleen, relieved that she didn't speak Russian. She'd be as concerned as he was about Sonia's story. It didn't seem like she was acting at all.

Lipov approached Nick. The security light cast long shadows off Lipov's forehead and hairy eyebrows, and his eyes glistened in their dark sockets. He traced his barrel along Nick's forehead, parting his wet hair and daring him to move.

"Hello, young friend. What is your name?" Lipov spoke perfect English.

His vodka-fouled breath reminded Nick of Boris after a long night out. So this was the sonuvabitch who'd shot Bushka. And he'd broken into *his* house, *his* sabor. Well, Nick would return the favor. Just wait, there'd be a way out of this. Nick's heart pounded feverishly. He didn't answer.

Rasputin said, "He feels not for his actions, Nick Ivanovich. He is an affront to the Virgin, and She will see that he does not defeat us. We shall recover the icon and be gone."

Deep down, Nick agreed—but he also wanted to see Lipov bleed, fighting for breath like Bushka had. Just one chance, that's all he'd need.

Lipov shook his head but did not linger. He moved to Colleen, who was shivering. His eyes traveled up and down, to where her wet clothes clung and defined her shape. He put his pistol to her forehead and stood very close. "Are you cold?"

Colleen, too, was silent.

Lipov glanced back at his daughter and smirked. He moved over to Boris, nodding to him as if they were old friends. "(Hello, old one. You speak Russian, yes? I think so, I think perhaps you speak Russian with the mad monk, Rasputin? The mad monk, ha! Maybe you two are one and the same—no, you smell more like a mad *dog*, a piss-wet mad dog)!

"(So talk to me, old one. Tell me about your icon. What were you going to do with Her? Sell Her? Place Her in a church somewhere? Tell me, now, so that you might live) . . . " He slid the action on the pistol, cocking it, and put it near Boris' head.

Boris did not look worried. "(The Virgin has come to me. I am prepared to give my life to Her and the Motherland)."

Lipov laughed. "(So you *do* speak the language! Perhaps *you* are the real Rasputin, eh)?" He laughed again and lowered his pistol. "(Luckily I have no fear of dead monks, old one. Soon enough, we'll return you to your Maker)."

Lipov turned to walk away, but suddenly he spun around and slugged Boris hard in the abdomen. Boris' head fell forward, white hair tumbling. He grabbed his midsection and doubled over, gasping for breath, and dropped to his knees.

"(Do you remember my grandfather, old one? Igor Igorevich? He spits on you now)," Lipov spat angrily onto Boris. "(He would kill you twenty times over. Burn in hell, *pivo*)!"

Colleen dropped to Boris' side. She leaned him over and sat him down. She glared at Sonia. "Do something!" she yelled.

Sonia shook her head and smiled. She said, "(Father, you should have heard the story I told them)."

Then to Nick and Sonia, she added, "Stupid children. That icon is worth a fortune. Did you think I would just *give* it away? To peasants? To you, or to *anyone*?"

The Lipovs laughed.

CHAPTER 18

Nick stared at Sonia's gun. Everything was falling apart. How could Sonia have lied to them like that—and how could *he* have believed her? But she had, and he had. Now Rasputin was locked inside him and couldn't take over. And Boris was hurt. And Bushka was probably dead. He stared at Sonia, trying to read her. She was so cold, so impossible to figure.

Rasputin said, "She shall not return the icon to the *moujiki*, Nick Ivanovich. Her words were false. She is not one with the Virgin."

Nick swallowed hard. His fingers were cold before, but now they were laced-together frozen. There was no way he could move his hands fast enough to surprise the Lipovs.

Boris sat, forehead on knees, hands around shins. Colleen had her arm around his shoulders.

Lipov moved around, behind them. "(All these years, I have wondered how I would know when I met Rasputin, *pivo*. And now I have my answer—he will be an old man, white-haired, and too feeble to fight back. What a pity. I so enjoy the challenge of combat with a strong adversary. But with you? . . . no. You cannot defend yourself. Yet you are too dangerous to set free, yes? Who knows, one day you might appear on the television and try to charm our people? But such things are no longer allowed, *pivo*. It would be better to bid you farewell now. And my grandfather would agree, I am sure of that! Perhaps he will even tell you so, face-to-face— and when he does, please say hello for me)." Lipov put his pistol to the back of Boris' head.

Colleen glared up at Lipov. "No!" she yelled, "you don't have to kill him!" She shoved his pistol away, nuisance that it was.

Lipov laughed. He pulled back the weapon, holding it high as he walked about. Eventually he settled in one spot, between Nick and Colleen. She seemed not to notice, and she surely didn't see his kick coming, a blow that landed squarely below her ribs. She tumbled backward hard, wincing in pain and holding her sides.

While Lipov enjoyed Colleen's agony, his back was turned to Nick. It was his chance. "Now, Nick Ivanovich, now!" Rasputin yelled, "hit him in the back of the head!"

Boris stirred, turning to see what happened.

Time seemed to stand still to Nick. He couldn't move his fingers. The pistol was so big, and he would be *so* slow. His fist might bounce harmlessly off Lipov's head. Lipov could turn and shoot him point-blank.

Nick dared glance at Sonia. She was stonefaced, her eyes on him. But . . . almost imperceptibly, she nodded to him.

Rasputin saw it, too. "It is a sign! She says, 'Do it now, Nick Ivanovich!'"

Lipov lowered his pistol and again took aim at Boris' head. But he didn't fire. Instead, he half-turned to Sonia and asked, "(You would like the honor, daughter)?"

Sonia shook her head. "(I'll take care of the other two, father. Avenge our family name)."

Lipov chuckled.

Nick looked again at Sonia, and this time she met his gaze with a raised eyebrow. She nodded again, more obviously.

Lipov said, "(The time has come, mad monk. I protect Russia from you now)."

"Now, Nick Ivanovich, now!" yelled Rasputin.

Nick worked to move his fingers, but they were stiff and unbending. He thought about the cowboys who were going to wail on Boris in the Sudspot. No way he could hit like they could. They were mean and hard, all sinew and spitty leather. And he'd never hit a fully-grown man before, especially not a hairy foreigner like Lipov. He *must* be a great fighter—and aren't all spies and secret agents trained to fight to the death?

Colleen was lying on her side in the dirt, arms around herself, eyes shut, face red and teary. *Ei Bogu*. A spark flicked. Nick's fingers came apart. He saw the puddle of blood beneath Bushka, felt its sticky warmth. His fist was too small and light, he pumped his arm to make it grow. He had to make this count. He shifted his weight. Sonia's gun was aimed right at him, she was following his movements. Colleen had kissed him so softly, his heart had nearly leapt from his chest. And she'd slapped him pretty hard, too. His fist tightened. Lipov was within reach.

"Behind the ear, little one," repeated Rasputin, over and over, until Nick finally heard it. He swallowed dryly. Bushka, she spit so far out into the dirt. Mom and Dad. On the swing. Their flattened car. Nick reared back and swung, a haymaker off the farm. Lipov's head snapped sideways. The gun shot one round, a quiet poof, and a light cloud lifted into the night. Lipov crumpled in front of him. Nick's head started to clear, he could see and hear and think and smell again.

"The gun, Nick Ivanovich, get his gun!" Rasputin yelled.

Nick stooped over and grabbed it from Lipov's limp hand. He tossed it to Sonia; he surely didn't need the thing.

"Quick," she said, watching her father, "there's rope by the front door. Get it, would you?"

Nick looked over at Colleen. She was righting herself, straining to rise. He wanted to go to her, but she nodded him toward the cabin and said, "Go, Nicky."

'Nicky' never sounded so sweet. He tried to dash off, but his legs were wobbly and unsure, and getting to the cabin was an uphill struggle. Finally, though, there was the rope, coiled behind the door. He grabbed it and leapt from the porch on his way back.

"My God! Boris!" Colleen shrieked, kneeling and lifting his head. His face was pale, and the side of his shirt was drenched with blood.

Nick dropped beside her. Lipov's stray shot had hit near Boris' shoulder and traveled sideways through him, exiting his side under his ribcage. It was a miracle he was even alive.

"Quick, get him inside," Sonia said. "I've *got* to tie up my father."

Nick nodded, shocked at the amount of blood on his grandfather's shirt. He scooped him up like he was weightless.

"I shall pray to the Virgin, Nick Ivanovich," Rasputin said, "May the light shine upon Boris Grigorevich."

"Start water boiling," Sonia called out, "I'll be right there." Impassively, fast and well-practiced, she bound her father's wrists and ankles and then hog-tied them together with a short rope behind his back. She ran to the car for duct tape and stuck a six-inch piece across his mouth, then dashed for the cabin.

Colleen ran ahead and opened the door, and they lay Boris out on the double bed. Nick ripped open his shirt and tried to cover the gaping hole with his hand, but it was pointless. Blood squirted everywhere.

Colleen ran to the bathroom and cranked open the hot tap in the bathtub, then jumped back out to the kitchen. There had to be a big pot somewhere! She found one under the sink and ran back and filled it from the tub, then sloshed it to the stove and flipped on the burner—but that would take forever, so she rounded up rags and towels and stuck them under the steaming tub spigot. She rushed them out to Nick.

Sonia burst in. "Just keep pressing hard, Nick . . . " She grabbed another towel and started wiping the entry wound clean. "We'll get him through this. And by the way, you did a great job out there. Here, let me take over . . . "

Nick stepped aside, shaking his head and wiping blood onto his pants. "I don't do these things every day like you do." He took his grandpa's hand. "He's bleeding pretty bad. I was too late, I took way too long."

"It's not your fault, Nicky," Colleen said. "I thought you were great."

"I don't know. I don't think I did anything at all," he said. "I think Rasputin hit him, not me."

But Rasputin didn't respond—he was praying loudly in Nick's head, and Nick crossed himself absentmindedly at just the right times.

Boris still wasn't moving; his breaths barely lifted his chest. Nick closed his eyes. First Bushka, now Grandpa. What could happen next? He looked out the window and saw Lipov on the ground, bent back awkwardly. Good. The sonuvabitch deserved it. Maybe he *had* knocked the crap outta him; yeah, it felt good, too. He could do it again. He could do it all day long.

Sonia pressed another towel onto Boris' wound. She turned to Nick. "It could be worse," she said somberly, "but not by much. We've *got* to get him some help. If I could tourniquet his chest, I would."

Suddenly, paused in prayer without Nick realizing, Rasputin said, "Only the Virgin can save Boris Grigorevich now, little one. She must work through my hands, just as She did for young Tsarevich Alexei. We pray for this now, we must try again to switch places."

Nick swallowed back his fear. He wanted so badly for this nightmare to be over, and he nodded.

But, again, nothing happened.

Nick couldn't believe it. "Grisha, what's wrong?!" he cried out loud. "Why is this happening? What are you doing in my head if you can't do what you're supposed to be doing?"

"It is the Virgin's way, Nick Ivanovich. Anger will not help. It is as She wishes."

"What?" asked Nick incredulously. Colleen and Sonia were staring at him weirdly, so he turned around. He needed to get this out, and he needed some semblance of privacy.

"Look, Grisha, I don't care what you say, this is *not* Her way—it's been *your* way, *your* way all along! This is *your* fault, Bushka and Grandpa getting shot. If you hadn't shown up, they'd still be fine—and don't try to tell me any different! *You're* the one who's screwed up everything!"

"I am but Her servant, little one. The Virgin asks us only for our . . . "

"God, shut the fuck up about the Virgin, would you?" he demanded. "I mean, you're always saying, 'the Virgin this' and 'the Virgin that', but only so you can get drunk and have sex! What a crock—what does *that* has to do with the Virgin?

"You know what? I think She's just tired of your crap! Think about it—She brought you here, and now She won't let you do anything! Why? 'Cause you've pissed Her off, that's why! *That's* why we can't switch places!"

"Nick Ivanovich, I feel your anger, but, still, we must work to save . . . "

"No! *You* work to save him, Grisha! Grow up and apologize to the Virgin! I would, if I were in your shoes, but I'm not the one who got sent back for another visit, now am I? And *I'm* not the one who's getting ignored, stuck in the back seat, now am I? In fact, if you ever *do* figure out what She wants, maybe She'll let you move on to your next life or do whatever you're supposed to be doing!"

"Nick Ivanovich, this is . . . " Rasputin paused, "difficult. I cannot answer you. You make me pause."

"Well, quit pausing! If you don't talk to Her, I will! 'I'm sorry, Virgin. I'm sorry my great-grandfather's such an idiot! I'm sorry he prays to you to get laid, and that he's too hung over the next day to do whatever he's supposed to do.' How's that? Good crap, I can't believe that *She's* never called you out on this before, and that no one else ever did, either. You're your own worst enemy. You probably always have been."

Rasputin answered quietly. "Perhaps She once 'called me out' so, Nick Ivanovich—I did not see Her light for many months. And yes, Iliodor once questioned my worship; the priests of Pokrovskoe did, too, and possibly there were others. But I never felt that they were one with the Virgin."

Nick couldn't believe it—Rasputin actually sounded contrite. It was like hearing a confession from a parent. He shouldn't be in a spot like this, but he was, and he needed to make sure he got his point across.

"One with *whose* Virgin—yours? Or theirs? So they were wrong and you were right. Did you ever consider that, maybe, *you* were the one who was full of shit the whole time?"

Rasputin again paused. "Nick Ivanovich, if you are right, I will apologize to Her. I am only a man, and I have been tempted oft . . . oh—*Ei Bogu*!" He gasped so loudly that Nick looked around the room. "Oh, my Lord, I *have* failed Her! She asked long ago that I 'avoid temptation' when I returned— and I have *not*! First with Leesha, then with Sonia . . . "

He moaned painfully in Nick's head, a shuddering cry of anguish so deep and profound that Nick knew there'd be no more forcing him to look in a mirror.

"Please . . . Nick Ivanovich," Rasputin was in tears, his voice choked with pain and sorrow. "We must pray! I must beg her forgiveness! You are so right, your years do not matter . . . it is clear to me now—I am a failure in Her eyes! She showed such faith in me, and now . . . oh, Lord, I am so sorry! My Irisha, my son . . . I have let you down! I am such a fool! Please Lord, hear my sorrow, bring me home! Take me now!" His anguish was profound, his heart truly ached.

Nick eyes were misty, too. This was difficult to witness. The confident Rasputin, the smooth talker, the priest, the traveler . . . now the admitted con man, doubting himself deeply, maybe for *really* the first time ever. But there wasn't time right now to let him bang his head for a couple of hours.

"My God, Grisha, get a grip, would you? She's not going to take you home right now. Just say a quick 'I'm sorry' and tell Her the long version later. Concentrate on Grandpa. Start the prayers, or do whatever things you do for stuff like this!"

Rasputin calmed himself, "Yes, Nick Ivanovich, you are right. We must pray for Boris Grigorevich. But there are no 'things'—She listens to my prayers and works through my hands, that is all. But if She is angry and does not listen to me . . . then perhaps She waits for you."

"For *me*?" Nick asked frantically. "How can I do anything? You said the Virgin will save him—*She* has to!"

"So She shall, Nick Ivanovich, for everything you said is true. It has made our path is clear . . . *you* are Her chosen one now, not me. *You* must have faith in Her, and trust in yourself. I can serve only as your guide. It is as She wishes."

"Oh, come on! There you go again!"

"No, little one, I do not 'go again'. We will do this together, but you must practice *zagovarivat'krov* with me, for only the old ways will save Boris Grigorevich today. Or would you rather bless him and say goodbye?"

Nick was quiet. So were Colleen and Sonia, though they both watched him intensely. Sonia changed towels again. She looked at Nick and shook her head.

From then it only took a moment, but Nick's irritation was obvious. "Okay, zaga-what*ever*. What am I supposed to do?"

Rasputin began to talk, slow and soothing, as Nick took over for Sonia. He described how he had soothed injured horses over the years, praying for them until the twinkling light had stilled their flowing blood.

"And now you must do the same, Nick Ivanovich. Pray to Her, and tell Her of your devotion. There is no greater love than Hers, and no brighter light will ever burn within you.

You shall see—Her love will flow through you and into those you touch."

Nick closed his eyes and searched for the truth. He wanted to feel a love that could fill his heart, he wanted to know his prayers were heard and could be answered—but right now, his doubts about Rasputin overshadowed everything else. How was *this* going to work? Was he being played for a fool?

Well, he figured, who better to ask than the Virgin Herself? So he launched into full-body prayer, chanting from his core with thoughts of the Savior in his head. Her image was beautiful, Her Child was lustrous—he told Her this and much more. He told Her his doubts and he asked Her his questions—even those concerning Her. What made Rasputin's return really happen? What was the point, and why was he inside Nick? Was it because of his family? How could they be *that* important? And if they were, why wasn't Anyone watching out for them? Were Bushka and Grandpa sacrificed for the good of Russia? What about his own parents? Were they part of this, too? Had he been orphaned as part of a much grander scheme?

Still the towel reddened with blood.

Suddenly Rasputin interrupted, "The icon! We *must* have 'The Weeping Virgin' brought before us—She works miracles! Ask that She be placed before us!"

Nick asked Sonia to find the icon, and luckily there weren't a lot of hiding places in the cabin. She found it wrapped in towels in a suitcase under the bed. Nick asked her stand it on the far nightstand.

Her beauty captured him. Her ebony skin and large eyes glowed with love, tracks of past tears were plainly visible. He thought of the small Child in Her arms, of how one day He rose above his doubters in eternal victory—and how ironically appropriate *that* was.

Without realizing, Nick was growing stronger and focused. He wasn't worried about anything else now, he just had to get the bleeding stopped. One simple thing. He concentrated. It seemed easy enough. He pictured the blood flow slowing, slowing, and eventually clotting. He thought of Boris healthy again, on his bicycle, long white hair blowing behind him.

He gazed again upon the Virgin, and he prayed to Her. He asked that She give his grandfather a chance to work in Her name. Nick remembered what Boris told Lipov earlier, 'The Virgin has come to me. I am prepared to give my life to Her and the Motherland.' That didn't sound like the old Boris, and Nick told Her so. She must save him. He was the son of Rasputin, after all. He would work in Her name like few ever had. But She didn't have to make it as difficult as She had with Rasputin, bringing him back in the future and all that. No, if She liked, She could simply leave Boris in the here and now and let him get on with his new calling. Nick smiled. Was he allowed to joke with the Virgin of Kazan, the Virgin Mother Herself?

Nick closed his eyes and apologized if he had offended Her. Of course She would do as She saw fit. If it was Boris' time to go home . . .

He opened his eyes, thinking it might be the last time he'd see his grandfather. But something had changed. Boris' face seemed lighter, like it was glowing in the sun. No, wait . . . there was light over him, above him, a twinkling, sparkling glow that was not of this world. Nick watched, mesmerized. His eyes could not leave it, he could not look away to see if the girls, too, were witnessing the magic.

"Ha!" he cried, shrilly, like a child, breaking the silence and startling even himself.

Ecstatically, Rasputin blurted, "The light! She has saved . . . "

But suddenly there was a crackling sizzle and a flash of light at the wall outlet near the nightstand lamp. Nick jumped, shying away, and in that instant an arcing bolt of electricity shot from it and landed squarely on the towel on Boris' wound, lighting it afire and filling the room with pungent smoke.

"Eeaaaahhhh!!!" Nick backhanded the towel to the floor a few feet away and stomped down the tall flames. Strangely, though, neither of the girls seemed to notice his dangerous fire-dance. They were silent and still, backs toward him.

Nick wormed his way in to see what was so important— he saw that Boris' bare chest was smoking slightly, a burnt, crusted sore marking the spot where the bullet had torn its way out. Boris' head was turned toward them. His eyes were open. He looked straight at Nick and blinked.

"*Ei Bogu!*" exclaimed Rasputin.

Nick crossed himself without thinking, and then Rasputin whispered, "Nick Ivanovich—look up."

Nick broke free of Boris' gaze and glanced upward. Dark smoke from the fire still hung there, but there was a glittery, twinkly presence to it; it seemed almost alive.

"Look," Nick said aloud to the girls, pointing up. The twinkles had grown to tiny diamonds just that fast, sparkling like fireflies in a fog of coal dust.

Shaking his head, Nick looked back at Boris. There was still a smile on his face. This couldn't be. It just couldn't be.

His head felt light, he needed to sit. This was too much to digest. He wished Rasputin would take over again so just he could sit back and catch his breath.

And this time, it happened. They switched places, and Nick didn't care how or why. It didn't matter. It was Her way, and he was happy with it. He joined Rasputin in prayer, a comfortable fit if there ever was one.

"Nicky . . . ?" But Colleen couldn't form a question to ask what she wanted to know.

Nick understood, but how could *he* explain it?

Suddenly Rasputin glanced at the icon. "*Ei Bogu!*" he shouted, pointing at the icon, "She cries! She cries again for Mother Russia!"

They all looked. The tears were unmistakable. And there was no rain pouring through the ceiling or anything else to explain it. Rasputin raced to the other side of the bed and knelt before Her. He bowed his head to the floor and began to chant.

"Nicky?" Colleen asked, but her senses were overloaded. She couldn't take her eyes off him, and tears began to well.

Then, without looking up, Rasputin pointed to the ceiling. "She arrives!" he announced.

The smoke above had lightened. The diamonds moved freely about and began to spin, twinkling and pulsing, whirling, gaining speed, becoming an eddy above their heads. And from it shot a bolt of light, diving, exploding to the floor in a white curling mist. A magical, majestic human shape formed within the rising whiteness, one that rested not on feet below.

Rasputin turned to witness Her arrival, and the girls stood shocked with awe. Nick heard none of Rasputin's continuing prayers, he was too fascinated with Her face and Her Child's face, both so radiant, so dark-skinned, so luminous they took his breath away. It was beauty in the Lord's own image, lustrous and glowing, too ethereal to capture in an icon. Soon She smiled and extended Her right hand in blessing.

"Kneel before the Virgin, little ones," said Rasputin, and Colleen and Sonia did so. They crossed themselves, Catholic, Russian Orthodox, it didn't matter. They were oblivious to all but Her love.

Nick felt so lost. He wanted to ask Her so much, to tell Her so many things, but the urges quickly vanished. She already knew.

He joined Rasputin, Colleen and Sonia in prayer. It was the only action he felt capable of, and only because the words and rhythms were already in his head. It was so satisfying when Rasputin touched his forehead to the ground. The prayers felt true in his soul, better than ever before. He never would have guessed this could happen. The Virgin Herself. No way. He thought of Boris' smile, and he *saw* Her smile. She was very happy with him, it was a warm feeling he had deep, deep inside.

She motioned with Her hand ever so slightly and the three of them rose to their feet. Colleen took Nick's hand. Tears stained her cheeks, but she was smiling broadly. Nick wanted to hold her in his arms and say, 'See? She *is* real, She <u>is</u> beautiful,' but it didn't seem necessary . . . Colleen had figured it out for herself. Sonia took her other hand. They were one before Her.

The Virgin bestowed Her blessing upon them with a slight, docile wave of Her fingers, yet they fully felt Her touch, warm and supple-soft, as if She had actually caressed them. Words seemed so . . . unnecessary, a mortal inconvenience. They bowed their thanks.

The Virgin's gaze fell upon Colleen. She spoke without lips that moved, yet they could clearly hear, "Colleen Elaine, you have honored Us, and We are proud. Your faith and courage bring Us happiness. Be blessed now, and your children blessed, and their children blessed." Her right hand bestowed the blessings with a gentle downsweep, but to Colleen it was a warm brush she felt wholly and physically, upon her cheek yet deep within her at once. Her ribs were pained no longer, and she happily bowed, beaming through flowing tears.

The Virgin turned to Sonia and 'spoke' again. "Sonia Mikhailevna, you fight for a Tsar and you have sacrificed all. Know now that you are not alone, for even your ancestors honor such courage. Continue now. Do not waver in your commitment. The Grace of God goes with you." As with Colleen, the Virgin swept Her fingers down ever-so-slightly, and Sonia bowed beneath Her soft, sweet touch.

The Virgin gazed upon Boris, prone and repentant. With a fluid, elegant grace She extended Her arm and swept away the remnants of his wound. No trace remained. "Boris Grigorevich, your path has been difficult, but the power of change is within you. Remember always that you are blessed. Cherish this, and care for your loved ones. Render prosperous your land. The Lord shall call you home when it is time." She nodded and blessed him, smiling.

Boris crossed himself, closed his eyes and prayed.

The Virgin turned to Nick. "Grigory Efimovich, I return you to your flesh. You may emerge."

And so Grigory Efimovich Rasputin sprang from Nick's body, whole and intact, hair and clothing wet, corded draperies from the basement of Prince Yussupov's palace still wrapped about him. He landed on his feet beside Nick like an upright bolt of sopping purple velvet, but he could not balance as such and fell to his rear. His eyes opened wide with the shock of the fall, the sensation of pain, the breath of fresh air in his lungs.

Nick jumped to Rasputin's aid, lifting him from behind with a Heimlich drapery maneuver. Once up, Rasputin twisted free of his shroud and ropes. He still wore the simple garments from his hideously long night so many years ago—a simple *bluza* decorated with flowers by the Tsarina, shapeless dark breeches, one foot bare and the other in an old, oiled boot. His fingernails were long and dirty, his beard scraggly and sticking out every-which-way, his hair plastered wet and flat, combed as if by a garden rake. He shook himself free of water for what seemed forever.

"Hey!" Nick cried, retreating from the dank shower.

But Rasputin didn't care. He chased Nick down and clamped him in a great bear-hug, then gave him three kisses, and then three more.

Nick hugged back with all he had. Stinky old thing, this *was* his great-grandfather, after all.

Soon Nick and Rasputin felt the touch of the Virgin upon their shoulders. They turned, and She addressed them. "Nikolas Ivanovich, no man could have borne the spirit of Grigory Efimovich as you have, and no other could have taught him what he needed to learn. The Motherland is indebted to you, and the story of your honor shall not leave the hearts of True Russians.

"Go now on your path of life. Know that you are blessed, Nikolas Ivanovich, as are your children and their children."

With a sweep of Her fingers She intoned Her blessing. To Nick, it felt like a kiss on the cheek. Maybe too much so—he had the urge to jokingly wipe it off, like he used to do with his mom. But he bowed instead, wide-eyed and a little shaky. The Virgin Herself. She'd blessed him and all his family to come. *Ei Bogu!* he thought—looking up quickly, though, to ensure his words hadn't offended Her Holiness.

They hadn't. She was already greeting Rasputin, smiling upon him like an old friend.

"Grigory Efimovich. With a little help you have fulfilled your destiny. True Russians will again unite behind 'The Weeping Virgin', and they will have you to thank. Your name shall become one with the coming Russian Renaissance."

Rasputin bowed deeply. "I have learned from my mistakes, Matushka. I am sorry you had to endure me for so long. I live now only for You and the Motherland."

"You have grown, Grigory Efimovich. I commend you. Your humility will serve you well in the house of Our Father.

"And now it is time. Many await you beyond—Praskovia Dubrovina and the children, Nikolas and Alexandra, the Tsarevich and his sisters . . . and one more."

From behind the Virgin stepped Irina. She was unmarked and whole, and no blood stained her nightshirt.

Nick knew instantly what it meant, and he burst into tears. "Bushka!" He rushed to her and embraced her, taking care not to hurt her. He couldn't move, he didn't want her to go away.

"(I love you so, my Nikisha)" she whispered in his ear. "(Please forgive me . . . I wanted you to turn out strong, like your grandfather and father before you.)"

Still Nick held her. He was trying to sniff back his tears and regain his composure. It wasn't working.

"(You have much to live for, Nikisha. Please, don't mourn me long. Be happy in knowing that I dance again)."

She allowed him to take his time. As they parted she took his hands into her own.

"(You've been a such good boy, Nikisha, you've made me <u>so</u> proud—and you'll take good care of each other now, yes)?"

Nick glanced at Boris and nodded—and Boris nodded back. Their respect felt *so good*. Finally he felt he could release her, and their hands parted. She went to Boris and they held each other just as tightly.

"Grigory Efimovich," the Virgin continued, "I asked for your faith and service, and you have delivered such unto Me. Come now. Become one with Us."

Rasputin nodded. As he started toward Her, he looked back at Nick.

Aw, jeez. Nick intercepted him with one last bear-hug. "Don't go singing at night," he told Rasputin. "They don't allow that up there."

Rasputin laughed. He nodded toward Colleen, "She is yours for the taking, little one," he half-whispered, loud enough for her to hear. "Make me proud . . . " but at that the Virgin cleared Her throat, if it could be said as such, and Rasputin added with a wink, "by making Her proud first."

With a smile and a slight shake of Her head, the Virgin extended Her hand and drew Rasputin to Her like a wayward child. Then, in a sparkling swirl, She lifted and left, with Rasputin and Irina trailing in Her misty wake. They looked back only briefly. They were smiling, not hesitant in the least, then their eyes turned and fixed on whatever lay before them.

"Goodbye, Bushka," Nick whispered, "Thank you, Grisha." He looked over at Colleen and Sonia; they were as dumbstruck and tearful as he was. And Boris was chanting, praying for them all.

EPILOGUE

5 weeks later

Monday, August 26

12:15 p.m.

"Nicky, are you stuck under that car again?"

Nick slid from underneath and squinted outside, into the sun. Colleen was back, dusty boots and jeans, hands on hips.

He grinned and looked for a rag. "Hey," he said, standing and wiping his hands. "Yeah, but working on this thing's been great. It's so normal, so predictable . . . it's been like therapy, I guess, after all the stuff that happened this summer."

"Well, therapy's different for everybody, Nicky, so I'm glad you found something that works for you. Personally, I keep thinking someone's gonna call me in for a head exam."

Nick smiled and tapped his temple. "Well, if they do, you know *I'll* vouch for you. Both me and Grisha will."

She broke up, laughing. "Omigosh . . . why do I believe that?"

Nick laughed, too. It was good to have her back.

She reached over and kissed him on the cheek. "Eww—so you *and* your therapy car stink like gas. Can we go outside? Wanna go sit by the river?"

Nick nodded, "Sure."

She took his hand and pulled him outside, onto the path to the picnic table.

"So how was vacation and barrel-chasing and everything?" he baited along the way.

"Oh, Nicky, you know it's barrel-*racing*! You do that on purpose. Anyway, the week in Oklahoma was dry and hot, and I was on one of *their* horses, I've got to tell you about *that*, and then driving for a week with my parents drove me crazy, clear to Florida to see grandma and all that," she paused for half-a-breath, "then we flew to New York, thank goodness, and that was just me and Mom, so it was cool, and it was out in the country New *York*, not the city *New* York, which I think was a whole lot better. So we had fun there, yeah, and that's about it. But how about you? What have you been doing, like anything *fun*?"

Nick answered in a dipstick drawl, "Nuthin'—plowing the back forty, cleanin'-n-cookin'—*nuthin'* as fun as running a horse in little circles, chasing cans . . . .yee-hah!"

She tried to slap him as they sat, but he caught her hand. "Jeez, Brody, you are *so* full of it . . . whoa! Whaddya got here?"

The edge of an envelope had risen out of his pocket, and she could see a Maltese Cross beside the return address. She grabbed it instantly.

Ugh! She was hopeless! "Nothing." But obviously *that* wasn't going to work.

"'Order of the Maltese Cross', huh? This is nothing? What's up, Nicky? Did something happen to the icon? Is it okay?"

Nick shook his head, "No! I mean, yeah! Every-thing's okay, it's just, um . . . a letter."

"Can I read it, then? I mean, is it private or something?"

He sighed. How could every question she asked always be answered 'yes' and 'no' at the same time? Well, who cared, but she was going to make a lot bigger deal out of this than she needed to. "How come you're always so curious?" he asked. "It's going to get you in trouble some day."

"It will and it has, Nicky. Jeez, you sound like my Dad." She pulled the letter from the envelope and read aloud:

Dear Nikolas,

The Order of the Maltese Cross thanks you for your courage and service to Mother Russia. Were it not for you, 'The Weeping Virgin' icon would never have been returned to Her people.

Yet we mourn with you in the loss of your great-grandmother, Irina Ivanevna. Her sacrifice for the Holy Mother and the Motherland showed great courage. We pray you find comfort in knowing she rests with the Virgin.

Please allow us to honor her inspiration with an annual scholarship in your family's name. Each year, our proposed Brodyaga Award will fund a deserving student's university studies, stipulating only that he or she provide tangible benefit to the Motherland upon graduation.

There could be no better recipient of our first scholarship than you, Nikolas. Your contribution to the Motherland is already known: it is seen in the *moujiki* who pray to 'The Weeping Virgin', in those who take spiritual comfort in the return of Father Grigory, and in those who lead Mother Russia's search for a new Tsar.

Congratulations, Nikolas. Complete your upcoming year of high school studies, and consider carefully your choice of universities. Your great-grandmother would be proud of you. We certainly are.

S. M. Lipov, Director

"Nicky!" she squealed, the letter shaking in her hands, "this is great! How come you're not excited?"

Nick shook his head, staring off. "I don't know. Maybe it's too soon. I just want life to be normal for a while. I don't feel like going anywhere."

"Well, you've got a whole year to get normal again. Wow — you've got it made! Free college! So if you *wanted* to go somewhere, where would you go? And what would you major in?"

Nick shook his head. He didn't answer.

Colleen stared in disbelief. Finally she had to know, "You do *want* the scholarship, don't you? I mean, you *are* going to college . . . right? You've *always* said you were!"

"I don't know." Nick stared across the river. "Maybe it's not something I *have* to do now. I've got my car, I've got this place, and somebody's got to take care of Grandpa and the herd. What would happen to everything if I took off for four years?"

"Herd? What herd? Your five scraggly cows? They win out over free college? I don't believe you said that! Let's see, you'll live here with Boris and the cows, I guess, all your life. Hmm. How attractive. Your beautiful wife and children are really going to *love* that!"

He turned and glared. "Wife? Who said anything about a wife?"

"I did! And children, too—remember? The Virgin said they would be blessed, and their children would be, too. So they're in the works, Nicky . . . duh! It's all coming in the future, one way or another, and you'd better be ready to provide for them!"

Nick stared off again. "Look, the stuff with Rasputin is history. It happened. He returned like they said he would, and the icon's back in Russia now. Isn't that what everyone wanted?"

Colleen shook her head gently. "No, Nicky, only *some* people wanted that. But *no one* wanted your Bushka gone. Is that what this is all about, her being gone now?"

"Christ no, Colleen."

"Well, what then? Why are you being so weird about this?"

He swallowed hard. "It's a personal thing, Colleen. It's my family, you know? It's *us*, and I don't want *us* put under some huge microscope. I mean, say I take the scholarship . . . the Order will have some big ceremony, and a bunch of strangers will want to hear the Rasputin story, over and over. And it'll be the same wherever I go, at whatever school I pick. Always *my* family. Hey, why don't *you* take the scholarship instead? You were there, too, so you deserve it just as much as I do. And you won't have to talk about *your* family all the time."

Colleen shook her head. "That's silly, Nicky. You're the hero, like it or not, and you will be wherever you are. But people will understand that you lost a loved one, too. They're not going to hassle you to tell the story like you think."

"Well, I *know* they won't around here, Colleen, not in Rushing Wells. I mean, everybody here already *knew* my family was nuts. And I don't *care* what they think, anyway. But everywhere else, it's just gonna be insane—"

Jovial whistling and footsteps on the path cut their conversation short. Boris had an old John Deere hat atop his pony-tailed white mane, and he wore the same stained bib overalls and dirty knee-waders as every other farmer for miles around.

"So my timing is perfect . . . ?"

They didn't answer, and Boris ignored the tense silence. "Lunch is ready on the stove. Nick, the barbed wire and cracked riser in the front pasture are both fixed, so please find something else to do this afternoon."

Nick nodded his thanks, but the return address on the envelope on the bench caught Boris' eye, too.

"The Maltese Cross—is everything all right?"

Nick looked at Colleen as he answered. "Just a letter from the Order . . . " Nick paused, testing Colleen, but she cleared her throat with an 'I'll-tell-him-if-you-don't' threat.

He sighed. "It's a scholarship, Grandpa. The Order wants to start a 'Brodyaga Award', a college scholarship. And they picked me as the first winner.

Boris nodded. "Well, bless Sonia and her friends. And congratulations to you, Nick. So what is the problem? I would *enjoy* your not being a fly in my ointment any longer."

Nick shook his head. "I don't know. I've got some thinking to do. This'll mean we're right back in the news again."

"Well, perhaps I can help, Nick. Let me see . . . no more of your dirty dishes, endless laundry or teenage TV shows . . . hmm. I say that you take the scholarship, and to heck with the news."

Nick rolled his eyes. "C'mon, Grandpa, I'm not that bad. At least I don't watch <u>Hee-Haw</u> reruns from 1927 like you do."

Boris nodded like he was admitting it, then he changed the subject. "There was something in the paper today that you two might find interesting . . . " he pulled a folded page of <u>Pravda</u> from his back pocket and put on his reading glasses.

"' . . . and so, in spite of protests from President Yeltsin, the Duma has scheduled the vote for a new Tsar for May 16 . . . '"

Nick's eyes opened wide.

"Cool!" said Colleen.

Boris continued, "'Yeltsin, however, stressed that the new Tsar will be limited to ceremonial duties. 'We must not forget how Tsarist Russia lost wars and drove our economy to tatters', he warned the Duma.'"

Boris paused, trying to find the next part, " . . . blah, blah . . . 'a driving force in the push for a new Tsar has been the Order of the Maltese Cross, a group derived from the former Corps of Pages Military Academy in St. Petersburg. Their spokesman, Sonia Mikhailevna Lipov, countered Yeltsin, stating that 'a figure-head Tsar is not the people's goal — we want Russia's new Tsar to become President! Only then will the Motherland find peace and prosperity in today's world.'

"' . . . but Yeltsin quickly downplayed the Order's plans, calling them 'out-of-date and irrelevant' to Russian society.'"

Nick shook his head. "Yeltsin's worried, isn't he?"

Boris nodded, and Colleen chimed in, "Go, Sonia!"

"I say that Russia is already in the hands of the Virgin," Boris said. "She is working to put the Motherland in or—"

But an angry steer interrupted, trumpeting like an elephant behind him. "Well, perhaps all is not good in the pasture. I now return to work, little ones. Good day," He put the paper back in his pocket and trudged off.

Colleen held her tongue as long as she could, then leaned over and whispered, "What a change!"

"I know!" answered Nick. "He doesn't drink anymore, he prays to the Virgin, he works all day — who'd have guessed?"

"That's great—and he doesn't need you here anymore, does he? So you can start sending out your applications, right . . . ?"

Nick nodded. She was right. Again. He needed to accept the scholarship, it was huge and he knew it. "I guess so, Colleen. But I don't know where to apply. Around here, or . . . ?"

"Well, I think *anywhere,* but we'll find out for sure—now that you've come to your senses!" she added sarcastically. "We'll get some college catalogs coming right away."

She hesitated for a moment. "You know, I don't mind helping you, Nicky, but you're kind of hard-headed. Shouldn't you be thanking me for my good advice?"

Nick fought a smile. She was pushing it. He stared straight ahead and scratched his chin, a pondering, thinking man.

She gave him an extra moment, then unloaded. "Oh! You're impossible, you know that? Why is thanking me so hard? I give *good* advice, and Lord knows you need it! So here's some more—I advise you to pick me up at six tonight. We need to go out."

"What? You've been gone for three weeks . . . don't you want to stay at home for even one night?"

"Oh, hello—!" Colleen groaned, "would you get a clue? I've been on the road for three weeks with my parents! I need to get out and have some fun. Maybe we'll go bowling or something.

"But right now, I've gotta get home. We're still unpacking, and there's a ton of chores to get caught up on. But your night is mine—got it?" she smiled menacingly.

Nick nodded. "I've got it! I've got it," he faked his fear with a few steps back, but then it struck him, "Hey, Colleen, the Camaro should be done by then. We'll take it into town and cruise too, huh?"

She turned up her nose, less than overjoyed. "It stinks."

He threw up his hands in protest. "No, Colleen, really! That was a leaky hose, and I'm fixing that right now. It'll be fine! I've got everything else done—it runs great, you'll see."

Colleen shook her head. "That would really amaze me, Nicky. I mean, I know you do good work, but you don't always have time to fix all the little things—like, remember the door handles on your old truck? I know it's because you're a busy guy and you've got a lot of things to take care of, but I don't want you to go overboard rushing stuff for me, okay? I'll just tell Dad we're borrowing his truck tonight, it'll be a lot easier on you."

Nick was adamant. "No way! I'll be there at 6. And I'll be driving 'Grisha'."

Her eyes and mouth opened wide and she started laughing. "What—'Grisha'? You named your car 'Grisha'? Why in the world would you do *that*? I mean, what were you saying about people making a big deal out of things—what'll they say about *that*?"

He hadn't expected it to be so funny; he rolled his eyes in protest. "They're not gonna know, Colleen—it's a personal thing I thought I could share privately with you. But if not, just say so, and I won't tell you anything personal again."

She was still snickering, "Oh, Nicky, you can trust me with your secrets. I won't tell anybody about 'Grisha', I promise."

Nick tried to look past her giggles; he wanted his logic to make perfect sense. "Look, I got to thinking one day—the Camaro's always had potential, but it needed fixing up. Just like Grisha did. And, we took turns in the driver's seat while he was here. And, there's still fine-tuning needed for the finished product, each little thing being a headache—just like he was! So *now* do you see? I thought 'Grisha' was a good name for it."

She started laughing again. "Oh, Nicky, you're too much. Okay, I'll go out with you and 'Grisha' tonight, but I don't want any breakdowns! And it can't sing, and I won't get in it if it stinks! And I do *not* want to have to pray to get rescued! Oh, you're such a *nut*! Goodbye!" She kissed him on the cheek and pranced off.

Nick couldn't believe her. *Ei Bogu!* That girl! He worked with a vengeance and had the gas line fixed in minutes. This was going to be so cool . . . Colleen was gonna flip out! This was gonna be one sweet ride, especially once he got this one last thing done . . . .

The license plates were still lying on the bench, wrapped in paper—it was a miracle she hadn't grabbed them, too. He stripped the paper off. Perfect. ONE WTV—one for the front bumper, one for the back. Nick grinned as he screwed them on. Colleen would figure 'em out, but it didn't matter who else did. He hopped in. The engine fired right up—*yes!* He carefully backed out, turned around and crunched down the drive toward the blacktop. This felt *good*. He hit the gas, cranked the wheel and chirped onto the long open road before him.

THE END

A Guide to Russian Names

Friends and family might use 'pet' names:
'Leon' could be called 'Lisha'

Casual associates use each others' first and middle names:
"Hello, Leon Igorovich!"

A man's **middle** name is his father's **first** name
with an added '-ovich' or '-evich'

Leon Smith, son of Igor Smith =
Leon Igorovich Smith

A woman's **middle** name is also her father's **first** name
but with an added '-evna' or '-ovna'

Maria Smith, daughter of Igor Smith =
Maria Igorevna Smith

Glossary

Babushka - (bah-boosh'-kah). Grandmother.

balalaika - (ball-uh-like'-uh). A Russian stringed instrument, similar to a lute or small guitar.

Batiushka - (Bah-tweesh'-kah). Father.

bluza - (bloo'-zhah). A peasant's blouse, often coarse cloth.

Bolsheviks - A political group (also known as the Red Russians) eventually led by Vladimir Lenin. Overpowered the Mensheviks (White Russians) and rose to power following the October Revolution of 1917.

Brody, Ivan Borisevich - (1952—1980). Father of Nick Brody. Shortened surname to reflect American patriotism during McCarthy era. Killed with wife Cathy in car accident near family farm.

Brody, Nikolas Ivanovich - "Nick", "Nikisha", "Nicky" (1974--). Orphaned child of Ivan and Cathy Brody. Lives on family farm in Rushing Wells, Idaho, with grandfather and great-grandmother.

Brodyaga, Boris Grigorevich - "The Gravedigger" (1918--). Father of Ivan Brody, divorced. An infamous Idaho local, alcoholic, prone to religious and burial oddities.

Brodyaga, Irina Ivanevna - "Bushka", "Irisha" (1896--). Mother of Boris Brodyaga, Great-grandmother of Nick Brody. Matriarch of the Brody/Brodyaga family. Escaped Russian Revolutions of 1917 and established the family farm near Rushing Wells, Idaho.

caftan - Russian peasant's overcoat, often greased to help repel moisture.

Cheka - (Chayk'-ah). First of the Communist national police forces, originally termed the **Vecheka**. Replaced the **Ohkrana**, preceded the **KGB**.

Dillinger, Colleen Elaine - (1974--). Daughter of Nick Brody's neighbors, Rocco and Diane Dillinger.

Duma - The Russian Congress, 2 chambers of elected and appointed officials based in St. Petersburg, the capitol of Russia.

Dunia - (1866-1919). The Rasputin family's housekeeper. Joined Rasputin and his daughters living in St. Petersburg in 1913.

Ei Bogu - mild Russian expletive, loosely translated "My Lord!".

Federal Security Service - Today's national Russian police force, headquartered in the Kremlin, Moscow. Formerly known as Russian Security Agency, KGB, Vecheka, Cheka and Ohkrana.

Iliodor of Tsaritsyn, Father - (1876-1944). A disillusioned one-time friend of Rasputin, later one of his greatest adversaries.

KGB - Longtime national police force in Communist Russia. Had origins in the **Ohkrana** and post-revolution **Vecheka & Cheka**. Became the **Russian Security Agency** in the post-Cold War era, known today as the **Federal Security Service**.

Khlysty - (Khlist'-ee). Religious cult with a sexual component, a banned offshoot of the Russian Orthodox faith.

Lazovert, Doctor Stanislaus Andreyevich - (1849-1933). Russian Army doctor, Corps of Pages graduate. Summoned to St. Petersburg by Purishkevich to aid in the assassination of Rasputin.

Lipov, Captain Igor Igorevich - (Lip'-of) (1873-1951). Undercover officer in the Ohkrana, graduate of The Corps of Pages military academy, confidant of Vladimir Purishkevich, member of the gang that assassinated Rasputin. Grandfather of Mikhail Vladimirovich Lipov.

Lipov, Colonel Mikhail Vladimirovich - (1954--). Former KGB officer, today a Field Colonel in the Russian Security Agency.

Lipov, Captain Sonia Mikhailevna - (1973--). Administrative officer in the former KGB and its successor, the Russian Security Agency. Traveled to Idaho with her father to settle a security threat and a matter of family honor.

Lipov, Tatiana Valentinyevna - (1876-1956). Wife of Captain Igor Igorevich Lipov, St. Petersburg social butterfly.

Maltese Cross - X-shaped cross tattooed onto chests of graduates of St. Petersburg's Corps of Pages Military Academy, symbolizes service and 'loyalty to the death' to the Tsar. Also the symbol of a covert Russian group working to return a Tsar to power.

matroishka - (ma-troish'-ka). A nesting set of egg-shaped dolls, each sharing a common theme.

Matushka - (Mah-toosh'-ka). Mother.

Mensheviks - (White Russians). A political group that rose in challenge to the Tsar. Eventually overtaken by the Bolsheviks.

molebin - (mo-layb'-in). A purification and/or blessing performed in the presence of one of the Russian Orthodox miracle-working icons.

moujik, moujiki (pl.) - (moo-zhik', moo-zhik'-ee). The peasant class, laborers, farmers. Unorganized and poor, but rich in tradition.

Novaya Derevnya (Noh-vie'-uh Dehr-ehv'-knee-uh). A gypsy camp outside St. Petersburg where Irina Brodyaga met Rasputin.

Ohkrana - (Oak-rah'-nah). Russian Secret Police under the Tsarist government. Became **Vecheka,** then **Cheka** after revolution.

Order of the Maltese Cross - Today's descendants of graduates of The Corps of Pages military academy. An underground group dedicated to the traditions and ideals of Tsarism.

Peterhof - Summer Palace of the Royal Family, near the Gulf of Finland.

pivo - pig.

Pokrovskoye, Siberia - (Pock-rov'-skoy'-a). Boyhood home of Grigory Rasputin, located in Central Russia's Tobolsk Province.

Purishkevich, Vladimir Mitrofanovich - (Pur-ish'-kev-ich), (1851-1934). Elected to Duma, graduate of The Corps of Pages military academy, co-planned Rasputin's assassination.

Rasputin, Grigory Efimovich (Novyhk) - "Father Grigory" "Grisha" (1873—1916). Son of Efim Andreyevich Novyhk, bestowed with healing powers, had an uncommon knowledge of the Russian Orthodoxy. Was given the nickname of 'Rasputin' at 16--could be translated as 'debauched one', but more likely 'ill-behaved child' or 'where two rivers meet'.

Rasputin, Praskovia Svetlana - "Pasha" (1869—1924). Tolerant wife of Grigory Rasputin. Mother of their 4 children: 1) Dmitri, who died very young, 2) Dmitri ("Misha"), named in tribute to his late brother and whose mind was affected by scarlet fever, 3) Maria, and 4) Varya.

Romanov, Tsar Nikolas II - "Nicky" "Nikisha" (1868—1917). King of all the Russias. Born to Tsar Alexander III, reigned from 1885-1916.

Romanov, Tsarevich Alexei Nikolayevich - "Alyosha" (1904—1917). Lone male heir to the throne, youngest child of the royal family. Chronic hemophiliac relieved of suffering by Rasputin.

Romanov, Tsarina Alexandra - "Alex" (1872—1917). Nikolas' German-born wife, prone to superstitious and mystical beliefs.

Romanov, 4 daughters: Olga Nikayevna, Tatiana Nikayevna, Maria Nikayevna, Anastasia Nikayevna - (1895 and on—1917).

Romanov, Grand Duchess Anastasia - (1874—1942). Wife of Grand Duke Paul Nikolayevich Romanov, sister of Militsa, spiritual adviser to Tsarina Alexandra.

Romanov, Grand Duchess Militsa - (1875—1939). Wife of Grand Duke Peter Nikolayevich Romanov, sister of Anastasia, spiritual adviser to Tsarina Alexandra.

Romanov, Grand Duke Dmitri Pavlovich - "Misha" (1885—1931). Flamboyant son of Grand Duke Paul Romanov, cousin of Tsar Nikolas II. Sexual deviate, member of the gang that assassinated Rasputin.

Romanov, Grand Duke Paul Nikolayevich - (1870—1941). Cousin of Tsar Nikolas II, brother of Grand Duke Peter Nikolayevich, husband of Grand Duchess Anastasia Romanov.

Romanov, Grand Duke Peter Nikolayevich - (1871—1940). Cousin of Tsar Nikolas II, brother of Grand Duke Paul Nikolayevich, husband of Grand Duchess Militsa Romanov.

Rushing Wells, Idaho - Small town near the Snake River Canyon of Southern Idaho, hometown of the Brody/Brodyaga family.

Russian Security Agency - Post-cold war national police force in the country of Russia. Replaced the Soviets' KGB. Known today as the **Federal Security Service**.

sabor - (sah-boar'). Small chapel or shrine, usually underground and accessed from a kitchen's root cellar. Adorned with religious icons, candles, lamps and prayer rugs.

samovar - A two-stage Russian tea kettle. Strong tea is brewed in a teapot atop a warming tube (charcoal or pinecone embers) that rises through a central water chamber. The concentrated tea is diluted with 10 parts hot water from the large, lower unit.

Spala, Poland - Home of a Royal Family retreat, scene of one of Rasputin's greatest healings of young Tsarevich Alexei.

starets, staretsi (pl.) - (sta-rets', sta-rets'-ee). A former strannik who has found his path in life, then retires to a monk-like solitude and meditation.

staroveri - The Old Believers, Russian Orthodox priests who were swept aside in radical reforms of the church.

strannik, stranniki (pl.) - (stran-ik', stran-eek'-ee). A wandering man in search of his path in life, living by the words of the Bible and from the generosity of the country's peasants.

tovarishch - (to-vahr-ish'). Friend.

troika - (troy'-ka). A 3-horse team used to pull a carriage.

Tsarskoe Selo, Russia - (Zhar-skoy'-ah Sa'-lo). Russian Royal Family compound south of St. Petersburg. Location of the Tsar's residences: the Alexander and Catherine Palaces.

Union of Tears - Group formed by Prince Felix Yussupov in 1916 to provide 'The Weeping Virgin' for worship by all Russians--and to pray for the 'return' of Rasputin.

Vecheka - (Veh-chayk'-ah). First of the post-revolution national police forces, headquartered in St. Petersburg.

verst - Approximately one kilometer.

'Virgin of Kazan' icon - A renowned, miracle-working icon depicting a dark-skinned Madonna with Child. Once lost, then unearthed in Russia's Kazan Province in the 1400's. Known to have 'shed tears' at times of national sorrow, thus gaining the nickname, 'The Weeping Virgin'. This icon's whereabouts are unknown today.

vozhd - A lay preacher.

Vyrubova, Anna Taneyeva - "Anyushka" (186x—1917). Best friend and Lady-in-Waiting to Tsarina Alexandra, lived in a guest house near the Winter Palace in St. Petersburg, often vacationed with royal family.

'Weeping Virgin' icon - See 'Virgin of Kazan' icon.

Yussupov, Prince Felix Felixovich - "Felisha" (Yoos'-oo-pof). Youngest child of the St. Petersburg Yussupovs, married to the Tsar's niece, Irina Pavlovna Romanov. Sexual deviate, member of gang that assassinated Rasputin.

zagovarivat'krov - (zha-go-vair-ih-vaht'-krof). The Russian art of blood-stilling, performed with a blend of prayer, touch and faith. Rasputin was taught the art by his father.

zubrovka - (zhu-brof'-kah). A homemade, strongly-scented vodka, warmed with hot water from a samovar. Rasputin used it to measure a man's honesty, nicknamed it 'Rasputin's Revenge'.